LEGEND OF THE GALACTIC HEROES

VOLUME 1
DAWN

YOSHIKI TANAKA

HAIKA SORU

SAN FRANCISCO

LEGEND OF THE GALACTIC HEROES

VOLUME 1
DAWN

WRITTEN BY
YOSHIKI TANAKA

Translated by Daniel Huddleston

Legend of the Galactic Heroes, Vol. 1: Dawn
GINGA EIYU DENSETSU Vol.1
© 1982 by Yoshiki TANAKA
Cover Illustration © 2007 Yukinobu Hoshino.

Cover and interior design by Fawn Lau

HAIKASORU
Published by VIZ Media, LLC
P.O. Box 77010
San Francisco, CA 94107

www.haikasoru.com

Library of Congress Cataloging-in-Publication Data

Names: Tanaka, Yoshiki, 1952– author. | Huddleston, Daniel, translator.
Title: Legend of the galactic heroes / written by Yoshiki Tanaka ; translated
    by Daniel Huddleston.
Other titles: Ginga eiyu densetsu
Description: San Francisco : Haikasoru, [2016]
Identifiers: LCCN 2015044444 | ISBN 9781421584942 (v. 1 : paperback) |
    ISBN 9781421584959 (v. 2 : paperback)
Subjects: LCSH: Science fiction. | War stories. | BISAC: FICTION / Science
    Fiction / Space Opera. | FICTION / Science Fiction / Military. | FICTION /
    Science Fiction / Adventure.
Classification: LCC PL862.A5343 G5513 2016 | DDC 895.63/5—dc23
LC record available at http://lccn.loc.gov/2015044444

Printed in the U.S.A.
First printing, March 2016

MAJOR CHARACTERS

GALACTIC EMPIRE

REINHARD VON LOHENGRAMM
Senior admiral. Count. Age 20.

SIGFRIED KIRCHEIS
Reinhard's trusted advisor. Captain.

ANNEROSE
Reinhard's elder sister. Countess—
or Gräfin— von Grünewald.

MERKATZ
Admiral. Highly experienced
admiral in the imperial military.

STADEN
Vice admiral.

FAHRENHEIT
Rear admiral.

LICHTENLADE
Minister of State. Marquis.

GERLACH
Minister of Finance. Viscount.

THOMA VON STOCKHAUSEN
Commanding officer of Iserlohn
Fortress. Admiral.

HANS DIETRICH VON SEECKT
Commanding officer of the Iserlohn
Fleet. Admiral.

PAUL VON OBERSTEIN
Staff officer serving in the Iserlohn
Fleet. Captain.

WOLFGANG MITTERMEIER
Commanding officer serving in
Reinhard's fleet. Vice admiral.

OSKAR VON REUENTAHL
Commanding officer serving in
Reinhard's fleet. Vice admiral.

KARL GUSTAV KEMPF
Commanding officer serving in
Reinhard's fleet. Vice admiral.

FRITZ JOSEF WITTENFELD
Commanding officer serving in
Reinhard's fleet. Vice admiral.

FRIEDRICH IV
36th Emperor.

ERWIN JOSEF II
37th Emperor. Age 5.

RUDOLF VON GOLDENBAUM
Founder of the Galactic Empire's
Goldenbaum Dynasty.

FREE PLANETS ALLIANCE

YANG WEN-LI
Staff officer serving in the Second
Fleet. Commodore. Age 29.

JULIAN MINTZ
War orphan and ward of Yang. Age 14.

PAETTA
Commanding Officer of the Second
Fleet. Vice admiral.

JEAN ROBERT LAPPE
Staff officer serving in the Sixth Fleet.
Lieutenant Commander.

JESSICA EDWARDS
Lappe's fiancee.

ALEX CASELNES
Top aide and second-in-command
to the Director of Joint Operational
Headquarters. Rear admiral.

SIDNEY SITOLET
Director of Joint Operational
Headquarters. Marshal.

JOB TRÜNICHT
Chairman of the Defense Committee.

BUCOCK
Commanding officer of the Fifth Fleet.
Vice admiral. Highly experienced
admiral in the Alliance military.

EDWIN FISCHER
Vice commander of the Thirteenth
Fleet. Master of fleet operations.
Commodore.

MURAI
Chief Staff Officer of the
Thirteenth Fleet. Commodore.

FYODOR PATRICHEV
Assistant Staff Officer for the
Thirteenth Fleet. Captain.

MARINO
Captain of the Thirteenth Fleet's
flagship. Captain.

OLIVIER POPLIN
Spartanian pilot. Lieutenant.

WALTER VON SCHÖNKOPF
Captain of the "Rosen Ritter"
regiment. Captain.

FREDERICA GREENHILL
Aide to the Thirteenth Fleet's
commanding officer. Sublieutenant.

DWIGHT GREENHILL
Deputy Director of Joint
Operational Headquarters. Admiral.
Frederica's father.

ANDREW FORK
Chief Intelligence Staff Officer for
the Expeditionary Force to Imperial
Territory. Rear admiral.

ARTHUR LYNCH
Deserter who abandoned the civilians
of Planet El Facil. Rear Admiral.

PHEZZAN
DOMINION

ADRIAN RUBINSKY
The fifth Landesherr. Known as the
"Black Fox of Phezzan."

NICOLAS BOLTEC
Rubinsky's aide.

TABLE OF CONTENTS

PROLOGUE:
AN OUTLINE OF THE HISTORY OF THE GALAXY

IT WAS IN AD 2801 that humanity declared the formation of the Galactic Federation and relocated the crux of its political authority from Terra (the third planet of the solar system) to Teoria (the second planet of the Aldebaran system). In this same year, humanity reset its calendar to Space Era 1 and began to expand inexorably into the inner reaches and frontiers of the galaxy. After the wars and the chaos that had been so starkly characteristic of the 2700s—which had brought development of space to a standstill—the energy that came bursting forth was all the more explosive.

Subspace jump theory, gravitational control, and inertial control technology—these were the Three Graces that made interstellar flight possible, and they were refined day by day as humankind spurred its starships toward unknown horizons and set sail upon oceans brimming with stars.

"Onward! And onward still!"

These were familiar words to the people of those days. It was plain to see that the consciousness of the human race itself had entered a period of exuberance.

And so with a resolute will and a dazzling passion, humanity grappled with every difficulty that came its way.

Even in the face of great hardships, it didn't indulge in the consolations of pessimism; instead it overcame obstacles with good cheer. Humanity in that age was what might perhaps have been called a legion of hopeless optimists.

"A golden age! Overflowing with enterprise and renewal!"

Perhaps. But although that period may well have been described in such terms, it does not mean that its veneer was without a number of scratches. Foremost among these was the existence of interstellar pirates. These were the malformed progeny of privateers that had once been employed by Terra and Sirius when they battled for dominance in the 2700s. Among these pirates were a number of individuals who stole from the rich, gave to the poor, and sang the praises of freedom. They, and their battles with the federal navy that pursued them, provided endless fodder for 3-D solivision programs.

The facts, however, were more prosaic. The majority of these pirates were nothing more than criminal syndicates, colluding with corrupt politicians and businessmen in order to collect and consume ill-gotten gains. For the people who lived on the frontier worlds in particular, they were nothing less than a Pandora's box of troubles. Naturally, they often haunted the shipping lanes connecting the outlying systems. Starships just put into service were destroyed, deliveries of supplies were delayed, and what goods did make it to their destinations were exorbitantly priced since the cost of protection money was being piled onto the original prices. The seriousness of this problem cannot be underestimated. As the dissatisfaction and uncertainty mounted, confidence in the federation's ability to govern was eroded, and the result was an eroding of the people's enthusiasm for developing the frontier.

In SE 106, the government finally put forth a serious effort to eliminate the pirates, and thanks to the efforts of admirals M. Chuffrin and C. Wood, this objective had been all but achieved two years later. It was by no means easy. As Admiral Wood, known for his sharp tongue, later wrote in his memoirs,

I had competent enemies in front of me, incompetent allies behind me, and had to fight with both of them at once. Hell, I wasn't even entirely sure I could count on myself!

After Admiral Wood moved into the world of politics, he was known as "that insensitive, stubborn old geezer" who waged a tireless, tenacious war against corrupt politicians and businesspeople.

These societal diseases continued to flare up without interruption. However, they were—if we consider the whole of humanity as a single individual—really nothing more than the equivalent of minor skin irritations. There is no way to prevent them completely, just as it is impossible to fully eliminate abrasions to one's skin. But as long as proper treatment is applied, there is no reason at all for such ailments to lead to a patient's death. And so it was that without ascending the operating table, humanity continued on in mostly good health for the next two centuries.

Left behind by this prosperity and development was Terra, once the suzerain of all humanity. This planet had already been scoured for every last bit of its resources, suffering the loss of both its real and potential political and economic power. Its population had plummeted, leaving it nothing more than a used-up and useless old state relying on faded traditions—its sovereignty still recognized, just barely, thanks to its harmlessness.

The interstellar colonies that Terra had wrested from Sirius and others, the accumulated wealth it had possessed during the days when it still dominated the galaxy—all had been lost somewhere along the way.

And so at last the cancerous cells began to multiply, and the shadow of a so-called medieval stagnation fell across the face of human society.

The hearts and minds of the people came to be ruled not by hope and ambition, but by exhaustion and weariness. Activity, optimism, and initiative gave way to passivity, pessimism, and protectionism. In the fields of science and technology, new discoveries and inventions ground to a halt. The democratically elected government of the republic lost its ability to maintain self-discipline and declined into an oligarchy interested in nothing but concessions and political infighting.

Plans for the development of the frontier regions were scrapped. The potential bounty of countless habitable worlds was foresaken, along with half-constructed facilities that were left abandoned. Social lifestyles and culture steadily decayed. People lost sight of their proper values and gave themselves over to drug abuse, alcoholism, promiscuity, and mysticism. Crime rates skyrocketed, while arrest rates fell in inverse proportion. The tendency to make little of human life and to ridicule morality grew increasingly pronounced.

Of course, there were many who lamented these phenomena, who could not stand to sit idly by while humanity in its decadence marched toward the same miserable fate that had awaited the dinosaurs.

They believed that drastic treatment of humanity's collective illness was needed, and in this they were not mistaken. But when they selected their favored form of medication, the majority opted not for the kind of long-term therapy that requires endurance and perseverance—instead, they quaffed a fast-acting elixir that came with many side effects.

This was the powerful drug called "dictatorship."

And so the stage was set for the ascent of Rudolf von Goldenbaum.

Rudolf von Goldenbaum was born into a military family in SE 268, and just as one would expect, he entered the military service as well.

While at the Space Force's officer school, he was the very picture of a top-ranked student. With a powerful body 196 centimeters in height and weighing in at ninety-nine kilograms, people who saw him often had the feeling that they were gazing up at a steel tower.

Von Goldenbaum's towering form contained not a trace of fat, nor the slightest hint of vulnerability. He received his commission as an ensign at age twenty, and was attached to a guard unit patrolling the Rigel shipping lanes as its legal affairs officer. There he applied himself to the enforcement of military discipline, driving out the "four evils" of alcohol, gambling, drugs, and homosexuality. Even when these problems entangled his superior officers, he showed no mercy, pursuing them with unassailable logic and regulations brandished high. His embarrassed senior officers responded by promoting him to lieutenant junior grade, then transferring him out toward Betelgeuse.

This was a dangerous region often called the "Space Pirate's Main Street," but Rudolf von Goldenbaum went into it in high spirits. In time, the pirate syndicate there was driven to destruction by his ingenious and unsparing attacks, bearing witness to the shrewd ways of he who came to be called "the second coming of Admiral Wood."

Von Goldenbaum's enthusiasm for ferocity—even those who wished to surrender and face trial were incinerated along with their ships—was, naturally, a target of some criticism, but the voices praising his escapades were far louder.

The citizens of the Galactic Federation knew well the suffocating feeling of life as part of a generation that was going nowhere, and they joyfully welcomed this young and spirited new hero. Rudolf's appearance came like a shining supernova to a world that had been enshrouded in thick fog.

In SE 296, Rudolf von Goldenbaum, who had made rear admiral at age twenty-eight, resigned from the military and entered the political arena, winning a seat in parliament. When he became leader of a political party called the National Reformation Alliance, he brought in many young politicians by virtue of his popularity.

By the time a few more election cycles had passed, von Goldenbaum's power had grown by leaps and bounds, and amid a complex brew of fervent support, uncertainty, opposition, and decadent unconcern, he succeeded in building a firm political foundation.

He was elected prime minister by popular vote, and then—by exploiting vague wording in the constitutional article that banned holding multiple offices simultaneously—was also appointed head of state by parliament. It had been an unwritten rule that no individual should hold more than one office at a time. These two positions possessed only limited powers alone. But when both were united in the person of a single individual, a fearsome chemical reaction took place. Now there was essentially no one left who could stand in the way of Rudolf von Goldenbaum's political power. As historian D. Sinclair would write a generation later:

> Von Goldenbaum's ascension was striking historical evidence that, fundamentally, people do not prefer independent thought and the accompanying responsibility, but rather orders, subordination, and the accompanying exemption from responsibility. In a popular democracy, the masses who elect unfit rulers are to blame for bad government, but that is not the case in a monarchy. Rather than reflecting upon their own mistakes, the people are free to enjoy speaking ill of leaders who are even more irresponsible than they.

Regardless of his theory's validity or lack thereof, it is certain that the people of von Goldenbaum's generation were on his side.

"Strong government! Powerful leaders! Order and revitalization!"

Somewhere along the way, the young, powerful leader who had cried out these slogans came to be a dictator called "Administrator for Life," and he did not permit the existence of any criticism. By SE 310, when he attained the title of "Sacred and Inviolable Emperor of the Galactic Empire," not a few citizens found themselves cursing their stupidity for failing to learn the lessons of history. As for those who had been consistently critical all along, no one could blame them for feeling deeply resentful. But the numbers shouting for joy had been so much greater.

Hassan el-Sayyid—one of the politicians of the republican faction of that time—wrote the following in his diary on the day of the coronation: "Here in my room, I can hear the crowds outside shouting 'Hail, Rudolf!' I wonder how many days they'll need to realize that they're cheering their own hangman."

The publication of the diary was later suppressed by the imperial authorities. It was also on this day that the SE calendar was abolished, and the first year of the imperial calendar was begun. Here the Galactic Federation collapsed, and the Galactic Empire—and the Goldenbaum Dynasty—were born.

It cannot be doubted that this man—who as Emperor Rudolf I of the Galactic Empire had become the first absolute monarch of the political system uniting all humanity—was possessed of extraordinary talents. With the boundless strength of his political leadership and the fortitude of his will, he enforced discipline, improved the efficiency of government, and purged corrupt officials.

This was all according to standards which Rudolf set himself, but the "vulgar, decadent, fallen, and unhealthy" way of life and entertainment vanished, and the rates of crime and juvenile delinquency plummeted in the face of severe—even cruel—judicial activism. In any case, the evil that had enshrouded human society was blown away.

And yet, the "Steel Giant" (as some liked to refer to Rudolf) was still not satisfied. His idealized society was one with a high degree of unity, regulated and managed in an orderly fashion by powerful leaders.

For Rudolf—who relied greatly on himself and had utmost faith in the justice that he himself executed—critics and opponents were nothing but foreign contaminants disrupting the unity and order of society. As a natural consequence, the cruel suppression of opposition forces began.

In Year 9 of the imperial calendar, this created the opportunity for the Genetic Inferiority Elimination Act to be promulgated.

The strong consume the weak! The fittest survive! Excellence is victorious while inferiority is defeated! This is the providence of the universe!

So Rudolf expressed his beliefs to his "subjects."

Human society is no exception. When the number of aberrations exceeds a critical mass, society loses its vitality and declines into

*weakness. My ardent desire is for humanity's everlasting pros-
perity. Therefore, the elimination of those elements that would
weaken humanity as a species is my holy obligation as ruler of
humanity.*

Specifically, this meant forced sterilization for the physically handicapped, those below the poverty line, and those who "did not excel." It
meant euthanasia for the mentally handicapped. It meant that societal
measures for the support of the weak were all but eliminated.

For Rudolf, weakness was the unforgivable sin, and the weaker members of society who "use their weakness as a shield, then demand to be
taken care of" were nothing more than objects of his hatred.

When this bill was shown to the people, even the throngs that had
thus far worshipped and followed Rudolf blindly were ashamed of themselves, as might be expected. The number of those who could confidently
declare themselves to be superior beings was not so great. Everyone was
thinking, *Isn't this a little too high-handed?*

Politicians of the all-but-vanished republican faction still hung on
in parliament, and they gave voice to the will of the people, lambast-
ing the emperor. To this, the emperor determined to make a decisive
counterstrike.

He immediately and permanently dissolved the parliament.

The following year, the imperial Ministry of the Interior created the
Bureau for the Maintenance of Public Order, which came to wield fierce
power against political crime. Ernst Falstrong, who was Minister of the
Interior as well as a close associate of Rudolf's, ran the bureau himself,
arresting, incarcerating, imprisoning, and punishing—not according to
law, but according to his own judgment.

Such was the unholy matrimony of authority and violence. These two
soon gave birth to the infant known as "state terrorism," which grew in
no time to be a giant that engulfed all of human society.

At that time, a blackly humorous joke was making the rounds: "If you
don't want to be executed, don't get arrested by the police. Get yourself
caught by Public Order instead, because they don't execute anybody!"

It is a fact that of all those whom the bureau arrested for political and thought crimes, not a single one was ever formally executed. However, those who were shot dead without trial, who died under torture, who were "disappeared" to barren penal asteroids, who were left disabled by lobotomies or massive doses of drugs, who died in prison of "illnesses" or "accidents"...the combined tally of these climbed to four billion. But because this number was only 1.3 percent of the Galactic Empire's total population of three hundred billion, the bureau was able to spuriously claim, "We have eliminated a handful of dangerous elements for the sake of the absolute majority."

Of course, that "absolute majority" did not include the four billion who shuddered in fear for their fates or the countless others who swallowed their objections amid the oppressive silence.

Rudolf crushed those who opposed him, and at the same time selected and granted special privileges to certain "people of superior ability," creating an aristocracy to support the imperial family. But was it a sign of the inferiority of Rudolf's own knowledge that all of them were white people who bore old Germanic family names?

Based on his strong service record, Falstrong also received the title of count, but on his way home he ran into a terror attack carried out by an underground republican group. In the flash of a neutron bomb, he met a tragic end. Rudolf mourned, and with the execution of twenty thousand suspects, he sought to comfort the soul of one who had served him well.

In the forty-second year of the imperial calendar, Rudolf's life of eighty-three years came to an end. It was said that his huge frame had been stronger than ever, but psychological distress had cast a heavy burden on his heart.

The emperor did not die in full satisfaction. Of the four children he and his empress Elizabeth had, all were girls, and he was left without a male heir. Late in life, his concubine Magdalena gave birth to a baby boy, but it is said that the child was born an idiot.

Of this episode, the public records of the empire are silent, but we may surmise that the rumors circulating at the time were almost certainly true, because not just Magdalena, but also her parents, her siblings, and even the doctors and nurses who had attended her birth were afterward all put to death.

It must have come as a stinging blow for Rudolf, who had promulgated the Genetic Inferiority Elimination Act and sought the development of a superior form of humanity.

For Rudolf, the gene decided everything, and to prevent the collapse of his belief system, Magdalena had had to die. It simply could not be that Emperor Rudolf had a genetic makeup that produced retardation. The fault had to lie completely with Magdalena.

After the death of Rudolf, the imperial crown of the Galactic Empire came to rest upon the head of Sigismund, eldest son of Rudolf's eldest daughter, Katharina. And so at the age of twenty-five, with the assistance of his father Joachim, Lord of Neue-Staufen, this young emperor came to rule the galaxy.

With the death of Rudolf I, republican rebellions erupted in every quarter. It was believed that with the loss of Rudolf's leadership and fierce personality, the empire would soon crumble; however, that kind of thinking was too optimistic. The aristocrats, military leaders, and bureaucrats that Rudolf had been nourishing at his side for the past forty years made up a troika far stronger than the republicans' hopeful estimation.

These forces were led by Lord Joachim of Neue-Staufen, who was both the emperor's father and prime minister. Displaying the composed, cool leadership that might be expected of a man chosen by Rudolf as groom for his daughter, Joachim crushed the weaker forces of insurrection as though they were eggshells beneath his heel.

More than five hundred million who had participated in the uprisings were killed, and of their families more than ten billion had their citizenship revoked and were thrown into serfdom. "In the suppression of opposing forces, be unsparing," said the imperial regulations, and they were followed to the letter.

The forces of republicanism were once again made to endure a long winter.

In the face of such powerful dictators, it was thought that this harsh winter would stretch on forever. After Joachim's death, Sigismund ruled directly. And after his death, Sigismund was succeeded by his eldest son Richard, who was in turn succeeded by his own eldest, Ottfried. The highest position of authority passed only to the descendants of Rudolf, and it looked as if heredity was the only thing that could determine the transition of power.

However, deep beneath the thick ice, a watery convection current was silently moving.

In IC 164, the republicans of the Altair system—who had been denounced as a rebel clan, reduced to slave status, and set to hard labor—succeeded in escaping, using a spaceship they had constructed themselves.

Their plan was not like the ones that their forebears had been carefully refining for generations. The number of such plans that had been proposed was equal to the number that had ended in failure. The grave markers of republicans had only increased, and in place of elegies, only the cruel laughter of the Bureau for the Maintenance of Public Order resounded among the graveyards. It was a cycle that had repeated itself endlessly. Yet finally, there was success. And from conception to execution, it had only taken three standard months.

It had literally begun as child's play. A child of two slaves who were mining molybdenum and antimony in the cruel cold of Altair 7 had dodged out of the sight of his overseers and was playing at carving small boats from the ice, which he then floated out onto the water. A young man named Ahle Heinessen had been watching him absently, and this image reverberated in the back of his mind like a divine revelation. Wasn't this lonely planet, after all, a bottomless storehouse of shipbuilding materials?

On the seventh planet, the overall amount of water was not so great; it abounded more in natural dry ice than in frozen water. Heinessen chose a gargantuan mass of dry ice that was entirely buried in a certain valley. Its dimensions were 122 kilometers in length, forty kilometers in width, and thirty kilometers in height. After hollowing out the center, he made a propulsion area and a living area, and soon it began to look like it could fly. The most difficult part of the plan was the question of how to get materials to actually build a spaceship. It was no good trying to obtain materials illegally, for if the Bureau for the Maintenance of Public Order got wind of it, they would simply arrest and slaughter everyone involved.

However, this world also had natural resources that would not draw the bureau's attention. In the absolute zero cold of outer space, there was no fear of dry ice sublimating into gas. If they could just isolate the heat that would be generated by the propulsion and living areas, a considerably long-term flight would be possible. During that time, they could search asteroids and uninhabited planets for the materials needed to build an interstellar spaceship. There was no need to keep flying in the same ship in which they had departed.

And so their glittering white spaceship of dry ice was christened the *Ion Fazegas,* named after the boy who had made that toy boat out of ice. Four hundred thousand men and women entered that vessel and escaped from the Altair system. This was the first step on a journey that historians would later dub the Long March of 10,000 Light-Years.

After shaking off the ruthless pursuit of the Galactic Empire's military, they hid themselves beneath the surface of a nameless planet and there constructed eighty interstellar spacecraft. Then they set out into the inner core of the galaxy. Here the escapees faced an immensity brimming with deadly giant stars, dwarfs, and variables. Here the ill will of the Creator crashed down on their heads time and time again.

In the midst of this journey of hardship, they lost their leader Heinessen to an accident. His dear friend Kim Hua Nguyen took over as leader. By the time this man grew old and his eyesight faded, they at last passed out of the dangerous regions and found their future in a stable cluster of main sequence stars. More than half a century had passed since they had left Altair.

To the stars of their new world they gave the names of the gods of ancient Phoenicia: Baalat, Astarte, Melqart, Hadad, and others. They made their base on the fourth planet from Baalat, to which they gave the name of their fallen leader Heinessen, that his deeds might be forever honored.

The conclusion of the Long March of 10,000 Light-Years occurred in IC 218, but these people—who had escaped the yoke of the dictatorship—chose to abolish the imperial calendar and revive the SE calendar instead. In this, they prided themselves that it was they who were the rightful heirs of the Galactic Federation. Rudolf and his ilk were nothing more than contemptible traitors to democratic rule.

In this manner, the establishment of the Free Planets Alliance was solemnly declared. It took place in SE 527. The first generation of its citizens numbered around 160,000. More than half of their comrades had perished during the Long March.

It was far too small a number to truly say that humanity had been divided, but the founders of the Free Planets Alliance possessed incomparable diligence and passion, and by their power, material fulfillment was rapidly attained. Childbearing was encouraged, and the population grew. A national establishment was put in order, and the agricultural and industrial production capacity steadily increased.

It was as if the golden age of the Galactic Federation had returned.

Then, in SE 640, the forces of the Galactic Empire and the Free Planets encountered one another for the first time in the form of a clash between battleships of both sides.

From the standpoint of the Free Planets, such an encounter was a possibility for which they had long been preparing themselves. To the imperial side, however, it came like a bolt from the blue, and so victory in the battle went to the Free Planets. However, just before a direct hit from a neutron-beam cannon turned the imperial warship into a fireball of destruction, an emergency communiqué leapt away toward the capital of the empire.

Imperial bureaucrats there extracted old records from computer archives and learned that more than a century before, there had been an incident involving slaves escaping from Altair. So they had not died out in space after all; they lived and even prospered! A force was assembled to put down this insurrection. Great battleships were dispatched to the stronghold of those rebels.

And there those warships were utterly defeated.

There are many reasons why the imperial military was so soundly beaten despite its superior numbers. For one thing, the long-distance campaign caused physical and mental exhaustion to set in on the empire's soldiers and officers. For another, the issue of resupply was taken too lightly. In addition, the imperial military knew too little about the area in which they were fighting. They also underestimated both the enemy's strength and will to fight. Their strategy was careless. The Free Planets' military had capable commanders. Et cetera, et cetera.

Pao Lin—commander in chief of the alliance military—was a womanizer, a heavy drinker, and a glutton, and although the statesmen of the alliance—who placed great importance on an ancient and puritanical simplicity of lifestyle—were apt to cast a cold eye on his behavior, the man was a genius when it came to tactics and strategy. Yusuf Topparole—his chief of staff, who assisted him in this work—was also known as "Griping Yusuf," for he was constantly crying foul in matters large and small, saying, "Why do you have to give me such a hard time?"

Topparole, however, was also a precise and accurate theorist who might well have been called a living, breathing computer. Both men were still in their thirties when—on the outer fringes of the Dagon system—they conducted the greatest envelopment operation in history, annihilating the enemy and becoming the greatest heroes of the alliance since its founding.

For the Free Planets, this was an occasion for material expansion. When malcontent elements within the Galactic Empire learned of the existence of an independent power resisting the hegemony, they fled the empire in droves. Seeking a home where they could live in peace, they came flooding into the alliance.

In the three centuries following Emperor Rudolf's death, the establishment—firm as it had once been—had become somewhat more lenient, and the influence of the Bureau for the Maintenance of Public Order, which had once spared no effort in oppressing the people, had faded as well. Voices of discontent within the empire were growing louder.

The men and women who flowed into the Free Planets Alliance were accepted in a spirit of "he who comes shall not be turned away," but not all of these people held to republican ideals. Among this number there were even some aristocrats and members of the imperial family who came, having been on the losing side of court intrigues. With such people being allowed entry, and with the Free Planets growing too quickly, it was an inevitable progression, perhaps, that the nature of the alliance should begin to change more and more.

The Galactic Empire and the Free Planets Alliance had been in a chronic state of war since first contact, but from time to time they were visited by periods of uncertain peace as well. A product of this was the Phezzan Land Dominion. This was a sort of city-state in the Phezzan star system, which lay almost exactly between the two powers. It was under the sovereign rule of the Galactic Emperor and paid tribute to the empire, but when it came to its internal affairs, it was almost entirely self-governing—above all, in that it was permitted to have diplomatic relations and trade with the Free Planets Alliance.

The Galactic Empire, in making itself out to be the singular, absolute ruler of all humanity, did not acknowledge the existence of any legitimate authority outside the sphere of its influence. In official documents, the Free Planets Alliance was not referred to by its formal name; "the rebel entity" was written instead. The alliance's military were "rebels" as well, and the chairman of the High Council (the alliance's head of state) was "that deplorable rebel warlord." With state regulations such as these in place, diplomacy and trade with the alliance should have been out of the question, but Leopold Raap—a powerful merchant of Terran birth—was possessed of a passion that might be called extraordinary, and drove forward the establishment of this most peculiar dominion. With petitions and persuasion—and above all, very large bribes—the matter was decided.

Representing the dominion was the *landesherr*, or domain lord, who as vassal of the emperor ruled there in his name, oversaw commerce with the alliance, and occasionally even played the role of diplomat. By monopolizing foreign trade, the dominion accumulated massive stores of wealth, and small as it was, its power became impossible to ignore.

It would be untrue to say that no one ever worked for amity between empire and alliance. Manfred II, who was enthroned in IC 398 (SE 707) was one of Emperor Helmut's numerous illegitimate children. After slipping through the clutches of assassins, he came to spend his early childhood in the Free Planets Alliance and grew up in a more liberal atmosphere.

Because of this, it appeared that his enthronement might soon bring about peace and fair trade between the two powers, as well as political reform within the empire. However, these hopes soon came to nothing, as this young and popular emperor was assassinated within a year, and relations between the two powers immediately cooled. Manfred II's assassin was a reactionary aristocrat, but there is also a compelling argument suggesting that behind the scenes, the hands of Phezzan were at work, seeking to preserve its monopoly on the right to foreign commerce.

And so at the close of the eighth century SE and the fifth century IC, the Galactic Empire—undisciplined and uncontrolled simply because of its immense size—and the Free Planets Alliance—having lost the ideals of its founding period—continued on with their struggle mainly out of inertia, with Phezzan in their midst. According to the calculations of certain economists, the relative national power of the three states was as follows:

Galactic Empire	48 percent
Free Planets Alliance	40 percent
Phezzan Dominion	12 percent

The balance of power was precarious.

Moreover, the total population of humanity, which had numbered three hundred billion at the height of the Galactic Federation's prosperity, had by this time plummeted to forty billion, due to the long years of chaos.

The distribution was twenty-five billion living in the empire, thirteen billion in the Free Planets, and two billion in Phezzan.

"It would be nice if something would work out, but it doesn't look like it will."

That was a statement that described the situation nicely.

What turned that situation on its head was the appearance of one young man on Odin, the third planet of the Valhalla system. Named after the chief deity of Norse mythology, Odin was the *hauptplanet* to which Rudolf had relocated the capital of the Galactic Empire. The name of that young man of icy beauty and fearless countenance was Count Reinhard von Lohengramm.

Reinhard von Lohengramm's last name was originally Müsel, and in IC 467 (SE 776) he was born into an impoverished family that was aristocracy in name only. Reinhard's life changed when he was ten years old, and Annerose—his elder sister by five years—was taken away to the inner palace of Emperor Friedrich IV. Reinhard, a youth with golden hair and ice-blue eyes, became lieutenant commander of a division of imperial guards at age fifteen, receiving accelerated promotions thanks both to his own talent and to Annerose's favor with the emperor.

When he reached the age of twenty, he received the title of Count von Lohengramm and was promoted to the position of senior admiral in the Imperial Navy. This sort of extreme personnel management is typical of dictatorships, but with rank also comes responsibility. Had he been a noble of fine ancestry, there would have been no great need to prove himself, but because Reinhard was nothing more than "the little brother of the emperor's favorite," he had no choice but to do so.

At almost the same time, the Free Planets Alliance gained a new strategist. This was Yang Wen-li, who was born in SE 767 and enlisted at age twenty. Yang Wen-li had never aimed for a career in the military, and if a series of coincidences hadn't pushed him in the right direction, he would have reached the end of his life not as a creator of history, but as a spectator.

"There are things you can do and things you can't do."

That was Yang's pet philosophy. Toward fate, he had a much more passive disposition than Reinhard, but on the other hand, he had great adaptability and inventiveness. Even so, he remained uncomfortable with war and the soldier's job of prosecuting it, and for the rest of his life, the military authorities were never free of his requests to "chuck my rank and retire."

At the start of SE 796 and IC 487, Reinhard led a fleet numbering twenty thousand vessels on an expedition. His goal was to bring the rebel forces—who so audaciously referred to themselves as the Free Planets Alliance—to heel, and through that achievement establish his own personal position.

The alliance's military had organized a fleet of forty thousand ships to intercept him. One of the staff officers in that fleet was named Yang Wen-li.

Count Reinhard von Lohengramm, was twenty years old that year, and Yang Wen-li was twenty-nine…

CHAPTER 1:

I

Imperial Navy captain Siegfried Kircheis froze for a moment when he stepped onto the bridge, standing riveted in place in spite of himself. The depths of space were before him, scattered with countless points of light—overwhelmingly massive, seeming to envelop his entire body.

For a moment, he stood there silent, but an instant later, the illusion that he was floating in an infinity of blackness disappeared. The bridge of the battleship *Brünhild,* Kircheis knew, was designed in the form of a gigantic hemisphere, the upper half of which was a single display screen. Dragging his senses away from the sky and back down to the ground, Kircheis took another look around the bridge.

The illumination in the vast chamber was extremely muted, creating a crepuscular dimness. Crew were moving to and fro amid countless screens, consoles, meters, computers, and communication devices of all sizes. The movements of their heads and limbs brought to mind schools of migratory fish swimming in the currents.

Kircheis's nostrils detected the faint tang of an almost imperceptible odor. It was one with which soldiers in space were well acquainted, produced by the blending of recycled oxygen, ozone given off by machinery, and adrenaline secreted by tense soldiers who would soon be facing combat.

The young red-haired man turned to face the center of the bridge and walked toward it with long strides. Although he held the rank of captain, Kircheis was not yet twenty-one. When he was out of uniform, he was "nothing but a handsome, redheaded beanpole," as the female officers in the rear service whispered. From time to time, it bothered him that his age and his rank were so out of proportion to one another. He wasn't able to accept his circumstances in the cool, calm way that his commanding officer did.

Count Reinhard von Lohengramm had his command chair tilted backward and was staring intently into the sea of stars that flooded over the display screen above. Kircheis felt a soft resistance from the air as he drew near. A soundproof force screen was up. Conversations taking place within a five-meter radius of Reinhard would be inaudible to anyone on the outside.

"Stargazing, Excellency?" he asked.

A moment after hearing Kircheis's voice, Reinhard shifted his line of sight and returned his chair to an upright position. Although he was still sitting down, his uniform—functional and black, with silver highlights here and there—made clear the tight masculinity of his slender, well-balanced limbs.

Reinhard was a handsome young man. One might even say that his good looks were without peer. His white, oval face was adorned on three sides with slightly curling golden hair, and his lips and the bridge of his nose had an elegance that brought to mind a sculpture carved by the hands of some ancient master craftsman.

But what could never be captured in lifeless sculpture were his eyes— ice-blue eyes that shone with light like the blade of a keenly polished sword, or the gleam of some frozen star. "Beautiful ambitious eyes," gossiped the ladies at court. "Dangerous ambitious eyes," whispered the men. Either way, it was certain that those eyes possessed something other than the inorganic perfection of sculpture.

Looking up at his faithful subordinate, Reinhard answered, "Yes, I love the stars." Then he added, "Have you gotten taller again?"

"I'm the same 190 centimeters that I was two months ago, Excellency. I don't think I'm going to grow any taller."

"Seven centimeters taller than me is certainly plenty," Reinhard replied. In the sound of his voice was the ring of an overcompetitive schoolboy. Kircheis smiled faintly. Until about six years ago, there had been virtually no difference in their heights. But when Kircheis's growth spurt had begun to put a distance between himself and Reinhard, the blond-haired lad had been genuinely frustrated. "Are you going to leave your friend behind and just grow up by yourself?" he had sometimes complained. That was the childish side of Reinhard, of which only Kircheis—and one other—knew.

"I see," Reinhard replied. "So, what business brings you up here?"

"Yes, sir. It's the battle formation of the rebel military. According to reports from three of our surveillance craft, they are closing in on our forces from three directions at uniform velocity. May I use your console's display?"

The young senior admiral nodded assent, and Kircheis moved his hands rhythmically over the console. On the display screen occupying the left half of Reinhard's command console, four arrows floated into existence, positioned at the top, bottom, left, and right sides of the screen, and all were advancing toward the center. Only the arrow at the bottom of the screen was colored red. The other three were green.

"The enemy's Fourth Fleet lies directly ahead of us, and we estimate that its force numbers twelve thousand vessels. Its distance from us is 2,200 light-seconds. At our current velocities, we will make contact in about six hours."

Kircheis moved his finger around the screen. On the left side was the alliance's Second Fleet, with a force of fifteen thousand vessels, approaching from a distance of 2,400 light-seconds. On the right side was the Sixth Fleet, numbering thirteen thousand vessels, advancing from a distance of 2,050 light-seconds.

With the development of the antigravity field system—along with all manner of radar-permeability devices, ECM waves, and materials that rendered radar useless in determining the position and strength of enemy forces centuries ago, the militaries of the galaxy had turned back to reliance on classical methods such as manned surveillance craft and observation satellites. After calculating the time differences and factoring in the element of distance, intelligence gathered in this manner could then be used to learn the enemy's position. Add to this the estimated levels of heat emission and mass, and a usable—if imperfect—calculation of force size could also be obtained.

"So in total forty thousand ships, eh? Twice the size of our fleet."

"They're attempting to envelop us by coming in from three directions."

"And I suppose our senile old generals have all gone pale in their faces...or red, perhaps." Reinhard allowed a spiteful smile to flash across his fair-skinned face. Though he had just been told that he was being surrounded by a force twice the size of his own, not a hint of panic was visible in Reinhard's expression.

"Pale, without a doubt," replied Kircheis. "The five admirals have come here in haste to request a meeting with Your Excellency."

"Oh? After they shot off their mouths saying they didn't even want to see my face?"

"Do you decline to meet with them?"

"No, I'll see them. In order to enlighten them."

The five men who appeared before Reinhard were Admiral Merkatz, vice admirals Staden and Fogel, and rear admirals Fahrenheit and Erlach. These were the "senile old generals" of whom Reinhard had spoken, though perhaps that term was too harsh. Merkatz—the eldest of them— was not yet sixty, and the youngest—Fahrenheit—was only thirty-one. It was not that they were too old, but that Reinhard and Kircheis were too young.

"Our thanks, Your Excellency," Merkatz said, speaking for all of them, "for permitting us to offer our opinions." Merkatz had joined the service long before Reinhard had been born, and was rich in knowledge and experience of both combat and military administration. His medium-height, thick-boned build and sleepy-looking eyes gave him the appearance of an unremarkable middle-aged man, but his record and reputation were far greater than those of the likes of Reinhard.

Taking the initiative, Reinhard politely replied, "I understand what you wish to say, milords." In form only, he was following the etiquette that Merkatz had displayed. "You wish to bring our disadvantaged circumstances to my attention."

"We do, Your Excellency," answered Vice Admiral Staden, advancing a half step forward. Staden was in his midforties, slender as a knife, and gave the impression of a man with a very sharp mind. As a soldier, he was the "staff officer" type who excelled in tactical theory and speech-making.

"The enemy has double the number of ships that we do. Moreover, they are attempting to envelop us from three directions. This means that in terms of battle readiness, we are trailing behind the enemy already."

Reinhard's ice-blue eyes gleamed coldly as he looked straight at the vice admiral. "In other words, you are saying that we will lose?"

"I said nothing of the sort, Excellency. But it is a fact that we are at a disadvantage in terms of preparedness. If you'll look at your display screen, you'll understand."

Seven sets of eyes focused on Reinhard's console display.

The positions of the two opposing forces, as Kircheis had shown to Reinhard, were indicated there. From outside the sound-deadening field, a number of soldiers were casting deeply curious glances at the high-ranking commanders. Then, at a glare from Vice Admiral Staden, they all hurriedly averted their eyes. After pausing to clear his throat, the vice admiral began to speak again.

"Many years ago, a fleet that was the pride of the empire was delivered a most regrettable defeat by the rebels of the so-called Free Planets Alliance. This is the same formation that they used then."

"You speak of the Dagon Annihilation, correct?"

"I do. It was a truly regrettable defeat." A deep, heavy sigh escaped the vice admiral's lips. "Victory in that battle rightfully belonged to humanity's true ruler—His Highness, the emperor of the Galactic

Empire—and to his faithful servants, the officers and soldiers of our military. But they were caught off guard by the rebel forces' cunning trick, and in the end, a million of our bravest, best, and brightest died meaningless deaths. If—in the coming battle—we were to follow in the footsteps of those who came before us, it would be certain to bring grief to His Highness, so—it was my foolish thinking, but would it not be wiser to make an honorable withdrawal now, rather than rushing impetuously forward in pursuit of achievement?"

Foolish thinking indeed, you worse-than-incompetent blatherer, Reinhard thought. But when he opened his mouth, he said, "I acknowledge your eloquence, milord. Your argument, however, I cannot accept. Withdrawal is out of the question."

"But…why? May we hear your reasoning?"

The look that rose up in Vice Admiral Staden's eyes seemed to append, *you unteachable whelp*, but taking no mind of it, Reinhard replied, "Because we are in a position of overwhelming tactical advantage over the enemy."

"What do you mean?" Staden's eyebrows quivered noticeably. The admirals all stared at the handsome young commander—Merkatz dumbfoundedly, and Fogel and Erlach in utter shock.

Only Fahrenheit—the youngest of the five—had a look of interest brimming in his light-aquamarine eyes. Born into lower-class aristocracy, Fahrenheit openly professed that he had become a soldier in order to eat. He had an established reputation as a planner of high-mobility, high-speed attacks, though it was also said that he was lacking in tenacity when it came to intercepting attacks.

"It would seem you have an opinion that is difficult for dullards such as ourselves to understand. We would be grateful if you could explain your meaning in more detail."

Vice Admiral Staden's voice grated on Reinhard's ears. Thinking to himself, *I'll rip that irritating tongue of yours out the day after tomorrow*, Reinhard granted his request: "I said that we have the advantage for two reasons. First, the enemy forces are divided along these three vectors, while our forces are concentrated in one place. While the enemy has the advantage in terms of overall numbers, we have the advantage over any of these three divisions."

The admirals listened, saying nothing.

"Secondly, when it comes to moving from one battlespace to the next, our force—which is located in the center—is able to take a shorter route than any of them. In order for them to move to another battlespace without fighting us, they will have to make a wide detour. This makes both time and distance our allies."

The silence of the admirals stretched on.

"In other words, we exceed the enemy in both mobility and concentration of firepower. If these are not the conditions for victory, what would you call them?"

In a sharp, cutting tone of voice, Reinhard finished speaking. Kircheis thought for a moment that the five admirals had frozen into crystal on the spot. Reinhard had turned the thinking of the older, more experienced military men on its head.

Reinhard transfixed the shocked, unmoving Vice Admiral Staden with an ironic gaze, pressing his advantage.

"We are in no danger of envelopment. We have a fine opportunity to destroy the enemy on each vector. You tell me not to make the most of this opportunity and to make a meaningless withdrawal, but to do so would not be merely passive—it would be criminal. Why? Because our mission is to do battle with the rebel forces and destroy them. 'An honorable withdrawal,' you said. But where is the honor in failing to complete the mission with which His Imperial Highness has charged us? Does this not resemble the self-justification of a coward, milord?"

At the mention of "His Imperial Highness," a ripple of tension ran through the bodies of four of the admirals, excluding Fahrenheit. Reinhard thought it all absurd.

"So you say, Commander," began Staden, attempting to plead with him. "But although Your Excellency may call this a 'fine opportunity,' you are the only one here who believes it to be so. Even from the standpoint of commonsense tactics, it is impossible to accept. For a strategy which has no proven track record—"

This one's not just incompetent, he's an imbecile, Reinhard concluded. *An unprecedented operation can't have a track record. Its record will begin with the coming battle, will it not?* Speaking aloud, he said, "Then tomorrow, milord, you will verify its record with your own eyes. Is that not acceptable?"

"Are you certain of success?" asked Staden.

"I am. But only if all of you follow my strategy faithfully."

"What kind of strategy?" Staden asked, making no attempt to hide his suspicion.

Reinhard glanced at Kircheis for a moment and then began to explain the operation.

Two minutes later, the interior of the soundproof field was filled with the sound of Staden's shouts.

"That sounds fine on paper, but there is no way it will actually work, Excellency. This kind of—"

"Enough! There's no need for further debate. His Imperial Majesty named me as commander for this operation. Your obedience to my commands must needs be interpreted as proof of your loyalty toward His Majesty. Is that not the duty of a soldier of the empire? Do not forget: I am your commanding officer."

A moment passed in silence.

"All authority over your lives rests in my hands. If you wish of your own accord to defy the will of His Highness, very well. I will simply use the authority he has vested in me to relieve you of duty and to punish you severely as insubordinates. Are you prepared to go to those lengths?"

Reinhard glared at the five men standing before him. They did not answer.

II

The five admirals departed. They neither accepted nor consented, but they did find it difficult to oppose the authority of the emperor. Only Fahrenheit's expression could have been interpreted as favorable toward Reinhard's plan for the coming operations, but the expressions of the other four were to varying degrees saying, "How dare that brat brandish the emperor's authority!"

For Kircheis, circumstances were forming in which it was a bit difficult to remain silent. Even without all this, Reinhard had a bad reputation as an overly young upstart. From the standpoint of these veteran commanders, Reinhard was nothing more than a weak little asteroid, giving off no light of his own, using the influence of his sister Annerose to borrow the power of the emperor.

It was not as though this were Reinhard's first campaign, though. In the five years since he had enlisted, he had already emerged victorious in a number of battles. But if someone were to tell that to the commanders, they would only say something like, "He was in a good unit" or "The enemy was too weak."

And because it was difficult to say that Reinhard was humble and courteous in all matters, their antipathy toward him had been amplified, and now in the shadows he was widely referred to as "that impudent golden brat."

"Are you sure about this?" the red-haired youth asked Reinhard, a look of anxiety rising up in his blue eyes.

"Leave me alone," his commanding officer said calmly. "What can they do? They're cowards who can't even make a nasty remark individually—they have to come in a group. They haven't the courage to defy the emperor's authority."

"But what little courage they have may gather in the shadows."

Reinhard looked at his aide-de-camp and gave a low, amused laugh. "You're still the same old worrier. But there's nothing to fret about. Even though they're full of grievances now, that situation will change in a single day. And I'll show that idiot Staden a framed copy of the 'track record' he loves so much."

Saying that he'd had enough of such talk, Reinhard rose from his chair and invited Kircheis to come to his cabin for a break. "Let's have a drink, Kircheis. I've got some good wine. It's supposed to be a rare 410 vintage."

"That sounds wonderful."

"Well, then, let's go. And by the way, Kircheis—"

"Yes, Excellency?"

"That 'Excellency' thing. There's no need to go around calling me that when nobody else is with us. Talk to me like you always have."

"I understand what you're saying, but—"

"If you understand it, then do it. Because when this battle is over and we return to Odin, people will be calling you 'Excellency' as well."

Kircheis said nothing.

"You'll be promoted to commodore. Look forward to it."

Leaving the bridge to Captain Reuschner, Reinhard set out for his private room. Following behind him, Kircheis ruminated over what his commanding officer had said to him.

When this battle is over and we return, you'll be made a commodore... It seemed that defeat wasn't in the young, blond-haired admiral's mind at all. To anyone but Kircheis, those words would surely be taken for hopeless arrogance. But Kircheis knew that Reinhard had only been speaking out of affection for a dear friend.

A thought suddenly occurred to Kircheis: *Has it already been ten years since we first met?* In meeting Reinhard and his sister Annerose, his destiny had changed forever.

Siegfried Kircheis's father was a minor official who worked in the Ministry of Justice. Harried about every day by bosses, paperwork, and computers, he earned forty thousand imperial marks a year. He was a kind, ordinary man whose only two pleasures were raising some sort of Baldurian orchid in his narrow garden and drinking black beer after dinner. As for his little redheaded son, the boy somehow managed to dangle at the lower edge of the honor roll at school, was a powerhouse in sports, and was his parents' pride and joy.

One day, a man and his two children moved into the house next door, which had been as good as abandoned.

Young Kircheis had been shocked when he first heard that the dispirited, middle-aged man was of the aristocracy, but when he saw the golden-haired brother and sister, he believed it. *They're so beautiful!* he had thought.

The next day, he met the younger brother. The boy named Reinhard was the same age as Kircheis, born only two months later according to the standard Space Era calendar. When the red-haired boy gave his name, the blond-haired boy's well-shaped eyebrows had shot upward.

"Siegfried? What a vulgar name."

At such an unexpected reply, the red-haired boy had been shocked and at a loss for how to reply.

Then Reinhard had continued, adding, "But Kircheis is a good last name. Very poetic. So I've decided to call you by your last name."

On the other hand, his elder sister Annerose had abbreviated his given name, calling him "Sieg." The features of her face bore a strong resemblance to those of her younger brother but were a step more delicate, and her faint little smile was infinitely gentle. When introduced to her by Reinhard, she had given him a smile that was like dappled sunlight streaming through the trees.

"Sieg, please be a good friend to my brother."

From that day until now, Kircheis had obeyed her request faithfully.

A lot had happened since then. One day, a luxurious landcar that Kircheis had never seen before stopped in front of the house next door, and a middle-aged man wearing fine clothes stepped out. All through the night, the tearful voice of the indomitable Reinhard had lashed out unceasingly against his father.

"You sold my sister!" he cried.

The next morning, when Kircheis went over on the pretext of asking Reinhard to walk to school with him, Annerose had said with a gentle, sad smile, "My brother can't go to school with you anymore. I know it was just for a short time, but thank you for being his friend."

Then the beautiful young girl had kissed him on his forehead and given him a homemade chocolate torte. That day, the red-haired boy hadn't gone to school. Instead, he had carefully carried the torte to a nature preserve, and, taking care not to be spotted by any patrol robots, had sat down in the shadow of some conifers—"Martian pines" they were called, for reasons no one knew—and there he had stayed for a long time, eating the torte. As he contemplated being separated from Annerose and Reinhard, tears had welled up in his eyes, and he had wiped them with his hands, leaving dark-brown stripes across his face.

When it was dark, he had returned home, preparing himself for a scolding, but his parents had said nothing. The lights were out at the house next door.

One month later, Reinhard had without warning come suddenly to visit, wearing the uniform of the Imperial Military Children's Academy. The blond-haired boy had spoken to the shocked, thrilled Kircheis in the affected tones of an adult. "I'm going to be a soldier," he had said. "It's the fastest way to get ahead. And I have to get ahead in the world so I can set Annerose free. Kircheis, come to the same school as me, won't you? They're all louts at the Children's Academy."

His parents were not opposed to the idea. Perhaps they had been hoping that their son would be able to get ahead in the world that way, or perhaps they had realized that their son had already been stolen away from them by the brother and sister from the house next door. At any rate, Kircheis made the decision in his youth that he would walk the same road as Reinhard.

Most of the students at the Children's Academy were the offspring of aristocrats, and the rest were all sons of eminent civilians. It was clear that Kircheis had only been admitted due to Reinhard's earnest desire and Annerose's intercession.

Reinhard's marks usually put him at the top of his class, and Kircheis also placed high. Not just for his own sake, but also for Reinhard and Annerose, he could not afford to let his grades slip.

From time to time, the fathers and elder brothers of students would come to visit the school. All of them were aristocrats of high status, but Kircheis had no respect for them. He could smell the stench of men who had become arrogant in their privilege.

"Look at them, Kircheis," Reinhard would whisper. Whenever he saw such nobles, his voice filled with an intense hatred and scorn. "They didn't get to be where they are today through any effort of their own... They inherited their authority and fortune from their fathers only by reason of blood, and they aren't even ashamed of it. The universe does not exist to be dominated by such people."

"Reinhard..." Kircheis would begin.

"It's true, Kircheis! There's not a shred of reason why you and I should have to stand downwind of their ilk."

This kind of conversation had passed between them not a few times, but on one occasion, Reinhard said something that gave his red-haired friend the shock of his life.

They had just made a polite salute—a salute that was the sacred duty of all subjects of the empire—before one of the many statues of Emperor Rudolf that towered haughtily above every quarter of the capital. They dared not do otherwise, for the eyes of these statues were elaborate video cameras, and the Ministry of the Interior was ever watchful for dangerous elements who flouted imperial authority. It was after this salute that Reinhard began to speak passionately.

"Kircheis, have you ever thought about this? The Goldenbaum Dynasty doesn't go all the way back to the dawn of humanity. It was founded by that arrogant, overbearing Rudolf. And the fact that there was a founder means that before he came to power, there was no imperial family, and he amounted to nothing more than a single, solitary citizen. There at the beginning, Rudolf was an ambitious upstart and nothing more. But in time, he ended up claiming titles like 'Sacred and Inviolable Emperor.'"

What is he trying to tell me? Kircheis had wondered as his heart began beating faster.

"Do you think that what was possible for Rudolf," Reinhard had asked, "is impossible for me?"

Then, with thoughts that took his breath away, Kircheis had looked back into the gaze of Reinhard's ice-blue, jewellike eyes. It had been winter, just before they entered the military service.

III

...from the twentieth century through the twenty-first century AD, one can produce many examples of the rampant technological development which threatened to rob humanity of

its identity. In particular, the replication of human beings by cloning—one of the fruits of genetic engineering—was once mistakenly believed to be a guarantee of eternal life, despite the fact that only its theoretical possibilities had been demonstrated. When cloning was brought together with ideas of social Darwinism, fearsome ideologies that took a very light view of human life ran rampant across the face of the planet known as Earth. The opinion that those possessing inferior genes were unqualified to bear children and that inferior races should be weeded out for the qualitative improvement of the human race began to hold increasing sway. This was truly the first budding of the assertions that Rudolf von Goldenbaum would make in latter times...

The passage that was displayed on the console's tiny screen suddenly dimmed and faded out. Faster than one could push a control button, another passage appeared.

"Commodore Yang, the commander is calling for you. Please report to the conn as quickly as possible."

His reading interrupted, Commodore Yang Wen-li grabbed his uniform beret and ran a hand through his unruly head of black hair. He was a junior staff officer in the Free Planets Alliance's Second Fleet, occupying a seat in a corner of the bridge of its flagship, *Patroklos*. Since he had been enjoying his private reading on a console originally intended as a tactical computer, there was no sense in feeling annoyed.

Yang's Name Notation Type was "E." This was a tradition carried over from the days of the federation. People whose family names came before their given names were designated "E," which stood for "Eastern." Those whose given names came before their family names were called "W," for "Western."

Of course, in this day and age, with the races having mixed as thoroughly as has they had, a person's name was only a vague indicator of his or her direct ancestry.

The twenty-nine-year-old Yang, with his black hair, black eyes, and medium height and build, gave more the impression of an easygoing scholar than that of a soldier. At least that's the impression one might describe if pressed. Most people who looked at him saw nothing more than a very quiet-natured young man. Most couldn't believe their ears when they heard his rank.

"Commodore Yang, reporting as ordered, sir."

The fleet commander, Vice Admiral Paetta, turned his unfriendly eyes on the young officer saluting him. He was a middle-aged man with stern, forbidding features that made it impossible to imagine him in any line of work but the military.

Observing Yang again, he simply said, "I've looked over the tactical plan you submitted," though what he wanted to say was, *How in the world can a sissy-looking kid like you be only two ranks below me?!* "It was a fairly interesting idea," he continued. "But too cautious. And I wonder if it wasn't just a bit too passive."

"You don't say," Yang answered. He said it in a very quiet tone of voice, but on reflection, it might have seemed a pretty rude thing to say to a commanding officer. Vice Admiral Paetta hadn't noticed it, though.

"As you yourself noted," he continued, "it would be pretty hard to lose with this strategy. But there's no point in simply not losing. We've gotta win. We're closing in on the enemy from three directions. And on top of that, we've got twice their numbers. All the conditions are lined up for a big win, so why are you thinking up ways to avoid losing?"

"Well, yeah, but it's not like they're surrounded already."

This time Paetta did notice. His eyebrows drew together in irritation, making a splendid vertical crease in the midst of his forehead.

Yang was as relaxed as ever.

Nine years ago, when he had graduated from the National Defense Force Officers' Academy, Yang had been an unremarkable, newly minted ensign. He had graduated 1,909th in his class of 4,840. But now, he could certainly not be called an unremarkable commodore. He was one of only sixteen officers in the entire alliance who had reached admiralty while still in their twenties.

It was impossible that Vice Admiral Paetta was unaware of the young commodore's service record. In nine years, Yang had participated in over a hundred combat operations. And even though he hadn't often been in large-scale battles involving thousands of vessels like this one, he hadn't been just some kid playing with firecrackers, either. Above all else, he had been the shining hero of the so-called El Facil Evacuation.

Though he was young, he was the hero of a historic battle, and yet Vice Admiral Paetta didn't get that impression from him at all. Still, when the officers' salaries were calculated in the rear service at headquarters, it was clear that he was being well paid in accordance with his record.

"At any rate, this tactical plan is rejected."

Paetta held the papers out to Yang, then added unnecessarily, "Let me also just say, this is nothing personal."

IV

Yang Wen-li's father, Yang Tai-long, was known as a man of great ability among the many traders and merchants of the Free Planets Alliance. Beneath his inoffensive little smile, the wheels of a keen mind for business were turning, and since the day he had set out as the owner of a small commercial vessel, his fortune had grown steadily.

"It's because I dote on my money," he would say to friends who asked him the secret of his success. "It goes out into the world and makes its fortune, and then it comes back home like a faithful child. Bronze coins turn into silver ones. Silver ones turn into gold. It all depends on their upbringing!"

As he himself seemed to think that this was a sharp-witted joke, he went around telling it every chance he got, eventually acquiring the nickname "The Financial-Parenting Expert." It would be difficult to claim that this title was always spoken with affectionate intent, but Yang Tai-long himself was apparently quite happy with it.

In addition, Yang Tai-long was a collector of antique art. His residence was piled high with stacks of paintings, sculptures, and ceramics from the days when the AD calendar was still in use. Before he came to occupy an office and command a fleet of interstellar commerce vessels, he was always busy at home admiring and polishing his antiques.

After this hobby had metastasized, there were rumors that he had even chosen an antique as his spouse. For after divorcing his first wife—who had had a penchant for wasting money—he had married another woman of considerable beauty, who was, however, the widow of a certain soldier. Then his son, Yang Wen-li, had been born.

Yang Tai-long had been in his study at home when he received the news that it was a boy. His hands had paused for a moment in their polishing of an old vase, and he had muttered, "Huh. So when I'm gone, all these works of art will be his."

Then his hands had resumed their polishing.

When Yang Wen-li was five years old, his mother died. The cause was acute heart disease, and since she had always been healthy up until that point, her sudden death understandably came as a shock to Yang Tai-long. He dropped a bronze lion ornament to the floor but then unexpectedly picked it back up and incensed his wife's entire family by uttering these words:

"Thank goodness I wasn't polishing something breakable..."

Yang Tai-long had now lost two wives—one to divorce and one to death—and he had no wish to marry again. He assigned a maid to take care of his son, but when the maid was on break or when the boy became difficult to manage, Yang Tai-long would set him down beside himself, and together they would polish a vase or something.

When the relatives of his late wife came to visit and found father and son wordlessly polishing vases in the study, they were horrified, and in the end the assertion emerged that the child should be rescued from living with such an irresponsible father. When they had cornered the father and asked him which was more important to him—his son or his antiques—he had replied:

"Well, the art required a lot of capital, you know..."

But on the other hand, I got my son for free, being the implication.

The entire family, driven into a rage by these words, was preparing to take the matter of the boy's custody to court, but Yang Tai-long guessed what they were up to, and carrying the boy with him, boarded an interstellar trading ship and disappeared from the capital of Heinessen. The family, realizing how absurd it would be to allege that a father had kid-napped his own son, shrugged their collective shoulders and did nothing beyond tracking where in the starry sky the spaceship had gone. "Oh well," they said. "The fact that he took the boy with him must mean he at least has a beating heart."

In this way, Yang Wen-li came to spend the greater part of his first sixteen years inside the hulls of starships.

In the beginning, the young Yang Wen-li would become ill and run fevers every time he experienced warp, but eventually he got used to it and was able to calmly accept his circumstances. Once he had generally satisfied his interest in engineering, he turned his attention in another direction: history.

The boy watched videos, read e-copies of old books, and loved listen-ing to reminiscences about the past, but in particular, he held a deep interest in "the most wicked usurper in all of history," Rudolf.

Because Yang Wen-li was in the Free Planets Alliance, Rudolf was naturally made out to be the very incarnation of evil, but in listening to what people said about him, the boy had begun to have his doubts. If Rudolf had really been such a villain, he wondered, then why had people supported him and given him power?

"Because he was dishonest to his marrow. He had the people fooled."

"Why were the people fooled?"

"Because Rudolf was an evil man, y'see."

These answers didn't quite satisfy the boy, but his father's view differed somewhat from those of the others he talked to. He answered his son's inquiry in this way:

"Because the people wanted to have it easy."

"Have it easy?"

"Exactly. They didn't want to solve their own problems by their own effort. They were all waiting for some saint or superman to show up from somewhere and shoulder all their troubles by himself. And that's what Rudolf took advantage of. Listen. I want you to remember this: it's the ones who empower a dictator who deserve most of the blame. But the ones who don't support him actively—who watch it happening without saying anything—they're just as much to blame. But listen, don't you think you should turn your interests in a more profitable direction than this kind of stuff?"

"More profitable?"

"Like money or artwork. Art for the soul, money for the pocket."

Despite comments such as these, Yang Tai-long never forced his business or his hobbies on his son, and Yang Wen-li became more and more absorbed in history.

A few days before his son's sixteenth birthday, Yang Tai-long died. It was the result of an accident involving his ship's nuclear-fusion furnace. Yang Wen-li had decided to take the entrance examination for Heinnessen Memorial University's history department, having only just recently gotten his father's approval.

"Ah, why not?" he had said. "It's not like there's never been anyone to make money at history."

With those words, the father had given his son his blessing to walk the path that he loved.

"Don't ever despise money, though. If you've got it, you can get by without bowing your head to people you don't like, and you don't have to compromise your principles just to get along in life, either. But just like politicians, it's best if we manage it well and not just do as we please with it."

At the end of his forty-eight years, Yang Tai-long left behind his son, his company, and his huge collection of artwork.

After Yang Wen-li had finished with his father's funeral, he was kept busy with mundane matters such as inheritance and taxes. And then he discovered the terrible truth: the works of art that his father had so passionately collected prior to his death were, almost without exception, counterfeit.

From the Etrurian vases to the rococo-style portraits to the bronze horses from imperial Han China, everything was "worth less than a single dinar," as the government's public appraiser told him by way of an expressionless underling.

And that wasn't all. Prior to his death, his father had mortgaged his ownership of the company in order to cover his debts. In the end, Yang was left out in the cold with nothing but a mountain of junk.

But just as he had done when he was a child, Yang accepted the situation with a wry smile, mingled with a sigh. He did think it was rather odd that his wheeler-dealer of a father should lack an eye for value only when it came to his beloved works of art. If—just if—he had been knowingly collecting forgeries, Yang felt like that would have been just like his father. As for his father's company, Yang had never had any desire to take over the business anyway, so he didn't mind losing it one bit.

At any rate, there was an even bigger problem. He didn't have enough money left on hand to afford the cost of going to the top-tier university he was supposed to be attending soon.

Because of the chronic state of war with the Galactic Empire, hugely expensive military appropriations were putting a strain on the national budget, and funding for education in the humanities—which had no direct military applications—kept getting cut. It was hard to get a scholarship.

It seemed as if there would be no school anywhere where one could study history for free . . . and yet there was one.

And the National Defense Force Officers' Academy, with its Department of Military History, was it.

Just before the deadline, Yang sent off his application, and although his entrance exam results placed him far indeed from the head of the class, he somehow managed a passing score.

∪

In this way, Yang Wen-li entered officer's school entirely as an expedient. Despite the fact that he was a stranger to both patriotism and belligerent militarism, his course had been set.

Almost all of the mountain of junk he had inherited from his father he threw away—though he did put some of it into storage—and he moved into the officer's school dormitory quite literally empty-handed.

His motives being what they were, there was no way Yang was going to be a top-level student. He diligently studied his military history—and all the wide range of nonmilitary history that made up its background—but he skimped as much as possible on his other subjects.

Particularly in the areas of weapons training, flight class, and mechanical engineering—the boring subjects—he was perfectly happy getting grades that hovered just above failing.

If he did fail, though, there was the danger of being expelled, and even if he weren't expelled, the makeup tests would take up precious time. The point being that as long as he didn't fail, it was okay. His goal was not to be the director of Joint Operational Headquarters, the secretary of the space srmada, or the superintendent general of staff. He wanted to be a researcher at the Military History Collation Office. He had practically no interest at all in advancement as a soldier.

His grades in Military History were outstanding, and combined with his nap-of-the-earth marks in all the practical subjects, produced a total that was the very picture of "average." However, Yang's marks in Strategic Tactical Simulations weren't bad at all. Grades in this class were determined by having the students face off against one another in VR simulations. The instructors were shocked one day when the class's top student—a boy named Wideborn, who was touted as the most brilliant student the school had seen in the last decade—was soundly defeated by Yang Wen-li.

Yang focused all of his forces on one point, cut his opponent's supply lines, and then switched over to a purely defensive posture. Wideborn, using a variety of tactics, penetrated deep into Yang's ranks, but when his supplies ran out, he had no choice but to retreat. Both the computer's judgment and the instructor's scoring awarded the victory to Yang.

Wideborn, whose pride had been wounded, was furious. "I'd have won if he'd played it straight and fought me head-on. I mean, all he did was keep running back and forth to get away, right?"

Yang didn't argue. For him, this class was making up for his low marks in Mechanical Engineering, and with that, he was satisfied in full.

That satisfaction, however, was to be short-lived.

At the end of his second year, Yang was summoned by an instructor and ordered to switch his major to Military Strategy.

"It's not just you," the instructor had said, trying to be consoling. "They're doing away with the whole military history department, so every student there has to change majors. You beat that Wideborn fellow in the simulation. That's an achievement. You should change departments anyway, just to make the most of your talents."

"I came to this school because I wanted to study military history," Yang objected. "I don't think it's fair to recruit students and then scrap their department before they graduate."

"Cadet Yang, you may not be on active duty yet, but from the moment you entered this school, you became a soldier. This is how petty officers get treated. And as a soldier, you have to follow your orders."

Yang said nothing.

"But listen, there's no way this is a bad deal for you. Military Strategy is a department that's packed with top-level students. Students who try to get into Strategy but don't make it flow into other departments. That's the reality here. It's a rare thing for someone to flow the other way."

"I'm honored, sir, but . . . do I sound like a top-level student to you?"

"Watch it with the sarcasm. Anyway, if you don't like it, you've got the right to quit, naturally. Of course, if you do that, you'll have to pay back all the tuition and school fees you've accrued thus far. Only soldiers get to study for free."

Yang was dumbstruck. He couldn't help remembering what his late father had said about money. Truly, with people being people, you could never be free in this life.

At age twenty, Yang graduated from the military strategy department with average grades and received his commission as an ensign. A year later, he was promoted to sublieutenant, but that was normal for graduates of the Officer's Academy. It didn't mean that his service record was particularly outstanding.

He was assigned to an office at the Joint Operational Headquarters called the Office of Records and Statistics, and no one distinguished themselves in combat there. But for Yang, it was rather pleasant to have a job where he could be around old records.

However, simultaneous with his promotion to sublieutenant, Yang received orders for frontline duty. He departed for his new post as a staff officer for forces stationed in the territory of El Facil.

"When one thing goes crazy, everything goes crazy," the young lieutenant junior grade grumbled.

Even though he had never once actively sought to become a soldier, here he was, wearing a black beret with a white five-pointed star mark, an ivory-white scarf tucked into the collar of his black jumper, black shoes, and slacks the same color as his scarf: an extremely functional military uniform.

That year, in SE 788, the Battle of El Facil greatly accelerated the course of Sublieutenant Yang Wen-li's life.

The curtain rose on this battle with a scene of outrageous disgrace for the Free Planets Alliance's navy. To the battle itself, both sides had dispatched in the neighborhood of a thousand vessels each, and after both sides had taken about 20 percent casualties, they had temporarily called it off. Yang did nothing during the engagement. All he did was sit in his station chair on the bridge of the flagship and watch the battle. He was not even asked for his opinion.

However, as the alliance ships were beginning their return to base, they were unexpectedly attacked from behind. The Imperial Navy, while pretending that they too were returning to base, had executed a rapid reversal of course and charged against the Alliance Navy, which had relaxed its guard and shown them its flank.

Spears of energy ripped through the blackness of space, and miniature novas flashed and vanished in an instant. The energies unleashed by destroyed vessels became a maelstrom, tossing other ships to and fro. Rear Admiral Lynch—the commander of the alliance fleet—must have panicked. Without trying to calm the confusion of his allies, his flagship fled back toward El Facil at full speed.

Upon learning that their commander had turned tail, the alliance fleet naturally lost its will to fight, and the ships that had been waging isolated battles with the enemies close at hand began to peel off and run from the field of battle, one after another. Some of them chose their routes of retreat independently and fled from the El Facil territory altogether, while others followed their flagship and escaped to the planet of El Facil itself. Ships that were late in retreating faced one of two fates: annihilation or surrender. Nearly all of them chose surrender.

Those surviving forces that had escaped to El Facil still numbered as many as two hundred vessels and fifty thousand soldiers, but the Imperial Navy afterward reinforced itself, building its forces up to three times that number, planning to leap at the chance to "liberate the El Facil territory from the clutches of the rebel forces" in one fell swoop. El Facil's civilian population of three million cowered in the midst of this tense situation. It was already too late to stop El Facil from falling.

The civilians came to negotiate with the military, seeking the creation and implementation of a plan for planetwide evacuation. The officer in charge who appeared before them was Sublieutenant Yang Wen-li.

He was too young, and his rank was low. Was the military even taking them seriously? The civilians had their doubts, but Yang did a good job with everything he was supposed to do, even though he kept scratching his head in a way that didn't inspire confidence. Amid the chaos of the impending imperial invasion, Yang procured civilian and military vessels and made preparations for the evacuation.

Even if Yang had not been there, any competent military officer could have done that much. Yang apparently calmed the impatient civilians while awaiting the chance to depart.

The next day, an urgent message came through that shocked everyone. Rear Admiral Lynch was in the process of fleeing from El Facil with his direct subordinates and the military provisions. He had abandoned the civilians and his other subordinates.

To the panicked civilians, Yang finally gave instructions to evacuate . . . in the direction opposite of Lynch's course.

"There is no need for concern," he told them. "The rear admiral is drawing away the Imperial Navy's attention for us. We can escape now if we just ride the solar wind in a leisurely way and avoid using radar permeability devices or anything like that."

With that casual decision, the young sublieutenant transformed his own fleet commander into a decoy.

And his prediction was dead-on. Rear Admiral Lynch and the others were spotted by the Imperial Navy, which had been sharpening its claws in anticipation of him trying just such a thing. After being run to and fro like hunted animals, the alliance vessels finally raised a white flag and were taken captive.

Meanwhile, the convoy of vessels led by Yang was leaving the El Facil system and making a beeline for territory to the rear. They were spotted on the Imperial Navy's detection grid, but thanks to the pre-conceived notion that evacuation ships would be equipped with some kind of antidetection system—and the fact that they did show up on radar—the ships were thought to be not man-made objects, but a large swarm of meteors, and thereby they slipped out right under the enemy's noses.

Later, when the officers of the imperial fleet learned about this, wine-glasses that had been raised in victory toasts were smashed to the floor. Yang arrived in territory to the rear of El Facil with three million civil-ians, and cheers of welcome were waiting.

Like a meteor shower, words of praise for Yang's composure and dar-ing rained down from the high chiefs of the military. They had no choice. After all, their navy had lost the battle, fled from the enemy, and finally abandoned the very civilians that they were supposed to be protecting. In order to wipe out such a blot of disgrace and dishonor, the leadership needed a military hero. Hence: "Yang Wen-li: a paragon of the fighting men of the Free Planets Alliance." "A warrior shining with the light of justice and humanity." "Let all the soldiers of the alliance praise this young hero!"

That year, on June 12 of the standard calendar, at 0900, Yang was promoted to full lieutenant. On the same day at 1300, he was made a lieutenant commander. Military regulations stated that special double promotions were not permitted for living officers, but this unusual treat-ment was arranged by the upper echelons.

The man himself was far less excited than those around him. Shrugging his shoulders, he just muttered, "What in the world is all this?" and that was that. The only thing he was happy about was that he got a pay raise with the promotions, which meant he'd be able to fill his library with the history books he'd always wanted.

However, this was also the time when Yang first felt a real interest in military strategy.

Basically, the fundamental nature of combat hasn't changed at all since three, four thousand years ago, Yang thought, comparing his experiences to his knowledge of military history. *Before you get to the battlefield, resupply is what counts. And after you get there, it's the quality of the commanders. Victory or defeat hinges on these two things.*

There were many ancient proverbs that emphasized the importance of commanders. "A fearless general has no cowardly soldiers," for example, or "A hundred sheep led by a lion will triumph over a hundred lions led by a sheep."

The twenty-one-year-old lieutenant commander knew better than anyone the reason for his success. It was because the imperial military—and that of the alliance as well—had a blind faith in scientific technology, and the result of it was preconceived notions such as, "If it shows up on radar, it must not be an enemy ship."

Nothing was more dangerous than ossified wisdom. And when he thought about it, wasn't that also the reason he'd been able to beat Wideborn in the simulator back in his academy days? He'd been able to surprise an opponent who had clung to the idea of a decisive frontal assault.

Know the psychology of your enemy. That was the most important point of military strategy. And after that was the point that on the battlefield, resupply is absolutely essential in order to make good use of your resources. Taken to extremes, you didn't even need to strike the enemy's main force at all—it was enough if you could just cut their supply lines. If the enemy couldn't fight, they'd have no choice but to withdraw.

Yang's father had emphasized the value of money in every aspect of his life. If you treated the entire military as a single individual, money would be the supply line. When he thought about it that way, his father's words turned out to be pretty valuable after all.

After this, nearly every other time that Yang participated in combat operations, he would mark up an unexpected achievement of some kind. And with those achievements came promotions to commander, then captain, and by age twenty-nine, commodore. His old classmate Wideborn was a rear admiral, but that was because as a captain he had stuck to orthodox strategy, taken a surprise attack head-on, and thus received a special double promotion posthumously.

And now Yang Wen-li was in the Astarte Stellar Region.

Suddenly, a commotion broke out on the bridge. Not a pleasant one. It had been caused by an urgent message received from the surveillance craft.

"The imperial fleet is not in the area we predicted. They are accelerating rapidly and will intercept the Fourth Fleet."

"What?!" Paetta cried. His voice was shrill and tinged with hysteria. "That's insane...They wouldn't!"

Yang reached over to his console and picked up the document lying almost shamefacedly there. A paper document. Four thousand years had passed since the ancient Chinese had invented the stuff, but humanity had still not come up with anything better for writing on. The document was the operations plan he had submitted earlier. He fanned through the pages. Lines of text written in the impersonal letters of his word processor jumped out at him.

> ...if the enemy wishes to take aggressive action, they may view these circumstances not as a threat of envelopment, but as a prime opportunity to attack our divided forces and destroy them individually. Should this happen, the enemy will first take the offensive against the Fourth Fleet, which is positioned directly ahead of them. The Fourth Fleet is numerically the smallest and therefore the easiest to attack and defeat. Furthermore, after defeating the Fourth Fleet, the enemy will then be able

to target the Second Fleet or the Sixth Fleet at its discretion. One way to resist this strategy is as follows: After meeting their challenge, the Fourth Fleet should return mild resistance for a time, then begin a slow withdrawal. As the enemy pursues them, the Second and Sixth fleets will strike them from behind. When the enemy turns to engage, the Second and Sixth fleets will return mild resistance while withdrawing, and then this time, the Fourth Fleet will strike from behind. Repeat until the enemy is exhausted. Then surround and destroy. This strategy has a very high probability of success, but close attention to force concentration, communication, and flexibility in advance and pullback is essential.

Yang closed the folder and glanced up at the ceiling's wide-angle monitor. Hundreds of millions of stars were glaring back at him coldly.

The young commodore almost started whistling but stopped himself and began working busily at his console.

CHAPTER 2:

THE BATTLE OF ASTARTE

I

Vice Admiral Pastolle, commander of the Alliance Navy's Fourth Fleet, was flummoxed when he heard the report: "Imperial warships closing rapidly!"

The entire display screen of fleet flagship *Leonidas* was being covered in points of light as they swarmed into being, their luminosity climbing by the moment as they swelled ever larger. It was a sight filled with menace—the hearts of all who saw it were set racing, and their mouths went dry.

The vice admiral sat up straight in his command chair. "What's going on here?" he growled in a low voice. "What do the imperials think they're doing? Why would they—?"

Some of those present thought it was a ridiculous question, though they numbered just a few. The imperial force intended to bring its full power to bear on the Fourth Fleet—that much should have been obvious. But the alliance leadership had never imagined such a daring assault being launched by an enemy being hemmed in on three sides.

Caught in an enclosure formation, facing a more numerous enemy, the imperial fleet would yield to its defensive instincts, they'd reasoned, contracting their battle lines and concentrating their force into a tight formation. Against this, the alliance forces could then pour in from three sides at uniform velocity, surround them like a finely woven net, and concentrate their firepower to slowly—but most assuredly—shear away their capacity for resistance.

That was how the Dagon Annihilation had been fought 156 years ago, and praises were sung to this day of the two great generals who had emerged victorious then. This enemy, however, had not acted at all in accordance with the alliance military's calculations.

"What in blazes is this? Has their commander even studied tactics? Who would fight a battle like this?" Foolish words came streaming from the vice admiral's mouth. He stood up from his command seat and wiped sweat from his brow with the back of his hand. A steady temperature of 16.5 degrees was maintained throughout the ship; he shouldn't have been breaking out in a sweat . . .

"Commander, what do we do?"

The voice of the staff officer calling him was shrill and lacking proper reserve. The tone grated on the vice admiral's nerves. Hadn't his staff officers been the ones insisting that the three-way advance was *the* unbeatable tactic? It only followed that contingency planning was their responsibility as well. What did they mean, 'What do we do?'! Still, this was neither the time nor place to be losing his temper.

The fleet of imperial warships numbered twenty thousand, and the alliance's Fourth Fleet only twelve thousand. The alliance's plans had been utterly derailed. They were supposed to surround and attack an enemy force of twenty thousand ships with three fleets totaling forty thousand—but now the Fourth Fleet was going to have to fight alone against an overwhelmingly larger force.

"Emergency messages to Second and Sixth Fleets: 'Engaging enemy in sector $\alpha7.4$, $\beta3.9$, γ minus 0.6. Requesting immediate support.'"

The vice admiral gave the order, but Lieutenant Commander Nann, communications chief of the flagship *Leonidas*, responded with desperate actions and an expression to match. Jamming signals from the imperial fleet were eating into the alliance fleet's comm network voraciously.

Floating in the void of outer space, tens of thousands of electromagnetic jamming bouys, deployed on Reinhard's orders, were hard at work.

"In that case, send out courier launches! Two of them to each fleet!" As he shouted those words, a flash of light from the display screen turned the vice admiral's face white for an instant. The enemy attack had begun, their neutron-beam cannons firing synchronized volleys. Their vast outputs of energy and the accompanying bursts of light were such that it seemed the fundi of the soldiers' eyes might be scorched.

Flashes of sparkling, rainbow-colored brilliance—the sparks that flew in those instants when enemy beams struck energy-neutralization fields—erupted throughout the alliance's fleet. Low-energy particles collided at terrific speeds, annihilating one another in a cannibalistic phenomenon.

Arms waving wildly, the vice admiral shouted, "Vanguard formation, return fire! All ships, get ready for all-out war!"

Vice Admiral Pastolle's order had not been intercepted, but on the bridge of the imperial fleet's flagship *Brünhild*, ripples of cold contempt danced in Reinhard's ice-blue eyes as he said to no one, "Your responses are slow, you incompetent fool!"

"Launch fighters! We're switching to close-quarters combat!" ordered Rear Admiral Fahrenheit. A keen vitality shone in his face and resonated in his voice, born of the exultation of battle, coupled with a confidence that came of seizing the initiative. *Even if the "golden brat" ends up taking the credit, the important thing is still to win!*

The single-seater, cross-winged fighter ships known as *walküren* launched from their giant carriers one after another. In the instant when they cut loose from their carriers, they had—due to momentum—already reached speeds exceeding those of the carriers; neither catapult nor runway was needed. The walküren were small craft, and so their firepower was not as great, but they excelled in maneuverability and were extremely effective in a dogfight.

The alliance also had single-seat fighters corresponding to walküren; these were known as spartanians.

Flashes of exploding fusion furnaces ripped across every quarter, and maelstroms of unleashed energies shook the ships of both sides in chaotic swells. New clusters of energy beams lashed across the battlespace, and dodging between them the walküren soared, four-winged angels of death clad in glistening silver. The alliance's spartanians did not trail the walküren in fighting ability, but a terrible disadvantage dominated all beyond their nose cones, and they found beams awaiting them the moment they separated from their carriers, aiming to destroy both fighter and pilot together.

One hour after the start of the battle, the Fourth Fleet's vanguard had been almost entirely destroyed by the withering onslaught of the Imperial Navy squadron under Fahrenheit's command.

Of the 2,600 vessels composing the vanguard, not even 20 percent were still participating in combat. Some ships had been vaporized by fusion-furnace explosions, others had avoided exploding but had been too severely damaged to continue fighting, and others still had light structural damage but now drifted uselessly through space, having lost most of their crew. In this dreadful condition, the front line's collapse seemed not a half step away.

In the case of the battleship *Nestor,* the damage was limited to a single spot on the vessel's underbelly, but the neutron warhead that had penetrated there had exploded inside, unleashing a great swell of raging, killing particles that had swept through the entire ship, in an instant turning *Nestor* into a coffin for 660 officers and soldiers.

For this reason, crewless *Nestor* continued to follow the final course input by its astrogator, and as it hurtled along on invisible rails of inertia, it grazed the nose of its confederate, *Lemnos,* just as *Lemnos*'s main front cannons were unleashing a volley of fire at an enemy ship. *Nestor* intercepted the photon-cannon volley at point-blank range and exploded soundlessly an instant later, the energy of the exploding fusion furnace ripping through its neutralization field and hitting *Lemnos* head-on.

There were two flashes of white light, one following the other like twins being born, and by the time they had faded, not even a fragment of inorganic matter remained. The crew of *Lemnos* had destroyed an allied vessel and received death as their recompense.

"What are you people doing?!"

That cry was Vice Admiral Pastolle's.

But the one who disdainfully murmured, "What are *you* people doing?" was Rear Admiral Fahrenheit.

Both had been looking on at that scene through the screens of their respective flagships. In the words of one was a cry of hopelessness and panic; the words of the other mocked, with all the confidence that comes of a comfortable margin. The difference in those two voices was at the same time the difference between the circumstances of their respective forces.

II

At that moment, the Second and Sixth Fleets of the Alliance were reeling from shock, having only just learned of the sudden change of circumstances. Even so, they had not decided to veer from the original plan and were still advancing toward the battlefield at the same velocity as before.

Vice Admiral Paetta, commander of the Second Fleet, was sitting in the command chair of the flagship *Patroklos,* jiggling one knee outside the crew's line of sight. Irritation and impatience kept it rocking nonstop. The fleet commander's psychological state was reflected in his subordinates, and the air on the bridge felt charged with electricity.

Amid all that, the vice admiral noticed one man, and one man only, who didn't look especially bothered. After the slightest of hesitations, he called out his name: "Commodore Yang!"

"Sir?"

"How do things look to you? Your opinion, please."

Yang, having risen from his station chair, removed his beret again and lightly scratched through his black hair with one hand. "The enemy is probably trying to destroy our forces individually before we can rendezvous. Since the Fourth Fleet is numerically smallest, it's only natural they'd try to get rid of them first. The ball's in their court as far as which target is most pressing, and they're making the most of the initiative."

"Do you think the Fourth Fleet can hold out?"

"Both forces have clashed head-on. Which means the advantage lies with the side outnumbering its opponent, and moreover, with the side that strikes the initial blow."

Yang's expression and tone of voice seemed indifferent. As Vice Admiral Paetta observed him, he kept opening his fist and then squeezing it shut, trying to exorcise his annoyance.

"In any case, we need to get to the battlefield ASAP to reinforce the Fourth Fleet. With any luck, we should be able to strike the enemy from behind. If we do that, we can turn the tide in one fell swoop."

"That probably won't work, sir."

Yang sounded unconcerned as ever, which almost made Paetta let his words pass by unacknowledged. The vice admiral had started to turn his head back toward the screen, but he stopped and looked again at the young staff officer.

"What makes you say so?"

"The fighting will already be over by the time we get there. The enemy will leave the battlefield, and before the Second and Sixth Fleets can rendezvous, they'll circle around to the rear of one or the other and launch an attack there. Since the Sixth Fleet is the smaller of the two, it's almost certain they'll be the ones targeted. The empire's taken the initiative, and at present they've still got it. I don't think we need to keep doing what they expect any further."

"Well then, what do you propose?"

"That we change tactics. Instead of rendezvousing with the Sixth Fleet in that battlespace, we go rendezvous with them now—without a moment to spare—and prepare a new battlespace in that sector. If we combine the fleets, we'll have twenty-eight thousand vessels, and after that we can challenge them with better than fifty-fifty odds of victory."

"...Meaning, you want me to just look the other way as the Fourth Fleet is massacred?"

A note of deliberate reproach was apparent in the vice admiral's tone. *That is one cold-blooded thing to say*, he was thinking.

"Even if we left right now, we wouldn't get there in time."

Yang's tone was curt, whether he knew what was going on in the vice admiral's head or not.

"But I won't abandon a friendly force."

At the vice admiral's words, Yang shrugged his shoulders lightly. "Then ultimately, their tactic of attacking each group separately will make easy prey of all three fleets."

"Not necessarily. The Fourth Fleet won't go down without a good fight. If they can keep holding out . . ."

"I just told you it was hopeless, but—"

"Commodore Yang, reality is made up of more than just cold-blooded calculation. The enemy commander is Count von Lohengramm. He's young and inexperienced. But Vice Admiral Pastolle is a seasoned warrior forged in countless battles. Compared to that—"

"Commander, he's inexperienced as you say, but his tactical planning—"

"Enough, Commodore." The vice admiral cut him off, displeased. He couldn't hold back his disgust for this young staff officer who just wouldn't give him the answer he wanted.

The vice admiral motioned for Yang to sit back down and turned his head back toward the screen.

III

Four hours had passed since the start of battle. By this point, the Fourth Fleet of the Alliance Navy could hardly be called a fleet at all. There was no tidy, well-organized battle formation. No unified chain of command. It was nothing more than scattered pockets of desperate resistance: isolated, cut off, single ships in every quarter waging a losing battle.

The flagship *Leonidas* was now a colossal hunk of metal wandering in the void. Within, there was nothing left that lived. The body of Commander Pastolle had been sucked out into the vacuum by the air-pressure differential in the instant that concentrated enemy fire had opened up a large crack in the bridge's hull. What condition his corpse was in and where in space it was drifting, nobody knew.

Meanwhile, Reinhard knew by this point that he had just secured a complete victory. The report came in from Merkatz by way of his comm screen.

"Organized resistance has ended. From this point forward we're to switch over to mop-up operations, but..."

"No need."

"Sir?" Merkatz's narrow eyes narrowed further.

"The battle's only one-third finished. You can leave the remnants be— we need to save our strength for the next battle. Further instructions will follow. Until then, get our formations reorganized."

"As you wish—Your Excellency."

With a solemn bow of his head, Merkatz's image vanished from the comm screen.

Reinhard looked back at his redheaded chief adjutant.

"Even he's changed his attitude just a little."

"Yes, he must have little choice."

This is a great first-round victory, Kircheis thought. *Even the admiralty will have to admit Reinhard's tactical plan worked well. The soldiers will take heart, and the enemy will be stunned when they see their unbeatable formation destroyed.*

"Which fleet do you think we should attack next, Kircheis? The one to starboard or to port?"

"It's possible to circle around to the aft of either, but surely you've made up your mind already?"

"Pretty much."

"Their Sixth Fleet, positioned to starboard, must have the weaker force strength, correct?"

"Exactly." A satisfied smile appeared around the mouth of the young, blond-haired commander.

"The enemy may be expecting that. That's the one slight concern that I have, but..."

Reinhard shook his head. "There's no danger of that. If they do guess what we're doing, they won't continue with a battle plan that uses divided forces. They'll try to rendezvous as early as they possibly can. After all, together they still outnumber us vastly. That they aren't doing so is proof they don't understand our fleet's intent. We'll circle around to the Sixth Fleet's aft starboard flank and attack them there. How many hours will we need?"

"Less than four."

"Look at you, you'd worked it out already." Reinhard smiled again. When he smiled, his face was like a boy's. But what wiped that smile from his face in a heartbeat was the realization that several sets of eyes were looking intently his way. Reinhard would not show his smile easily to anyone but Kircheis.

"Relay that to the whole fleet. Gradually shift our course clockwise as we proceed, and attack the enemy's Sixth Fleet on its aft starboard flank."

"As you wish," Kircheis replied, but he was looking at his blond-haired senior officer as though he still had something to say.

Reinhard drew his brows together in suspicion and returned the stare. "You have some objection?"

"It isn't that. I was just wondering if we might let the men have a break since we now have some time to spare."

"Oh, that's right. I hadn't realized."

Reinhard issued orders that the soldiers be given breaks of an hour and a half each, to be taken in two shifts. During that time, they were to eat and rest up in their tank beds.

A tank bed was essentially a large aquarium made of light plastic and filled to thirty centimeters' depth with strongly salinated water, the temperature maintained at a constant 32 degrees centigrade. Anyone who lay floating in its interior would enjoy a state of perfect peace and quiet, isolated from all color, lighting and heating, sound, and other external stimuli. Spending one hour in the tank was said to have the same effect on one's mind and body as eight hours of sound sleep. There was nothing like it for quickly restoring soldiers worn down in body and spirit by combat.

In small squads where tank bed facilities were lacking, stimulants were sometimes used, but oftentimes these were not just dangerous to the body, they had a bad effect on the military organization itself.

Drug-addicted soldiers had absolutely no value as a human resource, so accordingly, this measure was taken only in the worst of circumstances.

The wounded were also being treated. It had been widely known since the late 1900s on the AD calendar that electrons could stimulate the body's cells, increasing their natural healing abilities by leaps. Add to that the development of cyborg technology, and an age had arrived in which 90 percent of wounded soldiers who managed to see a military doctor could be saved. Though of course it was possible to be driven to a state wherein death would be better...

In any case, the crews of the Imperial Navy vessels were visited by a temporary period of peace and tranquility. Cheerful bustle swirled through the mess halls of every vessel. Though alcohol was forbidden, the crew members were in thrall of a drunkenness born of battle and victory, and the food tasted better to them than it actually was. "Even our young commander's actually pretty good, don't you think?" whispered some back and forth. "I was thinking he was just here as a decoration, with nothing going for him but his looks, but he's really quite the tactician. Maybe even the best since Admiral Wood in the old days..."

The question of why, and for whom, they and their unseen, unknown enemies were killing one another was nowhere to be heard among the soldiers at that time. They were simply and honestly rejoicing in their survival and their victory. But within the next few hours, a portion of these survivors would be added to the ranks of the newly dead.

IV

"Vessel's shadow sighted at 4:30. Identification impossible."

When the report was received from a destroyer in the rear guard, Vice Admiral Moore, commanding officer of the Alliance Navy's Sixth Fleet, was in the middle of a meal with his staff officers. Knife hovering over his gluten cutlet, the vice admiral scowled at the officer who had delivered the message. Riveted by a gaze sharper than the knife, the officer felt frightened. Vice Admiral Moore was widely known to be a fair-minded but coarse man.

"At 4:30, you say?"

The vice admiral's voice was a match for his gaze.

"Y-yes, sir. At 4:30. We can't tell yet if it's friendly or not."

"Oh? Well, which 4:30 are we talking about? Morning or afternoon?"

Caustic remarks notwithstanding, Moore broke off his meal and stepped out of the officers' mess. Looking back at his alarmed staff officers, his burly shoulders quivered as he laughed.

"Will you look at these deer-in-the-headlight faces! The enemy's in the same direction we're headed—they can't rightly be at 0430, now can they?"

The vice admiral continued to speak in a loud voice. "We're rushing toward the battlefield. The Second Fleet's no doubt taking the same action. That being the case, we can hit the enemy from behind from both starboard and port. We have a very good chance of winning—no, in fact, we will definitely win. From the perspective of numbers, from the perspective of formation..."

"But, Commander—"

The man interrupting the vice admiral's foray into eloquence was one of the staff officers, Lieutenant Commander Lappe. He was wiping grease from his mouth with a handkerchief.

"What?"

"What if the enemy's moved the battlespace? Such a thing is certainly not outside the realm of—"

"You want to abandon the Fourth Fleet?"

"This is difficult to say, sir, but the junior officers are projecting that the Fourth Fleet has been defeated already."

The vice admiral's excessively lush eyebrows drew together. "That's a bold and most disagreeable projection, isn't it, Commander? All that grease seems to have your mouth running like a well-oiled machine."

Embarrassed, Lieutenant Commander Lappe put away his handkerchief.

By that time, they had ridden the intraship beltway as far as the bridge, when unexpectedly the gravitational-control system lagged for a moment, and they both nearly stumbled. It had been forced by an acute change of course, though a measuring device was registering directional energy sufficient to destroy the ship just beyond the hull.

"Enemy attacking aft starboard flank!"

The comm channels of the Sixth Fleet erupted in surprised cries, which were immediately erased by static.

Officers shuddered, for the confused transmissions themselves testified eloquently to the fact that the enemy was positioned very near.

"Don't lose your heads, people!"

Vice Admiral Moore's pep talk was half directed at himself. His regrets slapped him hard across his thick jowl.

The fleet's cutting-edge warships were not deployed in the rear guard. There was no way the older vessels there could withstand an assault from behind.

The imperial force is behind us! Did that mean the Fourth Fleet was destroyed? Or had the empire readied a large, separate force?

"Intercept and open fire."

As confusion welled up in his heart, the vice admiral issued a bare minimum of orders, not yet able to resolve his confusion.

The imperial force commanded by Merkatz, a seasoned full admiral, had assumed a neat and orderly attack formation and launched the assault on the Alliance Navy's Sixth Fleet. Neutron-beam cannons slung glittering flashes of death against the low-output force fields cast by the older alliance vessels, piercing the fields and impaling the ships.

Through his viewscreen, Merkatz looked on at a scene of dazzling fireballs, blossoming and fading amid the darkness eternal. It was a sight that had become familiar over the last forty years, but this time he felt something deep and powerful that he had never felt before.

Merkatz was no longer looking at Reinhard as merely that "blond porcelain doll." That initial victory had been no fluke. It was the proper result of a bold change in thinking, based on keen insight and careful decision making. Allowing one's forces to be attacked from three directions, just to launch separate attacks on a divided force before it could close the net.

There was no way he could have done that. His comrades in arms from the old days were the same. This was only possible for a young man, one not yet shackled by convention.

The era of old soldiers like us may have passed on already. Unwittingly, he had actually thought such a thing.

Even during his moment of reflection, the battle was growing more fierce.

The imperial force drilled into the ranks of the alliance like an auger, steadily gaining the upper hand both in exchanges of cannon fire and in close combat. It looked like the whole force was riding high, making the most of the advantage that came with drawing first blood. The alliance force was launching a desperate counterattack, but with the commanders unable to recover from their confusion, there was little hope for much of a rally.

Vice Admiral Moore, standing frozen like a temple sculpture in the midst of the bridge floor, shouted, "All ships, come about!" At last he had made up his mind. Up until then, he had only been saying, 'What's going on?' over and over.

"Commander! Even if we turn around, we'll cause nothing but confusion. I think we should proceed full speed ahead while executing a clockwise change of course—plow into the enemy from behind."

Lieutenant Commander Lappe's suggestion collided with the vice admiral's burly frame and bounced off meaninglessly.

"By the time we hit the enemy's back side, most of our ships would be destroyed. Turn and fire."

"Yes, but—"

"Be quiet!"

Vice Admiral Moore gave an angry shout that made his whole body quiver, and the lieutenant commander closed his mouth, understanding clearly that his commanding officer had lost his head.

When the giant hulk of *Pergamum,* flagship of the Sixth Fleet, began to come about, the other vessels following behind it did likewise. But it was not an easy maneuver to accomplish while under fire. The seasoned Merkatz leapt on his enemy's confusion right away.

The beam cannons of the imperial force struck hard with cascades of glowing beams that streaked across the sky like meteor showers. In every quarter, energy-neutralizing force fields overloaded and collapsed, and the alliance's vessels were destroyed.

The surging billows of energy already seen in the previous battlespace were beginning to form again in this one, and Vice Admiral Moore and Lieutenant Commander Lappe alike had the feeling that only the ships of the alliance were being tossed by them.

"Multiple small vessels closing rapidly on *Pergamum,*" an operator shouted. One of the screens was showing a large swarm of walküren, and in no time at all they occupied the screens of numerous consoles. Nimbly demonstrating their maneuverability, they came in firing beams at point-blank range.

"It's gonna be a dogfight. Launch the spartanians."

This order as well came too late and cost them dearly. The walküren had been waiting for the instant when the spartanians would separate from their carriers. When a flood of glowing beams burst mercilessly forth, the alliance's fighter craft blew apart in balls of fire, deprived even of the right to die in battle.

"Commander, look at that!" An operator was pointing at one of the screens. An imperial battleship was closing in on them. And behind it, and behind what was behind it, one overlapping with the next, could be seen the shadows of more vessels. The bridge was suffused by an oppressive air of menace.

Pergamum was now surrounded by multiple rings of ships.

"They're sending a flash signal," the operator reported in a near whisper.

"See if you can decode it." Vice Admiral Moore was silent; the prompting came from Lieutenant Commander Lappe. Even his voice was low and dry.

"Decoding... 'You are completely surrounded and without any means of escape. Surrender, and I promise to treat you graciously.' "

The decoded message repeated once and then ended, and countless stares and countless silences stabbed into the massive frame of Vice Admiral Moore. Every one of them was urging a decision from the fleet commander.

" 'Surrender,' he says..." The vice admiral's face turned a dark red as he growled out his answer. "Forget it! I may be a washout, but I won't be a coward."

Twenty seconds later, a white flash enveloped him.

V

The accumulated store of unease was just about to reach saturation point.

An invisible thunderhead seemed to hang over the bridge of *Patroklos*, flagship of the Alliance Navy's Second Fleet. When would a blistering discharge come arcing down from it? As orders to assume a stage-one battle formation were issued, all crew were changing into space suits. Still, the unease was passing right through their suits, making them break out in gooseflesh.

"The Fourth and Sixth Fleets have apparently been destroyed."

"We're all alone out here. And by now the enemy's force is larger than ours."

"I want information. What's going on? What's the present situation?"

Speaking out of turn was prohibited, but if they didn't say something, the unease would be unbearable. This wasn't in the plan. Weren't they going to catch an enemy half their size in a three-way pinch, wipe them out, and raise a song of victory...?

Suddenly, an operator's voice rang out across the bridge from his microphone. "Enemy fleet closing."

"From either one or two o'clock..." Yang murmured. Though he spoke only to himself, the following report came as if in answer:

"Bearing 0110, elevation minus eleven degrees, closing at high speed."

Yang did not respond to the tension that then gripped the bridge of the flagship *Patroklos* in its talons.

This was all as he'd anticipated. The imperial force had struck the alliance Sixth Fleet on its aft starboard flank and bored right on through to emerge from the fore on its port side, tracing a natural curve as it now turned its spearhead toward its last remaining enemy, the Second Fleet. With the Second Fleet advancing straight ahead, it only followed that the imperial fleet should appear from somewhere between one and two o'clock.

"Battle stations!" ordered Vice Admiral Paetta, and Yang thought, *You're too slow.*

To wait for the enemy to come to you and then fight back was the orthodox tactic, but in this case, it was impossible to ignore the fact that Paetta's thoughts were locking up. Measures that needed to be taken also needed proper timing to work. With rapid maneuvers, it wouldn't have been impossible to hit the enemy force from behind and then coordinate with the Sixth Fleet to catch them in a pincer movement.

In battle, it was impossible to sacrifice no one. Yet at the same time, the effect of victory was lessened in inverse proportion to mounting losses. It was in finding the point that made both propositions compatible that tactics as a discipline found its raison d'être. In other words, it meant getting the maximum effect for the minimum losses, or to put it more coldly, finding the most efficient way to murder your comrades. Yang wondered doubtfully whether his commander understood that.

It was too late to do anything for those sacrificed already. And from the start, this wasn't something that could be swept under the rug by saying, "It couldn't be helped." The military leadership should be hanging their heads in shame for their poor tactical leadership. But that would come later, after all was said and done—what they had to think about now was how to prevent an expansive reproduction of their mistake and how to come up with some way of turning a disaster into a blessing.

If regrets could bring back slain officers and soldiers, the brass should be shedding tears by the kiloliter. But ultimately, they would be doing nothing more than playing at sorrow, wouldn't they?

"All ships, open fire!"

Whether that order came before or after, no one could tell. A flash of light strong enough to make people think their retinas had been fried stole the vision of all who were on the bridge.

With a lag of half an instant, *Patroklos'* body was jostled by an explosive burst of energy, then tossed and turned in every direction.

Noises of things falling over and objects colliding overlapped with screams and shouts of anger. Not even Yang was able to avoid falling down. He took a hard blow to the back and had the wind knocked out of him. As his helmet communicator picked up a chaotic jumble of noises and voices and a fierce flow of air from the surrounding area, Yang straightened out his breathing and covered his sightless eyes with the palms of his hands—protecting them, albeit after the fact.

And who needed a dressing-down over that one? Failing to adjust the screens' photoflux capacity was not an easy blunder to forgive. If this kind of thing kept happening, it would be a wonder if they didn't lose.

"...this is aft turret! Bridge, please respond. Awaiting orders!"

"—engine room. This is the engine room. Bridge, respond please..."

At last Yang opened his eyes. An emerald fog hung over his whole field of vision.

He sat up and noticed the person lying next to him. A thick and sticky, deeply hued fluid covered everything from his mouth down to his chest.

"Commander," Yang said in a low voice, staring closely at the vice admiral's face. He planted both his legs firmly and got to his feet.

A fissure now ran through one section of bulkhead, and the air pressure was dropping rapidly. It looked like a few who hadn't had their magnetic boots switched on had been sucked out. The opening, however, was being rapidly sealed by a vaporized bonding agent blown against it from the self-repair system's operations gun.

Yang looked around the bridge. This was a mess; hardly anyone was still standing. After confirming that his helmet communicator still worked, Yang started giving out instructions.

"Commander Paetta is injured. Would a navy surgeon and paramedics come to the bridge, please. Operations officers, find out how badly we're damaged and begin repairs—you can report in later. Please hurry. Aft turrets, all ships are already in combat, so you shouldn't need any particular instructions—perform your assigned duties. Engine room: did you say something?"

"I was worried about things on the bridge, sir. No damage here."

"Well, thank goodness for that." There was a note of sarcasm in his voice. "The bridge is operational, as you can hear. Now I want you to calm down and focus on your duties."

He took another look around the bridge.

"Is there an officer here who isn't injured?"

One man stepped forward with a slightly perilous gait. "I'm all right, Commodore."

"You are, um…"

"Lieutenant Commander Lao, of the staff officer team." The small-eyed, small-nosed face peeking out of the space suit's helmet looked about the same age as Yang. In addition, two astrogators and one operator raised their hands and stood, but that was all.

"Nobody else?"

Yang slapped his helmet over where his cheek was. The Second Fleet's leadership had been essentially wiped out.

A naval surgeon came running in with a team of paramedics. Quickly and efficiently, they checked out Vice Admiral Paetta and told Yang that a broken rib had punctured his lung when his chest slammed into the corner of a control panel.

"He's had some pretty bad luck," the doctor opined unnecessarily. On the other hand, one couldn't deny that Yang's luck had been good.

"Commodore Yang…" Vice Admiral Paetta called his young staff officer, assailed by torments both physical and mental. "You take command of the fleet…"

"Me, sir?"

"You're the highest-ranked officer who's still in one piece. Show me… what you've got as a tactician…" The vice admiral stopped speaking suddenly—he had lost consciousness. The navy doctor called a robot car that served as an ambulance.

"He thinks highly of you, doesn't he?" said Lieutenant Commander Lao, impressed.

"Does he? I wonder."

Lieutenant Commander Lao, unaware of the clashes of opinion between the vice admiral and Yang, gave a doubtful glance at that answer. Yang walked over to the comm board and flipped on the switch for external communication. It seemed the machines were built more sturdily than the people.

"Attention, all ships. This is Fleet Commander Paetta's next-in-command, staff officer Commodore Yang."

Yang's voice raced through the empty spaces, piercing the void.

"The flagship *Patroklos* has taken a hit, and Commander Paetta is seriously injured. On his order, I'm taking over command of the fleet."

Here he paused for the space of a single breath, giving his comrades the time they needed to recover from the shock.

"Don't worry. If you follow my orders, you'll be all right. If you want to get back home alive, I need you to remain calm and do as I say. At the present moment, our side is losing, but the only thing that matters is to be winning in the last moment."

Hoo-boy, even I'm talking awfully big. Yang was smiling wryly, but only on the inside; he didn't let it come to the surface. In the position of commander, you had to puff out your chest even when you felt like hanging your head.

"We're not going to lose. All ships: concentrate on destroying your targets one by one until I send further instructions. Over."

That transmission was being monitored by the imperial forces as well. On the bridge of the flagship *Brünhild*, Reinhard raised his finely shaped eyebrows slightly. "You're not going to lose? If they follow your orders, they'll be all right? It seems the rebel forces have people who can spout a lot of bluster, too." A cold glint like that of a shard of ice sheltered in his eyes. "At this point, how do you intend to make up for your weaker force?...Hmm, never mind. Let's just go with 'Show me what you've got.' Kircheis!"

"Sir."

"Regroup our ranks. Tell all ships to assume spindle formation. You understand why?"

"You intend a frontal breakthrough?"

"Correct, as I've come to expect from you."

Through Kircheis, Reinhard's order was transmitted to every vessel in the imperial force.

But for his helmet, Yang would have taken off his beret to scratch through his black hair at that moment. When there was little difference in force strength, the most effective tactic for the attacking side was either the frontal breakthrough or the partial encirclement. He'd been guessing they would choose the more aggressive of the two, and it looked like he'd managed to hit the nail on the head.

"Lieutenant Commander Lao."

"Yes, Acting Commander, sir."

"The enemy's assuming a spindle formation. They're going to go for a frontal breakthrough."

"A frontal breakthrough!"

"They're in high spirits after wiping out the Fourth and Sixth Fleets. The imperial force probably won't even think of anything else."

Lieutenant Commander Lao glanced forlornly toward Yang as he provided his commentary. The faintheartedness in the alliance force—of which Lao's expression was representative—was the real fruit of the empire's aggressive tactics, Yang reflected.

"How do you plan to counter it?"

"I've got something in mind."

"But how do we communicate with the other ships? There's a danger that the enemy's listening to our transmissions. Flash signals have the same problem, and shuttles would take too long."

"Don't worry—use multiple channels and tell all vessels to open the C4 circuits of their tactical computers. That'll be enough. If that's all we say, the enemy shouldn't understand even if they pick it up."

"Acting Commander, sir, does that mean...Your Excellency had already worked out a plan and input the data...long before this battle even started?"

"Though I'd rather have seen it go to waste," said Yang. Perhaps in his tone of voice there was a slight note of self-justification. Icy glares had been standard recompense for prophets of defeat, even when Cassandra was queen in Troy. "Never mind that—hurry up and relay my instructions."

"Yessir, right away."

Lieutenant Commander Lao hurried off at a jog toward the reoccupied communications officer's seat. With only five officers left unharmed, running the bridge was impossible, so about ten men were summoned from other departments. Warships didn't carry excess personnel, so that meant *Patroklos* would be shorthanded elsewhere. It couldn't be avoided, though.

Taking its time, the imperial force prepared its spindle formation and then began its charge. The alliance ships met them with guns blazing, but the imperial ships paid them no mind. As the distance between the two narrowed, erupting beams began to weave countless patterns of crisscrossing bars.

Commanded by Fahrenheit, the empire's vanguard squadron didn't slow as it came plunging into the ranks of the alliance.

"All enemy ships are charging us!"

The operator's voice was shrill and sharp.

Yang looked up at the panel on the ceiling. A 270-degree wide-angle monitor was inset there. As the enemy vessels accelerated and closed the distance, they seemed to be leaping ferociously toward the throat of the alliance. Their movements were dynamic and precise. In the face of that, the alliance forces intercepting them couldn't help appearing sluggish and lackluster.

Well, let's see what happens.

In the command chair, Yang crossed his arms. He wasn't really as composed as he appeared to be. At present, the enemy's actions were within the bounds of Yang's predictions. The problem was what his allies would do. All would be fine if they went along with his plan, but one misstep and things would likely spin out of control, and the whole force would be put to flight. And what would he do then?

Scratch my head and pretend to look embarrassed, Yang told himself, answering his own question. He couldn't predict everything, nor was there an infallibly correct move he could make. He wasn't responsible for things beyond his power.

VI

The projection panel that made up the ceiling was covered in pulsating lights. The battleship *Patroklos* was now in the midst of a whirlpool of particle beams. Beams came at them from fore and aft, port and starboard, up and down, in thickness resembling clubs more than lances.

Patroklos itself had opened fire as well, sending out exhalations of death and destruction that slammed against its enemies. An immense waste of human energy—or material energy—was being justified as the path toward victory and survival.

"Enemy battleship closing! Judging by its model, it's probably *Wallenstein.*"

Wallenstein had already taken considerable structural damage, having apparently charged straight through the fire. Its half-ruined main battery took aim at *Patroklos* from straight ahead, but *Patroklos*'s response, this time, came swiftly.

"Fire all main cannons! Target is right in front of us!"

The order came from Lieutenant Commander Lao, who was temporarily doubling as gunnery chief.

Patroklos's front cannons spat out synchronized beams of neutrons, scoring a direct hit on *Wallenstein,* dead in its midsection.

After an instant's agonized buckling, the Imperial Navy's gargantuan battleship blew apart. Cheers rang out in the comm circuit of Yang's helmet, but their end notes transformed into cries of renewed horror. Crashing haughtily though the shining white whirlpool of the fusion explosion, the next enemy vessel, *Kärnten,* revealed its stately form. Yang acknowledged anew the dignity and grandeur of the Imperial Navy's formation, as well as its strong fighting spirit.

It was clear that their powerful will to fight was one born of their overwhelming victories. For a moment, Yang was captivated by the thought that he might be witnessing the moment in which a great general was born.

"Some generals are called 'wise' and others 'fierce,' but a commander who transcends those categories—who inspires in his men a faith unbreakable—is one whom I call 'great.'" Yang had read those words in a history book. *Reinhard von Lohengramm must still be quite young, but at the very least, he's on his way to being 'great.' He's a threat to alliance forces, and to the old power structures in the Imperial Navy, he's most likely a threat as well.*

Yang crossed his arms the other way and savored what small satisfaction he could in the thought that he was probably sitting right in the midst of history's current.

Even during that interval, the state of the battlefield was changing moment by moment.

Kärnten and *Patroklos* had exchanged fire, but amid the confusion of battle, they had moved apart, with neither having delivered a killing blow.

Yang shifted his gaze to the simulated-battlefield model that the tactical computer displayed on his monitor. Simplified shapes showed the distribution and condition of both forces.

Backward rippling motions were occasionally running through the alliance fleet, but overall the display showed the imperial force's advance and the alliance force's retreat.

Those movements were gradually increasing in velocity. The empire advanced, the alliance fell back. The tiny, reverse-propagating ripples vanished, and the more the simulated image was simplified, the more the effect was amplified. To most anyone's eyes, the empire appeared ready to take victory by the hand, and the alliance defeat by the tail.

"Looks like we've won," murmured Reinhard.

Meanwhile, Yang was also nodding toward Lieutenant Commander Lao.

"Looks like it's going to work," he said, not vocalizing his relieved *Thank heavens!*

What had been worrying Yang was whether or not the ships on his own side would follow their instructions. He had confidence in the planned operation itself. At this point there was no longer any way to win. It was, however, still possible to finish this without losing. But that could only happen if the other ships followed the plan.

There were no doubt obstinate squadron commanders who scorned the idea of obeying a young and inexperienced commander like Yang, but in the absence of any other effective battle plan, there was little choice but to accept Yang's orders. If the desire for survival motivated them more than any sense of loyalty, though, Yang had not the slightest objection.

A hint of puzzlement began to appear on Reinhard's face.

He stood up from his seat, put both hands on the command console, and glared up at the overhead screen. Irritation was beginning to boil up all through his body.

His allies were advancing, and his enemies retreating. Hit by the frontal breakthrough attack, the alliance's fleet was being split to the left and right. The scenes on the screen, the simulation that the tactical computer was reconstructing on his monitor, the status reports coming in from the vanguard—all were describing exactly the same situation.

Yet even so, a sound of distant thunder was beginning to rumble faintly in the back of his mind. He became aware of a sick feeling eating away at his nerves—the kind you get right before you realize that some dirty trick has just been played on you.

He put the fist he'd made with his left hand up against his mouth, resting his teeth lightly on his index finger's second joint. And in that instant, for no reason whatsoever, he intuited what his enemy had in mind.

"No!"

That low cry, drowned out by the shouts of operators, reached the ears of no one.

"Their force has split apart to port and starboard! They're—they're going to rush past us along both flanks!"

Amid a shocked stir, Reinhard cried out for his red-haired adjutant. "Kircheis! We've been had. The enemy wants to separate on both flanks and come around on our back side. They're using our frontal breakthrough against us. *Damn them!*"

The golden-haired youth slammed his fist down against the command console.

"What shall we do? Reverse course and intercept?"

Kircheis's voice had lost none of its cool self-possession. That had a calming effect on the nerves of his momentarily enraged commanding officer.

"Don't be absurd. You want me to be a greater imbecile than that Fourth Fleet's commander was?"

"In that case, all we can do is advance."

"Exactly." Reinhard nodded and gave orders to his communications officer. "All ships, full speed ahead! Clamp on to the back side of the enemy rushing past us. Bear to the right. And hurry!"

VII

Thirty minutes later, both formations were spread out in the shape of a ring. It was a strange sight. The alliance's vanguard was engaged in a blistering assault on the imperial fleet's tail end, while the imperial vanguard was attacking one tail end of the forked alliance fleet.

Viewed from far away in the depths of space, it might have looked like two glittering, gargantuan serpents trying to swallow one another, each from the other's tail upward.

Staring at the simulated model on the screen, Lieutenant Commander Lao said admiringly in Yang's direction, "I've never seen a battle formation like this."

"I'd imagine not . . . It's a first for me, too."

But Yang's words were only halfway true. Back when humanity had lived only on the surface of a backwater planet called Earth, this kind of formation had appeared on battlefields any number of times. Even the brilliant tactics employed by Count von Lohengramm had precedent in ground wars. Since ancient times—for better or worse—military geniuses inevitably took the stage during eras of war, turning on its head what had been orthodox tactical thought until their arrival.

"Look at this miserable excuse for a battle formation!"

The enraged cry rang out on the bridge of *Brünhild*. Reinhard suppressed his voice and snarled. "Won't this mean a battle of attrition . . . ?"

A report was delivered to him of the death of a high-ranking officer.

Rear Admiral Erlach had been blown away with the ship he had been aboard. Ignoring Reinhard's order to go full speed ahead, he had been trying to turn around and intercept the alliance force when in midturn his ship had taken a direct hit from a neutron-beam cannon.

What sort of imbecile tries to turn a ship around right in front of enemies that are snapping at his heels! He has only himself to blame. Yet even so, there's no denying this casts a slight pall over the empire's victory.

Yang had understood from the moment he launched this operation that it would turn into a battle of attrition. The imperial fleet's commander, Count von Lohengramm, was no fool. He wasn't likely to continue a fruitless battle that did nothing but increase the bloodshed and destruction. That had been the plan: to force the enemy into making that decision...

"The enemy should start pulling out soon," Yang said to Lieutenant Commander Lao.

"Are we going to pursue?"

"...Let's not." The young commander shook his head. "Let's follow their lead—when they withdraw, so do we. We've done all we can up till now—there's no way we can continue fighting."

A conversation was being held on the bridge of *Brünhild* as well.

"Kircheis, your thoughts?"

"It might be about time for a tactical withdrawal..." It was a reserved but unambiguous answer.

"You think so, too?"

"If we do continue to fight, the damage on both sides will only increase. That would serve no military purpose."

Reinhard nodded agreement, though a shade of dissatisfaction drifted across his youthful cheeks. Even if he accepted the reasoning, he wasn't satisfied emotionally.

"Is that frustration?"

"Nothing of the sort, though I did want a more unambiguous victory. It's just a pity is all, like leaving off the finishing touches of a painting."

That's just like you, thought Kircheis, an unconscious half smile forming around his mouth.

"You annihilated two of their fleets by attacking their forces separately, even while being hemmed in on three sides by a force twice the size of our own. And although the remaining fleet did swing around and get our back, you still fought them to a standstill. Isn't that enough? To hope for any more would be what we call 'just a little greedy.'"

"I know. And there's also the idea of leaving something to look forward to on another day."

Though the two fleets continued to fire away at one another, the formation was at last spreading gradually outward horizontally as the two forces began putting distance between one other. The rate of fire slowed as well, and the density of the energies being unleashed thinned out precipitously.

"He's quite good. Better than I had expected." In Reinhard's voice there was blended both irritation and praise. The young commander with the golden hair was deep in thought, and after a few minutes he called out for his adjutant.

"What was the name of the Second Fleet's commander—the man who took charge midway through?"

"Commodore Yang Wen-li."

"That's right—Yang. Send him an e-gram in my name."

Kircheis, smiling, asked, "What sort of message shall I send?"

"'My compliments to you, Commander, on a battle bravely fought... Be well till the day of our next encounter...' Something along those lines should be fine."

"As you wish."

Kircheis relayed Reinhard's order to the communications officer, who responded with a slight, quizzical tilt of the head. Kircheis returned a pleasant smile. "Like you, Officer...I'm in no hurry to fight such a tough opponent again. Better to have easy wins than run into enemies we have to praise."

"Absolutely, sir," the comm officer replied with a nod.

New orders from Reinhard rang out: "We're returning to Odin. All ships, get into formation."

After appending a few additional commands—"We'll put in at Iserlohn Fortress along the way...Calculate the damage to friends and foes ASAP"—Reinhard lowered the back of his command chair until he was facing the hemispherical ceiling almost directly and closed his eyes.

He felt exhaustion come bubbling up from beneath the surface of his consciousness. *It should be all right to sleep for just a little while. Just a short rest. Kircheis would wake me if anything were to happen. Just leave the settings for the trip home to the inertial astrogation system…*

For the leader of a defeated force, delegating squad operations to lower-ranking commanders and taking a nap were luxuries not permitted. Yang's greatest obligation was the recovery of those who remained, so he had to rush from battlespace to battlespace seeking survivors of the Fourth and Sixth Fleets. *Like with most things, the hardest part is picking up the pieces when it's over,* thought Yang as he pulled off the helmet of his space suit and drank protein-enriched milk from a paper cup.

"You have an e-gram from the imperial fleet, Assistant Staff Offi—I mean, Acting Commander, sir…"

The face of Lieutenant Commander Lao, who had come to inform him, was brimming with curiosity. *This battle has been nothing but surprises from start to finish,* his expression was saying.

"Read it for me."

"Um, all right. Here goes: 'My compliments to you, Commander, on a battle bravely fought…Be well till the day of our next encounter. Senior Admiral Reinhard von Lohengramm, Galactic Imperial Navy. Over.'"

"'Bravely fought,' he says? I'm so honored."

Next time we meet I'm gonna grind you into powder, was how Yang took the message.

Childishness was what he should probably call it, but it failed to arouse any ill will on his part.

"What should I do? Shall I send a reply?"

Yang answered Lieutenant Commander Lao's question in a halfhearted tone. "I doubt they're really expecting something like that. Never mind, just ignore it."

"...Yes, sir."

"Instead, hurry up and get the survivors aboard. I want to save as many as we can."

After taking his leave of Lieutenant Commander Lao, Yang turned his gaze to his console. The operations proposal he had submitted to Vice Admiral Paetta before the start of combat was lying on the floor beneath it. A bitter smile adorned Yang's mouth. He had never hoped to be proven right like this. How high would the death toll climb? Yang could imagine the faces at military HQ, every hair on their heads standing on end.

It was in this way that the Battle of Astarte was concluded.

On the side of the empire, 2,448,600 personnel participated in combat; the alliance fielded 4,065,900. The empire deployed over twenty thousand vessels, and the alliance more than forty thousand. Deaths on the side of the empire numbered over 153,400; for the alliance that number exceeded 1,508,900. Over 2,200 imperial ships were either lost or destroyed, while the alliance lost more than 22,600. The losses of the alliance climbed to between ten and eleven times those of the empire. The empire's invasion of the Astarte system, however, had been deflected just narrowly.

CHAPTER 3:

THE EMPIRE'S FADING GLOW

I

Beyond a gracefully curving wall made of specialized glass, a dense pro-fusion of strangely shaped boulders jutted upward, resembling nothing so much as temple bells. Twilight was unfolding her wings without a sound across the backdrop of sky, and to those looking on, particles of arid atmosphere seemed to have tinted the whole field of view with unplumbed depths of blue.

The man standing motionless by the wall, hands folded casually behind his waist, turned only his head as he looked back into the room. At the end of his line of sight was a large, chalk-white console, beside which was a man in late middle age was standing with impeccable posture.

"So what you're telling me, Boltec," the man by the wall rumbled sol-emnly in a deep, masculine voice, "is that the empire won but didn't win to excess."

"That is correct, Landesherr. The alliance was defeated, but it did not result in a total collapse of their military force."

"So they recovered their footing?"

"They recovered their footing, they fought back, and they even man-aged to bloody the empire's nose just a little. All in all, it made little difference to the empire's victory, but since the alliance didn't just lie there and take it, either... I believe I can say it was a satisfactory outcome for we of Phezzan. But what say you, Landesherr?"

The man by the wall—Adrian Rubinsky, fifth to hold the title of landesherr in Phezzan—now turned fully around to face the room's interior.

He was an unusual-looking man. Though he appeared to be around forty years of age, he had not a single hair on his head. His skin was dark. His eyebrows, eyes, nose, and mouth were all large, and though he could hardly be called handsome, he had a look that couldn't help leaving a vivid, powerful impression on others. His body brimmed with overwhelming spirit and vitality, and was blessed not only in stature, but also in its wide shoulders and sturdy ribs.

Five years in office, scorned by empire and alliance alike as the "Black Fox of Phezzan," he was ruler for life of this middleman trading state.

"I can't be all that satisfied, Boltec." There was irony in both the glance and the tone with which the odd-looking landesherr responded to his trusted aide. "This result was brought about by chance, not because we worked for it. We can't rely on good luck always being there in the future. We need to step up our data collection and analysis, and fill our hand with more trump cards for the future."

Rubinsky, dressed casually in a black turtleneck and light-green suit, was hardly the picture of a nation's ruler as he approached a console at a leisurely stroll.

Boltec's hands danced across the board, and in the console's central display, a chart appeared. "This is the distribution of both militaries, shown from directly overhead. Have a look, please." It was the exact chart Kircheis had shown Reinhard three days prior. Imperial forces were red and alliance forces green. From fore, port, and starboard, three green arrows were closing in on a red one. If the arrows were changed to points, it would look like a single dot of red within a triangle whose vertices were green.

"In terms of numbers, the empire had twenty thousand, and the alliance forty thousand altogether. Numerically, the alliance had an over-whelming advantage."

"They did in terms of positioning as well. They were poised to encircle the imperial force from three different angles. Except...wait a minute. Isn't this—" Rubinsky pressed a thick finger against the side of his forehead. "Isn't this the same formation the alliance used in the Dagon Annihilation over a hundred years ago? So that's it—they wanted to live that dream one more time, did they? Those people never evolve."

"Though from a tactical standpoint, the plan made sense."

"Hah! On paper, every plan is perfect. But in a real fight, the opponent is what matters. The empire's fleet commander—it was that 'golden brat' I've been hearing about, right?"

"Yes, sir. Count von Lohengramm."

Rubinsky gave a smug laugh. Five years ago, when his predecessor Walenkov had died suddenly, and Rubinsky, then thirty-six, had first taken over the reins of power, the opposition had backed a seasoned candidate in his fifties, raising a loud ruckus about how a man in his thirties was too young to be head of state. And now here was Count von Lohengramm, sixteen years younger than he had been at that time. For old soldiers who could do nothing but speak of precedent and custom, it seemed a most unpleasant age had begun.

"Can the landesherr guess how Count von Lohengramm got himself out of this trap?"

Something in Boltec's tone said he was enjoying this.

The landesherr glanced at his aide and stared into the display. Then, as though it were the simplest thing in the world, he stated his conclu-sion: "He took advantage of their divided forces and took them out one by one. It's the only way."

The landesherr's aide gazed back at the object of his political fidelity, looking like he'd just been slapped across the face. "It was just as you say. Your keen insight amazes me, sir."

Rubinsky, with a relaxed—even brazen—little smile, accepted the compliment.

"There are often situations where the pros can't keep up with the amateurs. They see the minuses more than the pluses, and the dangers more than the opportunities. A specialist will look at this formation and think defeat is inevitable for the encircled imperial force. But the net hasn't been pulled shut yet, and you can see how it's actually the scattered alliance forces that are vulnerable."

"It's just as you say."

"In short, what happened is that the alliance underestimated Reinhard von Lohengramm's ability as commander. Not that I can say I really blame them. Anyway, can you give me a detailed rundown of how things developed?"

The image on the display, obeying Boltec's commands, came to life and began to change. The red arrow turned toward one of the green arrows and made a beeline for it at high speed, then after crushing it, turned to another green arrow and destroyed it in turn. The landesherr narrowed his eyes and watched intently as it turned yet again to face the third green arrow. He ordered Boltec to stop and, still staring at the display, gave a sigh.

"A perfect one-two punch. An active, dynamic strategy. It's splendidly executed, but..." He trailed off and tilted his head. "But if things got to this point, the empire should have had a near-perfect win. To get back in the game after things had gone this far south wouldn't be easy for the alliance. The obvious end of this is the alliance force completely falling apart and being set to flight. Who was commanding that third alliance formation?"

"Vice Admiral Paetta, at the start. But after the battle began, he was seriously injured when his flagship took a hit. Afterward, Commodore Yang Wen-li, a staff officer who was next in line, took over for him."

"Yang Wen-li? I've heard that name somewhere..."

"He was in charge of evacuating El Facil eight years ago."

"Oh yeah, that fellow," Rubinski acknowledged. "I remember thinking at the time that the alliance had a pretty interesting man in its ranks, too. So, how did the hero of El Facil move his forces?"

In response, Rubinsky's top aide manipulated the display to show his superior the final stage of the Battle of Astarte.

The green arrow divided to the right and left. As if trying to preempt that, the red arrow charged forward, attempting a frontal breakthrough. The green arrow, looking as though it had been split in half, raced backward along both sides of the red arrow, merged back together behind it, and launched an attack from its rear...

Rubinsky made a low tone in the back of his throat. He had not expected to see an alliance commander using tactics this refined.

Moreover, the fact that he could grasp the situation and handle it so composedly, even while facing the prospect of his force completely crumbling, meant he was no more an ordinary commander than Count von Lohengramm was.

The fifth landesherr of Phezzan had had his gaze riveted to the display for some time. "That was some pretty exciting magic I just saw."

At last, Rubinsky motioned to have the display turned off. After doing so, Boltec took a step back and awaited his next instructions.

"Yang Wen-li, was it? Get in touch with the office of our high commissioner on Heinnessen, and tell them to gather data on that commodore ASAP. What happened on El Facil was no fluke—that I can see very clearly now."

"I'll see to it, sir."

"No matter what the organization, no matter what the machine, what runs it, ultimately, is the personnel. The skill and competence of the ones in charge can turn a tiger into a cat, and can even do the opposite. And what the tiger sinks his fangs into is up to the tamer as well. It's vital we get a profile on this man."

And in so doing, Rubinsky was thinking as he sent his aide from the room, *we find a way to use him.*

The star known as Phezzan was attended by four planets. Three were gas giants, with the second planet alone possessing a hard planetary crust. The composition of its atmosphere—nearly 80 percent nitrogen and almost 20 percent oxygen—differed little from that of humanity's birth-place. The biggest difference was that it had originally lacked carbon dioxide, so plant life had never existed there.

There wasn't much water, either. Even the terragreening, having advanced from blue-green algae to disseminating the seeds of higher plants, had not yet turned the whole of the landscape into fertile, verdant fields. Only the well-irrigated regions of the planet's surface were adorned in colorful belts of green. The red regions were wastelands of boulders and sand, where weathered landscapes boasted spectacular vistas of bizarre geographical features.

Phezzan was the name of the star as well as the name of the second planet. It was also the name of the system as a whole and the name of its autonomous governing body, established in year 373 of the empire, which held it as its territory. Its military force consisted of only a small fleet of patrol vessels, and its two billion Phezzanese, their passions ever bent on increasing profits, had long dominated the trade routes between the Galactic Empire and the alliance. While subordinate to the empire as a formality, it retained a de facto political independence that was nearly complete, and in terms of economic power, displayed a vigor surpassing that of the two great powers.

However, the long road that had led to this day had not been a smooth one, and every landesherr since Leopold Raap—the first landesherr—had struggled with the political maneuvering necessary to secure Phezzan's position. Phezzan's national policy could be summed up in the phrase, "Not so weak as to be taken lightly, and not so strong as to be feared," and it was because the numerical balance of power—Empire, forty-eight; Alliance, forty; Phezzan, twelve—had not changed at all in the last half century that the hard work of Phezzan's political authorities had been most vividly realized.

If the power of the empire and Phezzan were combined, they would be in an advantageous position over the alliance, but even so, destroying the alliance would be no easy task. On the other hand, if the alliance and Phezzan were to form a coalition, it would be possible to thwart the empire, though not to the point of overwhelming it.

It was in the upkeep of this precarious, even artistic, balance that Phezzan's politico-military strategy showed its true worth. Phezzan mustn't become too strong. That could arouse opposition from both the empire and the alliance, putting both on their guard, causing them to eye an alliance with one another to wipe Phezzan from the face of the universe. If the empire and alliance were to join forces, they would command 88 percent of the power balance and could destroy Phezzan in a single battle. On the other hand, if Phezzan were too weak, its continued existence would lose its value, and it would become unable to compel either the empire or the alliance to respect its independence.

When the empire plotted to rob it of its autonomy, Phezzan would display intent to go over to the alliance. When the alliance conceived ambitions against it, Phezzan would turn with flirtatious eyes toward the empire. Providing both sides with needed supplies, pushing into the imperial and alliance interiors, and ensnaring those in power, Phezzan had long survived by its wits.

It was he, Adrian Rubinski, who was the fifth ruler of this shrewd and cunning people.

It would mean trouble if either the empire or the alliance were to succeed in conquering the other. Both powers needed to exist, maintaining their balance; if one were to fall, Phezzan would need to have the other fall at the same time—and without dragging Phezzan down with it.

Phezzan charted the course of history, and without the exercise of military power; instead it used strategy and the power of its wealth. Building gigantic warships and huge cannons, through bloodshed ultimately inviting the exhaustion of national power and the ruin of society—that sort of foolishness they could leave to the two great powers. Lacking any means of protecting themselves save through slaughter and destruction, were not the Galactic Empire, with its absolute monarchy, and the Free Planets Alliance, with its democratic republic, both in essence imbeciles driven by hidebound custom? Then let them both dance in the palm of Phezzan's hand, intoxicated by the legitimacy of their respective orthodoxies.

Even so, there was something about Count von Lohengramm and

about Yang, about their respective ascents to the galactic stage, that seemed to augur the coming of a new age. Phezzan would need to watch both of them carefully from now on. Though he might be overestimating them, it was always best to keep one's nose to the ground and one's hand full of trumps.

II

Night was enfolding the western hemisphere of Hauptplanet Odin in soft and gentle hands.

Whether imperial territory or alliance, the revolving worlds could never escape the changing guard of night and day. Not even the great Emperor Rudolf, who had sought to dominate galactic space and all that was in it, could stop the revolution of heavenly bodies. Moreover, the motion of these heavenly bodies had no uniform periods; while one planet might rotate once every eighteen and a half hours, the rotational period of another might be forty hours, each asserting its own precious individuality.

On the other hand, even when humanity had dwelt on its original birthplace of Sol III, the internal body clocks of humans had been running on a twenty-five-hour cycle—one hour longer than that world's rotational period. Each individual adjusted this for a life lived in twenty-four-hour increments. It was as a custom that the twenty-four-hour clock had been established. When humanity achieved interstellar flight, that had meant facing the difficult problem of adjusting psychologically to days and nights of widely varying length.

Inside spaceships, in cities in floating in space, on planets that for any number of reasons required an artificial environment, this was not much of a problem. They simply synchronized the environment to the twenty-four-hour lifestyle. Artificial lighting made the daytime bright and the night dark. In these kinds of places, they could adjust the temperature to be lowest just before dawn, and between summer and winter change not only the temperature, but also the length of the nights.

Furthermore, on worlds where the periods of rotation were extremely long or short, a twenty-four-hour day could be enforced by regulation.

People would start to say, "It'll be night all day today. I hear the sun comes up tomorrow," or "On this planet, you can see sunsets twice a day."

The trouble occurred rather on planets with near-Earthlike rotational periods of 21.5 hours or 27 hours, where after much trial and error, the population would divide into one faction in favor of splitting the orbital period into twenty-four equal divisions and using the planetary local time, and another in favor of enduring the various inconveniences of using the standard twenty-four-hour system. Whatever they settled on, there would be nothing else to do but steel one's nerves and get used to it.

Twenty-four hours is a day, and 365 days is a year. This so-called standard calendar was used both in the empire and in the alliance. January 1 in the Galactic Empire was January 1 in the Free Planets Alliance as well.

"There's no need to remain shackled by the bonds of Earth forever," was a common refrain. "Humanity doesn't revolve around Earth any longer, and the Space Era calendar is already in force. Shouldn't we set up new standards for keeping time?"

There were those among the "old equals bad" set that made such arguments, but when asked what these new standards should be, there was never any answer that everyone could agree on. Ultimately, the age-old custom received the greatest—if not necessarily the most enthusiastic—amount of support, and continued even to this day.

The "bonds of Earth" extended to weights and measures as well. One gram was equal to one cubic centimeter of water, weighed under Earth's gravity at 4 degrees centigrade. In like manner, one centimeter was roughly equal to one four-billionth the length of the Earth's circumference. These units as well were in common use by the entire star-spanning society of humanity.

Emperor Rudolf had made an effort to change the units of weights and measurement. Seeking to standardize all the units, he had defined the height of his own body as one kaiser-faden and his own body weight as one kaiser-centner. However, this system was never put into action.

Not because it was altogether illogical, though. Kläfe, who was lord of the treasury at the time, was granted an audience with the emperor, at which time he respectfully submitted a single datum. It was a trial calculation of the expenditure that would be necessary to change the units of weights and measures, based on the assumption that doing so would necessitate swapping out every computer chip and measuring device throughout the whole of the settled galaxy. At that time, the unit of currency had only just been changed from credits to imperial marks, and the story goes that the number of zeros lined up on that paper had been sufficient to daunt even the ever-obstinate Rudolf.

In this way, the meter and the gram were suffered their continued existence, though the current prevailing theory was that Kläfe's estimate had been an obviously inflated figure and that Kläfe, whose meekness had been considered his only saving grace, had in fact dared a subtle show of resistance to Rudolf's boundless self-deification.

The stately Neue Sans Souci Palace, residence of the emperor of the Galactic Empire, revealed itself beneath the night sky.

Buildings large and small, freestanding and interconnected, innumerable fountains, natural and artificial forests, sunken rose gardens, sculptures, flower beds, gazebos, and an endless successions of lawns were enveloped in pale silver light by ingenious illumination effects designed with care not to irritate the optic nerve.

This palace was the political crossroads of a government that ruled more than a thousand star systems. Government offices were laid out around its perimeter, but there was not a tall building among them to be found. Their main offices were underground, for it was an unforgivable act of disrespect for a subject to look down from a high position upon the emperor's palace. Even the many satellites that orbited Odin's skies never, ever passed directly over the palace.

Over fifty thousand chamberlains and ladies-in-waiting worked at the palace. It was an age when the use of people to perform easily automated tasks proved the height of one's position and the greatness of one's authority. Cooking, cleaning, guiding visitors, maintaining the gardens, caring for the free-roaming deer—all of these were accomplished by human hands. This was the luxury of a king.

There were no beltways or escalators at the palace. You had to use your own legs to walk its corridors and ascend or descend its staircases. This was true even for the emperor himself.

"Rudolf the Great" had believed that physical strength, too, was a requisite of rulership. How could one shoulder the burden of this vast empire if he couldn't even walk on his own two feet?

Within the palace were several audience chambers, and that evening the Black Pearl Room was packed with high officials beyond counting. A ceremony would be held tonight to bestow the scepter of an imperial marshal upon Count Reinhard von Lohengramm, who had smitten the brutish rebel forces at the Battle of Astarte and there caused the light of the emperor's authority to shine gloriously.

An imperial marshal was not merely one rank above senior admiral, nor did the rank come only with a lifelong pension of 2.5 million imperial marks per year. An imperial marshal was also not punishable under criminal law for any offense save high treason and could establish an admiralität, or bureau, in which he was free to hire or dismiss staff at will.

At present, there were only four imperial marshals who enjoyed these privileges, though tonight they would become five when Count Reinhard von Lohengramm was added to their number. Moreover, it was going around that Count von Lohengramm would also be made vice commander in chief of the Imperial Space Armada, placing half of its eighteen fleets under his command.

"Next he'll be made one of the peerage. From count to marquis," some were whispering thus to one other off in the recesses of the vast Black Pearl Room. Along with fire, humanity's great friend down through the ages had been gossip. Those who adored this friend existed in every era under every circumstance, ceasing neither in luxurious palace nor in homely ghetto.

Positioned nearest the emperor's throne, those who held the highest positions in the empire stood motionless—highborn aristocrats, high-ranking civilian and military officials, and those holding multiple titles. Separated by a red carpet six meters wide—two hundred craftsmen had woven it over the course of 450 years—they had formed two ranks. On one side was a row of civil officials, with Marquis Lichtenlade occupying the highest position.

Marquis Lichtenlade, the imperial government's minister of state, was presiding over cabinet meetings as acting imperial prime minister. He was an old man of seventy-five, with a pointed nose and silver hair like newfallen snow, possessed of a glint in his eye more stern than penetrating.

Moving downstream from him were Minister of Finance Gerlach, Minister of the Interior Flegel, Minister of Justice Lump, Minister of Science Wilhelmj, Minister of the Palace Interior Neuköln, Chief Secretary of the Cabinet Kielmansek—they and others like them were sitting in rows.

On the opposite side were rows of military officials: Imperial Marshal Ehrenberg, who was minister of military affairs; Imperial Marshal Steinhof, the secretary-general of Imperial Military Command Headquarters; Imperial Marshal Krasen, the commissioner of staff; Imperial Marshal Mückenberger, commander in chief of the Imperial Space Armada; Senior Admiral Ofresser, commissioner of Armored Grenadier Corps; Senior Admiral Ramusdorf, commissioner of the Imperial Guard; Admiral Klammer, commissioner of military police; the commanding officers of the eighteen fleets…

At the clear, resounding blare of an old-fashioned trumpet, the whole assembly began to straighten their posture. There was a rustling as of leaves in the wind, and then it quieted. The coordinator of ceremonies' voice pounded the attendees' eardrums, announcing the entrance of the Highest Honored.

"Ruler of all humanity, sovereign of all the universe, defender of the order and laws that govern the heavenly realm, kaiser of the sacred and inviolable Galactic Empire, His Highness, Friedrich IV!"

The solemn melody of the empire's national anthem swelled up on the heels of his last word. All present bowed their heads deeply, as though something were pressing down on their necks.

Perhaps some of them were counting under their breaths. When they slowly raised their heads, their emperor was sitting in his gilded, luxurious seat.

Friedrich IV, thirty-sixth emperor of the Galactic Empire. At age sixty-three, he was a man who gave an impression of being oddly worn out. Though he wasn't quite elderly, there was something about him that made people want to call him "old." He had almost no interest in the affairs of state. Nor did he seem to have the ability or will to actively use the absolute power that he had. Emperor Friedrich IV: a feeble man who bore the twilight gleam of his mighty ancestor Rudolf, his polar opposite.

The emperor had lost his empress ten years prior. It had not been some intractable disease—just a cold that had gotten worse and developed into pneumonia. Cancer had been conquered in distant antiquity, but driving the common cold from the list of maladies had, as one historian of the alliance so maliciously put it, been impossible "even for the glory and power of Rudolf the Great."

Since then, the emperor had bestowed on one of his mistresses the title of Countess—or Gräfin—Grünewald, making her his de facto wife, although he refrained from making her empress. But because that mistress was not highborn, she refrained from attending official state functions and as usual did not show her lovely face before the court that night. Countess von Grünewald's real name was Annerose.

In a sonorous voice, the coordinator of ceremonies called for the man of the hour to come forth.

"Lord Reinhard, Count von Lohengramm!"

This time there was no need to bow deeply, so all those assembled turned their eyes toward the young military officer walking across the carpet toward them.

There were sighs of admiration from among the noble ladies. Even those who harbored hostility toward Reinhard—to wit, the greater part of the attendees—couldn't help acknowledging his incomparable good looks.

His face was like that of a doll crafted from the finest *baici* porcelain, though his eyes were too piercing for a doll's, his expression too intense and strong. If not for the emperor's indulgence with Reinhard's elder sister Annerose and the expression Reinhard wore at that moment, backbiting gossip of sovereign-subject sodomy would likely have been inevitable.

With a brisk step befitting an officer of the military, Reinhard passed through the jumble of onlookers' varied emotions, coming at last to stand before the throne, where with a reverence felt nowhere in his heart, he bowed to one knee.

In that posture, he waited to be graced by the words of his sovereign. At official functions, subjects were not allowed to address the emperor.

"Count von Lohengramm, your recent military exploits have been truly splendid," the emperor said, speaking in a voice devoid of originality or character.

"If I may be so bold, it was done wholly through the grace of Your Majesty's authority."

Reinhard's answer had also been lacking in originality, but that was due to calculation and self-restraint. Even if he were to say something clever, he was not talking to someone capable of understanding cleverness, and doing so would only stoke the hostilities of those in attendance. To Reinhard, that one piece of paper that the emperor took from the conductor of ceremonies and began reading aloud was far more important.

"In recognition of thy success in the subjugation of rebel forces in the Astarte star system, I hereby appoint thee, Count Reinhard von Lohengramm, to the office of imperial marshal. Furthermore, I do name thee vice commander of the Imperial Space Armada and place half its vessels under thy command. March 19, Year 487 of the Imperial Calendar, Friedrich IV, Emperor of the Galactic Empire."

Reinhard rose, ascended the steps, and, bowing deeply, received his letter of appointment. At the same time, the scepter of an imperial marshal was given him. In that instant, Count Reinhard von Lohengramm became an imperial marshal.

Even as a brilliant smile surfaced on his face, Reinhard felt no satisfaction at all inside. This was nothing more than the first step on the long road he had to travel—the road toward taking the place of that bumbling fool who had used his power to steal away his sister.

"Hmph. A twenty-year-old imperial marshal?"

That low murmur had come from Senior Admiral Ofresser, commissioner of the Armored Grenadier Corps. He was a large, well-built man in his late forties; a scar carved into his left cheekbone by an alliance soldier's laser was a vivid purple. Deliberately left partially unhealed, it announced to the world that he was a fierce and battle-hardened general.

"Since when was the glorious Imperial Space Armada reduced to being a toddler's toy, Excellency?"

The man to whom he so provocatively whispered was the one who had just had half the men under his command stolen from him by Reinhard.

Imperial Marshal Mückenberger, commander in chief of the Imperial Space Armada, arched a graying eyebrow just slightly.

"So you say, milord, but you can't deny that the golden brat is a talented tactician. It's a fact he destroyed rebel forces despite being outnumbered, and his talents have even silenced battle-hardened veterans like Merkatz."

"Indeed, the man does look like he's had his fangs pulled." Casting a glance toward Admiral Merkatz, standing silent amid a row of military officers, Offresser gave a merciless critique. "While it's true the brat did defeat them, one victory by itself might just be a fluke. If you ask me, all I can think is that the enemy just didn't know what they were doing. Victory and defeat are ultimately relative, after all."

"You're speaking rather loudly."

Though he spoke reprovingly, the imperial marshal had not denied the content of what the senior admiral had said. Reinhard's achievement was not an easy thing for highborn nobles and old guard admirals to accept.

The time and place being what it was, however, the imperial marshal apparently felt a need to change the subject. "About that particular enemy, by the way, have you ever heard of a commander by the name of Yang?"

"Let me think... I don't remember anyone by that name. What about him?"

"In the recent battle, he was the man who stopped the rebel force from completely disintegrating and brought about the death of Rear Admiral Erlach."

"Oh?"

"He seems to possess quite an aptitude for the work of a general. I have information that even our blond-haired whelp had his nose tweaked by the man."

"And you're not glad to hear it?"

"I would be if this were only about Reinhard. But do you think they pick and choose who to fight when they go to battle?"

As might be expected, there was a note of disgust in the imperial marshal's voice, at which Ofresser awkwardly shrugged his thick shoulders.

In the Black Pearl Room, music was beginning to play again. It was "Thy Courage Doth Walküren Adore," a piece composed in praise of the military officers who gave their all in service of king and country.

The curtain was now beginning to fall on what for the highborn nobles had been a most unpleasant ceremony.

Captain Sigfried Kircheis, together with the other soldiers of the field officer class, was waiting in the Amethyst Room, which was separated by a wide corridor from the site of the ceremony itself.

Kircheis, as he was neither a noble nor an admiral, lacked the qualifications needed for entrance into the Black Pearl Room. It had been decided over the past two days, however, that he would be promoted to rear admiral, skipping over commodore to a position in which he would be called "Excellency." When that happened, he would be excluded no longer from elegant ceremonies.

Every time Reinhard climbs a rung in the hierarchy, I get pulled up behind him... Kircheis trembled just slightly. Although he didn't think of himself as lacking in talent, the speed of his rise was certainly extraordinary, and it would be disastrous to think it due entirely to his own ability.

"Captain Sigfried Kircheis, correct?" said a soft voice from his side.

An officer who looked to be in is early thirties was standing in Kircheis's line of sight. He wore a captain's insignia. He was a tall man, though not so tall as Kircheis, with pale-brown eyes, a sickly white complexion, and lots of early gray in his dark head of hair.

"That's right, and who might you be?"

"Captain Paul von Oberstein. This is my first time meeting you."

Just as he spoke these words, Kircheis was startled to see a strange light well up in his eyes.

"I beg your pardon…" murmured the man calling himself von Oberstein. He had read from Kircheis's expression what had happened. "Something must be wrong with my artificial eyes. I'm sorry if I startled you. I'll make it a point to have them replaced, tomorrow maybe."

"They're artificial? I'm sorry, then—I'm the one who should beg your pardon."

"No, not at all. Thank to these things, with their integrated photonic computers, I can get along without any disability whatsoever. They just don't seem to last very long, do they?"

"Were you wounded in battle?"

"No, I've been like this since birth. Had I been born in Rudolf the Great's generation, I'd have been caught and disposed of by that Genetic Inferiority Elimination Act."

Vibrations of air became sound that just barely reached the lower limits of human hearing, and yet that was enough to make Kircheis gasp. It went without saying that comments sounding critical of Rudolf the Great were grounds for charges of lèse-majesté.

"You have a fine commander, Captain Kircheis," von Oberstein added in a slightly louder voice, yet it was still nothing more than a whisper. "And by a fine commander, I mean someone who can make the most of the talents of his subordinates. There are so very few of them in the service right now. Count von Lohengramm is different, though. He's most impressive for one so young. It's a hard thing for the powerful highborn families to understand, though, caught up in their lineage-obsessed mentality…"

Kircheis's trap detector was ringing like mad in the back of his mind. How could he be sure this man von Oberstein wasn't some marionette sent by someone hoping for Reinhard to slip up?

"So tell me, what unit are you serving in?" he said, casually changing the subject.

"Up until now, I've been in the Data Processing Department at Command HQ, but just recently I received orders to serve as a staff officer in the fleet stationed at Iserlohn."

Von Oberstein smiled thinly after his reply. "You seem to be on your guard, Captain."

At that instant, an embarrassed Kircheis was just about to say something when he caught sight of Reinhard coming into the room. The ceremony was over, it seemed.

"Kircheis, tomorrow…" Reinhard began to say, but then he noticed the pale man standing next to his subordinate.

Von Oberstein saluted and introduced himself, then after brief and conventional words of congratulation, turned and departed.

Reinhard and Kircheis went out into the corridor. Tonight they would be staying in a small guesthouse in an out-of-the-way corner of the palace grounds. It was a fifteen-minute walk through the gardens to get there.

"Kircheis," Reinhard said as they came out underneath the night sky, "I'm meeting my sister tomorrow. I'm sure you're coming too?"

"It's all right for me to come along?"

"Why so reserved at this point? We're family." Reinhard smiled like a young boy but then reeled himself back in and lowered his voice just a little. "By the way, who was that man just now? Something about him bothers me a little."

Kircheis gave a brief overview of the situation and further opined that he was "somehow a mysterious fellow."

Reinhard's perfectly formed brows had furrowed slightly as he was listening. "A mysterious fellow indeed," he agreed. "I don't know what he has in mind cozying up to you like that, but it would pay to be on your guard. Of course, with as many enemies as we have, being on one's guard isn't exactly easy either."

Both of the men smiled together.

III

The residence of Countess Annerose von Grünewald was located in another nook of Neue Sans Souci Palace, though visiting it required a ten-minute ride in a flamboyantly decorated landcar used only at court.

For someone like Kircheis, walking would have been easier, but when a landcar was sent round by the Ministry of the Palace Interior as a token of His Imperial Highness's generosity, there was nothing to do but get in. The mansion they were bound for was by the shore of a lake grown thickly about with lindenbaum trees, built in a simple, clean style of architecture that fit its mistress well.

When he spotted Annerose's slender, elegant figure standing out on the porch, Reinhard leapt from the still-moving landcar and hurried to her at a trot.

"Annerose! My big sister!"

Annerose greeted her younger brother with a smile that was like sunlight in the spring.

"Reinhard! It's wonderful you've come. And even Sieg is here."

"The important thing is that you're looking well, too, Miss Annerose."

"Thank you. Now come inside, both of you. I've been waiting for you for the past few days now."

Ah, she hasn't changed a bit since old times, thought Kircheis. *That gentle kindness, that unaffected purity ... impossible to mar, though all the emperor's might be brought against it.*

"I'll put on some coffee. Have some kelsey plum cake too. I baked it myself, so I'm not sure if it'll be to your tastes or not. Try this and tell me."

"We shall align our tastes to it," Reinhard answered, laughing. The living room was just the right size, and a relaxed, friendly atmosphere filled its space. The three young people shared equally in the illusion that the spirits of time had moved that room alone back ten years in time.

The clink of coffee cups as they touched one another, the clean tablecloth, the aroma of a slight touch of vanilla essence that was mixed into the kelsey cake…glimpses of a singular joy were reflected in all of these things.

Annerose was wearing a little smile as she sliced and parceled out the cake with deft, fluid movements.

"Every once in a while, someone will tell me the kitchen is no place for a countess, but no matter what they say, I enjoy it so much I just can't help myself. Though it is a lot of hard work not relying on machines very much."

The coffee was brewed and the cream poured in. There was homemade cake and conversation without the slightest concern of ulterior motives. For once, their hearts were at ease.

"Reinhard always wants to have his way, Sieg. I can only imagine all the trouble he must put you through."

"No, not at—"

"You can say what you think."

"Reinhard, stop teasing him. Oh! I just remembered. I have some delicious *vin rosé* that Viscountess Schafhausen gave me. It's in the cellar, so I wonder if I could have you go and get it? Sorry to send His Excellency the Imperial Marshal on errands, though."

"Now you're the one teasing me. But yes, milady—whether for errands or whatever else, consider me at your service."

Reinhard stood and departed, relaxed and at ease.

Annerose and Kircheis stayed behind. Annerose turned her little smile toward her younger brother's best friend.

"Sieg, thank you for always being there for my brother."

"It's nothing at all. I'm the one who's always being looked out for. Since I'm not an aristocrat, it seems a bit much for me, making captain at my age."

"You'll be a rear admiral soon enough. I've heard the news. Congratulations."

"Thank you very much."

Kircheis's earlobes started to feel hot.

"My brother never says so, and maybe he doesn't realize it himself, but

Sieg, he really does depend on you. So please, somehow, take good care of him from now on, too."

"I'm honored . . . that someone like me—"

"Seig, you should recognize your own talents more. My brother has a talent. Probably a talent that no one else has. But he isn't as mature as you are. He's a bit like an antelope that gets so caught up in the speed of his legs that he runs right off a cliff. I've known him since he was born, so I can say things like that."

"Miss Annerose . . ."

"Please, Sieg, I'm begging you. Watch over Reinhard—don't let him lose his footing on those cliffs. If you see the signs of it, scold and nag. If the warning comes from you, he'll listen. The day he stops listening to you is the day my brother is finished. He'll have proven all by himself that no matter how much raw talent he may have had, he lacked ability to perfect it."

That little smile had disappeared already from Annerose's lovely countenance. In her sapphire eyes, a deeper blue than those of her brother, there hovered the shadow of something like sorrow.

An invisible blade glided over Kircheis's heart. *That's right, things aren't the same as ten years ago. Reinhard and I aren't neighborhood boys anymore, and Annerose isn't that domestic-minded little girl anymore. The emperor's favored mistress, the imperial marshal, and his top aide. The three of us, standing amid the fragrance and stench of imperial power . . .*

"If it's within my ability, I'll do anything, Miss Annerose."

Somehow, Kircheis's voice managed to obey the will of its master as he struggled to contain his emotions.

"Please believe in my loyalty toward Reinhard. I will never do anything that would betray your wishes, Miss Annerose."

"Thank you, Sieg. I'm sorry—I'm always asking too much of you. But other than you, there's no one I can rely on. Please, find some way to forgive me?"

I want the two of you to rely on me, Kircheis murmured in his heart. *Ever since that moment ten years ago when I heard you say, "Please be a good friend to my brother," it's what I've always wanted . . .*

Ten years ago! Again, Kircheis felt that pain in his heart.

If he had been his present age ten years ago, he would never have handed Annerose over into the emperor's hands. No matter what the cost, he would have taken those two siblings and fled, probably to the Free Planets Alliance. And by this time, he might even be an officer in the alliance military.

But back then, he hadn't the ability and had lacked even a clear grasp of his own desires. Now things were different. But ten years or more in the past, there had been nothing he could do. Why couldn't people be the ages they needed to be at the most important moments in their lives?

"You could've put this in an easier place to find."

Those words announced the return of Reinhard.

"Yes, your hard work is much appreciated. But your efforts in seeking it out bring their own reward. I'll go get the glasses."

Times such as these were fleeting, though to have them at all was to be counted a blessing. Kircheis told himself that. The next battle, which would surely be coming, was not something he could allow himself to shrink from.

CHAPTER 4:
THE BIRTH OF THE THIRTEENTH FLEET

I

Stretching from fifty-five floors above ground level to eighty floors beneath it, located in the deciduous climatic zone of the northern hemisphere of Planet Heinessen, was the Free Planets Alliance Joint Operational Headquarters building. Positioned in orderly fashion all around it were buildings for Science and Technology Headquarters, Rear Service Headquarters, the Space Defense Command and Control Center, the military academy, and the Capital Defense Command Center. These buildings formed a zone that was the hub of military affairs, about one hundred kilometers away from the heart of the capital city of Heinessenpolis.

In an assembly hall that occupied space on four of the Joint Operational Headquarters building's underground floors, a memorial service for those who had died in the Battle of Astarte was about to begin. It was a beautiful afternoon with clear blue skies, two days after the alliance force dispatched to the Astarte system had returned as an exhausted remnant, having lost 60 percent of its force strength.

The lane heading toward the hall was packed with crowds of attendees. The families of those lost were present, as were the related governmental and military personnel. Among them was also the figure of Yang Wen-Li.

As he made appropriate responses to the people who came to speak to him, Yang looked up at the vast spread of blue sky. Although he could not see them, countless military satellites soundlessly flew overhead in space above the many layers of atmosphere.

Among them were the twelve interceptor satellites that together formed "Artemis's Necklace," that giant engine of murder and destruction controlled by the Space Defense Command and Control Center, of which alliance military leaders were given to boast: "As long as we have this, Planet Heinessen is impregnable." Every time he heard that, Yang would remember past history and how most fortresses dubbed "impregnable" had collapsed amid devouring flames of judgment. Did they really believe that being strong militarily was something to brag about?

Yang lightly slapped both cheeks with his hands. It felt like he wasn't completely awake. He'd slept for sixteen hours straight but stayed awake for sixty hours before that.

He wasn't eating right either. His stomach wasn't feeling all that well, so all he had consumed was some vegetable soup that Julian had warmed up for him. He had collapsed into bed as soon as he had returned to the official housing, then left to come here not even an hour after waking, and now that he thought about it, he could not remember having had any decent conversation with the young boy whose guardian he had become.

Oh well, guess this makes me a failure as a parent...

As he was thus thinking, someone tapped him on the shoulder. When he turned around, Rear Admiral Alex Caselnes, his upperclassman from the academy, was standing there, smiling.

"It looks like the hero of Astarte hasn't completely woken up yet."

"Who's the hero?"

"The person standing in front of me. You probably haven't had time to see the news yet, but that's what the whole field of journalism is writing about you."

"Me? I'm a defeated general."

"That's right," said Caselnes. "The Alliance Navy was defeated. Which is why we need a hero. Though if we'd won big, I wouldn't go so far as 'need,' you know? That's because when we lose, we have to avert the public's eyes from the big picture. It was probably the same thing with El Facil."

The ironic tone was characteristic of Caselnes. A man of thirty-five, of middling height with a healthy-looking stoutness, he worked as top aide and second in command to Marshal Sidney Sitolet, director of the Alliance Military Joint Operational Headquarters. With more experience at desk work than frontline service, he was a man of great ability when it came to things like organizing projects and dealing with bureaucracy; there was little doubt that the director's chair at Rear Service HQ lay in his future.

"Is it really okay for you to come over here, though?" asked Yang. "What with 'top aide' really meaning 'errand boy,' I figured you'd be busy, but…" Under light counterattack, the capable military bureaucrat returned a subtly formed smile.

"Well, this show is being run by the Bureau of Ceremonies. It's not for the soldiers and not really even for the families. The one most excited for all this is His Excellency the Defense Committee Chairman. Because if I may say so, this whole thing is a political show for the chairman, as he is aiming to run the next administration."

The face of Defense Committee Chairman Job Trünicht rose up in both of their recollections.

A tall, handsome, youthful politician of forty-one. An energetic, argumentative hard-liner against the empire. Half of those who knew him praised him as an eloquent orator. The other half loathed him for a sophist.

The alliance's current head of state was Supreme Council Chairman Royal Sunford. An elderly politician who had risen out of political strife to play the role of moderator, he was in all things devoted to respect for precedent. Since he was somewhat lacking in vigor, the spotlight was beginning to shine on Trünicht as the leader of the next generation.

"But having to listen to that man's tasteless rabble-rousing at length is worse than pulling an all-nighter," Caselnes said disgustedly. Although he was in the military, he was in the minority opinion on this. A publicity hound Trünicht may have been, but he spoke passionately of providing ample facilities for the military and of crushing the empire, and among those whose affection he garnered, many were uniformed soldiers. Yang, too, was one of the minority.

Inside the auditorium, the two men were seated far apart. Caselnes sat behind Director Sitolet in the seats reserved for honored guests, while Yang was front and center, right beneath the podium.

The ceremony had begun in a conventional manner, and in a conventional manner it was proceeding. Chairman Sundford left the stage after an emotionless, monotone delivery of a script prepared by bureaucrats, then Defense Committee Chairman Trünicht stepped lightly onto the stage. At the mere appearance of the man, the air in the auditorium became charged, and a round of applause rose up, even louder than the one for Chairman Sundford.

Trünicht—who wasn't holding a script—called out to the sixty thousand attendees in a rich and sonorous voice.

"Citizens and soldiers! What is the purpose for which we've all come rushing out to assemble in this place? It is to give comfort to the heroic spirits of those 1,500,000 who so valiantly gave their lives in the Astarte Stellar Region. For it was to protect the freedom and the peace of their country that they offered up their precious lives."

He was only this far into the speech, and Yang was already wishing he could plug his ears. He wondered, had this situation—of listeners cringing at empty, flowery words, even as their speaker feels perfectly at ease rattling them off—been a part of humanity's heritage since the days of ancient Greece?

"I just said, 'their precious lives.' And truly, life is something that must always be respected. But, friends, they died to show those of us left behind that there exist things more precious still than the life of the individual. What are these? They are country and freedom! Their deaths were beautiful, precisely because they set aside themselves and gave their lives for the sake of a great and noble cause. They were good husbands. They were good fathers, good sons, and good boyfriends. They had a right to lead long, fulfilling lives. Yet casting that right aside, they departed for the field of battle and there laid down their lives! Citizens, if I may be so bold as to ask... why did 1,500,000 soldiers die?"

"'Cause the leaders' operational command sucked," Yang muttered, his voice a little loud for a private commentary. Shocked expressions appeared on the faces of a few of the people around him, and a young black-haired officer shot a glance his way. Yang's eyes met that glance head-on, and its owner, flustered, quickly looked back toward the podium.

And from where he was looking, the defense committee chair's speech was still dragging on. Trünicht's face was flushed red, a gleam of self-intoxication in his eyes.

"Yes, I have said the answer already. It was in the defense of country and of freedom that they gave up their lives! Is there any death more worthy than this of the word 'noble'? Is there anything else that speaks to us so eloquently of what a petty thing it is to live for oneself only, and die for oneself only? You must all remember that the country is what makes the individual possible. That is the thing that exceeds even life in importance. Bear that truth in mind! And what I want to say most loudly is this: that country and freedom are worth protecting, even at the cost of human lives. That our battle is a just one! To those of you who are self-styled pacifists, demanding that we make peace with the empire... to those of you who are self-styled idealists, thinking that it's possible to coexist with tyrannical absolutism, I say, awaken from your delusions! Whatever your motivation for what you do, it results in a sapping of the alliance's strength, and it benefits the empire. In the empire, antiwar and pacifist ideologies are suppressed. It's because our alliance is a free nation that opposition to national policy is even permitted. Don't just take advantage of that! There's nothing easier than advocating for peace with words."

There is one thing, thought Yang. *Hiding in a safe place and advocating for war*. Yang could feel the excitement of the surrounding crowd all over him, increasing by the moment like a rising river. He had had enough of it, but agitators, it seemed, were never wanting for support, no matter what the era or the times.

"If I may be so bold, all of those who oppose this righteous war to bring down the Galactic Empire's tyrannical absolutism are undermining the country. They are unworthy of their citizenship in our proud alliance! Only those who fight fearlessly in the face of death to protect our free society and the national establishment that guarantees it are true citizens of the alliance. The cowards who lack that readiness shame these heroes' spirits! This alliance was forged and built by our ancestors. We know the history. We know how our ancestors paid for their freedom in blood. Our homeland, with its grand history! Our free homeland! Will we not stand and fight to defend the one thing worth defending? Let us fight, now, for the homeland! Hail the alliance! Hail the republic! Down with the empire!"

With each shout of the defense committee chairman, the listeners' reason was being blown away like chaff. Churning waves of exuberance lifted the bodies of sixty thousand people as they rose from their seats to join Trünicht in his hails, their mouths opened so wide he could probably see all the way back to their molars.

"Hail the alliance! Hail the republic! Down with the empire!"

A forest of arms beyond counting sent berets dancing high up into the air. There was a capriccio of applause and cheers.

In the midst of it, Yang remained silent, resolutely staying seated. His black eyes were fixed coldly on the warrior at the podium. Both of Trünicht's arms were raised high in response to the excitement of the full auditorium, and then his gaze fell down to the front row of spectators.

For an instant, the gleam in his eye became hard, showing disgust, and the corners of his mouth drew tight. He had recognized that one young officer in his field of view who was still sitting. If Yang had been seated in the back, he probably wouldn't have been noticed, but he was in the front row, a shameless rebel sitting right beneath the nose of sublime patriotism incarnate.

A jowly middle-aged officer shouted at Yang, "Officer, why aren't you standing?!" He was wearing commodore's insignia, same as Yang.

Shifting his gaze, Yang quietly answered. "This is a free country. I ought to be free to not stand up when I don't want to. I'm just exercising that freedom."

"Well then, why don't you want to stand up?"

"Exercising my freedom not to answer."

Yang knew that was a smart-aleck response, even for him. Caselnes would have probably laughed and said, *That was rather awkward, even as a show of resistance.* Yang, however, had no enthusiasm for behaving like a grown-up here. He didn't want to stand up, he didn't want to clap his hands, and he didn't want to shout "Hail the alliance!" either. If not being moved by Trünicht's speech was enough to merit criticism of his patriotism, what response could there be except, "Whatever you say"? The adults were never the ones to cry out that the emperor had no clothes; it was always a child.

"What are you trying to—"

Just as the middle-aged commodore was starting to yell at him again, Trünicht, at the podium, lowered his arms. He gestured lightly toward the crowd, both hands open, and as he did so, the level of excitement dropped off, and a quiet stillness began to smother all the noise. The people lowered their heads.

Even the middle-aged commodore who had been glaring at Yang took his seat, his thick, meaty cheeks trembling in discontent.

"Ladies and gentlemen?"

The defense committee chair opened his mouth again at the podium. Between his shouting and his long-winded speech, his mouth had dried out, leaving his melodious voice hoarse. After coughing once, he began to speak began.

"Our most powerful weapon is the unified will of all the people. With our free country and our democratically elected system of republican government, we cannot force on you any goal, no matter how noble. Every one of you has the freedom to oppose the state. But this much should be obvious to all conscientious people: true freedom means casting aside our petty egos, banding together, and advancing as one toward a common goal. Ladies and gentlemen..."

The reason that Trünicht closed his mouth at that point was not because of his dry mouth. It was because he had noticed a woman walking down the aisle toward the podium, alone. She was a young woman with light-brown hair, and pretty enough to probably turn the heads of half the men she passed on the street. From both sides of the aisle down which she strode, there arose low, suspicious stirrings of whispers, spreading outward through the crowd like ripples.

Who is that woman? What's she doing?

Yang, like the other listeners, looked toward the woman as well, figuring anything was better than looking at Trünicht's face, but when he saw her he couldn't help but raise his eyebrows slightly. It was a face he remembered all too well.

"Defense Committee Chairman?" she said, calling toward the podium in a mezzo-soprano voice that had a nice, lingering ring. "My name is Jessica Edwards. I am—or, I was—the fiancée of Jean Robert Lappe, a staff officer in the Sixth Fleet, who died in the Battle of Astarte."

"Why, that's..." The eloquent "leader of the new generation" found himself at a loss for words. "...that's a terrible shame, ma'am, but..."

His words going nowhere, the defense committee chairman looked meaninglessly around the vast assembly hall. The crowd of sixty thousand listeners reciprocated with sixty thousand silences. All of them were holding their breath as they stared at this young woman, bereaved of her fiancé.

"I don't need your consolation, Chairman, because my fiancé died a noble death defending his country."

Jessica quietly calmed the chairman's discomfiture, and an unguarded expression of relief rose up on Trünicht's face.

"Is that so? Well then, you should be considered a role model for all the young women on the home front. Such a laudable spirit is sure to be rewarded richly."

At this point, Yang wanted to shut his eyes on that shameless man. All he could think was, *Nothing is impossible if you have no sense of shame.*

Jessica, on the other hand, appeared composed.

"Thank you very much. I came here today because there's a question—just one question—I'd like to have the chairman answer."

"Oh? What kind of question might that be? I hope it's one I can answer..."

"Where are you now?"

Trünicht blinked his eyes. So did most of the onlookers, unable to grasp the question's intent.

"Ah, what did you say?"

"My fiancé went to the battlefield to protect his country, and now he isn't anywhere at all in this world. Chairman, where are you now? You, with your praise of death, where are you?"

"Young lady..." The defense committee chairman appeared to be flinching from everyone's gaze.

"Where is your family?" Jessica continued relentlessly. "I offered up my fiancé as a sacrifice. You, who preach the need for sacrifice to the people, where is your family? I don't deny a single word you've said here today. But are you living it yourself?"

"Security!" Trünicht called out, looking toward the right and then the left. "This young lady is very upset. Escort her to another room. Conductor, my speech is over. National anthem! Play the national anthem."

Someone took hold of Jessica's arm. She was about to try to shake it off when she saw the man's face and gave it up.

"Let's go," Yang Wen-li said quietly. "I don't think this is a place you need to be..."

Stirring music, abounding in a sense of exaltation, was beginning to fill the assembly hall. It was "Freedom's Flag, Freedom's People," the national anthem of the Free Planets Alliance.

> *My friends, someday, the oppressor we'll o'erthrow,*
> *And on liberated worlds,*
> *We'll raise freedom's flag.*
> *Now, we fight for a shining future;*

Today, we fight for a fruitful tomorrow.
Friends, let us sing; the soul of freedom praise.
Friends, let us sing; the soul of freedom show.

The crowd began to sing along with the music. Unlike the chaotic cries of just moments ago, this was a unified and rich melody.

From beyond the darkness of tyranny,
With our own hands, let's bring freedom's dawn.

Backs turned on the podium, Yang and Jessica walked up the aisle toward the exit. Attendees glanced at the two of them as they passed, then immediately turn their gazes back toward the podium and continued singing. When the door that had opened silently before them had closed on their backs, they heard the final line of the national anthem:

Oh, we are freedom's people,
Through eternity unconquered…

II

The last gleam of the setting sun faded, and all the land was covered in the cool air of a relaxing evening. The silvery blue light of gorgeous swarms of stars was beginning to shine. At this time of year, a constellation said to resemble a spiral belt of silk was particularly vivid.

The spaceport in Heinessenpolis was filled with hustle and bustle.

In its vast lobby, people of all sorts were crowded together. Those who had completed their journeys, those about to depart on them. Those who had come to see someone off, those who had come to pick someone up. Regular citizens wearing conventional suits, soldiers in black berets, technicians in their combination suits. Security officers standing still at strategic points and looking irate at the heavy crowds, overworked spaceport employees walking quickly, children running wild with excitement. Robot cars threaded their way like mice through gaps in the interposing walls of humans, carrying baggage.

"Yang," Jessica Edwards said to the young man sitting by her side.

"Hmm?"

"You must have thought I was a horrible woman."

"What makes you say that?"

"Most of those bereaved families were sitting there in silence, enduring their grief, but I went and caused a scene in front of all those people. It's only natural you should take offense."

There's not a single example of things getting better thanks to silently enduring it, Yang thought. *Somebody needs to criticize the leadership and hold them responsible.* But when he opened his mouth to speak, all he said was, "No, not at all."

The two of them were sitting side by side on one of the sofas in the spaceport lobby.

Jessica had said she was heading back to Heinessen's neighboring world of Terneuzen on a liner leaving in about an hour. There she worked as an elementary school music teacher. If Lieutenant Commander Jean Robert Lappe had survived, she had planned to quit that job upon her marriage.

"You've really come a long way, haven't you, Yang?" said Jessica, staring as a family of three passed by in front of her.

Yang didn't answer.

"I heard all about what you did at Astarte. And your achievements before that . . . Jean Robert was always impressed. You're the pride of his graduating class, he'd say."

Jean Robert Lappe was a good man. Jessica made a wise decision in choosing him, Yang thought with just a touch of forlornness. Jessica Edwards: daughter of the Officers' Academy purser, who had been attending music school. Now a music instructor who had lost her fiancé . . .

"Aside from you, the whole admiralty should be ashamed. Due to their incompetence, over a million people are dead from a single battle. Morally, too, they should be ashamed."

That's not quite right, Yang thought. Acts of barbarism such as truce breaking and the slaughtering of noncombatants aside, there was no fundamentally high or low ground morally between a great general and a stupid one. When a foolish general got a million allies killed, a great general killed a million enemies. That was the only difference, and if viewed from the standpoint of absolute pacifism—the kind that said, "I will not kill, even if it means being killed myself"—there was no difference between the two. Both were mass murderers.

What the stupid general had to be ashamed of was his lack of ability; the issue was utterly divorced from the concept of morality. This, however, was something Jessica was unlikely to understand even if Yang explained it, nor did Yang think it was something for which understanding should be sought.

The spaceport's boarding announcements pulled Jessica up from the sofa. The departure of the liner she was on was growing near.

"Goodbye, Yang, and thank you for seeing me off."

"Take care."

"Go as far as you can in the service, all right? And as far as Jean Robert could have gone, too."

Yang watched intently as Jessica disappeared into the boarding gate.

Go far, eh? Wonder if she realizes that's the same as telling me, "Go kill even more people." Probably—no, definitely—not. That would also be the same as telling me to do to the empire's women the same thing that was done to her. And when that happens, who will the empire's women take out their sadness and anger on...?

"Excuse me, but might you be Commodore Yang Wen-li?" said a voice. Yang slowly turned around, to find an elderly, refined-looking lady with a boy of five or six in tow.

"Um, that's right, er..."

"Ah yes, I thought so. Here, Will, this man is the hero of Astarte. Say hello to him."

Shyly, the boy hid behind the old lady's back.

"I'm Mrs. Mayer. Both my husband and my son—my son was this boy's father—were soldiers and died honorably in battle with the empire. I was very moved to hear of your exploits on the news, and to be able to meet you in a place like this is more than I could have hoped for."

Yang had no idea what to say.

I wonder what in the world kind of look is on my face right now, he thought.

"This child also says he wants to be a soldier. That he's going to beat the empire and avenge his daddy...Commodore Yang, I know it's an impudent thing to ask, but I wonder if you might let him shake the hand of a hero? I think that shaking hands with you would be an encouragement for him for the future."

Yang couldn't look at the old lady straight on.

Perhaps taking his lack of an answer for assent, the old woman tried to push her grandson to stand before the young admiral. The boy, however, clung tight to his grandmother's dress and wouldn't let go, although he was looking at Yang in the face.

"What's the matter, Will? You think you can become a brave soldier acting like that?"

"Mrs. Mayer," said Yang, mentally wiping away sweat. "When Will becomes an adult, it's going to be peacetime. There's not going to be any need to make himself become a soldier...Take care, kid."

With a slight bow, Yang turned on his heel and got out of that place, walking rapidly. In short, he fled. This was one retreat in which he saw no dishonor.

III

When Yang got back to his officer's house on Block 24 Silver Bridge Street, his watch was showing 2000 Heinessen Standard Time. The whole area was a residential district for high-ranking officers who were either single or had small families, and the refreshing scent of natural chlorophyll drifted on the breeze.

Even so, the buildings and facilities could not necessarily be called new or luxurious. There was plenty of land and an abundance of green plants, but that was owing to a chronic lack of funds needed for new construction, additions, and renovation.

After getting off the low-speed sidewalk, Yang crossed a poorly kept common lawn. Creaking with complaints of overwork, the front gate, equipped with ID scanners, welcomed in the master of Officers' Residence B-6.

It's about time to have this thing replaced, even if I have to pay for it out of my own pocket, Yang thought. *Even if I negotiated with Accounting, it wouldn't get me anywhere.*

"Welcome back, Commodore." Young Julian Mintz came out to the porch to meet him. "I was wondering if you might not be coming back. Good thing you did, though. I've made that Irish stew you like."

"Makes it worth coming home on an empty stomach. But why'd you think I wasn't coming back?"

"Rear Admiral Caselnes contacted me," the boy answered, taking Yang's uniform beret. "'That rascal ducked out in the middle of the ceremony hand in hand with a beautiful woman,' he was saying."

Yang grimaced as he stepped into the foyer. "Why, that son of a…"

Julian Mintz was fourteen years old and was Yang's ward. He was of average height for his age, with flaxen hair, dark-brown eyes, and delicate features. Caselnes and others at times referred to him as "Yang's page."

Two years prior, Julian had come to live under Yang's protection in accordance with the Law for Special Regulations Concerning Children of Soldiers. Commonly, this was called Travers's Law, after the name of the statesman who had proposed it.

The Free Planets Alliance had been in a state of war with the Galactic Empire for a century and a half. This meant chronic generation of war dead and other victims of war. Travers's Law had been conceived as one stone to kill the two birds of assisting war orphans with no next of kin and of procuring human resources.

Orphans were raised in the homes of soldiers. A set sum of money for child-rearing expenses was lent to their guardians by the government, and the orphans attended regular schools until fifteen years of age. Then it was up to them to choose their future course; however, if they volunteered for the military and became child soldiers, or enrolled in Officers' Academy or some technical or other school with military affiliation, repayment of the child support fees would be waived.

For the military, even women were an indispensable human resource in the Rear Service, vital in resupply, accounting, transport, communications, space traffic control, intelligence processing, and facilities management.

"In short, you can think of it like the apprentice system that's been around since the Middle Ages. More vicious maybe, since it uses money to try and restrict people's futures."

Caselnes, who at the time was assigned to Rear Service Headquarters, had explained it to Yang like that, with a healthy dose of sarcasm.

"In any case, people can't live without being fed. That's a fact, right? Which means we need a feeder. So come on—you can take in one at least."

"I don't even have a family of my own."

"Exactly, which means you're not fulfilling your societal obligation to support a wife and child. Look, the government even pays child support—it'd be a shame if we can't even get you to take on this much. Right, you swinging bachelor, you?"

"Understood. But only one."

"If you like, you can have two."

"One is plenty."

"Really? Well, in that case I'll have to find you one who eats enough for two."

Four days after that exchange had passed between them, the boy named Julian had appeared standing in the foyer of Yang's home.

That very day, Julian had secured for himself his station in the Yang household. Given that the household's erstwhile sole member was hardly what could be called a capable and industrious manager in the home, things were in a rather horrid state. Although Yang did own a handheld domcom, he always neglected to input the data needed to control his various household appliances; not only had it ended up a useless piece of junk, all his home tech had acquired a layer of dust as well.

For his own sake too, apparently, Julian had made up his mind to get the home's physical environment into shape. Two days after becoming a resident of the Yang home, its young master had left on a short business trip. When he returned a week later, he found his home under occupation by a federated force of neatness and efficiency.

"I've arranged the data on your domcom into six categories," the twelve-year-old commander of this occupying force had reported to the head of the house, who had stood there frozen with a stunned look on his face. "Let's see, 1 is home management, 2 is appliance control, 3 is security, 4 is data collection, 5 is home study, and 6 is entertainment. Household accounting and daily menu selection are under 1; air-conditioning, cleaning devices, and the washing machine are under 2; the burglar alarm and fire extinguisher are under 3; and news, weather, and shopping information are under 4…Please remember these, Captain."

Yang had been a captain at the time. Wordlessly, he had sat down on the sofa in what doubled as his living room and dining room, wondering what he was going to say to this innocently smiling little invader.

"I went ahead and cleaned that, too. And the bedsheets are also washed. I, ah, think I've managed to get things shipshape indoors, but if there's anything you're not happy with, please tell me. Is there anything I can do for you?"

"Can you get me a cup of tea?"

Yang had asked this because he was thinking, *I'll wet my whistle with my favorite tea, and then I'll start with the griping,* but the boy had hurried off to the kitchen and come back carrying a tea set that was now so clean it looked practically brand-new. Then, before his very eyes, Julian had brewed Shillong-grown tea with a startling dexterity.

Yang had taken one sip of the tea set out before him, and then he had decided to surrender to the young boy. That's how good the aroma and flavor were. Julian said that his late father had been a lieutenant in the space armada. Being even more of a tea-ceremony aficionado than Yang, he had taught his son all about tea varieties and brewing.

Six months after Yang had accepted Julian-style housekeeping, Caselnes, who had come over for a game of 3-D chess, had looked around the room and thus opined: "This is the first time in recorded history that your place is clean, isn't it? I guess it's true what they say, that a child is as mature as his parents are incompetent."

Yang had made no argument.

Another two years had gone by. Julian had grown more than ten centimeters taller and was starting to look just a little bit like a grown-up. His grades were apparently fine. "Apparently," because his guardian had always said that as long as he wasn't failing, he didn't need to report every little thing, and also because his ward would from time to time come home with awards, medals, and the like. In Caselnes's words, he was a "student who had surpassed his teacher."

"Today at school, they asked me what I'd be doing from next year on."

It was unusual for Julian to say something like that while Yang was eating. Yang's spoon stopped moving in the midst of scooping up some stew, and he glanced at the boy.

"Graduation's in June of next year, isn't it?"

"There's a system where you can gain credits and graduate six months early."

"There is?" said his irresponsible guardian, impressed. "So, you plan on becoming a soldier?"

"Yes, I'm a soldier's child, after all."

"There isn't any law saying a child has to continue in his parent's career. Actually, my dad was a trader."

"If there's some other kind of work you want to do, you should do it," Yang told him. He remembered the ingenuous face of Will, the boy he had met in the spaceport.

"But if I don't enter the military, you'll have to pay back all that child support…"

"So I'll pay it back."

"You'll what?"

"Don't sell your legal guardian short here. I've got enough saved to cover that. Now, first of all, there's no need for you to be graduating early. How about having a little fun instead?"

The young boy's smooth cheeks flushed with embarrassment. "I couldn't possibly leave you with such a burden."

"Don't talk back to me, kid. The thing about children is this: sponging off adults is how they grow."

"Thank you very much, but still…"

"But what? You want to be a soldier that badly?"

Julian looked at Yang's face suspiciously. "Somehow, you sound like you don't like soldiers."

"I don't."

Yang's clear, concise reply bewildered the young man. "But, if that's true, why did you become one?"

"Very simple. I had no talent for anything else."

Yang finished his stew and wiped his mouth with his napkin. Julian cleared the table and used the domcom to turn on the dishwasher in the kitchen. Then he brought in the tea set and began brewing reddish tea from Shillong leaves.

"Anyway, think it over a little more before you decide. There's nothing at all to be in a hurry over."

"Yes, sir. I'll do that. But, Commodore, they were saying on the news that Count von Lohengramm joined the military when he was fifteen."

"That's true, apparently."

"They showed his face, and he was incredibly handsome. Did you know that?"

Yang had seen the face of Count Reinhard von Lohengramm any number of times—not directly, but in holograms and such. He had even heard rumors that the man was more popular than any officer in the Alliance Armed Forces among the female officers at Rear Service HQ. It seemed likely enough. Yang had never seen a young man with as handsome a face, either.

"But even I can't be all that bad-looking. Isn't that right, Julian?"

"Would you like milk with your tea, or would you prefer brandy?"

"Brandy."

That was when the security system's lamp began to flash and make a nervous sound. Julian flipped on the monitor. Many human forms were displayed on its infrared-enhanced screen. All of them wore white hoods over their heads, with only their eyes exposed.

"Julian."

"Yes, sir?"

"Is there some kind of fad these days where clowns like that make home welfare visits en masse?"

"They're the Patriotic Knight Corps."

"I don't know any circus by that name."

"It's an extremist group of nationalists. They do all kinds of things to harass people who say or do things against the country or the war. They're pretty well-known lately...But this makes no sense—why would they come barging in here? You've even been praised by them. There's no reason they should criticize you, is there?"

"How many are there?" asked Yang casually.

Julian read out a number in the corner of the screen. "Forty-two have come onto the premises. Ah, forty-three...and now forty-four."

"Commodore Yang!" A loud voice blaring from a megaphone caused a wall of reinforced glass to vibrate slightly.

"Yeah, yeah, I heard ya..." Yang mumbled, though there was no way he could have been heard outside.

"We are the Patriotic Knight Corps—a band of people who truly love their country. We condemn you! You have displayed actions both disruptive to the unity of the military's aims and harmful to its fighting spirit. Perhaps your military accomplishments have made you arrogant. I'm sure you know what we're talking about."

Yang could nearly feel the gaze of a surprised Julian landing on his cheek.

"Commodore Yang, you showed contempt for a sacred memorial service. When everyone in attendance answered the defense committee chairman's passionate speech by vowing to bring down the empire, did not you, and you alone, by remaining seated assume an attitude of ridicule toward the determination of the entire nation? We condemn your arrogance! If you have anything to say for yourself, come out here and say it in front of us. I should mention that calling for security is useless. We have a way of disabling your communication system."

I see, Yang acknowledged. *Looks like that enchanting temptress of patriotism, His Excellency Trünicht, is lurking behind these Patriotic Knights or whatever it is they're called. Both of their speeches are thinner than cheap consommé—and remarkably similar in their exaggerations alone.*

"Did you really do that, Commodore?" asked Julian.

"Er, yeah, kinda."

"Not again! Why do you—! Even if you're against it in your mind, things like this wouldn't happen if you'd just let them see you stand and clap! Strangers can only see the surface, you know."

"You sound like Caselnes, kid."

"You don't have to bring Admiral Caselnes into this—even children have that much common sense."

"What's the matter?" called the voice from outside. "Not coming out? Still have a little shame left in your heart? But even if you do repent, we can't acknowledge your sincerity unless you say so definitively in front of us."

Yang clucked his tongue and was about to stand up when Julian pulled on his sleeve.

"Commodore, no matter how angry you are, you mustn't use any weapons."

"Stop jumping to conclusions like that, kid. First of all, what makes you think I don't intend to have a talk with them?"

"But . . . you don't."

Yang didn't have an answer for that.

At that moment, the window of reinforced glass cracked with a loud noise. This wasn't the kind of glass that could be broken by throwing rocks at it. A moment later, a metal ball the size of a person's head came flying into the room and slammed into a display shelf on the opposite wall, where it shattered several ceramic vessels lined up on it. The ball rolled off the shelf and fell to the floor with a heavy thump.

"Take cover! It's still dangerous!"

As Yang cried out and Julian leapt lightly behind the sofa with the domcom in his hand, the metal sphere blew apart into shrapnel. Discordant sounds rang out simultaneously from every corner of the room as lighting fixtures, plates, and chairs were shattered.

Yang was left speechless. The Patriotic Knights had used a grenade launcher to fire the sort of powder-free bomb that military engineers used to flatten small-scale buildings when there was a fire hazard.

That there had been as little damage as there was meant it had been set to its lowest level of destructive power. Otherwise, everything in the room would have been reduced to heaps of wreckage. All that aside, what were civilians doing with that kind of military-grade equipment?

An idea occurred to Yang, and he snapped his fingers, though it didn't make a very good sound.

"Julian, which one is the switch for the sprinkler system?"

"It's 2-A-4. Are you fighting back?"

"I need to teach them a thing or two about manners."

"Catch!"

"How about it! Ready to talk to us now? If you don't answer, we'll send another—"

The increasingly forceful voice from outside suddenly turned into a shriek. The sprinklers, with their water pressure set to maximum, struck the white-masked men with thick lashes of water. Soaking wet, as though caught in an unexpected downpour, they ran to and fro through the curtains of water in all directions.

"Starting to see now why it's a scary thing to get a gentleman pissed at you? You're just relying on numbers, you hoodlums!"

As Yang grumbled to himself, the distinctive siren of the security police grew audible in the distance. Residents in the other officers' houses had called it in, most likely.

Even so, the fact that the authorities had not mobilized until now might well mean that those self-styled, self-righteous Patriotic Knights were an unexpectedly powerful group. If Trünicht was indeed behind them, it would not be hard to imagine why.

The Patriotic Knights hurriedly dispersed. They probably wouldn't be in the mood to sing any songs of victory tonight. The police officers, who finally arrived in their blue combination suits, afterward described the Patriotic Knights as a group of people with an ardent love for their country, to which Yang took offense.

"If they're like you say they are, then why don't they volunteer for military service? Is surrounding a house with a minor inside at night and raising a huge ruckus something patriots do? And besides all that, if what they're doing is on the up-and-up, doesn't hiding their faces in itself go against common sense?"

While Yang was refuting the police officers, Julian had cut off the sprinklers and was starting to clean up the terrible mess inside.

"I'll help, too," said Yang, after he had ushered the useless policemen out.

Julian shooed him away with his hand. "No, you'll just get in the way. I know—sit on top of that table, please."

"On top of the table?"

"I'll be finished in no time."

"What should I do on the table?"

"Well, I'm going to put on some tea, so please just drink it."

Yang, grumbling to himself, climbed up on the table, crossed his legs, and sat—but soon grew indignant when he saw Julian pick up a ceramic potsherd.

"That's red Wanli porcelain. The only piece in my dad's things that was real."

When Caselnes called on the visiphone at 2200, Julian was mostly finished with cleaning up the room.

"Hey there, kid, can you put that guardian of yours on for me?"

"He's over there."

Julian pointed at the table, where the head of the Yang household was sitting cross-legged, sipping his tea. Caselnes stared at this scene for about five seconds, then slowly asked, "Sitting on tabletops *was* a custom in your house, wasn't it?"

"Only on certain days of the week," Yang answered from the top of the table, making Caselnes grimace.

"Well, whatever. A pressing matter's come up—I'd like you to come over to Joint Operational Headquarters right away. A landcar's been sent to pick you up. It should be there any minute."

"Right now?"

"The order comes straight from Director Sitolet."

When Yang returned his teacup to its saucer, the clink was just a little louder than usual. Julian was frozen to the spot for a moment, but then he came to himself and hurried off to fetch Yang's uniform.

"What's the director want with me?"

"All I know is that it's urgent. I'll see you soon at headquarters."

Caselnes ended the call. Yang crossed his arms and sank into thought for a short while. When he turned around, Julian was standing there holding Yang's dress uniform in both hands. While he was changing, the official car from HQ arrived. Yang couldn't help thinking that this was a busy night in several respects.

As he was about to leave the foyer, Yang glanced back at Julian. "I'm probably gonna be pretty late. Don't wait up."

"Yes, sir, Commodore," replied Julian, though Yang somehow got the feeling that the boy wasn't going to do as he was told.

"Julian, what happened tonight is probably going to be something we laugh about eventually. But in the short term, maybe not. Little by little, it looks like we're heading into some pretty bad times."

Yang himself didn't consciously understand why he had said such a thing so suddenly. Julian looked straight back at the young admiral.

"Commodore, I . . . I say a lot of things that may be uncalled for, but please don't worry about things like that. I want you to walk the path you think is right. I believe, more than anyone else, that you're right."

Yang stared at the young boy, and though he wanted to say something, in the end he just silently tousled the boy's flaxen hair. Then he turned his back and set off walking toward the landcar. Julian didn't move from the porch until the vehicle's tail lamps had melted into the womb of night.

IV

Marshal Sidney Sitolet, director of the Free Planets Alliance Military Joint Operational Headquarters, was a middle-aged black man who was nearly two meters tall. Though he was not the type whose talents were immediately evident, he was reliably capable both as a manager of military organizations and as a strategist, and people trusted in his plain but dignified character. While not wildly popular, he enjoyed wide support.

Director of Joint Operational Headquarters was the highest peak to which men and women in uniform could aspire, and in wartime the individual who held this position was also given the title of deputy commander in chief of Alliance Armed Forces. The commander in chief was the chair of the High Council, who was the head of state. Under him, the chair of the Defense Committee was in charge of military administration, and the director of Joint Operational Headquarters oversaw military command.

Unfortunately, in the Free Planets Alliance these two were not necessarily on good terms. The head of military administration and the head of military command had to cooperate with one another. Unless they did so, it was impossible to make the wheels of the military turn smoothly. Even so, their personalities clashed, and with nothing to be done about the fact that they just didn't like each other, the relationship between Trünicht and Sitolet was often described as one of armed neutrality.

When Yang stepped into his office, Marshal Sitolet greeted him with a nostalgic smile. Back when Yang was a student at Officers' Academy, the marshal had been headmaster.

"Have a seat, *Rear Admiral* Yang."

Yang did as Sitolet said without reservation. The marshal delved straight into the matter at hand. "I had you come in because there's something I need to inform you of. Your letter of appointment will be formally issued tomorrow, but you're about to be promoted to rear admiral. This is not an unofficial offer—it's already decided. You know the reason you're being promoted, I take it?"

"Because I lost?"

Yang's answer made the middle-aged marshal crack a pained smile. "Well, you haven't changed a bit since old times. A mild expression and a sharp tongue. You were like that when you were at Officers' Academy, too."

"But that's a fact, though, isn't it, Headmas—I mean, Director?"

"I wonder why you think so?"

"There's an ancient military treatise that says showering someone with rewards is proof that you're in dire straits. Apparently because there's a need to divert the people's eyes from defeat."

Yang spoke without a hint of apology and made the marshal grimace again. He crossed his arms and looked intently at his former student.

"In a sense, you are correct. We have suffered a huge defeat, as has not been seen in recent years, and military and civilians alike are very upset. In order to soothe them, a hero is necessary. In other words, you, Rear Admiral Yang."

Yang gave a little smile, but he didn't look at all pleased.

"You probably don't like it, becoming an artificial hero. But for a soldier, this is also a sort of mission. Besides that, your achievements really do make you suitable for promotion. If in spite of that we didn't promote you, it would call into question whether Joint Operational HQ and the Defense Committee really do reward success and punish failure."

"About the Defense Committee, what are Chairman Trünicht's wishes?"

"His wishes as an individual, in this case, present no problem. Even if he is the committee chairman, he has his position as a public figure to think about."

That was likely true regarding his public face. But it looked to Yang like Trünicht's personal side had encouraged the Patriotic Knights to mobilize against him.

"By the way, on a different subject, that operations plan you submitted to Vice Admiral Paetta before the start of combat . . . I wonder, do you think our forces could have won if it'd been executed?"

"Yeah, probably." Yang answered as modestly as he could.

Marshal Sitolet pinched his chin as though deep in thought. "But it's possible, isn't it, that we can use that plan on another occasion. And when that time comes, we can get back at Count von Lohengramm."

"That would be up to Count von Lohengramm. If his successes this time were to make him cocky, if he couldn't resist the temptation of trying to beat a large force with a small one again, then that plan could probably be revived. However . . ."

"However?"

"However, I don't think anything like that is going to happen. Defeating a large force with a small one, at first glance, certainly looks spectacular, but it's out of step with tactical orthodoxy and really more in the realm of magic tricks than military strategy. I find it hard to believe Count von Lohengramm doesn't know that. The next time he comes to attack, he'll probably be leading an overwhelmingly large force."

"That's true—putting together a larger force than your enemy's is the foundation of military tactics. Amateurs, however, are more welcoming of what you call magic tricks—they'll think you're incompetent if you *can't* destroy a large force with a small one. So when you've lost big to an enemy half your size…"

Yang could perceive anguish in the marshal's dark features. Regardless of how Yang himself might be perceived, it was only natural that the government and the citizenry were taking a dim view of the military as a whole right now.

"Rear Admiral Yang, if you think about it, our forces made no mistake in terms of the tactical fundamentals. We sent double the enemy's force strength to the battlefield. Why did we lose so disastrously in spite of that?"

"Because we screwed up the application of that force strength." Yang's answer was simple and to the point. "In spite of preparing superior numbers, we failed to make the most of that advantage. We probably felt secure in the size of the force."

"And?"

"Excluding the age of so-called push-button warfare and that period of freakish development in radar electronics, there have always been two fixed principles for the use of troops on the battlefield: concentrate your force, and move it quickly. Both of these. To sum it up in one sentence, 'Never create an unnecessary force.' Count von Lohengramm practiced that to perfection."

"Hmm…"

"On the other hand, look at our forces," Yang continued. "While the Fourth Fleet was being crushed by the enemy, the other two were wasting time sticking to the initial plan. Reconnaissance of the enemy's movements and the analysis of that intelligence were also insufficient.

All three fleets had to fight the enemy alone and without reinforcement. That's what happens when you forget the principles of force concentration and rapid mobilization."

Yang shut his mouth. For him to become so talkative was, lately, a rarity. Was it because he was feeling a little bit jittery?

"I see. And I see your powers of discernment." The marshal nodded repeatedly. "However, there's one other thing, and this one is not decided—it's an offer. Some organizational changes are going to be made in parts of the military. New forces will be added to the remnants of the Fourth and Sixth Fleets to create the Thirteenth Fleet. And you are to be appointed as its first fleet commander."

Yang cocked his head to one side. "Don't appointments to fleet commander come with vice admiralships?"

"The new fleet is about half the size of a normal one. Around 6,400 vessels and seven hundred thousand personnel. And the first mission of the Thirteenth Fleet is the capture of Iserlohn Fortress."

The director's tone of voice was utterly casual.

After a moment, Yang slowly opened his mouth to confirm what he'd just heard. "With *half a fleet*, you're telling me to go take Iserlohn?"

"That's right."

"Do you believe that's possible?"

"I believe that if you can't do it, it's impossible for anyone else."

"I believe in you." "You can do it." The old traditional clinchers, thought Yang. There was no telling how many people had had their egos tickled by that sweet whisper and ended up ruining their lives attempting the impossible. The ones who did the sweet-talking were never held responsible, either.

Yang remained silent.

"You're not feeling confident, I take it?"

When the director said that, Yang was all the more unable to answer. If he were lacking confidence, he would have said so right away. But Yang had both confidence and a hope of success. If he had been in command of the assaults on Iserlohn, the Alliance Armed Forces would surely not have borne the dishonor of being beaten back six times in the past and of losing so many men. The reason that he couldn't answer in spite of that was that he didn't like being played by Marshal Sitolet.

"If you were to achieve the outstanding feat of leading the new fleet and capturing Iserlohn Fortress," Director Sitolet said, looking intently, almost suggestively, at Yang's face, "then regardless of what he may think of you personally, even Defense Committee Chairman Trünicht will have no choice but to acknowledge your ability to get things done."

Which meant that Director Sitolet's position would be strengthened with respect to the chairman. What was going on was evidently more within the realm of political than military strategy. *He was a crafty fox, the director!*

"I'll do what little I can," Yang replied after quite a long pause.

"Really? You'll do it?" Director Sitolet nodded, looking satisfied. "Well, then, give orders to Caselnes to hurry up and get the new fleet organized and equipped. If there are supplies that you need, requisition them from him, whatever they are. I'll help you out as much as I possibly can."

When do we leave for the battlefield, I wonder, thought Yang. *The director must have another seventy days or so left in his term. And being that he's aiming for reappointment, that means the operation to take Iserlohn will have to be completed before then. If we assume thirty days needed for the operation itself, then it looks like we'll be leaving Heinessen in forty days at the latest.*

Trünicht was unlikely to oppose these personnel decisions for the operation. This was because surely there was no way to take Iserlohn with only half a fleet, and when the mission ended in failure, he would be able to dispose of both Sitolet and Yang publicly. He might even raise a toast, saying that Yang and the others had dug their own graves.

Once again, Yang was going to be unable to drink tea brewed by Julian for a while. For him, that was a bit of a shame.

CHAPTER 5:

I

Iserlohn.

That was the name given to this vital stronghold of the Galactic Empire. Located 6,250 light-years from the imperial capital of Odin was Artena, a star in the prime of its life, originally a solitary sun with no planets of its own. It was its astrographical importance that had led the Galactic Empire to construct in its orbit an artificial world sixty kilometers in diameter for use as a base of operations.

When the galaxy was viewed from directly "above," Iserlohn appeared situated near the tip of a triangular region where the Galactic Empire's influence was reaching out toward the Free Planets Alliance. This entire swath of territory, a difficult region for astrogation, was the interstellar graveyard known as "Sargasso Space," where the founders of the Free Planets Alliance had once lost many of their comrades. Later, this bit of history, which imperial VIPs found most satisfactory, had even played a role in strengthening their resolve to build a military stronghold in this region from which to threaten the alliance.

Variable stars, red giants, irregular gravitational fields…through dense concentrations of these, there ran a narrow thread of safety, and Iserlohn was sitting right in the middle of it. To travel from the alliance to the empire without passing through this area meant using a route that went through the Phezzan Land Dominion, and use of that route for military operations was problematic to be sure.

The Iserlohn Corridor and the Phezzan Corridor. Statesmen and tacticians of the alliance alike had taken pains to find out whether a third route connecting the alliance and the empire could be discovered, but defects in their star charts and interference both seen and unseen from the empire and Phezzan had long frustrated those intentions. From Phezzan's perspective, the very worth of its existence as a middleman trading post was at stake, and the discovery of a "third corridor" was not something they were going to stand idly by and let happen.

Because of this, the realization of the Alliance Armed Forces' plan—summed up in the words, "We've gotta invade imperial territory!"—was dependent on the fight to capture Iserlohn. Across four and a half centuries, they had dared six times to launch large-scale attacks to take the fortress, and repulsed every time, these failed attempts had birthed the imperial military boast, "The Iserlohn Corridor is paved with the corpses of rebel soldiers."

Yang Wen-li had twice taken part in operations attempting to topple Iserlohn. He had been a lieutenant commander at the time of the fifth operation and a captain at the time of the sixth. Twice he had witnessed massive fatalities and had come to know the stupidity of trying to push through on sheer force alone.

We can't take Iserlohn by attacking from the outside, Yang had thought in the midst of a fleet set to flight. *But given that, how could we do it?*

In addition to being a fortress, Iserlohn harbored a fleet fifteen thousand ships strong. The commander of the fortress and the commander of the fleet were both full admirals. Could there not be some kind of opening there they could take advantage of?

Count von Lohengramm's recent incursion had also used Iserlohn as a forward base of operations. No matter what, Yang had to topple this ominous military stronghold of the empire. And moreover, he had only been given half a fleet to do it with.

"Frankly, I didn't think you'd accept this mission," Rear Admiral Caselnes said as he thumbed through a troop organizational document. They were in his office at Joint Operational Headquarters. "The chairman and the director are both counting on this for their own respective reasons... Surely you can see through the both of them."

Sitting in front of him, Yang just smiled and didn't answer. Caselnes slammed his papers down on the table loudly and looked with deep interest at his underclassman from Officers' Academy.

"Our forces have tried *six times* to take Iserlohn, and six times we've failed. And you're telling me you're gonna do it with only *half* a fleet?"

"Well, I thought I'd give it a try."

The eyes of Yang's former upperclassman narrowed ever so slightly at this answer.

"So you do think there's a chance. What are you gonna do?"

"That's a secret."

"Even from me?"

"Getting to act all high and mighty about it is what makes you appreciate this kind of thing," Yang said.

"You got that right. Let me know if there're any supplies I can ready for you—I won't even ask for a bribe."

"In that case, one imperial warship, please—you ought to have one that's been previously captured. Also, if I can get you to ready about two hundred imperial uniforms..."

Caselnes's narrowed eyes opened wide.

"What's the deadline?"

"Within the next three days."

"...I'm not gonna ask you for overtime pay, but you're at least treating me to a cognac."

"I'll buy you two. And by the way, I've got one more request..."

"Make it three. What is it?" Caselnes asked.

"It's about those *extremists* called the Patriotic Knights."

"Oh yeah, I heard. That must have been awful."

Since Julian was going to be at home by himself, Yang requested that arrangements be made for military police to patrol the neighborhood in his absence. He had thought about leaving the boy with some other family, but it was unlikely that Julian, the household's commanding officer whenever Yang was out, would have stood for it. Caselnes said he would see to it right away, then looked at Yang again as though he had remembered something.

"Oh yeah, the high commissioner of Phezzan—lately he's been awfully curious about you."

"Oh?"

The special entity known as Phezzan held an interest for Yang that was a little different from what it held for others. That dominion had been the creation of a great merchant of Terran birth named Leopold Raap, but many things about his background and source of funds were unclear. Had someone for some reason caused Raap to create the entity known as Phezzan? Yang, having tried and failed to become a historian, thought about things like that as well. Naturally, though, he had not spoken of this to anyone else.

"Looks like you've caught the interest of the Black Fox of Phezzan. He may try to scout you."

"I wonder if Phezzan tea is any good?"

"Flavored with poison, most likely... Incidentally, how is the planning coming along?" Caselnes asked.

"Things that go according to plan are pretty rare in the world. That said, I can't rightly not make one."

So saying, Yang departed. A mountain of work was waiting for him.

It wasn't just that the ships and personnel of the Thirteenth Fleet numbered half what was usual. Most of its officers and soldiers were surviving remnants of the Fourth and Sixth fleets that had been defeated so soundly at Astarte; the rest were new recruits lacking in combat experience. An up-and-coming rear admiral their commander may be, but Yang was still just a twenty-something kid...and seasoned admirals' words of surprise, shock, and derision had reached his ears: *It seems a babe not yet out of diapers intends to beat a lion to death barehanded—that should be fun to watch. If you're forced into it, you're forced, but to go willingly—oh, dear!*

Yang didn't even get upset. *You'd have to be one heck of an optimist to not have doubts about this operation,* he thought.

The only one who had taken up for Yang was Vice Admiral Bucock, commanding officer of the Fifth Fleet. An unsociable, white-haired admiral seventy years of age, he was known as a stubborn individual with a short temper. When saluted by the likes of Yang, he would return a disinterested salute with a suspicious look in his eye that all but said, "Where'd this greenhorn come from?" At the White Stag—a club for high-ranking officers—his fellow admirals had been using Yang and the Thirteenth Fleet as fodder for jokes when that "scary old man" had said, "I hope you all don't end up with egg on your faces later. You might just be looking at a redwood sapling and laughing at it for not being tall."

They had all fallen completely silent. They had remembered the capability that Yang had displayed at Astarte and in battles prior. At the words of the elderly admiral, their group mentality had dissipated. The admirals had drained their glasses and gone their separate ways, an awkward feeling in the chest of each from having said something they couldn't quite patch over . . .

Yang, to whose ears that story had found its way, had made no particular effort to thank Vice Admiral Bucock. He had known that if he did attempt such a thing, he would be laughed to scorn by the white-haired admiral.

Though the admiralty's opposition had subsided for the time being, the overall situation had not taken that much of a turn for the better. The gloomy fact solemnly remained of the hybrid half fleet, composed of defeated survivors and green recruits, that was heading off to attack an impregnable fortress.

Yang put a great deal of thought into the selection of his executive staff. For his vice commander, he chose Commodore Edwin Fischer, a skilled, seasoned officer who had fought well in the Fourth Fleet. For chief staff officer, he chose Commodore Murai, a man lacking in originality but possessed of a precise and well-ordered mind. For assistant staff officer, he named Captain Fyodor Patrichev, who had a reputation as a good fighter.

Yang would get commonsense advice from Murai and make use of him as an advisor for ops planning and decision making. Patrichev he would have yelling at and encouraging the troops. And of Fischer, Yang wanted the fleet run steadily and soundly.

I think I can be satisfied with the postings so far, but it wouldn't hurt to find an aide-de-camp, Yang thought. He put in a request with Caselnes for an "outstanding young officer" and a communiqué arrived later that said, "I've got just the person. Graduated salutatorian from Officers' Academy in 794—one heck of a better student than you. Presently assigned to the Data Analysis Department at Joint Operational Headquarters."

The officer who appeared before Yang shortly thereafter was a beautiful young woman with hazel eyes and golden-brown hair that had a natural wave; even a simple black-and-ivory-white military uniform looked pretty on her. Yang took off his sunglasses and stared at her fixedly.

"Sublieutenant Frederica Greenhill reporting. I've been assigned to work as aide-de-camp to Rear Admiral Yang."

That was her introduction.

Yang put his sunglasses back on to hide his expression, thinking there must surely be a black, pointy tail hiding in the back of Alex Caselnes's uniform slacks. The daughter of Dwight Greenhill, assistant director at Joint Operational Headquarters, Frederica had a reputation as one who possessed astonishing powers of memory.

And so it was that the personnel assignments for the Thirteenth Fleet were decided.

II

On April 27 of SE 796, Rear Admiral Yang Wen-li, commander of the Free Planets Alliance Armed Forces Thirteenth Fleet set out on the path to topple Iserlohn.

Officially, this voyage was to be the new fleet's first large-scale maneuver, to be held in a backwater star system in the direction opposite that of the alliance's empire-facing border. They departed from Heinessen using 50-C pulse-warp navigation, headed in the direction opposite that of Iserlohn, and after continuing for three days, recalculated the route and executed eight long-range warps and eleven short-range warps, finally entering the Iserlohn Corridor.

"Four thousand light-years in twenty-four days. Not bad," murmured Yang. But it wasn't just not bad; the fact that this hastily assembled, prefab fleet had been able to somehow reach its destination without a single ship going missing was downright praiseworthy. Of course, this success was all due to the experienced hand of the vice commander, Commodore Fischer, lauded for his masterly performance in the operation of the fleet.

"The Thirteenth Fleet has an expert on that, so..." Yang would say, leaving relevant matters entirely up to Fischer. When Fischer said something, Yang would only nod approval.

Yang's mind was focused on one thing only: how to capture Iserlohn Fortress. When he had first revealed his plan to the fleet's three executive officers—Fischer, Murai, and Patrichev—they had been at a loss for words.

Fischer, in late middle age with silver hair and a mustache; Murai, a thin, nervous-looking man close in age to Fischer; and Patrichev, with long sideburns on his rounded face and a uniform that seemed fit to burst from the strain of holding in his body—all three of them for a while simply stared back at their young commander.

The moment passed, and then Murai asked the obvious question: "And if it doesn't work, then what?"

"Then all we can do is run away with our tails between our legs."

"But if we do that..."

"Then what? Don't worry about it. Taking down Iserlohn with half a fleet was an unreasonable demand from the start. The ones who end up embarrassed in front of everybody will be Director Sitolet and me."

After he dismissed the three of them, Yang called for his aide, Sublieutenant Frederica Greenhill.

In her position as his personal aide, Frederica had learned about Yang's plan before the three executive officers, but she had raised no objection, nor even shown any sign of anxiety. No, far from that, she had predicted success with a certainty exceeding that of Yang himself.

"What is it that makes you so confident?" Yang just couldn't help asking, though he was well aware what a strange thing that was to say.

"Because, Admiral, you were also successful eight years ago, at El Facil."

"That's still awfully flimsy grounds, though, don't you think?"

"Maybe . . . but at that time, Admiral, you succeeded in planting absolute trust in the heart of one little girl."

Yang gave her a quizzical look.

To her doubtful-looking superior, the officer with the golden brown hair said, "I was on El Facil with my mother at that time. My mother's ancestral home was there. I clearly remember the young sublieutenant who was nibbling on a sandwich while commanding the evacuation proceedings; he had hardly enough downtime to eat. That sublieutenant, though, has probably long forgotten the fourteen-year-old girl who brought him coffee in a paper cup when he choked on that sandwich, hasn't he?

Yang had no ready reply.

"And also what he said after his life had been saved by drinking that coffee?"

"What did he say?"

" 'I can't stand coffee. Would've been nice if you'd made it tea.' "

Feeling the start of a fit of laughter coming up, Yang cleared his throat loudly to drive it from his body. "Did I say such a rude thing?"

"Yes, you certainly did. As you were crushing the empty paper cup in your hand."

"Is that so? I apologize. You need to find a better use for that memory of yours, though."

The words sounded reasonable enough, though they were nothing more than sour grapes. Frederica had once discovered six slides out of fourteen thousand taken of Iserlohn in which the pre- and postbattle images did not match; she had proven already how valuable her powers of memory could be.

"Call Captain von Schönkopf for me," Yang said.

Exactly three minutes later, Captain Walter von Schönkopf appeared in front of Yang. He was captain of the *Rosen Ritter*, or "Knights of the Rose" regiment, which was affiliated with the Alliance Armed Forces ground battle commissioner's department. He was a man in his early thirties with a refined appearance, though those of his own gender often considered him a "pretentious SOB." Born to respectable imperial aristocrats, he would have ordinarily been standing on the battlefield in an imperial admiral's uniform.

The Rosen Ritter had been established primarily by the children of aristocrats who had defected from the empire to the alliance, and had a history going back half a century. That history was written partly in golden lettering and partly in blots of black ink. The regiment had had twelve prior captains in its history. Four of them had died in battle, fighting against their former homeland. Two had retired after rising to the admiralty. Six had fled to their former homeland— some stealing away quietly and others switching sides in the midst of combat.

There were those who averred, "That guy's unlucky. Since he's number thirteen, he's sure to become traitor number seven." As for why the number thirteen was unlucky, there was no general consensus. One theory said it was because the thermonuclear war that had nearly eradicated humanity on Terra (and provided the impetus for the survivors to completely abolish nuclear-fission weapons) had lasted thirteen days. Another claimed it to be because the founder of an old, long-extinct religion had been betrayed by his thirteenth disciple.

"Von Schönkopf reporting, sir."

His respectful tone of voice was a poor fit for his impudent expression. As Yang looked at this former imperial citizen three or four years his senior, he thought, *Taking a contrived attitude like that might be his way of sounding out others. Though even if it is, I can't bring myself to go along with it on every point . . .*

"There's something I need to talk with you about."

"Something important?"

"Probably so. It's about capturing Iserlohn," Yang said.

For a few seconds, von Schönkopf's line of sight wandered about the room.

"That would be extremely important. Is it all right to consult a junior officer like me?"

"It can't be anyone but you. I want you to listen close." Yang began to describe the plan.

Five minutes later, von Schönkopf had finished listening to Yang's explanation, and there was a strange look in his brown eyes. He seemed to be trying hard to suppress and conceal utter shock.

"Let me jump the gun and say this, Captain: this is not a proper plan. This is a trick—actually, it's a cheap trick," Yang said, taking off his black uniform beret and twirling it ill-manneredly on his finger. "But if we're to occupy the impregnable fortress Iserlohn, I believe it's the only way. If this doesn't work, then it's beyond my ability."

"You're right—there probably is no other way," said von Schönkopf, rubbing his pointed chin. "The more people depend on sturdy fortresses, the more they tend to slip up. A chance of success most certainly does exist. Except—"

"Except?"

"If, as the rumors suggest, I were to become traitor number seven, this will have all been for nothing. If that were to happen, what would you do?"

"I'd have a problem."

Von Schönkopf gave a pained smile at the sight of Yang's dead-serious look.

"Yes, indeed—that would be a problem. But is that all it would be? Surely, you'd think of some way to cope."

"Well, I did think about it."

"And?"

"I couldn't come up with any ideas. If you betray us, I throw up my hands and run home right then and there. There'll be nothing else I can do."

The beret slipped off Yang's finger and fell to the floor. The hand of the former imperial citizen reached out and picked it up, and after brushing away the dust that hadn't even clung to it, handed it back to the senior officer.

"Sorry about that."

"Don't give it a second thought. So, you're saying you have absolute trust in me?"

"To be honest, I don't have a lot of trust in myself," Yang replied flatly. "But unless I trust you, the plan itself will be over before it starts. So I'm going to trust you. That's the big prerequisite."

"I see," von Schönkopf said, though the look on his face said he hadn't necessarily taken Yang at his word. The commander of the Rosen Ritter regiment glanced toward the young senior officer again with a sort of look that was partly trying to penetrate Yang's real intentions, partly trying to figure out his own.

"May I ask you one question, Admiral?"

"Go ahead."

"The orders you were given this time were utterly impossible. They told you to take half a fleet—with undisciplined troops equivalent to a rowdy mob—and bring down Iserlohn Fortress. Even if you'd refused, there wouldn't have been many who would've blamed you. So the fact you agreed to this must mean that you already had this plan in mind. However, I'd like to know what was going on in your head underneath all that. Lust for honor? Or for advancement?"

The light in von Schönkopf's eyes was sharp and ruthless.

"I don't think it was any lust for advancement," Yang said. His reply was indifferent, as though he were talking about someone else altogether. "If I've got people calling me 'Excellency' before I turn thirty, then that's enough for me already. 'Cause first of all, if I'm still alive at the end of this mission, I intend to get out."

"Get out?"

"Yeah, well, I get a pension, and there's also a retirement allowance . . . It should be enough for me and one other to live a comfortable, if modest, lifestyle."

"You're saying you'll retire under these conditions?"

Yang smiled at the sound of von Schönkopf's voice; it as much as said he was struggling to understand.

"About those conditions: If our forces occupy Iserlohn, that will cut off what is pretty much the empire's only route for invading us. As long as the alliance doesn't go and do something stupid like using the fortress as a platform for its own invasion of the empire, the two militaries won't be able to clash even if they want to. At least not on a large scale."

Von Schönkopf listened, silently.

"At that point, it'll be up to the diplomatic skills of the alliance government, and since we'll have gained an advantageous foothold militarily, they may be able to manage a satisfactory peace treaty with the empire. As far as I'm concerned, I can retire with peace of mind if that happens."

"Though I wonder if that peace can be lasting."

"Lasting peace has never existed in human history, so I'm not gonna hope for that. Still, there have been peaceful and prosperous stretches lasting several decades. If we have to leave some kind of heritage for the next generation, the best thing we can ultimately give them is peace. And maintaining the peace that the previous generation handed to them will be the next generation's responsibility. If each generation remembers its responsibility to future generations, a long-term peace will be maintained. If they forget, then they'll squander that inheritance, and the human race will be back to square one. And hey, that's okay, too."

Yang lightly placed the beret he'd been playing with back on his head. "In short, all I'm realistically hoping for is peace for the next several decades. But even so, a peace that long would be a million times better than a wartime period one tenth as long. There's a fourteen-year-old boy living in my house, and I don't want to see him dragged into the battlefield. That's how I feel."

When Yang closed his mouth, silence fell. It didn't last long.

"Forgive me, Admiral, but you're either an exceptionally honest man or the biggest sophist since Rudolf the Great." Von Schönkopf flashed a wry smile. "At any rate, that's a better answer than I was hoping for. That being the case, I'll do my utmost as well. For a not-so-everlasting peace."

Neither of the two men were the type to clasp the other's hand in deep emotion, so from there the conversation delved immediately into businesslike matters, as they discussed the details of the operation.

III

There were two full admirals of the imperial military at Iserlohn. One was the fortress commander, Admiral Thomas von Stockhausen, and the other the commander of the Iserlohn Fleet, Senior Admiral Hans Dietrich von Seeckt. Both were fifty years of age, and while tallness was also a trait they both shared, von Stockhausen's waistline was a size more narrow than von Seeckt's.

They were not on friendly terms, but this had less to do with individual responsibility than with tradition. They were two commanding officers of equal rank in the same workplace. It was a wonder when they didn't lock horns with each other.

Emotional conflicts naturally extended even to the troops under their command. From the standpoint of the fortress's garrison, the fleet was like an obnoxious houseguest that would fight outside, then come running back when things got dangerous, looking for a safe place to hide—a prodigal son, as it were. And if you asked the fleet crewmen, they would say that the fortress garrison troops were a bunch of "space moles" holed up in a safe hideout and amusing themselves by playing at war with the enemy.

Two things just barely bridged the rift between them: their pride as warriors "supporting the impregnable fortress of Iserlohn" and their enthusiasm to do battle with the "rebel army." In fact, when enemy attacks came, they competed for success unyieldingly, even as they despised and cursed one another. This resulted in the achievement of enormous military successes.

Whenever the military authorities proposed combining the offices of fortress and fleet commander to unify the chain of command, the idea was squelched. This was because a decrease in the number of commander-level positions presented a problem for the high-ranking officers and also because there were no prior examples of the conflicts between the two leading to a fatal result.

It was May 14 of the standard calendar.

The two commanders, von Stockhausen and von Seeckt, were in their conference room. Originally, this had been part of a salon for high-ranking officers, but as it was equidistant from both their offices, it had been remodeled as a fully soundproof meeting room. This measure had been taken because neither was fond of going to the other's office, and since they were both within the same fortress, it wouldn't do to rely solely on televised communications.

For the past two days, communications in the vicinity of the fortress had been garbled. There was no room for doubt that a rebel force was approaching. However, there had been nothing like an attack yet. The two commanders were meeting to discuss what to do about this state of affairs, but the conversation had not advanced in a necessarily constructive direction.

"You say we should launch since they're out there, Commander, but we don't know where they are, so how are you going to fight them?"

Thus spoke von Stockhausen, to which von Seeckt countered:

"That's exactly why we *should* go out: to find out where they're hiding. If the rebels do come to attack, it's likely they'll mobilize a large force."

At von Seeckt's words, von Stockhausen gave a nod of complete self-assuredness. "Which will end with them being beaten back again. The rebels have attacked us six times, and six times they've been repulsed. Even if they're about to come again, it only means six times becoming seven."

"This fortress is truly amazing," the fleet commander said, implying, *It's not because you're particularly capable.*

"At any rate, it's a fact that the enemy's nearby. I'd like to mobilize the fleet and go find them."

"But if you don't know where they are, you've got no way of finding them. Wait a little longer."

Just as the conversation was beginning to go in circles, there was a call from the communications room. It said that a strange transmission had been picked up.

Although the jamming was fierce and the transmission faded in and out, at last it revealed the following situation:

A single Bremen-class light cruiser carrying vital communiqués had been dispatched to Iserlohn from the imperial capital of Odin but had come under enemy fire inside the corridor and was presently being pursued. They were seeking rescue from Iserlohn.

The two commanders looked at one another.

In a growl from the back of his thick throat, von Seeckt said, "It's unclear where in the corridor they are, but at this point we have no choice but to move out."

"But is that really a good idea?"

"What do you mean by that? My troops are a breed apart from space moles who only want security."

"What's that supposed to mean?"

The two of them arrived at the joint operations meeting room and took their seats, disgusted faces side by side.

Von Seeckt gave orders to launch the fleet to his own staff officers, and von Stockhausen stared off in another direction while he was explaining the situation.

When von Seeckt finished speaking, one of his staff officers stood up from his seat.

"A moment, please, Your Excellency."

"Ah, Captain von Oberstein…" said Admiral von Seeckt, without one iota of goodwill in his voice. He hated his newly assigned staff officer. That salt-and-pepper hair, that pale, bloodless face, those artificial eyes that emitted a strange glow from time to time—he didn't like any of it. *He's a very portrait of gloom,* he thought. "You have some opinion?"

At least on the surface, von Oberstein seemed unperturbed by his superior officer's halfhearted tone.

"I do."

"Very well, let's hear it," von Seeckt prodded reluctantly.

"Well then, I'll tell you. This could be a trap."

"A trap?"

"Yes, sir. To draw the fleet away from Iserlohn. We mustn't go out. We should observe the situation without making a move."

Von Seeckt snorted with disdain. "So what you want to say, Officer, is that if we go out, the enemy's waiting, and if we fight, we'll be defeated."

"That isn't what I meant."

"Well then, what did you mean? We're soldiers, and fighting is our duty. Rather than seeking our personal safety, we should think proactively about destroying the enemy. And more importantly, what can we do if we can't help a friendly ship that's in trouble?"

He felt antipathy toward von Oberstein, and he also had to consider his appearance in front of von Stockhausen, who was observing this development with an ironic smile. Also, von Seeckt was a guns-and-glory sort of leader, the kind who couldn't bear to wait on the sidelines when the enemy was before him; it was not in his nature to stay holed up in the fortress and wait for an assault. He believed that if he did that, a career spent on battleships would have been a waste.

"I don't know, Admiral von Seeckt—your staff officer does have a point. We know the precise positions of neither our enemies nor our allies, and the danger is great. How about waiting just a little bit longer?"

It was von Stockhausen's opinion from the sidelines that decided the matter.

Von Seeckt said so flatly.

At last the Iserlohn Fleet, composed of fifteen thousand ships large and small, commenced leaving port.

Von Stockhausen watched the departures via the screen of the port traffic control monitor in the fortress command room. The sight of the battleships like huge towers on their sides and sleek streamlined destroyers launching in orderly formations, departing for a battlefield in the void, was truly magnificent.

"Hmph. I hope you come back smarting," von Stockhausen murmured to himself. He could not bring himself to say things such as "die" or "lose," not even as a joke. That was his own way of exercising moderation.

About six hours passed, and then once again a transmission came in.

It was from the Breman-class light cruiser in question, and the following words were teased out from the static: "We've finally arrived near the fortress but are still under pursuit by attacking rebel forces. Request artillery bombardment to cover our approach."

As he ordered the gunners to make preparations for covering fire, von Stockhausen wore a deeply bitter expression. Where had that imbecile von Seeckt gone off to? It was a fine thing to talk a big game, but was the man not even capable of helping an ally who was all alone out there?

"Ship reflections on-screen!" reported one of his men. The commander gave orders to augment and project the image.

The Bremen-class light cruiser was approaching the fortress with all the unsteadiness of a drunkard. The multiple points of light that could be seen in its background were, of course, enemy vessels.

"Prepare to fire!" von Stockhausen ordered.

However, just before entering firing range of the fortress's main cannons, the ships of the alliance force halted altogether. They were floating—timidly, it seemed—beyond an invisible border, and when they saw the Bremen-class light cruiser heading into port, guided by a signal from the fortress's port traffic control room, they began turning their noses around in apparent resignation.

"Prudent fellows, you know it's hopeless."

The imperial soldiers broke out into raucous laughter. Their confidence was as unshakeable as the fortress was impregnable.

Having entered port and been moored there by magnetic fields, the Bremen-class light cruiser was a tragic sight to behold. Just by looking at its exterior alone, it was possible to make out a dozen or so damaged areas. White shock foam was sticking out of rents in the hull like the intestines of some animal, and the number of hairline cracks was impossible to count, even with the fingers and toes of a hundred soldiers.

Hydrogen-powered cars loaded with ground crew came racing toward it. These were not fortress troops, but troops under the Iserlohn Fleet's commander, and they sympathized from the bottoms of their hearts when they saw the ship's wretched condition.

A hatch on the light cruiser opened, and a youthful-looking officer appeared, white bandages wrapped around his head. He was a handsome man, but his pale face was sullied with a caked, reddish-black substance. "I'm Captain Larkin, commander of this ship. I'd like to see the commander of this fortress."

He spoke the official language of the empire clearly and articulately.

"Yes, sir," said one of the maintenance officers, "But what in the world is going on out there?"

Captain Larkin gave a frustrated sigh. "We aren't too sure ourselves. We came from Odin, you know. However, it looks like somehow your fleet has been destroyed."

Glaring sharply at the ground crew as they swallowed hard and peered at him in disbelief, Captain Larkin shouted, "It appears that somehow the rebel forces have come up with a new way to pass through the corridor. This threatens not only Iserlohn but the survival of the empire itself. Quickly, now, take me to the commander."

Full Admiral von Stockhausen, who had been waiting in the command room, rose from his chair when he saw five of the light cruiser's officers enter the room surrounded by security personnel.

"Explain the situation—what's going on out there?" As von Stockhausen walked toward the captain with long strides, his voice was pitched higher than usual. He had been informed already, and if the rebel forces had devised a way to pass through the corridor, it meant that the very significance of Iserlohn's existence would be called into question and it would be up to him to develop some way to counter the movements of rebel forces.

Since Iserlohn was itself a fixed-point construction, it was exactly for times like these that the Iserlohn Fleet was needed. And von Seeckt, that wild boar, had gone charging off with it! Von Stockhausen was having trouble maintaining a calm demeanor.

"This is what's happened…" The voice of this Captain Larkin was low and weak, so von Stockhausen, feeling impatient, drew near to the man. "This is what's happened: Your Excellency von Stockhausen, you have become our captive!"

A frozen instant melted, and by the time the security guards had with sharp curses drawn their blasters, Captain Larkin's arm was wrapped around von Stockhausen's neck, and a ceramic firearm—invisible to the fortress's security system—was pointed at the side of his head.

"Why, you..." growled Commander Lemmrar, head of the command room's security detail, his ruddy face growing even redder. "You're friends with those rebels. How dare you try such an outrageous—"

"I'm going to ask you to remember me. I'm Captain von Schönkopf of the Rosen Ritter regiment. I've got both hands full right now, so I can't wash off the makeup to greet you properly." The captain laughed as though invincible. "To be honest, I didn't think things would go this well. I made sure to forge an ID card before I came, but nobody even checked it. That's a good lesson to learn—that no matter how secure the system, it all depends on the people running it."

"And who is that lesson for, I wonder?" With these ominous words, Commander Lemmrar aimed his blaster at both von Stockhausen and von Schönkopf. "You planned on taking hostages, but don't think that you rebels are the same as imperial soldiers. His Excellency the Commander is a man who fears dishonor more than death. There is no shield here to protect you!"

"His Excellency the Commander seems annoyed at being so overestimated." Smiling scornfully, von Schönkopf shot a glance toward one of the four men encircling him. That man produced a ceramic disc, small enough to hold in his hand, from beneath his imperial uniform.

"You know what that is, right? It's a Seffl particle emitter."

Von Schönkopf spoke, and it was like an electric current had run through the wide chamber.

Seffl particles were named for their inventor, Karl Seffl. A researcher in applied chemistry, he had synthesized the particles for mining ores and performing civil engineering work on a planetary scale, so—to put it briefly—these particles were like a gas that would react to a set amount of heat or energy, setting off an explosion within a controllable range. Humanity, however, had always adapted industrial technologies to military use.

Commander Lemmrar's face looked almost completely dark. Blasters, which fired energy beams, had just become impossible to use. If anyone fired, everyone would go down together. The Seffl particles in the air would be ignited by the beam, reducing everyone in the room to ashes in an instant.

"C-Commander..."

One of the security guards had raised his voice in what sounded like a shriek. Commander Lemmrar, eyes brimming with a vacant light, looked at Admiral von Stockhausen. Von Schönkopf loosened his arm ever so slightly, and after taking two ragged breaths, the commander of Iserlohn Fortress surrendered.

"You win. It can't be helped—we surrender."

Von Schönkopf let out a sigh of relief in his heart.

"All right, everyone: you know what to do."

As instructed, the captain's subordinates set about their tasks. Port traffic control programs were altered, all manner of defense systems were deactivated, and sleeping gas was released throughout the fortress by way of the air-conditioning system. Technicians who had been hiding inside the Bremen-class light cruiser disembarked and executed these operations with skill and efficiency. While only a small group of people yet realized what was happening, Iserlohn was being invaded, as if by a cancer, and its functions shut down.

Five hours later, the imperial soldiers were released from a sleep as cloudy as bean soup and were stunned speechless to find themselves stripped of their arms and taken captive. Adding up all combat, communications, supply, medical, maintenance, traffic control, technical, and other personnel, their full number rose to five hundred thousand. With its gargantuan factories for production of food and other necessities, Iserlohn was equipped with an environment and facilities capable of supporting a population, including fleet personnel, exceeding one million. The empire's intention that Iserlohn must be an "eternal fortress" in both name and in fact was clear to see.

However, officers and troops of the Alliance Armed Forces Thirteenth Fleet were now in command.

Iserlohn Fortress, which in the past had like a vampire consumed the blood of millions of Alliance Armed Forces soldiers, changed hands without a single drop of new blood being shed.

IV

The imperial military's Iserlohn Fleet had been roaming about the corridor's obstacle- and danger-filled interior seeking the enemy.

The communications officers had been hard at work trying to raise the fortress, and at last, turning pale, they called for Commander von Seeckt. Having eliminated the persistent jamming waves, they had finally restored communications, but what they had received from the fortress was a transmission saying, "A mutiny has broken out among the men. Requesting assistance."

"A mutiny inside the fortress?" Von Seeckt clucked his tongue. "Can't that incompetent von Stockhausen even control his own men?"

Von Seeckt's feelings of superiority were being tickled by the polite request for aid. When he thought about how this would leave his colleague indebted to him in no small measure, he felt delighted all the more.

"Putting out the fire at our feet has priority. All ships, head back to Iserlohn immediately."

"Wait just a moment," someone replied to von Seeckt's order.

The voice was so quiet as to cast a pall of gloom over the bridge, and yet it riveted the entire room. When von Seeckt saw the officer who had come out before him, an expression welled up on his face of open hatred and opposition. *That salt-and-pepper hair, those deathly pale cheeks—it's Captain von Oberstein again!*

"I don't recall asking your opinion, Captain."

"I am aware of that. If I may, however?"

"...What do you want?"

"This is a trap. I think it may be better not to return."

Von Seeckt was silent for a long moment.

Without a word, the commander drew in his lower jaw and glared hatefully at an unpleasant subordinate who said unpleasant things in an unpleasant tone of voice.

"It appears to me that every little thing you see is a trap in your eyes."

"Excellency, please listen."

"That's enough out of you! All ships, come about and head for Iserlohn at combat velocity two. This is a great chance to put those space moles in our debt."

His broad back moved away from von Oberstein.

"Small men who are full of anger but have no true courage are not worth talking to."

He spat those words with cool contempt, and von Oberstein turned on his heel and left the bridge. No one tried to stop him.

After stepping into an exclusive elevator that reacted only to the voice-prints of officers, von Oberstein began to descend through the massive ship, equivalent in size to a sixty-story building, heading toward its lowest level.

. .   .
 .   .
        .

"Enemy fleet has entered firing range!"

"Main fortress cannons already charged and ready."

"Target acquired! We can fire anytime."

Tense voices filled the air of Iserlohn Fortress's command room.

"Draw them in just a little more."

Yang was at von Stockhausen's command table. He wasn't seated in the commander's chair—rather, he was sitting cross-legged atop the table, and in that unseemly position he was staring at an approaching cluster of shining points that covered the giant screen of the tactical display. At last, he took a deep breath and said, "Fire!"

The order Yang had given had not been spoken loudly, but via his headphones, it was transmitted accurately to the gunners.

They tapped their screens.

The gunners watched as masses of light—white, abounding in brilliance—leapt away and bore down upon the swarm of twinkling specks.

Over a hundred ships in the imperial fleet's vanguard took the assault from Iserlohn's main battery head-on and were instantly annihilated. The excess of heat and the high concentration of energy did not even give them time to explode. After organic and inorganic matter alike had been vaporized, there remained nothing except a near-perfect emptiness.

The ships that had exploded were those in the second rank of the imperial force and those flanking the vanguard. Ships on the periphery were buffeted by the energies and sent tumbling off course, and even ships positioned outside that region were shaken violently in the aftermath.

Shrieks and screams occupied the communications channels of those imperial ships that had survived that first attack.

"Why are they firing on allies?!"

"No, that's not right. It's gotta be those guys who mutinied—"

"What do we do?! We can't fight back. How do we maneuver away from those main guns?"

Inside the fortress, the alliance force's officers and troops alike had gasped and fallen silent, their eyes riveted to the screen. They had beheld for the first time the devilish destructive power of Iserlohn's main battery, dubbed "Thor's Hammer."

The entire imperial force was squeezed in the grip of terror. The fortress's main battery, which up until that moment had been their matchlessly powerful guardian deity, had become an irresistible bludgeon in the hands of an evil spirit, brought down upon their crowns.

"Counterattack! All ships, give me a synchronized barrage from main cannons!" Admiral von Seeckt's angry cry rolled out like thunder.

In its own way, that cry had the effect of restoring discipline to the confused servicemen. Pallid-countenanced gunners reached for their consoles, synchronized their automated targeting systems, and pressed the buttons on their touch screens. Hundreds of beams traced geometric lines across the void of space.

It was impossible, however, to destroy the outer hull of Iserlohn Fortress with only the power output by ship-based cannons. The bombardment struck the outermost hull, and the beams were deflected, scattering futilely.

The humiliation, defeat, and terror that the officers and crew of the

Alliance Armed Forces had in times past tasted was now amplified and fed back to the imperial forces.

Flares of light ten times as thick as the beams unleashed by the ship cannons burst forth once again from Iserlohn Fortress, and again wrought wholesale death and destruction. Gigantic holes had appeared in the columns of the imperial fleet, too wide to close easily, edges adorned with the ruined husks of ships and fragments of the same.

After being fired upon only twice, the imperial force was half paralyzed. The survivors had lost their will to fight, and they were only just barely able to remain where they were.

Yang looked away from the screen and rubbed himself around his stomach. His feeling was, *If we don't go this far, we can't win this.*

Captain von Schönkopf, watching the screen at Yang's side, gave a purposefully loud cough.

"This isn't what you call combat, Excellency. This is a one-sided massacre."

Yang, who turned toward the captain, wasn't angry.

"I know. You're exactly right. But we aren't going to behave like the empire does. Captain, try advising them to surrender. If they don't want to do that, tell them to retreat and that we won't chase them."

"Yes, sir." Von Schönkopf looked at the young senior officer with deep interest. Other soldiers might also go so far as to advise surrender, but they probably wouldn't tell the enemy to escape. Was this a strength or a weakness in this most rare of tacticians, Yang Wen-li?

On the bridge of the flagship, a communications officer cried out: "Excellency, there's a transmission from Iserlohn!" Von Seeckt glared at the man with bloodshot eyes, to which he said: "Iserlohn is occupied by the alliance—I mean, rebel—forces, after all. Their commander, Rear Admiral Yang Wen-li, says the following: "There's nothing to be gained by further bloodshed. Surrender.'"

"Surrender, he says?"

"Yes. And one other thing: 'If you don't want to surrender, then retreat—we will not pursue.'"

For a moment, faces all around the bridge came alive again. Running away! Finally, an intelligent option! Those lively expressions, however, were erased by a ferocious shout of anger.

"How could we do such a thing!" Von Seeckt stamped on the floor with his uniform boots. Yield Iserlohn to rebels, lose almost half the ships under his command, go back to face His Majesty the Emperor in defeat? Was that what this rebel commander was telling him to do? For von Seeckt, such a thing was impossible. Better to shatter as a priceless jewel, the saying went, than lead a long and shameful life as a worthless tile. The last honor that remained to him now was that of the shattered jewel.

"Communications Officer, transmit the following to the rebel forces."

As the officers and crew surrounding von Seeckt listened to the content of his message, the color drained from their faces. The fierce light in their commander's eyes shot right through their countenances.

"On my command, all ships will plot collision courses and charge Iserlohn. Surely none of you would begrudge our lives at a time like this."

The bridge was silent.

No one answered him.

Meanwhile at Iserlohn, von Schönkopf informed Yang, "There's a reply from the imperial forces."

He wore a frown on his face.

"The heart of the warrior thou knowest not; to die and honor's cause fulfill is the path we know; to live smeared with disgrace is a path we know not."

"Hmm," Yang said.

"What he means is that under these circumstances, all they can do now is charge ahead with all ships to die glorious deaths, and in so doing repay his Imperial Highness's favor."

"The heart of the warrior?"

Sublieutenant Frederica Greenhill sensed the ring of a bitter anger in Yang's voice. In fact, Yang was enraged. *Want to die to atone for defeat in battle? Fine and dandy. But if you're gonna do that, why can't you just die alone? Why take your subordinates with you by force?*

It's because of men like this that the war can't end, Yang thought. *I've had enough. Enough of dealing with men like this.*

"All enemy ships are charging!" cried an operator.

"Gunners! Concentrate fire on the enemy flagship!"

It was the first time Yang had ever given an order this incisive. Frederica and von Schönkopf stared at their commander, each with their own expression.

"This is the last barrage. If they lose the flagship, the rest of them will run."

With great care, the gunners targeted their quarry. Countless arrows of light were unleashed by the imperial force, but not even one had any effect.

The sights were aligned perfectly.

And that was when a single escape shuttle was ejected from the stern of the imperial flagship. The humble fleck of silver quickly melted away into the blackness.

Had anyone noticed it? After the space of another breath, rounded pillars of light came stabbing through the darkness a third time.

At their focal point was the imperial flagship, and it looked as though a circular region of space had been sliced out from the rest. Full Admiral von Seeckt, with his angry voice and hulking body, had been reduced to particulates measurable only in microns, along with his ill-fated staff officers.

As the surviving imperial ships realized what had happened, they began to swing their noses around one after another and withdraw from the firing range of Iserlohn Fortress's main battery. Since the commander calling for their noble and beautiful deaths had vanished, there was no reason to throw their lives away in reckless combat—or rather, one-sided slaughter.

In the midst of them was the shadow of the escape shuttle carrying Captain von Oberstein. As it advanced on semi-autopilot, he cast a glance back over his shoulder at the spherical shape of the colossal fortress that was dwindling in the distance.

In the moment before his death, did Admiral von Seeckt shout "Hail to his Imperial Majesty" or some such? How absurd.

Only the living can retaliate.

Ah well, von Oberstein murmured in his heart. If he had leadership skills and the power to get things done in addition to his resourcefulness, he could take the likes of Iserlohn back anytime. Or even if they just left Iserlohn in the alliance's hands as things stood, it would lose all its value when the alliance itself was destroyed.

Whom should he choose? There was no one with talent among the blue-blooded aristocrats. Should he pick that young, blond-haired fellow—that Count Reinhard von Lohengramm? There didn't seem to be anyone else...

Threading past the stricken, fleeing ships of her comrades, the shuttle flew away through the midst of the night.

Inside Iserlohn Fortress, however, a volcano of joy and excitement was erupting, and every open space was occupied by voices of laughter and song, heedless of key or scale. The only ones keeping quiet were the dazed-looking prisoners who had learned of their circumstances, and the director of the big show, Yang Wen-li.

"Sublieutenant Greenhill?"

When Frederica answered his call, the young, black-haired admiral was just stepping down to the floor from the command table.

"Contact the alliance homeland. Tell them that it's over, that we won, and even if I am told to do this again, I can't. Take care of the rest—I'm gonna find an empty room and get some sleep. At any rate, I'm bushed."

"Yang the magician!"

"Miracle Yang!"

A windstorm of cheers greeted Yang Wen-li, who had returned to the Free Planets Alliance's capital of Heinessen.

The great defeat in the Astarte Stellar Region that had happened just recently was promptly forgotten, and Yang's clever scheme and Marshal Sitolet's insightful judgment in appointing him were praised to the limits of what flowery language could be devised. At the carefully prepared ceremony and at the banquet which followed, Yang had a fabricated image of himself shoved into his face till he was sick of it.

When he was at last free, Yang returned home with an exasperated expression on his face and poured brandy into some tea that Julian had brewed for him. In the eyes of that young man, the amount seemed a little excessive.

"They're all the same—nobody understands," griped the hero of Iserlohn as he took off his shoes, sat down cross-legged on the sofa, and sipped his tea, which had become mostly brandy by this point. "Magic and miracles—they have no idea how hard people work. They just say whatever they feel like. The tactics I used have been around since ancient times. It's a way to separate the enemy's main force from their home base and take them out separately. I'm not using any magic—I just added a little spice to that, but if I slip up and fall for their flattery, I might be told next time to go to Odin unarmed and take it over alone."

And before that happens, I quit, he didn't say.

"But everyone's saying such wonderful things about you." As he spoke, Julian casually moved the bottle of brandy out of Yang's reach. "I think it's all right to be honestly glad, just like they want you to be."

"You're only praised while you're winning," Yang replied in a tone that was neither glad nor what Julian wanted it to be. "If you keep fighting, eventually you lose. Talking about how they turn on you when that happens can be fun if it's somebody else it's happening to. And by the way, Julian, can you at least let me drink as much brandy as I want to?"

CHAPTER 6:

TO EVERY MAN HIS STAR

I

Iserlohn is fallen!

At the sound of this disastrous news, a shudder ran through all of the Galactic Empire.

"But Iserlohn was supposed to be impregnable..."

With pallid countenance, Marshal Ehrenberg, minister of military affairs, murmured those words and afterwards sat motionless at his desk.

"I can't believe that. The report must be mistaken."

Fleet Admiral Steinhof, supreme commander at Imperial Military Command Headquarters, gave a hoarse groan, and after verifying the facts, retreated into a fortress of silence.

Even Emperor Friedrich IV, known for having little interest in or energy for affairs of state, had through Minister of the Palace Interior Neuköln demanded an explanation from Marquis Lichtenlade, the minister of state.

"The empire's territory must be sacred and inviolate to all external foes, and so in fact, it has ever been. Nevertheless, for our lack of foresight in having allowed such circumstances to trouble Your Majesty's heart, the shame we feel today knows no bounds."

Word reached the Lohengramm admiralität that the marquis had thus fearfully given answer.

"Something's wrong with that line of reasoning, Kircheis," Reinhard said to his trusted aide in his office. "Not an inch of imperial territory must be invaded by *external foes*, he says. But since when are the rebels an equal, external power? It's because he doesn't see things for what they are that he utters contradictions like that."

Reinhard, having opened his admiralität and secured under his command half the ships of the Imperial Space Armada, was struggling daily with personnel arrangements.

In the recruiting of young officers, preference was as a fundamental policy being given to low-ranking aristocrats and those of common birth. The average age of frontline commanders had plummeted. Energetic, youthful officers such as Wolfgang Mittermeier, Oskar von Reuentahl, Karl Gustav Kempf, and Fritz Josef Wittenfeld were now newly minted admirals, and the admiralität had come alive with youthful energy and spirit.

Reinhard, however, had for these past few days been unable to shake a feeling of dissatisfaction. He had assembled frontline commanders who had courage and tactical skill to spare but had been unable to find people to fill his staff positions.

Reinhard expected little of highborn staff officers who had been honor students in officers' school. He knew all too well that military skills were not something nurtured in the classroom. While natural-born soldiers were sometimes brilliant in their school days—as Reinhard himself had been—the opposite was never true.

He couldn't put Kircheis on staff. Reinhard needed him to function as his representative and at times take command of some of the fleets. When they were together, he would have Kircheis looking at the big picture, making decisions with him. That was the duty one's most trusted aide should perform.

Just a few days ago, Reinhard had dispatched Kircheis in place of himself to the Kastropf system on the occasion of the uprising there. This he had done to let Kircheis mark up some achievements of his own and make it clear to everyone that he was the Reinhard Corps's vice commander.

Reinhard had put in a request with Marquis Lichtenlade, minister of state, for orders from the emperor to be handed down to Kircheis.

At first, Marquis Lichtenlade had not looked favorably on this idea. However, the marquis had a parliamentary aide named Waitz who had offered this opinion: "Why not let him? Rear Admiral Kircheis is the very closest of Count von Lohengramm's close aides. If he should succeed in quelling Kastropf's rebellion, rewarding him—and putting him in your debt—may turn out to be profitable down the road. And if he fails, the blame will lie with Count von Lohengramm for recommending him. All you'll need do is again order the count to go subdue them, and if his subordinate has failed once already, he won't be able to go around boasting of it when the matter is settled."

"Hmm. That does make sense."

Accepting this reasoning, the marquis had set about the procedure by which the order to subdue Kastropf would be handed down from the emperor to Kircheis. Reinhard sent a gift of money to Waitz privately; the marquis never knew that Reinhard had asked Waitz to advise him as he had.

In this manner, Kircheis received his orders from the emperor directly. This meant that he was going places as a soldier of the empire. In Reinhard's admiralität, he leapt ahead of equivalently ranked colleagues, and it was recognized openly that he was now in the number two position. Naturally, this was nothing but a formality. In order to make it real, Kircheis needed some real military achievements.

It was in this way that the uprising in the Kastropf system had come about:

Earlier that year, the life of Duke Eugen von Kastropf had come to an unexpected end due to an accident aboard his private spacecraft.

As an aristocrat, he had held the right of taxation over his private domain and as a matter of course had boasted the power that came of plenteous wealth; also, as one of the chief vassals at court, he had served as minister of finance for roughly fifteen years. During his tenure, he had used the authority of that post to amass personal wealth, and had from time to time even been embroiled in shameful bribery scandals. When it came to the crimes of the aristocracy, however, the law's netting was of a terribly frayed weave. When things had reached the point at which even those holes were too small for Duke von Kastropf to slip through, he had nonetheless continued to avoid the hands of punishment through skillful application of his wealth and power.

Count Ruge, minister of the judiciary at the time, had sardonically described his abuses as "splendid hocus-pocus," from which it may be inferred that even in the eyes of highborn nobles like himself, the man had gone too far. As he was a pillar of the imperial government, they found it inconvenient that he would not follow the rules for public officials a little more closely. Public dissatisfaction with one chief vassal could easily grow into a distrust of the system as a whole.

Now, this duke of Kastropf had died. For the empire's Ministries of Finance and the Judiciary, this was what could be called a welcome opportunity. "Best to go right ahead and flog the deceased," was the general consensus. This was imperative in order to show the population that even the great noble families could not avoid the rule of law and also to rein in all the other innumerable little Kastropfs that existed within the aristocracy, thereby demonstrating the law of the empire and the strength of its public administration. Naturally, the public funds that Count von Kastropf had made his own and the bribes he had accepted amounted to a vast sum, and if that could be paid into the national treasury, the suffering of public coffers strained by military expenditures could, for a time at least, be eased.

Although there were some among the bureaucrats at the Ministry of Finance who spoke of taxing the aristocracy, that would mean changing a national policy in place since the days of Rudolf the Great and might also invite insurrections or a palace coup. If Duke von Kastropf were the sole target, however, there would be little opposition from the aristocracy.

Investigators from the Ministry of Public Finance were dispatched to Kastropf. And that was where the trouble began.

Duke von Kastropf had a son by the name of Maximilian, who, pending the emperor's approval via the minister of state, was to inherit the title and property of his late father. Due to present circumstances, however, the minister of state, Marquis Lichtenlade, had elected to postpone the succession process and only recognize inheritance of the estate after the Ministry of Public Finance had concluded its investigation and deducted the portion that the prior duke, Eugen von Kastropf, had wrongly obtained.

Maximilian opposed this. The child of a chief vassal and high-ranking aristocrat, this self-centered young man, long pampered in wealth and privilege, lacked his late father's political skills, even in the negative sense of the word. He quite literally set his hunting dogs loose on the investigators from the Ministry of Public Finance and then expelled them from his territory. These hunting dogs were "hornheads," which through DNA processing had come to have conical horns on their heads—they were savage beasts and symbolic of the violent side of aristocratic authority.

This unimaginative young man had no idea that his actions had been a slap across the cheek of an imperial government that placed great importance on prestige and the appearance of dignity. The slapped party, however, was not about to quietly tolerate that insult.

When a second team of investigators was also illegally expelled, Minister of Finance Viscount Gerlach sent a request to the Minister of State that Maximilian be summoned to court.

Upon receipt of that harshly worded summons, Maximilian realized for the first time that his actions were being viewed as problematic. Lacking balanced judgment, he was then overcome by extreme terror. He was certain that if he traveled to Hauptplanet Odin, he would never see his home again.

In the family of Duke von Kastropf, he of course had many relatives and in-laws, and concerned about the situation, they interposed themselves and tried to mediate a solution. This, however, only exacerbated Maximilian's suspicions.

When one of his relatives, Count Franz von Mariendorf—a man

known for his mild and unassuming nature—went to try to reason with him, Maximilian had him thrown into prison, and all hope for a peaceful resolution faded. Maximilian, having taken complete leave of his senses, began assembling a private army that consisted mainly of duchy security forces. That was when the imperial government decided to send a force to put down his insurrection.

This fleet, commanded by Admiral Schmude, departed Odin at about the same time that the militaries of the empire and alliance were clashing in the Astarte Stellar Region. Schmude's force was handily defeated.

Maximilian, failure though he was at responsible adulthood, still possessed a modicum of purely military talent, and the force sent against him had taken their opponent too lightly, engaging Maximilian in battle with little in the way of a strategy. While these were among the factors that had brought about defeat, the bottom line was that the force sent to restore order had been attacked just as it was landing, and Admiral Schmude had died in battle.

The second force sent to Kastropf had failed as well, and Maximilian, now getting carried away with himself, had proceeded to annex neighboring Mariendorf County and made plans to carve out a semi-independent fiefdom for himself in one corner of the empire. Although Franz, the head of Mariendorf's ruling family, had been incarcerated by Maximilian, his family security forces put up a sustained fight against Maximilian's invading army and appealed to Odin for aid.

That was where matters stood when Kircheis was ordered to go and quell the rebellion. It took him ten days to tame an uprising that had gone on for half a year.

First, Kircheis made a show of heading to the aid of Mariendorf County, and then he turned sharply and made for the Kastropf Duchy instead. A shocked Maximilian, not about to stand by and be robbed of his home base, broke his siege of Mariendorf County and rushed back toward Kastropf Duchy with all of his forces. With that, Kircheis had first rescued Mariendorf County from the danger it had been facing. Moreover, his making for the Kastropf Duchy had itself been nothing more than a diversionary tactic.

Maximilian, frantic over the threat to his main stronghold, was negligent in protecting his rear. Kircheis, having hidden his fleet in a treacherous region of an asteroid belt, let them go past, then launched a sudden assault on their undefended back side, delivering a devastating blow.

Maximilian withdrew from the field of battle, only to be murdered at the hands of subordinates hoping to lighten their own punishments. His remaining forces then surrendered.

Thus the Kastropf rebellion came to a swift ending. Though it was said to have taken ten days to quell, six of those days had been needed for the journey from Odin, and it had taken two to deal with the aftermath on Kastropf, so in fact only two days had been spent in actual combat.

The tactical ability Kircheis had displayed in this insurrection was extraordinary. Reinhard was satisfied, the admirals of his admiralität nodded their heads in approval, and the highborn nobles were astounded. It was one thing for Reinhard alone to possess such dazzling talent, but for his right-hand man to be similarly gifted was a bitter pill for them to swallow.

A military achievement, however, was still a military achievement. Kircheis was promoted to vice admiral and awarded a glittering, gold-colored *zeitwing*—a medal shaped like a two-headed eagle. In the capacity of acting imperial prime minister, Marquis Lichtenlade, minister of state, bestowed on Kircheis both the title and the medal, and praised his accomplishments, encouraging him to be grateful for His Imperial Highness's favor and to seek even greater devotion to His Majesty.

Kircheis knew all about what had happened behind the scenes, so to him, the sucking up to which Waitz had egged on Marquis Lichtenlade was merely absurd, though of course he let nothing of such feelings come to the surface.

Nevertheless, Kircheis was thinking, *You're asking the impossible, telling me to devote myself to the emperor.* Had it not been Emperor Friedrich IV himself who had kidnapped the object of his true devotion from before his very eyes and even now kept her all to himself? It wasn't the empire, the imperial household, or the emperor that Kircheis was fighting for.

Sigfried Kircheis, this tall redheaded youth, was quite popular with the women of the palace, from the daughters of dukes up above to the page girls running errands down below. He was completely unaware of this himself, though, and would have only found it a bother had he realized.

It was while Reinhard and Kircheis were in this way securing their respective footholds that there appeared before them Captain von Oberstein with his half-silvered hair.

II

I want staff officers! Lately, this desire of Reinhard's was growing stronger by the day.

But the sort of staff officers he was looking for were not necessarily specialists in military affairs. For that, Reinhard himself and Kircheis would suffice. Rather, he was looking for people with a strong aptitude for political maneuvering and plotting. Reinhard could foresee those sorts of struggles against the nobles at court—conspiracies and battles of wits, to put it bluntly—becoming ever more frequent from this point forward. Kircheis was unsuited to be Reinhard's confidant in such matters. This was not a problem of intellect; it was a problem of character and thought processes.

Reinhard checked his mental name card of the man who had just left his blaster with the guard and stepped unarmed into his office. There was nothing about him written on it that said he should view the man favorably.

"Captain von Oberstein, is it? What business might you have with me?"

"First, I would like you to clear the room," the uninvited guest requested, his attitude bordering on arrogance.

"There are only the three of us here."

"True, Vice Admiral Kircheis is here as well. Which is why I'm asking you to clear the room."

Both men stared at the visitor—Kircheis silently and Reinhard with a sharp gleam in his eye.

"Speaking with Vice Admiral Kircheis is the same as speaking with me. Did you not know that?"

"I am aware of that, sir."

"So you have something to talk about that you absolutely don't want him to hear. But when I tell him afterward, the end result will be the same."

"Your Excellency is of course free to do that. The labors of a conqueror, however, are not achieved without talented people of all different types. I believe one should tell A what A needs to hear, give B duties suited to B, and so on…"

Kircheis glanced toward Reinhard, and reservedly said, "Your Excellency, perhaps it might be best if I waited in the next room…"

Reinhard nodded with a pensive expression. Kircheis took his leave, and von Oberstein finally delved into what he had come to talk about.

"To be honest, Your Excellency, I am in a bit of a awkward position at present. I believe you're aware, but—"

"You're the deserter from Iserlohn. It's only natural that you be censured. This, despite word that Admiral von Seeckt died so heroically."

Reinhard's answer was cold. Von Oberstein, however, showed no sign of having been moved by it.

"To legions of commanding officers, I am a despicable deserter and nothing more. However, Excellency, I do have my own side of the story. I'd like you to hear it."

"You've come to the wrong person. Make your case to the military tribunal, not to me."

Von Oberstein, the sole survivor of the Iserlohn Fleet's flagship, was facing a maximum sentence for a single count of having lived. He had failed to perform his duty to assist his commanding officer and keep him from committing errors, and furthermore had sought only his own safety—these were the grounds for the impeachment and the icy stares, though there was also the fact that the circumstances required the scape-goating of some suitable individual present at Iserlohn's fall.

Upon hearing Reinhard's indifferent reply, von Oberstein unexpectedly touched his hand to his right eye. When he finally lowered that hand, a small, eerie hollow had appeared in one part of his face. The man with the half-silvered hair held a small object out to the young marshal—a tiny, almost spherical crystal resting in the palm of his right hand.

"Look at this, please, Your Excellency."

Reinhard looked but said nothing.

"You'll probably have heard from Vice Admiral Kircheis, but both my eyes are bionic like this one. If I had been born during the reign of Rudolf the Great, I would have been killed as a baby in accordance with the Genetic Inferiority Elimination Act."

After fitting his detached bionic eye back into its socket, the gleam in von Oberstein's gaze was directed at Reinhard head-on, seeming to bore right into the admiral's own line of sight. "Do you understand?" he said. "I hate them all. Rudolf the Great, his descendants, everything they've brought forth…the Goldenbaum Dynasty, the Galactic Empire itself."

"Those are bold words."

For just one instant, the young imperial marshal was seized with a claustrophobic tightness of breath. Illogical suspicions were even aroused in him, as he wondered if the functionality of von Oberstein's bionic eyes included the power to overwhelm the will of others or if perhaps he had activated some component that applied psychological pressure.

Though von Oberstein's voice was low and the entire room was furnished with soundproofing devices, his words carried like an out-of-season peal of spring thunder.

"The Galactic Empire—by which I mean the Goldenbaum Dynasty—must be destroyed. If it were possible, I would destroy it with my own hands. However, I lack the acumen, the power. What I can do is assist in the rise of a new conqueror, that's all. I'm speaking of you, Your Excellency: Imperial Marshal Reinhard von Lohengramm."

Reinhard could practically hear the crackling of the electrified air.

"Kircheis!"

As he rose from his seat, Reinhard called out for his friend and closest advisor. The wall opened up without a sound, and there appeared the tall figure of the redheaded youth. Reinhard's finger was pointed at von Oberstein.

"Kircheis, arrest Captain von Oberstein. He's spoken words of lawless rebellion against the empire. As a soldier of the empire, I cannot overlook it."

Von Oberstein's bionic eyes flashed intensely. The young redheaded officer had drawn his blaster faster than seemed humanly possible and taken aim at the center of von Oberstein's chest. Since his days in military preparatory school, few had surpassed Kircheis in terms of shooting skill. Even if von Oberstein had been holding a pistol and had tried to resist, the effort would have been futile.

"So in the end, that's your measure…" von Oberstein muttered. A bitter shadow of disappointment and self-reproach crept into a face that had had precious little color to begin with. "Very well, then—walk your narrow road with only Vice Admiral Kircheis to guide you."

His words were partly performance and partly heartfelt. He shot a glance at Reinhard's silent figure, then turned toward Kircheis.

"Vice Admiral Kircheis, can you shoot me? I'm unarmed, as you can see. Even so, can you fire?"

Though there was also the fact that Reinhard had issued no further orders, Kircheis—his aim still fixed on von Oberstein's chest—had hesitated to put strength into his trigger finger.

"You can't do it. That's the sort of man you are. Deserving of respect, but you can't claim that respect alone will see you through the work of conquest. Every light has a shadow that follows it…Does our young Count von Lohengramm still not see that?"

Still staring hard at von Oberstein, Reinhard motioned for Kircheis to put away his blaster. Ever so slightly, his expression was changing.

"You're a man who speaks his mind."

"I'm honored you should say so."

"And Admiral von Seeckt…how he must have hated you! Am I wrong?"

"The admiral was not a man to inspire loyalty in his troops," von

Oberstein answered, not batting an eye. He knew in this moment that he had won his gamble.

Reinhard nodded.

"Very well, then. I'll buy you from those nobles."

III

The minister of military affairs, the secretary-general of Military Command Headquarters, and the commander in chief of the Imperial Space Armada were known collectively as the three directors general of the Imperial Armed Forces. For an example of one man holding all three posts at once, one would need to go back nearly a century to the time of then crown prince Ottfried, the only man who had ever done so.

Ottfried had been imperial prime minister as well, but since that time, the ministers of state had come to be named as acting prime ministers, with the office itself never being officially filled—the reason being that vassals tended to avoid emulating any precedent set by that particular emperor.

In his days as crown prince, Ottfried had been a capable and promising young man, but after succeeding to the throne to become Emperor Ottfried III, he had found himself in a whirlpool of repeated palace conspiracies that nourished nothing but his suspicions. Four times he replaced his empress and five times his named successor, until at last a fear of death by poisoning caused him to abstain from food much of the time, and he died, emaciated, while only in his midforties.

The three directors general of the Imperial Armed Forces—Minister of Military Affairs Ehrenberg, Secretary-General of Military Command Headquarters Steinhof, and Commander in Chief of the Imperial Space Armada Mückenberger—submitted their resignations to the acting imperial prime minister, Marquis Lichtenlade, the minister of state. This they did in order to take responsibility for the loss of Iserlohn Fortress.

"You seek neither to avoid responsibility nor cling to position. I think your gracefulness in this matter is praiseworthy. However, were the posts of the three directors general to be vacated temporarily, that would probably mean at least one of them going to Count von Lohengramm. Surely you wouldn't trouble yourselves to pave his way for advancement? All of you are quite comfortable financially, so how about giving up your salaries for the next year or so, instead?"

When the minister of state had thus spoken, an anguished expression rose up on the face of Marshal Steinhof, and he replied:

"It's not that we haven't considered that, but we are also soldiers. The regret would be too great if it were said of us that we clung to our positions and erred in staying when we should have resigned... So, please, accept these letters."

Reluctantly, Marquis Lichtenlade headed to court and got Emperor Friedrich IV started on the resignation letters of the three directors general.

The emperor, who had been listening to the minister of state with the same apathy as always, gave instructions to his chamberlain to have Reinhard summoned from his admiralität. Going to the trouble of a direct summons when a visiphone call would have finished the task within minutes was just one of the formalities that the emperor's conspicuous showing of power required.

When Reinhard appeared at the imperial palace, the emperor showed the young imperial marshal the three letters of resignation, and with the same intonation used when letting a child choose a toy, asked him which job he wanted. After a brief glance toward the minister of state, who was standing by unmoving with an unhappy look on his face, Reinhard answered.

"I can't rob someone of his seat when it's not for any achievement of my own. The loss of Iserlohn was due to the mistakes of Admirals von Seeckt and von Stockhausen. Also, Admiral von Seeckt has paid for his sins already with his life, and the other is in an enemy prison even as we speak. I don't believe there's anyone else deserving of blame. I humbly beg Your Highness to please not blame the three directors general."

"Hmm. How magnanimous."

The emperor looked back at the minister of state, who was surprised at this unexpected turn of events.

"The count has spoken. What say you?"

"Your humble vassal is struck by the count's keen insight, far beyond tender years. The three directors general have done great things for the nation, and for my part, I too would like to ask that you deal with them graciously."

"If that's what the both of you have to say, then I won't hand down any harsh punishments. At the same time, however, it won't be possible to avoid punishing them altogether..."

"In that case, Your Highness, I wonder what you would say to having them give up their salaries for the next year and forwarding those funds to the Families of Fallen Soldiers Relief Foundation."

"Yes, something along those lines would be fine. I'll leave the details to the minister of state. Is this all you need to talk about?"

"Yes, Your Highness."

"In that case, the two of you may go. I have to get to the greenhouse to care for my roses."

Both men withdrew.

Five minutes had not passed, however, before one of them secretly returned. Since the seventy-five year-old Marquis Lichtenlade had returned at a half run, he needed a moment to catch his breath, but by the time he was standing in the emperor's rose garden, he had recovered his physical composure.

There, amid thick hedges of rose bushes that filled the greenhouse with wild, bounteous swirls of color and fragrance, the emperor stood unmoving, like a withered old tree. The aged aristocrat approached him and carefully eased himself down to his knees.

"If I may, Your Highness."

"What is it?"

"I say this with awareness that it may earn me your displeasure, but..."

"Is it about Count von Lohengramm?"

The emperor's voice was devoid of any edge, intensity, or passion. It was like the sound of windblown sand—the voice of a lifeless old man.

"You mean to say that I'm giving too much power and prestige to Annerose's younger brother."

"Your Highness knew that already?"

What also surprised the minister of state was how unexpectedly lucid the emperor's delivery of those words had been.

"The man knows no fear, and so he might not stop at wielding the power of a chief vassal—perhaps he'll get carried away and plot to usurp the throne. Is that what you're thinking?"

"It is only with the greatest of reservations that I even let it cross my lips."

"So what if he does?"

"Majesty?!"

"It's not as if the Goldenbaum Dynasty has been with humanity from its beginning. Just as there's no such thing as an immortal man, there's no such thing as an eternal state, either. There's no reason the Galactic Empire mustn't end in my generation."

His low, parched laughter sent a shudder down the spine of the minister of state. The depths of the gaping void he had just glimpsed chilled his soul to its core.

"If it's all going to be destroyed anyway, then its destruction should at least be spectacular…" The emperor's voice trailed off like a comet's ominous tail.

IV

The three directors general had to admit, however reluctantly, that they owed Reinhard a favor, offensive to them as that was. It followed, then, that they were in no position to refuse when Reinhard contacted them the following day to request Captain Paul von Oberstein's exemption from all responsibility regarding the loss of Iserlohn and his transfer to the Lohengramm admiralität. They could hardly take harsh measures against others while themselves basking in the grace of "the emperor's generosity." There was also the fact that they didn't view the retention or dismissal of a single captain as being terribly important anyway. In any case, it was a satisfactory outcome for von Oberstein.

Regarding Reinhard having willingly declined the seat of a director general, opinion among the elite was split fifty-fifty between the favorable—"Surprisingly unselfish, isn't he?"—and the negative—"He's just trying to look good in front of people."

Reinhard himself paid no mind to either evaluation. A directorship was his for the taking any time he liked. Until then, he was merely lending those positions out to feeble old men. Most importantly, that sort of position was nothing more than a stepping-stone as far as he was concerned.

On the day that Reinhard assumed that most noble of stations, there would be no satisfaction even in holding all three directorships at once.

"What is it, Kircheis? You look like you have something to say."

"You're not being very nice, are you? Pretending not to know what it is."

"Don't get upset. This is about von Oberstein, isn't it? I was suspicious myself for a while that he might be a tool of the highborn. But he's not the sort of man the aristocrats can handle. He's got a sharp mind but too many peculiarities."

"But can *you* handle him, Lord Reinhard?"

Reinhard tilted his head slightly. Whenever he did that, one lock of his brilliant, golden hair would slide to the other side.

"Hmm...I'm not expecting friendship or loyalty from that man. He's only trying to use me in order to achieve his own goals."

Reinhard stretched out his long, supple fingers and playfully tugged at his best friend's hair, as red as if dyed with molten rubies. Reinhard would do this sort of thing from time to time when no one else was around. During his boyhood, he would describe Kircheis's hair according to his whim: whenever they were quarreling—a state that never lasted very long—he would say mean things like, "What's with that red hair? It looks like blood." Then after they made up, he would praise it, calling it "really pretty, like a burning flame."

"...So in the same way, I'm going to use him for his brain. His motives are irrelevant. If I can't control a solitary man like that, I haven't a prayer of holding sway over the entire universe. Wouldn't you agree?"

Politics isn't about processes or systems—it's about the results, Reinhard believed.

Taking over the USG and making himself emperor wasn't what made Rudolf the Great so unforgivable; it was that he had used his vast, newfound powers for that most asinine of purposes—self-deification. That was the true face of Rudolf: a hunger for power masquerading as heroism. What a boon he might have been to the advancement of civilization if he had only used those vast powers in the right way! Instead of wasting its energy on conflicts arising from political differences, humanity could have been leaving its footprints all across the galaxy. Today, humanity ruled only a fifth of this vast realm of stars, even when taking the rebel power into account.

Responsibility for this roadblock in the path of human history lay solely at the feet of Rudolf's monomania. A "living god"? The best thing you could call the man was a plague-spreading devil.

Immense authority and power were necessary to destroy the old system and carve out a new order. But Reinhard would not make the same mistakes Rudolf had. Emperor he would become. However, he would not hand that title to his descendants.

Rudolf had been a blind believer in bloodlines and the gene. But genes were not to be trusted. Reinhard's father had been neither a genius nor a great man. Lacking in both the ability and the will to live according to his own efforts, he'd been a good-for-nothing who had sold off his lovely daughter to the powerful in order to lead a life of comfort and self-indulgence. Seven years ago, when excessive drinking and carousing had culminated in his father's sudden death, Reinhard hadn't had in himself the tears he should have cried. Though it had cut him to the heart to see pellucid drops running down and falling from his sister's porcelain cheeks, his grief and pain had been exclusively for his sister.

For an example of untrustworthy genes, one need look no further than the present state of the Goldenbaum imperial family. Who would imagine that even a milliliter of that giant Rudolf's blood was flowing in the decrepit body of Friedrich IV? The blood of House Goldenbaum was already clouded beyond recognition.

Every last one of Friedrich IV's nine brothers and sisters were dead. Starting with his empress, Friedrich IV had impregnated six women for a total of twenty-eight times, but there had been six miscarriages and nine stillbirths, and of the thirteen who had been born, four had died before their first birthday, five had died before reaching adulthood, and two had died as adults. Only two daughters yet remained: Marqesse Amalie von Braunschweig and Duchess Christine von Littenheim. Both were wed to powerful aristocrats from old families, and to both of them, one child had also been born, both of them girls. Aside from her, Crown Prince Ludwig, who had died in adulthood, had left one child behind. This was Erwin Josef, who was presently the only male child in the imperial family. As he had only just turned five, however, he was not even crown prince yet.

Emperor Friedrich IV, who had seemingly absorbed the whole of the palace's decadence into his person, was to Reinhard nothing but an object of bitter hatred and derision—yet on two points only, Reinhard was able to approve.

The first was that the emperor, having been through the deaths of many mistresses in difficult past childbirths, feared losing Annerose and had never made her pregnant. Another factor in that decision was pressure from aristocrats concerned about the succession struggle that might ensue if Annerose were to give birth. From Reinhard's standpoint, the thought of his sister bearing that emperor's child was too disgusting to even contemplate.

The other thing was that the number of claimants to the throne was so extremely small. There were only the emperor's three grandchildren. All he had to do was eliminate those three. Or he could use the strategy of marrying one of the two granddaughters—albeit just for appearance's sake.

Either way, von Oberstein would prove useful. With dark enthusiasm and tenacity, that man would envelop the aristocrats and imperial family with plots and schemes, and if it were necessary, would probably not hesitate to murder even a woman or child. It was likely because Kircheis had surmised this unconsciously that he loathed the man, but still, Reinhard had need of him.

He wondered if Annerose and Kircheis would look on him kindly now, having come to have need of a man like von Oberstein.

Yet still, this was something that he had to do.

⋃

Phezzan landesherr Rubinsky's briefing on economic strategy was held at his official residence.

"Universe Finance—a dummy corporation in the Free Planets Alliance that is operated by our government—has secured excavation rights for the solid natural gas on the seventh and eighth planets of the Bharatpur system," an aide said. "The total amount of extractable reserves comes to forty-eight million cubic kilometers, and they expect to be profitable within two years."

Watching as Rubinsky nodded, the aide continued with his report.

"Also, regarding Santa Cruz Line, one of the largest interstellar transport companies in the alliance, our percentage of acquired stock has reached 41.9 percent. Ownership is divided among more than twenty people, so they haven't realized what's happening. Still, we've already surpassed the state-run investment trust that's at the top of its shareholders list."

"Well done. But don't slack off until you've reached more than half."

"Certainly. Meanwhile, in the empire, our equity participation has been approved for the agricultural development project in the Seventh Frontier Stellar Region. That's the one we spoke of earlier—they say they're going to transport two hundred quadrillion tons of water from Eisenherz II to eight arid worlds and increase production of foodstuffs enough to support five billion people."

"What's the breakdown of equity participation?"

"Our government's three dummy companies together hold 84 percent, so we have de facto sole ownership. Now, on to the subject of Ingolstadt's metallic radium factory…"

After Rubinsky had listened to the rest of the report, he sent the aide away for a time and gazed up at the scenery beyond the wall, which showed off the beauty of a bleak and desolate landscape.

At present, all was smooth sailing. In the empire and the alliance alike, the leadership seemed to believe warfare was just battleships firing subluminal-velocity missiles at one another in space. That meant that while obstinate dogmatists were caught up in murdering one another, the foundations of both countries' socioeconomic systems would fall into Phezzan's hands. Even now, nearly half of the war bonds being issued by both countries were purchased directly or indirectly by Phezzan.

In every corner of the universe where humanity's foot trod, Phezzan ruled economically. One day, the governments of both the empire and the alliance would do nothing but generate economic gain for Phezzan and execute policies on its behalf. It would still take a little more time to reach that point, but when it happened, only a half step would yet remain before the final stage of their goal . . .

However, the political and military situation was not, of course, something that could be taken lightly. In short, should the empire and the alliance achieve political unification of their vast hegemonies, Phezzan's special position would lose all meaning. In ancient times, trading cities on both land and sea had yielded before the military and political power of newly arisen, unified dynasties, and that history could probably repeat itself.

If that happened, the road that led to the attainment of Phezzan's goal would be shut off permanently. The birth of something like a new Galactic Empire had to be prevented by any means necessary.

A new Galactic Empire . . .

The thought gave Rubinsky a fresh feeling of tension. The present Goldenbaum-dynasty Galactic Empire was already creaking with the degeneration of age, and to reinvigorate it was nearly impossible. Even if it split apart and turned into a cluster of little kingdoms, and even if a new order were to be born out of that, how many centuries would it take for it to happen?

The Free Planets Alliance, on the other hand, had lost the ideals of its founding and was drifting along on inertia. The stagnation in its economy and the lack of development in its society had given rise to discontent among the masses, and there was no end of hostility over economic inequalities among the various planets that made up the alliance. Unless one incredibly charismatic leader were to appear and reconstruct a system of centralized power, things would continue as they were with no exit in sight.

Five centuries earlier, a young Rudolf von Goldenbaum, his hulking body brimming with a lust for power, had taken over the political organization of the USG to become the sacred and inviolable emperor. Through legal means, a dictator had arisen. Would the day of his return ever come? If he were to take over the already-existing power structure, change was possible in a short period of time. Even if it wasn't legal…

A coup d'état. For those who were near to the crux of political and military power, there was this classical yet effective method. For that reason alone, the idea had its attraction.

Rubinsky pressed a button on his console and called up his aide.

"The odds of a coup d'état happening in both countries?"

The landesherr's question had surprised him.

"If that is your order, I'll see to the research immediately, but…have you received some sort of urgent communiqué suggesting such a thing?"

"Nothing like that. The thought only occurred to me just now. Still, there's nothing wrong with examining all kinds of possibilities."

It's offensive that those whose minds and spirits are so utterly corrupt can do as they please with power they don't even deserve, thought the ruler of Phezzan. Still, there was a need for the political systems of the empire and alliance to continue in their present forms for now. At least until the day that the true aims of Phezzan, which neither the empire nor the alliance could fathom, were achieved.

VI

The High Council of the Free Planets Alliance was made up of eleven councillors. The members included the council chair, the vice council chair who doubled as chair for the Domestic Affairs Committee, the clerk, the

Defense Committee chair, the Finance Committee chair, the chair of the Committee for Law and Order, the Natural Resources Committee chair, the Human Resources Committee chair, the Economic Development Committee chair, the chair of the Committee for the Development of Regional Societies, and the Intelligence Traffic Committee chair. They were all gathered together in a meeting room within a magnificent building whose outer walls were the color of pearl.

The Decision Room had no windows and was surrounded on all four sides by thick walls and other rooms. These included the Anti Room, for communicating with people outside the alliance; the Chart Room, where reports and other materials were compiled; the Intelligence Room, for data processing; and the Operations Room, from which the mechanism of the alliance was controlled. In addition, these were surrounded on the outside by the security guards' antechamber, which formed a doughnut shape around all of them.

Is this what you call the seat of open government? thought João Lebello, chairman of the Finance Committee, as he took his seat at a round table seven meters in diameter. This was not something he'd only just started thinking; every time he passed through all the infrared rays in the corridor to enter the Decision Room, that question preoccupied his thoughts.

That day, during the meeting of August 6, SE 796, one of the topics being taken up was the question of whether or not to approve or deny a troop-dispatch proposal that had been submitted by the military. This plan, to use occupied Iserlohn Fortress as a bridgehead for invading the empire, had been handed to the council in person by a group of young, high-ranking officers. To Lebello, this reeked of extremism.

The meeting began, and Lebello staked out a strong position against expansion of the war.

"It's a strange way to put it, but up to this very day, the Galactic Empire and our alliance have continued the war just barely within the range that our finances will tolerate. However..."

Survivor annuities for the families of soldiers killed in the Battle of Astarte alone were going to require a yearly outlay of ten billion dinars. If the flames of war were to spread further, neither the nation's finances nor the economy supporting them would be able to avoid fiscal collapse. Never mind that they were engaging in deficit spending even now.

Ironically, even Yang had contributed to the financial woes. At Iserlohn, he had taken five million prisoners of war, and just keeping them fed was turning out to be a considerable undertaking.

"To shore up our finances, we have the same two choices we've always had: increase the issue of bonds or raise taxes. There's no other way."

"What about increasing the amount of paper money?" asked the vice chairman.

"Without the finances to back it? Several years down the line, we'd be trading it by weight instead of the amounts written on the bills. Personally, I have no desire to be remembered as the infamous financier who didn't have a plan and ushered in an age of hyperinflation."

"But unless we win the war, we can never be sure we have tomorrow, let alone years down the line."

"Then in that case, we should put an end to the war itself."

Lebello spoke those words in a powerful voice, and the room fell dead silent.

"Thanks to the strategy of one Admiral Yang, we now have Iserlohn. The empire has lost its forward base for invading the alliance. Don't you think this is an excellent opportunity to conclude a peace treaty with them on favorable terms?"

"But this is a just war against absolute monarchy. We mustn't inherit the stars together with the likes of them. Do you seriously think we can just stop just because it isn't economical?"

Several people launched back with arguments of their own.

A just war? João Lebello, chairman of the Finance Committee for the government of the Free Planets Alliance, crossed his arms, dissatisfied.

Oceans of bloodshed, national bankruptcy, impoverished masses. If sacrifices such as these were essential to realizing justice, then Justice looked like a greedy god indeed, tirelessly demanding one sacrificial victim after another.

"Let's recess for a little while . . ." he heard the Chairman say in a voice devoid of all luster.

VII

After lunch, the meeting reconvened.

This time, it was Huang Rui—who as Human Resources Committee chair had administrative responsibilities involving education, employment, labor issues, and social security—who was taking a hard line. He was also in the antideployment camp.

"As Human Resources Committee chair, I must say—"

Huang was a small man, but he had a loud voice. With his ruddy complexion and his short but nimble-looking arms and legs, he gave the impression of a man who had energy to spare.

"To begin with, I can't help feeling uneasy about the present situation: there are too many talented people who end up being used by the military when they should be used to help grow the economy and improve our society. It's also troubling that the investments we make toward education and job training keep getting reduced. As evidence of laborers' declining skill levels, I'd like to point out that the number of workplace accidents has increased by 30 percent over the last six-month period. In a transport-convoy accident that happened in the Lumbini system, over four hundred lives and fifty tons of metallic radium were lost. It's plausible that shortened training periods for civilian astronauts had a lot to do with that. Moreover, astronauts are being overworked due to personnel shortages."

He had a clear and brisk way of speaking.

"On this point, I have a proposal: of the technicians presently being forced to work for the military, I'd like to see four million of the transport and communications personnel returned to civilian life. At a minimum."

Huang's gaze swept across his fellow councillors, coming to a rest on the face of Defense Committee Chairman Trünicht. His eyebrows twitched as he responded.

"Please don't make unreasonable demands. If we released that many from rear service work, the whole organization of the military would collapse like a house of cards."

"So the Defense Committee chairman says, but at the rate we're going, our society and economy will collapse before the military does. Do you know the current average age of an operator working in the capital's Lifestyle Supply Distribution Center?"

"...No."

"Forty-two."

"That doesn't sound like an unusual figure to me..."

Huang pounded the table forcefully.

"Because it's an illusion created by the real numbers! As many as 80 percent of them are either twenty and under or seventy and over. Average them, and you certainly do get forty-two, but in reality there is no backbone of experienced technicians in their thirties and forties. Throughout all the machinery of our society, there's an ongoing weakening of the software that makes it run. I hope I can impress on all of our wise councillors just how terrifying a thing that is..."

Huang closed his mouth and looked around at everyone once again. Aside from Lebello, there was no one who met that gaze head-on. One had his eyes turned down, another casually averted his gaze, yet another looked up at the high ceiling.

Lebello took over for Huang.

"In short, now is the time to let the people rest and rebuild their strength. With Iserlohn Fortress now in our hands, the alliance should be able to put a stop to the empire's invasions of its territory. And this situation should hold for the medium term. And that being the case, what possible need is there to willingly launch an attack from our side?"

Lebello made his appeal with fervor.

"To drive our citizens to even greater sacrifices than they've already made is to abandon even the basic principles of democracy. They cannot bear the burden."

Voices of refutation rose up, starting with Intelligence Traffic Committee Chair Cornelia Windsor, the only woman among the councillors. She had just been sworn in a week ago.

"There's no need to pander to the egotism of citizens who make no effort at understanding our great and noble purpose. And what great enterprise has ever succeeded without sacrifice?"

"Madam Windsor, the people are beginning to wonder if these

sacrifices might be too great." Lebello said this to counter an argument that came straight from a textbook, but his words had no effect.

"No matter how great the sacrifice—even if it were to mean death for every one of our citizens—we have something that we must do."

"Th-that's no longer a political argument." Lebello had raised his voice without realizing it.

Casually ignoring him, Madam Windsor turned toward the attendees and in a strong voice that carried well through the chamber, began imparting her opinions.

"We have a noble duty. A duty to bring down the Galactic Empire and rescue all humanity from its oppression. How can you say we're walking in the path of righteousness if we, intoxicated with cheap humanitarianism, forget that great purpose altogether?"

In her early forties, she was an attractive woman—graceful, with an intellectual sort of beauty—and in her voice there was a musical ring. That alone raised the danger Lebello sensed in her to another level. Was cheap heroism not clutching at her own ankles?

Just as Lebello was about to make another counterpoint, Chairman Sunford, who had remained silent till now, spoke up for the first time.

"Um...I have some materials here. Could everyone look at your terminal?"

Everyone was a little surprised, and for a moment all eyes focused on the chairman—he was oft said to cast "a thin shadow"—before turning to their terminals as instructed.

"This is the general public's approval rating for this council. It definitely isn't good."

The value displayed—31.9 percent—was not far off from what the attendees expected. Not so many days had passed since Madam Windsor's predecessor had fallen in a disgraceful bribery case, and as Lebello and Huang had pointed out, societal and economic stagnation was a very serious issue.

"And on the other hand, here is our disapproval rating."

There were sighs at the value: 56.2 percent. It was not unexpected, but the disappointment was unavoidable.

Observing the reactions of all present, the chairman continued. "At this rate, it's doubtful we can win in the elections early next year. I can see us being caught between the pacifist faction and the strongest hard-liners, and falling short of a majority. However..."

The chairman lowered his voice. Though it was hard to say whether this was intentional or not, it was greatly effective in drawing in the attention of his listeners.

"I've had the computer run some numbers, and it's almost certain that if we can secure an epoch-making victory over the empire within the next one hundred days, our approval rating will rise 15 percent at minimum."

There was a soft stir of voices in the room.

"Let's take a vote on the military's proposal," said Madam Windsor. After a few seconds, several voices were raised in agreement. Everyone was thinking about keeping their committee chairmanships versus returning to the opposition in the event of electoral losses, and it was only during this interval that there was silence.

"Wait a minute."

Lebello had half risen from his seat. Despite the fact that he was under a sunlamp, his cheeks were pale like an old man's.

"We have no such right. To launch a needless invasion just to maintain political power...no such right has been given to us..."

His voice trembled and cracked.

"My, you say such pretty things."

Madam Windsor's cold, brilliant laughter rang out. Lebello was at a loss for words as he looked on, stunned at the sight of policy makers about to pollute the spirit of democratic government with their own bloody hands.

From his seat some distance away, Huang was looking at the anguished figure of Lebello.

"I'm begging you, please don't lose your temper," he whispered, and stretched a thick finger toward the voting button.

Six in favor, three opposed, two abstaining. A two-thirds majority of valid votes cast was required for approval, and the yes votes had that number; it had just been decided to invade imperial territory.

However, the results of the vote shocked the councillors—not because the mobilization had passed but because one of the three votes against it had been cast by Defense Committee Chairman Trünicht.

The other two votes, cast by Finance Committee Chairman Lebello and Human Resources Committee Chair Huang, had been expected. But wasn't Trünicht acknowledged by all as a hard-line hawk?

"I'm a patriot. But that doesn't mean I stand for going to war in every case. I want you all to remember that I was against this mobilization."

That was the answer he gave to those who questioned him.

The very same day, Joint Operational Headquarters officially rejected the letter of resignation that Rear Admiral Yang Wen-li had submitted, issuing instead his letter of appointment to the rank of vice admiral.

VIII

"What you're saying is you want to quit, right?"

Marshal Sitolet's response when Yang had submitted his letter of resignation had not been a terribly creative one. Yang, however, hadn't exactly expected him to take the letter in one hand while with a flourish of the other handing him his retirement allowance and pension card, so he gave him the friendliest nod he could manage.

"But you're still just thirty years old."

"Twenty-nine." Yang put special emphasis on the *twenty*.

"But at any rate, you're not even up to a third of your average life span. Don't you think it's a little early to be putting your life behind you?"

"Your Excellency, that's not what I'm doing," objected the young admiral. He wasn't abandoning his life; he was getting it back on track. Everything up till now had been a detour forced on him against his will. From the start, he had wanted to be an observer of history, not a creator of it.

Marshal Sitolet laced the fingers of both hands and rested his sturdy-looking chin on top of them.

"What our military needs is not your erudition as a historian but your competence and capability as a tactician. And we need it desperately."

Haven't I indulged your flattery once already? Yang shot back in his heart.

Any way he looked at it, he had to be doing some serious overlending in his credit-debit relationship with the military. *Just for taking Iserlohn, I think I ought to have a little change coming my way,* Yang thought. Director Sitolet's assault was two-pronged, however.

"What's to become of the Thirteenth Fleet?"

At this offhanded but effective question, Yang's mouth opened just slightly.

"That's *your* fleet, and it's only just been formed. If you resign, what happens to them?"

"Well, they'll…"

To have forgotten about that could only be described as a careless mistake. He'd screwed up the operation, he had to admit. Once you got tangled up in something, getting loose again was no easy matter.

In the end, Yang withdrew from the director's office, leaving his letter of resignation with him, though it was clear as day it was not going to be approved. Indignant, he headed downstairs by way of a gravitational lift.

Sitting on a waiting room sofa, Julian Mintz had been glancing disinterestedly at the uniformed people passing this way and that, but when he spotted Yang at a distance, he rose energetically to his feet. Yang had told him to come by headquarters on his way home from school that day. "Why not eat out once in a while? Besides, I've got something I want to tell you." That had been all he had said to the boy. He had wanted to surprise him: "Actually, I just quit the military. From now on, it's the carefree life of a pensioner."

But now, however, his plans were still up in the air, so that blissful dream had vanished in a single puff of reality's bitter exhalation. *Well, what do I tell him now?* Unconsciously relaxing his pace, Yang was trying to come up with something when a voice from the side called out to him.

Captain Walter von Schönkopf was saluting him. Due to his recent exploits, von Schönkopf was now scheduled for promotion to commodore.

"I saw you coming out of the director's office, Excellency. Did you perhaps come in to tender your resignation?"

"I sure did. No question it'll be turned down, though."

"I should say so. There's no way the service is going to let *you* go."
The captain, once a citizen of the empire, was looking at Yang with an
amused expression. "In all seriousness, though, I do want to see people
like you staying in, sir. You're always on target in your appraisal of the
situation, and you're lucky as well. Serving under you, I might not ever
distinguish myself in battle, but at least the odds of survival seem high."

Von Schönkopf was calmly rattling off an evaluation of a superior
officer right in front of the man.

"I've made up my mind to close the curtains on my life by dying of old
age. I want to live to be 150, turn into a doddering old man, and then as
I breathe my last breath, hear my grandchildren and great-grandchildren
weeping happy tears to finally be rid of me. I have no interest in going
out in a blaze of glory. Please keep me alive long enough to do that."

Having said his piece, the captain saluted again and smiled at Yang,
who returned the salute with a demoralized demeanor.

"I'm sorry to have taken up your time. Look here, the boy can hardly
wait for you."

Caselnes and von Schönkopf alike possessed no small capacity for
sarcastic barbs, but it made no difference when Julian was around;
maybe there was something about him that made them simply sup-
portive instead.

As Yang and Julian walked side by side, Yang glanced over at the boy,
unable to suppress a degree of embarrassed bewilderment in his heart. It
was such a strange thing... To experience emotions like those of a father,
even without having ever been married.

The restaurant's atmosphere was far more relaxed than one might imagine
of a place called The March Hare. The old-fashioned decor tied all its
furnishings together, and there were also candles set out on tabletops
covered with handwoven cloths—Yang was delighted. However, his
reward for having neglected the task of making reservations—hardly even

worth calling a task, since a single call on the visiphone was all it took—was that he was not on good terms with the little fairies of luck that night.

"I'm terribly sorry, but we're filled to capacity."

So they were solemnly informed by an elderly waiter abounding in dignity, physique, and beautiful sideburns. Yang took in the restaurant's smallish interior with a glance, and it was clear right away that the waiter wasn't lying in order to angle for tips. Under the dim illumination, the glow of candlelight was flickering rhythmically on all of the tables. Candles were not lit for tables without customers.

"Oh well. Want to try somewhere else?"

As Yang scratched his head thoughtfully, someone stood up from one of the tables by the wall with movements so refined as to be called elegant. It was a woman. Her pearl-white dress shone in the candlelight, appealing to Yang's eye with a dreamlike effect.

"Admiral?"

When she called him, Yang unconsciously froze where he stood. His aide, Sublieutenant Frederica Greenhill, responded with a light smile.

"Even I have civilian clothes. My father says he'd like you to come join us, if you don't mind."

While she was speaking, her father rose and stood behind her.

"Well, good evening, *Vice Admiral* Yang."

In a friendly voice, Senior Admiral Dwight Greenhill, deputy director of Joint Operational Headquarters, called out to him. Inside, Yang felt a bit uneasy about sitting down with a superior officer, but at this point there was no refusing the invitation.

"It's rear admiral, Your Excellency," Yang said while saluting.

"You'll make vice admiral by next week at the latest. You may as well go ahead and get used to the new title, right?"

"That's wonderful! Is that what you wanted to talk about?" Julian's eyes shone. "I'd expected that much, but still, that's really wonderful news, isn't it?"

"Ha, ha, ha…" With a simple laugh, Yang distracted himself from extremely complex emotions, pulled himself together, and introduced his ward to Greenhill and his daughter.

"I see, so you're the famous honor student, are you? And you also won the gold medal for most points scored in the flyball junior division. Doing well in the classroom and the dome alike."

Flyball was a sport played in a dome where the gravity was set to 0.15 Gs. It was a simple sport in which the goal was to throw a ball into a basket that would at irregular intervals move at high speed along the wall. However, the same sort of charm also seen in dance could be seen in the figures that fought over the ball in midair, handling it as it slowly revolved.

"Julian, is that true?"

Julian's irresponsible guardian looked at the boy, surprised, and the boy nodded, flushing slightly in the cheeks.

"The admiral must be the only one who didn't know," Frederica said in a lightly teasing tone that made Yang blush. "Julian's something of a celebrity in this town."

They placed their orders. With three glasses of a 670 vintage red wine and one of ginger ale, they toasted Julian Mintz's award for scoring the most goals, and then the food was brought out. It was after many plates had been brought to their table that Senior Admiral Greenhill brought up an entirely unexpected topic.

"By the way, Yang, you still don't have any plans about getting married, do you?"

Yang's and Frederica's knives both screeched against their plates simultaneously, and the elderly waiter, an aficionado of traditional chinaware, raised his eyebrows unconsciously.

"That's right. When peace arrives, I'll think about it."

Saying nothing, Frederica was sawing away with her still-downturned knife and fork. There was an ever-so-slight element of violence in her handling of them. Julian was looking at his guardian with deep interest.

"I had a friend who died and left behind a fiancée. When I think about that, I just can't . . . not right now . . ."

He spoke of Lieutenant Commander Lappe, who had died at the Battle of Astarte. Senior Admiral Greenhill nodded and then changed the subject again.

"You know Jessica Edwards, don't you? She was voted in as a representative in last week's special election. For the Planet Terneuzen electoral district."

As with Marshal Sitolet, colorful, multipronged ambushes were also a strong suit of Senior Admiral Greenhill's, it seemed.

"Oh? I can imagine the support she must've gotten from the antiwar faction."

"That's right. And there were naturally attacks from the prowar side . . ."

"Such as from, say, the Patriotic Knights Corps?"

"The Patriotic Knights Corps? Listen, now, those guys are idiots. They've never even been worth talking about. You agree, right? . . . Mmm, this jelly salad's fantastic."

"I agree," said Yang, in reference to the jelly salad.

That the Patriotic Knights were idiots Yang was willing to allow, but one couldn't say with certainty that their exaggerated and caricatured actions were not the result of skillfully planned direction. After all, hadn't the young generation that had fanatically supported one Rudolf von Goldenbaum been greeted early on with grimaces and smiles of pity by the intelligentsia of the Galactic Federation?

Perhaps in the shadow of a thick curtain, outside the sight of the spectator seats, someone was wearing a satisfied smile even now.

IX

On the way back home, Yang was thinking about Jessica Edwards in the seat of a self-driving taxi.

"I want to keep going, to always continue asking those who hold authority: 'Where are you? When you are sending our soldiers into the jaws of death, where are you? What are you doing . . . ?'"

That had apparently been the climax of Jessica's speech. Yang couldn't help remembering the scene at the memorial service held after the defeat at Astarte. Not even Defense Committee Chair Trünicht, who prided himself on his eloquence, had been able to resist in the face of her accusations. That alone must have been enough to make her the focus of all the hatred and hostility of the prowar faction. One thing was certain:

the path she had chosen would be a road more treacherous than the Iserlohn Corridor.

The taxi screeched to a sudden halt. Normally, this should have never happened. Cars never moved in such a way as to let inertia exert unnecessary force on the human body—at least as long as the control system was running. Something very out of the ordinary had just happened.

Opening the door manually, Yang stepped out into the street. A police officer in a blue uniform came running up, his massive body swaying ponderously. He recognized Yang's face, and after expressing at length how moved he was to be able to meet a national hero, explained the situation.

"An anomaly's occurred in the traffic-control computer at the Municipal Traffic Control Center," he said.

"An anomaly?"

"I don't know the details—apparently it was simple human error that occurred during data entry. Anyway, just about every workplace is short on experienced people these days, so this sort of thing's nothing unusual."

The police officer laughed, but then, faced with Julian's direct and unfriendly stare, forced himself to pull together a solemn expression.

"Ah, ahem, but this is no time to be laughing about it. Because of this, every public transportation system in this district is going to be stopped for the next three hours. Even the slidewalks and maglev roads are at a total standstill."

"Total?"

"Yes, total."

From the officer's attitude, it almost seemed like he was proud of it. Although Yang found it humorous, this was no laughing matter. This accident and the officer's words added up to something that sent a chill through his heart. The system that was controlling and running their society had grown alarmingly weak. The war's negative influence was steadily eroding their society, more softly and yet more surely than the devil's footfalls.

From his side, Julian looked up at Yang. "What shall we do, Admiral?"

"Nothing else we can do—let's walk," Yang said, and so it was decided. "It's nice to do this every once in a while. On foot, we'll get back in an hour. It'll be good exercise."

"Oh, that's right."

The policeman's eyes opened wide at this. "Oh, I couldn't let you do that! Making the hero of Iserlohn walk home on his own two feet? I'll send for a landcar or an aircar. Please use that instead."

"I can't let you do that just for me."

"Please, don't be shy about it."

"No, I think I'm gonna be shy about it," Yang said.

It took a bit of an effort to keep his displeasure from showing in his face or voice.

"Let's go, Julian."

"Aye, aye, sir."

With that cheerful answer, the boy started out at a nimble skip, then came to a sudden halt. Yang looked back at him suspiciously.

"What's the matter, Julian? You don't like walking?"

Perhaps his voice was just a little sharp from his residual displeasure.

"No, it isn't that."

"Well then, why aren't you coming?"

"That's . . . the wrong direction."

Yang turned on his heel without a word. *As long as a space fleet commander doesn't get the fleet's heading wrong, there's nothing to worry about.* He considered saying that, or something similarly unsporting, then decided against it. Truth be told, his confidence even failed him on that point from time to time. That was why Yang prized the precision-tuned fleet management of Vice Commander Fischer so highly.

Long rows of stopped maglev cars stretched out to form long walls on the streets, and people who could do nothing about it were walking aimlessly around. Yang and Julian calmly threaded their way between them.

"The stars are really beautiful tonight, Admiral," said Julian, lifting up his gaze to the starry sky above. The gleaming lights of countless stars formed patterns too complex to take in, testifying with their continual twinkling to the existence of the planet's atmosphere.

Yang was unable to completely clear his mind of ill feelings.

Everyone was reaching up toward that night sky, trying to grasp the star that was given them. But people who knew their own star's exact position were few and far between. *And what about me—Yang Wen-li? Have I clearly determined where my own star is? Swept along by circumstance, have I lost sight of it? Or could I have been wrong all along about which one is mine?*

"Admiral?" said Julian in a crystal clear voice.

"What is it?"

"Just now, you and I were both looking at the same star. Look, that big blue one."

"Hmm, that star is..."

"What's it called?"

"It's on the tip of my tongue..." Yang said.

If he had started tracing back that thread of a memory, surely he could have arrived at the answer, but Yang didn't feel like forcing himself to do it. *There's not even the slightest need for this boy at my side to look up at the same star as me,* Yang thought.

A man should grab hold of a star that's for him and him alone. No matter how unlucky a star it may be.

CHAPTER 7:

A FARCE BETWEEN THE ACTS

I

In the Phezzan Land Dominion, the interests of the Galactic Empire were represented by the imperial high commissioner. Count Jochen von Remscheid was the holder of that office.

This white-haired aristocrat with near-colorless eyes had been sent there from Odin around the same time that Rubinsky had been sworn in as landesherr and was spoken of as the "White Fox" behind his back. It went without saying that this name was playing off of Rubinsky's "Black Fox."

That night, the site to which Rubinsky had unofficially invited him was neither the landesherr's office nor his official residence, nor was it even his private residence. It was a place that until four and a half centuries prior had been a bowl-shaped dip in a mountainous region with heavy salt deposits, but was now an artificial lake. On its shore, there stood a mountain cottage that had no legal connection to Rubinsky. Its owner was one of Rubinsky's many mistresses.

When someone had once asked him, "Landesherr, Your Excellency, just how many mistresses do you have?" Rubinsky, not answering right away, had thought about it with a serious expression on his face, until at last with a cheerful smile bordering on audacity he had said, "I can only count them by the dozen."

Although there was certainly exaggeration there, he was not entirely telling tall tales. His vitality of mind and body did not in the slightest belie the impression given by his outward appearance.

Rubinsky's philosophy was that life should be enjoyed grandly. Full-bodied spirits, foods that melted on the tongue, renowned melodies to make the heartstrings tremble, and graceful, supple beauties: he was a lover of them all.

These, however, were mere entertainments. His greatest amusement lay elsewhere—for games of political and military intrigue were played with the fates of men and of nations as the intangible chips, and neither wine nor women could compare to the thrill they delivered.

Even Machiavellian trickery, sufficiently refined, can be an art, Rubinsky reflected. *Only the lowest of the low resort to threats of armed force. The words on their placards may differ, but on that point there's little difference between the empire and alliance. Both are twin children born of a monster named Rudolf,* he thought with malice, *and share a mutual hatred for one another.*

"Well then, since Your Excellency the Landesherr has gone to such trouble inviting me out here tonight, there must be something you wish to discuss," Count von Remscheid prompted as he set his wine glass down on a marble table.

Enjoying himself as he looked back at the man's guarded expression, Rubinsky replied, "Indeed I do, and I believe the topic will interest you . . . The Free Planets Alliance is planning an all-out military offensive against the empire."

The imperial aristocrat needed several seconds to digest the meaning of that reply.

"Your Excellency means to say that the alliance—" was what the count started to say, but then his own words registered on him, and he corrected himself: "That the rebels are plotting lawless outrages against our empire?"

"It seems that after capturing the empire's proud fortress of Iserlohn, the alliance is boiling over with a lust for war."

The count narrowed his eyes slightly. "By occupying Iserlohn, the rebels now hold a bridgehead in imperial territory. That is a fact. But it does not perforce follow that they will launch an all-out invasion right away."

"Be that as it may, it's clear the alliance is drawing up plans for a large-scale attack."

"What does 'large-scale' mean?"

"A force over twenty million strong. Which might actually exceed thirty million."

"Thirty million."

The imperial aristocrat's near-colorless eyes shone white in the illumination.

Even the imperial military had never mobilized that large a force all at once. The difficulty in doing so was not merely a problem of numbers; it also involved organization, management, and the ability to run it all. Did the alliance have that kind of capability? Whether they did or not, this was certainly vital intelligence, but...

"But, Landesherr, Your Excellency, why are you sharing this information with me? What are your aims?"

"I'm a bit surprised Your Excellency the High Commissioner would ask me such a thing. Has our dominion ever once done anything that would put the empire at a disadvantage?"

"No, I've no recollection of such a thing. Naturally, our empire has the utmost confidence in Phezzan's loyalty and faithfulness."

It was an exchange with an emptiness and insincerity of which both sides were well aware.

At last, Count von Remscheid left. Watching his landcar as it hurriedly raced away on his monitor screen, a cruel smile appeared on Rubinsky's face.

The high commissioner would run to his office and send an emergency message to Odin. The intelligence Rubinsky had just fed him could not be ignored.

Having lost Iserlohn, the imperial military would blanch at this news and begin preparations to intercept the attack. Reinhard von

Lohengramm would almost certainly be the one sent out to meet them, but this time Rubinsky wanted him to win for the empire without winning too much.

If Reinhard didn't show, that would be a problem, actually.

Rubinsky had not informed the empire when he had received word that Yang was to attack Iserlohn with only half a fleet. For one thing, he'd never dreamed the attempt would succeed, and for another, he had felt like watching to see what kind of clever scheme Yang would come up with.

The conclusion had been such as could even surprise Rubinsky. *To think he had a trick like that up his sleeve!* he had thought, genuinely impressed.

He was not in a position, however, to simply be impressed and leave it at that. The balance of military power had tilted toward the alliance, and now he needed to nudge it back slightly toward the empire.

He needed them fighting each other—hurting each other—more and more.

II

Marquis Lichtenlade, the minister of state and acting imperial prime minister, received a visit one night at the estate where he lived from Viscount Gerlach, the minister of finance.

The occasion for the minister of finance's visit was to report that one stage of the Kastropf Uprising's mop-up had been completed. Having a subordinate send a report by visiphone from one's own home was not a tradition that existed in the empire.

"The disposition of Duke von Kastropf's lands and fortune is for the most part accomplished. After liquidation, the estate's value comes to roughly five hundred billion imperial marks."

"He certainly had been saving, hadn't he?"

"Most certainly. Although I do feel a slight twinge of pity for the man when I think of how diligently he'd saved just to pay it all into the national treasury..."

After enjoying sufficiently the full-bodied aroma of the red wine set before him, the minister of finance touched it to his lips. The minister of state set down his glass and changed his expression.

"By the way, there's a little matter I'd like to discuss with you."

"And what might that be?"

"A short while ago, I received an urgent communiqué from Count von Remscheid on Phezzan. He says that the rebel forces will stage a massive invasion of imperial territory."

"The rebel forces—!" The minister of state nodded at him. The minister of finance set his half-filled glass on the table, causing the remaining wine to churn violently. "This is a serious problem."

"It is. Yet at the same time, I can't say it doesn't present an opportunity." The minister of state crossed his arms. "We have a need right now to fight a battle and win. According to the minister of the interior's report, there's some sort of revolutionary mood being fomented yet again amongst the commoners. They seem to have some vague idea of our losing Iserlohn. In order to blow all that away, we have to destroy the rebels and restore the dignity of the imperial household. In conjunction with that, we need to let the commoners suck on a bit of candy as well. A special pardon for thought criminals, an easing up on taxation, a decrease in liquor prices—something like that."

"Indulge them too much and the commoners will take advantage of you. I've seen the radicals' underground writings—they're full of outrageous declarations. 'Humans have rights before duties,' and the like. Don't you think a special pardon would only spoil them?"

"It's as you say, but we can't govern exclusively by the stick," the minister of state said reprovingly.

"That's true, but pandering to the people more than necessary is . . . But no, let's leave that for another time. This report of the rebels invading our empire, was the source of it Rubinsky?"

The minister of state nodded.

"The Black Fox of Phezzan," said the minister of finance, clucking his tongue loudly. "Lately, I get the feeling the misers of Phezzan might be a much greater danger to the empire than the rebels are. There's no telling what they might be plotting."

"I agree," said Lichtenlade. "But for now, it's the rebel threat we need to deal with. Who should we assign to the defense . . . ?"

"The golden brat will probably want to do it," said Gerlach. "Why not let him?"

"It's best not to make an emotional decision. Suppose we let him: If he were to succeed, his reputation would rise to a whole other level, and the room we have to impede him would evaporate. If, on the other hand, he were to fail, it would mean a fight against rebel forces under extremely unfavorable conditions—within the core of the empire, most likely, against a huge horde of thirty million whose morale would be soaring because of their victory."

"Your Excellency is too pessimistic," said the minister of finance, who leaned forward and began to explain his own position.

"Even if the rebels are victorious, they won't come out of battle with Count von Lohengramm's force unscathed. The count is certainly no incompetent and will doubtless inflict considerable casualties on the enemy. Furthermore, the rebel force will be on a campaign very far from their home base, unable to resupply at will. On top of that, they will be lacking the geographical advantage.

"For these reasons, imperial forces will be able to head off a battle-weary enemy at their leisure. Given the circumstances, in fact, it may not even be necessary to go out and fight them at all. If we simply wage a battle of attrition, the enemy will suffer supply shortages and psychological strain, and in the end they'll have no choice but to withdraw. If the imperial forces wait for that moment to pursue and attack, victory will come with little difficulty."

"I see," said Minister of State Lichtenlade. "That settles that in the event the brat is defeated. But what if he wins? Between his military accomplishments and his exploitation of His Highness's favor, he's more than we can manage, even now. I can only imagine how much more spoiled he'd become if he were victorious."

"I think we should let him get spoiled. One man who's risen beyond his station? We can fry him up at our leisure. It's not as if he's with his troops twenty-four hours a day."

"Hmm..."

"Once the rebel fleet has been wiped out, the golden brat will fall as well," the minister of finance said coldly. "Shall we not make the most of his talents while we have need of them?"

III

It was August 12 of the standard calendar, SE 796. On the Free Planets Alliance's capital of Heinessen, an operations planning session was being held for the invasion of the Galactic Empire.

Gathered in an underground meeting room at Joint Operational Headquarters were the director, Marshal Sitolet, and thirty-six admirals, which meant that the commanding officer of the Thirteenth Fleet, newly minted Vice Admiral Yang Wen-li, was among them as well.

Yang didn't look well. As he had once told Captain von Schönkopf, he had believed the threat of war would recede if Iserlohn fell. The reality, however, had taken exactly the opposite shape—one that for Yang's part reminded him of the fact that he was young—or rather, naive.

Even so, Yang was naturally in no mood to acknowledge the logical soundness of arguments for this mobilization and expansion of the war.

The victory at Iserlohn had been nothing more than Yang's solo gambit paying off. It didn't mean that the Alliance Armed Forces were actually capable of defeating the empire. The true state of affairs was that the troops were worn out to the point of exhaustion, and the wealth and power of the nation supporting them was riding a downward curve.

However, this fact, which Yang himself acknowledged was one the political and military leadership just didn't seem to understand. Military victories were like narcotics, and a sweet drug called "occupied Iserlohn" seemed to have caused a sudden blooming of warlike hallucinations lurking in the hearts of the people. Even in the national assembly, where cooler heads should have prevailed, they were calling with one voice for "invasion of imperial territory." The government's manipulation of information was skillful, too, but...

Did we pay too little in taking Iserlohn? Yang wondered. *If it had come*

at the cost of a bloodbath that climbed into the tens of thousands, would the
people have said, "Enough, already!" instead?

Would they have thought, "We've won, but we're dead tired. Shouldn't
we rest for a while, reexamine the past, think about our future, and then
ask ourselves, is there really something out there that would make fighting on worth it?"

That hadn't happened. "Who would have imagined that victory could
be this easy?" the people had thought. "Who would have imagined that
the fruits of victory could be this delectable?" It was an irony that the
one who had put those thoughts in their heads had been Yang himself.
This was the last thing the young admiral had wanted, and these days
the brandy content of his tea was only increasing.

The expeditionary force's order of battle had not yet been announced
to the public, though it was decided already.

Marshal Lasalle Lobos, the Alliance Armed Forces Space Armada's commander in chief himself, was personally taking the post of supreme fleet
commander. As the number two man in uniform after Joint Operational
Headquarters director Sitolet, his competitive relationship with Sitolet
was one that stretched back over a quarter of a century.

The job of vice commander in chief had been left vacant, and taking
the seat of joint chief of staff was Senior Admiral Dwight Greenhill—
Frederica Greenhill's father. Under his command had been placed Vice
Admiral Konev, the operations chief of staff; Rear Admiral Birolinen, the
intelligence chief of staff, and Rear Admiral Caselnes, the rear service
chief of staff. This was the first duty on the front in quite some time for
Alex Caselnes, who was known for his outstanding knack for getting
things done in the office.

Under the operations chief of staff, there were five operations staff
officers. One of these was Rear Admiral Andrew Fork, a brilliant man
who had graduated top of his class from Officers' Academy six years ago;
this young officer was the original architect of the plan for the upcoming
expedition.

The intelligence staff and the rear service staff consisted of three
officers each.

To these sixteen were added high-level aides and essential communications, security, and other personnel, and together they formed the supreme command center.

To begin with, eight space fleets were to be mobilized as combat units:

The Third Fleet, commanded by Vice Admiral Lefêbres.
The Fifth Fleet, commanded by Vice Admiral Bucock.
The Seventh Fleet, commanded by Vice Admiral Hawood.
The Eighth Fleet, commanded by Vice Admiral Appleton.
The Ninth Fleet, commanded by Vice Admiral Al Salem.
The Tenth Fleet, commanded by Vice Admiral Urannf.
The Twelfth Fleet, commanded by Vice Admiral Borodin.
The Thirteenth Fleet, commanded by Vice Admiral Yang.

The Fourth and Sixth Fleets, having been dealt severe blows at the Battle of Astarte, had been recently joined with the remaining forces from the Second to form Yang's Thirteenth Fleet, so only two of the ten fleets that made up the Alliance Armed Forces Space Armada—the First and Eleventh—were being left behind in the homeland.

To these forces were added armored mobile troops known collectively as ground combat units, intra-atmosphere airborne combat squadrons, amphibious squadrons, naval units, ranger units, and all manner of other independently operating units. Heavy weapons specialists from the Domestic Security Corps were also going to participate.

As for noncombat personnel, the maximum number possible were to be mobilized from technological, engineering, supply, communications, space traffic control, maintenance, electronic data, medical, lifestyle, and other fields.

The total number mobilized came to 30,227,400 people. This meant that 60 percent of the Free Planets Alliance's entire military was to be mobilized all at once. That number also accounted for 0.23 percent of the alliance's full population of thirteen billion.

With an operational plan before them whose gargantuan scope knew no precedent, even admirals who had fought bravely in many prior battles were, here and there, conspicuously unable to clear their heads. They wiped nonexistent sweat from their foreheads, downed glass after glass of the ice water prepared for them, or whispered to colleagues in the seats next to them.

At 0945, Marshal Sitolet, director of Joint Operational Headquarters, entered the room with his top aide, Rear Admiral Marinesk, and the meeting got under way immediately.

There was no sense of grand exaltation in the expression or voice of Marshal Sitolet when he opened his mouth to speak: "The plan we're discussing today for a campaign into imperial territory has already been approved by the High Council, but..."

All of the admirals in attendance knew that he had been against this deployment.

"Detailed plans for the expeditionary force's actions are not yet established. The purpose of today's meeting is to decide on these. I need not remind you at this point that the Alliance Armed Forces is the free military of a free nation. I'm hoping that in that spirit, you'll carry out a vigorous exchange of ideas and discussion today."

There may have been some present who from the lack of enthusiasm in the director's remarks understood his anguish, and there may have been some as well who could perceive in his professorial intonation a passive-aggressive resistance. The director closed his mouth, and for a moment no one said anything. It was as if all present were simmering in their own thoughts.

In the back of his mind, Yang was replaying something he'd heard from Caselnes the other day:

"At any rate, there are unified regional elections coming up soon. On the domestic front, there's been a string of internal scandals going on for a while now, so if they want to win, they'll have to divert the public's attention to the outside. That's what this military campaign is all about."

That's an old trick rulers use to distract the people from their own bad governance, Yang thought. How the founding father Heinessen would have been grieved to know about this! His wish had never been to have a statue fifty meters tall erected in his honor; surely his hope had been for the construction of a governmental system that posed no danger to its people, where the rights and freedoms of citizens would not be infringed upon by the arbitrary whims of rulers.

But just as humans must eventually grow old and infirm, perhaps so, too, their nations must eventually grow corrupt and decadent. Even so, the notion of sending thirty million troops to the battlefield in order to win an election and retain power for another four years transcended Yang's comprehension. Thirty million human beings, thirty million lives, thirty million destinies, thirty million possibilities, thirty million joys and furies and sorrows and pleasures—by sending them into the jaws of death, by swelling the ranks of the sacrificed with them, those in safe places monopolized all the profit.

Though the ages turned, this outrageous correlation between those who made war and those who were made to make war had not improved in the slightest since the dawn of civilization. If anything, the kings and champions of the ancient world may have been slightly better—if only on the point of having stood themselves at the heads of their armies, exposing their own skins to the threat of physical harm. It could also be argued that the ethics of those forced to wage wars had only degenerated as well . . .

"I believe this campaign is the most daring feat attempted since the founding of our alliance. There is no greater honor for me as a soldier than to be able to participate in it as a staff officer."

Those were the first words that were spoken.

The flat, monotonous voice, like that of someone reading off a script, belonged to Rear Admiral Andrew Fork.

He was only twenty-six, but he looked a good deal older than that, and next to him it was Yang who seemed boyish. The flesh on his pallid cheeks was too thin, although he was not bad looking around the eyes and brows. However, his way of looking down at people and then sweeping his gaze upward conspired with the crook of his mouth to give him a rather gloomy impression. Though of course Yang—to whose experience the word "honor student" was nil—was perhaps given to regarding genius through lenses of prejudice.

The next to speak after Fork's long, flowery trumpeting of the military's grand design—that is to say, the operation he had drafted himself—was Vice Admiral Uranff, commander of the Tenth Fleet.

Uranff was a well-built man in the prime of his life, descended from a nomadic tribe said to have once conquered half the world of ancient Earth. He had a dark complexion and eyes that glinted with a sharp light. His courageous leadership made him stand out even among the admirals of the alliance and had brought him popularity among the citizenry.

"We're soldiers and as such will go anywhere if ordered. If that means striking the very seat of the Goldenbaum Dynasty's tyranny, we will go, and gladly. However, it should go without saying that there's a difference between a daring plan and a reckless one. Thorough preparation is essential, but first I'd like to ask what the strategic goal of this campaign is. Do we plunge into imperial territory, fight one battle, and then call it a day? Are we to occupy a part of the empire's territory militarily, and if so will the occupation be temporary or permanent? And if the answer is 'permanent,' will the occupied territory be turned into a military stronghold? Or are we to deal a destructive blow to the imperial military and not turn back until we've made the emperor swear an oath of peace? And before all that, is this operation itself considered short-term or long-term? It's a long-winded list of questions, but I'd like to hear the answers."

Uranff sat down, and Marshals Sitolet and Lobos both directed their gazes toward Rear Admiral Fork, prompting him to reply.

"We will penetrate deep into the empire's territory with a large force. That alone will be enough to strike terror into the hearts of the imperials."

That was Fork's answer.

"So, we withdraw without fighting?"

"I'm thinking we should maintain a high level of flexibility and deal with each situation as it comes our way."

Uranff's brows drew together, showing his dissatisfaction. "Can you not give us a few more specifics? This is far too abstract."

"What he means is, we just bumble around haphazardly, correct?"

The crook in Fork's lip grew more pronounced at that sarcasm-spiced comment. Vice Admiral Bucock, commander of the Fifth Fleet, was the one who had spoken it. He was a true veteran of the Alliance Armed Forces, several notches more so than Marshal Sitolet, Marshal Lobos, Senior Admiral Greenhill, and the like. He was not a graduate of Officers' Academy but had instead worked his way up from a raw recruit, and so although he was lower than they were in terms of rank, he exceeded them in age and experience. As a tactician, his reputation placed him in the bounds of "proficient."

Fork didn't reply; although he naturally felt some reserve toward the man, there was also the fact that Bucock had not been formally recognized to speak. On those grounds, Fork had apparently decided to politely ignore him.

"Does anyone else have anything…?" he said somewhat forcedly.

After a moment's hesitation, Yang asked to be recognized.

"I'd like to hear the reason the invasion has been set for this point in time."

Of course Fork wasn't going to say, "Because of the election." But how would he answer?

"For every battle, there exists something called the moment of opportunity," said Rear Admiral Fork, haughtily beginning an explanation of the matter to Yang. "Letting it pass, ultimately, would be to stand in defiance of destiny itself. Someday we might regretfully look back and say, 'If only we'd taken action then!' But by then it will be too late."

"So in other words, our best chance to go on offense against the empire is right now. Is that what you want to say, Commodore?"

Yang had a feeling it was ridiculous to ask for confirmation, but he asked anyway.

"On *major* offense," Fork corrected.

He sure does like his adjectives, Yang thought.

"The imperial military is in a panic over the loss of Iserlohn—they have no idea what to do. At this precise moment in history, what but victory could lie ahead for an alliance force of unprecedented magnitude, formed up into long, stately columns, forging ahead with the flag of freedom and justice raised high?"

There was a shade of self-intoxication in his voice as he spoke, pointing at the 3-D display.

"But this operation takes us too deep into the enemy camp. Our formation will get too long, and there'll be difficulties with resupply and communications. Also, by striking us on those long, thin flanks, the enemy will be able to divide our forces easily."

Yang's voice grew heated as he argued, though this was not necessarily in sync with what he was really thinking. After all, how much did the details of execution-level issues matter when the tactical plan itself wasn't even sound? Yet still he couldn't bear to not try telling him.

"Why is it just the danger of being divided that you're emphasizing? An enemy that plowed into the center of our fleet would be caught fore and aft in a pincer attack, and would no doubt be soundly defeated. The risk is insignificant."

Fork's optimistic arguments exhausted Yang. Fighting back the desire to say, "Go ahead, then—do whatever you want," Yang continued to counter him.

"The commander of the imperial force is most likely going to be Count von Lohengramm. There's something about his military expertise that's beyond imagining. Don't you think you should take that into account and come up with a plan that's just a little more cautious?"

After he finished speaking, Senior Admiral Greenhill answered before Fork was able to.

"Vice Admiral, I'm aware you have a high opinion of Count von Lohengramm. He's still young, however, and even he must make errors and mistakes."

Senior Admiral Greenhill's words didn't make much of an impression on Yang.

"That's true. However, the factors that result in victory and defeat are ultimately relative to one another . . . so if we make a bigger mistake than he does, it only stands to reason that he'll win and we'll lose."

And the main point, Yang wanted to say, *is that the plan itself is wrongheaded.*

"In any case, that's nothing more than a prediction," Fork concluded.

"Overestimating the enemy, fearing him more than necessary . . . that's the most shameful thing of all for a warrior. Considering how that saps our troops' morale and how their decision making and their actions can be dulled by it, the result is ultimately beneficial to the enemy, regardless of your intent. I do hope you'll be more cautious about that."

There was a loud noise from the surface of the meeting room table. Vice Admiral Bucock had struck it with the palm of his hand.

"Rear Admiral Fork, don't you think what you said just now was disrespectful?"

"How so?" As the elderly admiral skewered him with a sharp glare, Fork puffed out his chest.

"Just because he didn't agree with you and advised caution, you think it's acceptable to go around saying he's abetting the enemy?"

"I was merely making a general statement. I find it highly irritating to have that interpreted as the defamation of an individual."

The thin flesh on Fork's cheeks was twitching. Yang could see it clearly. He didn't even feel like getting upset.

"From the beginning, the purpose of this campaign is to realize our grand and noble purpose of liberating the twenty-five billion people in the Galactic Empire who are suffering under the crushing weight of despotism. And I have to say that anyone who opposes that is effectively taking the side of the empire. Am I mistaken?"

Those in their seats were growing quieter in inverse proportion to his increasingly shrill voice. It wasn't that they had been moved by his words; rather, the mood had been thoroughly spoiled.

"Even if the enemy had the geographical advantage, the greater troop strength, or even new weapons of unimaginable power, we could not use that as an excuse for being daunted. If we act based on our great mission—as a liberation force, as a force that's there to defend the people—then the people of the empire will greet us with cheers and cooperate willingly . . ."

As Fork's speech dragged on and on, Yang sank into silent reflection.

"New weapons of unimaginable power" were basically nonexistent. Weapons invented and put to practical use by one of two opposing camps had almost always been at least conceptually realized in the other camp as well. Tanks, submarines, nuclear-fission weapons, beam weapons, and so on had all entered the battlefield in this fashion, and the feeling of defeat experienced by the side that had lagged behind was verbalized not so much in the form of "How can this be?" as "I was afraid that might happen." Between individuals, there were great inequalities in human powers of imagination, but those gaps shrunk markedly when viewed as totals within groups. In particular, new weapons were only made possible through the accumulation of technological and economic power, which was why there had been no air raids during the Paleolithic.

Also, looking at history, new weapons had almost never been the deciding factor in war—the exception being the Spanish invasion of the Incan empire, but even that had been colored deeply by their having fraudulently exploited an ancient Incan legend. Archimedes, who had lived in the ancient Greek city-state of Siracusa, had devised all sorts of scientific weapons, but they hadn't been able to stop the Roman invasion.

"Unimaginable" was rather a word more likely to be uttered when a sea change took place in tactical thought. Certainly, there were times when these changes were triggered by the invention and introduction of a new weapon. Mass use of firearms, the use of air power to rule the sea, high-speed mobile warfare using combinations of tanks and aircraft—all of them were examples of this. But Hannibal's envelopment tactics, Napoléon's mounted charges against enemy infantry, Mao Tsetung's guerilla warfare, Genghis Khan's use of his cavalry units, Sun Tzu's psychological and informational warfare, Epaminondas's deep hoplite echelons...all these had been devised and implemented without any relationship to new weaponry.

Yang was not afraid of any new weapon of the empire. What he did fear was the military genius of Reinhard von Lohengramm and the alliance's own faulty assumption that the people of the empire were seeking freedom and equality more than they were peace and stability in their lives. That could neither be counted on nor forecast. There was no way that a factor like that should be included in the calculation of battle plans.

With a hint of gloom, Yang made a prediction: considering how unfathomably irresponsible the motivations behind this campaign were, that irresponsibility was going to extend to its planning and execution as well.

The distribution of the expeditionary force was decided. On point were Admiral Uranff's Tenth Fleet, and in the second column, Yang's Thirteenth.

General headquarters for the expeditionary force would be set up at Iserlohn Fortress, and for the duration of the operation, the supreme commander of the expeditionary force would also double as commanding officer of Iserlohn.

IV

The meeting drew to a close having borne no fruit as far as Yang was concerned. Just as he was about to head back home, though, Yang was stopped by Marshal Sitolet, director of Joint Operational Headquarters, and stayed behind. Without a sound, the dregs of wasted energy drifted like a convection current through the air.

"So, you must be dying to say I should've let you retire," said Sitolet. His voice had become corroded by a sense of labors come to naught.

"I was naive, too. I was thinking if we captured Iserlohn, the flames of war would recede afterward. Yet here we are."

Yang fell silent, having lost sight of the words he should say. Of course there was little doubt that in Marshal Sitolet's calculus, the arrival of peace would have secured his position and strengthened his influence, yet compared to the reckless adventurism and political maneuvering of the prowar faction, he was far easier to sympathize with.

"Ultimately, I guess I got tripped up by my own calculations. If Iserlohn hadn't fallen, the hawks might not be making a gamble this dangerous. At any rate, you could call this just deserts as far as it concerns me, but for you I've made a real mess."

"...Are you planning to retire?"

"Right now, I can't. Once this campaign is finished, though, I'll have no choice but to resign. Regardless of whether it fails or succeeds."

If the expedition failed, Marshal Sitolet, as the highest-ranking man in uniform, would of course be driven to take responsibility with his resignation. On the other hand, if it succeeded, there was only one higher post with which to reward Marshal Lobos, supreme fleet commander of expeditionary force, for his accomplishment: that of director of Joint Operational Headquarters. The fact that Marshal Sitolet had been against this campaign would also work against him; his expulsion would take the form of a graceful bow out to make way for Marshal Lobos. No matter which way the die rolled, his future was already decided. All that was left for Sitolet was to prepare himself for it gracefully.

"I'm only telling you this because the circumstances are what they are, but what I am hoping for is that this expedition fails with the smallest possible number of casualties."

Yang didn't say a word.

"If it's a rout, there'll of course be a lot of blood spilt over nothing. But what happens if we win? It's clear as day the hawks will pounce on the opportunity, and neither reason nor political calculation will be enough to make them accept subservience to civil governance any longer. Then they will stampede and eventually fall into a gorge. The history books are full of nations that were driven to ultimate defeat because they won a battle when they shouldn't have. You should know all about that."

"Yeah…"

"The reason I turned down your resignation was because I figured I could count on you to understand if things came to this. It's not like I foresaw our present circumstances, but as a result of them, your presence in the military has become even more vital."

Yang continued to listen in silence.

"You know a lot about history, and that's given you a certain contempt for authority and military power. I can't say I blame you, but no organized nation can exist free of those things. That being the case, political and military power should be placed in the hands of competent and honest people—not those who are the polar opposite—so the state can be reined in by reason and conscience. Being a soldier, I won't venture to speak of politics, but speaking strictly of his role in the military, Rear Admiral Fork is unfit."

The intensity with which he spoke those words surprised Yang.

For a moment, Sitolet looked like he was struggling to control his own emotions.

"He carried this operations plan directly to the chairman of the High Council's secretary by way of a private route. That he sold them on it as a strategy for staying in power is enough to tell me that he's motivated by a lust for personal advancement. He's aiming for the top seat in the military, but at present he has a rival who's just too strong, and he's chomping at the bit to mark an achievement that will put him ahead of that person. He graduated top of his class from Officers' Academy and has a funny thing about not losing to regular Joes."

Yang murmured a casual "I see" to show he was listening, and a smile appeared on Marshal Sitolet's face for the first time.

"You sure can be dense sometimes. His rival isn't somebody else—it's you."

"Me, sir?"

"Yes, you."

"But, Director, I—"

"This has nothing to do with however you may evaluate yourself. The problem is in what Fork is thinking and the method he's taken for achieving his goals. I have to say, it's too political, in the negative sense of the word. Even if it weren't for that"—here the marshal sighed—"you must have grasped something of his character from today's meeting. He displays his talents not in actual achievements but in eloquent speech, and what's worse, he looks down on others while trying to make himself look distinguished. He doesn't really have the talent he thinks he does, though…Entrusting anyone's fate to him other than his own is just too dangerous."

"Just now, you were saying the importance of my being here had increased…" Yang said pensively. "By that are you telling me to oppose Rear Admiral Fork?"

"Fork isn't exactly the only one. When you reach the highest position in the service, you'll be able to hamper and weed out people like him by yourself. That's what I'm hoping you'll do. Though I know it's nothing but aggravation as far as you're concerned."

Silence clung to the pair like a heavy wet robe. Yang had to physically shake his head in order to shrug it off.

"Your Excellency the Director is always assigning me tasks that are too big for me. Telling me to take Iserlohn was one of those, too, but—"

"But you did it, didn't you?"

"That time, I succeeded, yes, but…" Yang broke off and almost fell silent again, but he pushed on, saying, "It's not that I hold authority and military power in contempt—no, the truth is, those things terrify me. Most people who gain authority and military power turn ugly—I could give a ton of examples. And I don't have the confidence to say I wouldn't change as well."

"You said *most* people. Which is exactly right. Not everybody changes."

"In any case, I intend to be a man of discretion and stay the greater part away from valor. I want to do some kind of work within the range that I'm able and then live a relaxed, easygoing life—is that what they call lazy by nature?"

"That's right. Lazy by nature."

As he stared at Yang, who was at a loss for words, Director Sitolet broke into an amused smile.

"I've long struggled with this myself. It's not a lot of fun to work hard all alone and see other people living relaxed lives of ease. But first of all, if I can't get you to do the hard work suited to your talent, that's what I'd call unfair."

"…Unfair, sir?"

Aside from grimacing, Yang knew of no other way of expressing his emotions. In Sitolet's case, the director had probably decided to work hard willingly and of his own accord, but Yang didn't think he was like that. At any rate, the one certain thing was that he had lost his chance to resign.

∨

Before Reinhard were arrayed the young admirals attached to the Lohengramm admiralität: Kircheis, Mittermeier, von Reuentahl, Wittenfeld, Lutz, Wahlen, and Kempf, followed by von Oberstein.

Reinhard considered them the best of the best from the imperial military's human resource pool. However, he needed to assemble still more, of both quality and quantity. He needed it said of this admiralität that an appointment here meant recognition as a talented and capable individual. The admiralität's reputation was already significant, but Reinhard wanted the superiority of his admiralität to be universally apprehended.

"I've received the following report from imperial military intelligence," Reinhard said, looking around the assembly, and the admirals straightened their posture just slightly. "Recently, the frontier rebels of the so-called Free Planets Alliance have succeeded in stealing the empire's frontline base of Iserlohn. This much you know already, but since then, the rebels have been massing their forces at Iserlohn in vast numbers. According to our estimates, there are two hundred thousand vessels and thirty million troops—moreover, these are bare minimum estimates."

Murmurs of surprise and even admiration wended their way among the admirals. To command a giant fleet was a warrior's greatest ambition, and despite this one belonging to the enemy, they still couldn't help feeling impressed by its scale.

"What this means is as clear as day, nor can there be an iota of doubt: the rebels intend to launch an all-out assault directed at the core of our empire." Reinhard's eyes seemed to burn. "I have secret orders from the minister of state: the duty of intercepting and defending against this military threat is to be mine. Orders from the emperor will come down in the next couple of days. As a warrior, there is no greater honor I could hope for. I expect a good hard fight out of you all."

Up to this point, he had been speaking in a hard, formal tone, but here he smiled unexpectedly. It was a smile filled with energy and spirit, although it was not the purehearted, transparent smile that he showed only to Annerose and Kircheis.

"In other words, this means all the other corps are ornamental dolls decorating the imperial palace, and not to be counted upon. This is an excellent chance for promotions and medals."

The admirals smiled as well. Like Reinhard, they shared a common enmity toward highborn nobles who did nothing but gorge themselves on position and privilege; it had not been for their talents alone that Reinhard had selected these men.

"And now I'd like to talk with you about where we should intercept the enemy…"

Mittermeier and Wittenfeld expressed a shared opinion: The rebel attack would come by way of the Iserlohn Corridor, so why not hit them the moment they emerged from it into imperial territory? "We can ascertain the point where the enemy will appear, so it will be possible to strike their vanguard and create a half-envelopment formation, which will give us the advantage and make fighting them easy—"

"No…" Reinhard said, shaking his head. He then proceeded to explain that the enemy would be expecting an attack at the point where they exited the corridor and poured into the empire's core. Their elite forces would be positioned in the vanguard, and if the remaining force didn't emerge from the corridor when they were attacked, his force would be left with no means of attacking them further.

"We should lure the enemy in deeper," Reinhard argued, and after a brief discussion, the other admirals agreed. "We lure the enemy deep into imperial territory, and then when their ranks and supply lines are stretched to the breaking point, we hit them with everything we have. I'd say that with such a strategy, victory for the defending side is assured."

"But that will take a lot of time," said Mittermeier. He had a firm, if smallish, build and certainly looked like a sharp young officer. He had unruly, honey-colored hair and gray eyes. "As this is, in rebels of the alliance's own words, the most daring feat since their founding, it's sure they'll cut no corners when it comes to the preparation of their ranks, equipment, and supply lines. It will take a considerable amount of time for their matériel to be exhausted and for their fighting spirit to wane." Mittermeier's rather concerned opinion was only natural, but Reinhard swept his gaze across his admirals, and then with a gleam of utmost confidence in his eyes, said, "No, it won't take very long at all. I'd give it less than fifty days. Von Oberstein, explain the basics of the operation."

When called upon, the staff officer with the half-silvered hair stepped forward and began to explain. As he was doing so, an air of shocked disbelief spread out among the admirals without a sound.

On August 22, SE 796, General Headquarters for the Free Planets Alliance's Expeditionary Force to Imperial Territory was established within Iserlohn Fortress. Around that same time, thirty million troops from the capital of Heinessen and its surrounding star systems were assembling columns of warships and setting out toward a distant battlespace.

CHAPTER 8:

I

For the first month, a dazzling excitement was the constant companion of all the alliance's space fleets. Then the warmth of that friendship cooled, and what remained was disappointment and, even worse, anxiety and impatience. There was a question the men began asking one another—the officers in places where no enlisted men would hear and the enlisted men in places where there were no officers.

Why doesn't the enemy show themselves?

With Admiral Urannf's Tenth Fleet in the lead, the alliance force had penetrated roughly five hundred light-years into imperial territory. Two hundred star systems had fallen into their hands, and of those, over thirty were inhabited, albeit with populations whose levels of technological development were low. A total of about fifty million civilians were living on these worlds. The colonial governors, frontier counts, tax officials, and soldiers who were supposed to be governing these people had all fled, and the alliance had been met with virtually no resistance to speak of.

"We are a liberation force."

That was what the alliance's pacification officers announced to the throngs of abandoned farmers and miners.

"We promise you liberty and equality. You won't suffer anymore under the oppression of despotism. You'll be given full political rights and begin your lives anew as free citizens."

But to their disappointment, what they found waiting for them were not the fervent cheers they had envisioned. The crowds didn't show the slightest interest, in fact, and the pacification officers' impassioned eloquence rolled right off their backs. When the farmers' representatives spoke, they would say:

"Before you give us any kind of political rights, we'd appreciate it if you'd give us the right to live first. We've got no food here. There's no milk for our babies. The military took it all when they left. Before you promise freedom and equality, can you promise bread and milk?"

"O-of course," the pacification officers would reply, though inside they were disheartened by these prosaic requests. Nevertheless, they were a liberation force. Guaranteeing the necessities of life to multitudes groaning under the heavy yoke of imperial governance was a duty eclipsing even combat in importance. Foodstuffs were disbursed from each fleet's supply department, and at the same time, requisitions were sent to Supreme Command Headquarters on Iserlohn: 180 days' worth of food for fifty million people, seeds for upwards of two hundred varieties of crops, forty production plants for artificial protein, sixty hydroponics plants, and all the ships needed to carry them.

"This is the minimum needed to rescue the liberation zone from a state of perpetual famine. These figures will grow steadily larger as the liberation zone expands."

Rear Admiral Caselnes, the expeditionary force's rear service chief of staff, let out an involuntary growl at the sight of that annotation, which came attached to the requisition form. One hundred eighty days' worth of food for fifty million people? The grain alone would hit ten million tons. To move it would require fifty transport vessels in the two hundred thousand-ton class. Most importantly, that much food greatly exceeded the production and storage capacity of Iserlohn.

"Even if we empty every warehouse on Iserlohn, that only comes to seven million tons. And even with the artificial protein and hydroponics plants running at full capacity—"

Caselnes cut off his subordinate's report: "It won't be enough—I know."

The resupply plan, designed for the thirty million soldiers of the alliance, had been drawn up by Caselnes himself, and he had been confident regarding its implementation.

It would be a different story now, though, because on top of that they had to handle a noncombatant population nearly double the size of the entire expeditionary force. He would need to make corrections to the plan that would triple its scale, and he would need to do it fast. Caselnes could easily imagine the cries from the fleets' supply departments as they strained under the excessive burden.

"Still, are these pacification officers all imbeciles?"

What was sticking in his craw was that line in the note attached to the requisition form: *These figures will grow steadily larger as the liberation zone expands.* Didn't that mean the burden on the resupply effort was only going to get heavier? This was no time for childlike rejoicing over the expansion of seized territory. And furthermore, there was a faint suggestion of something else in all of this—of something that was terrifying.

Caselnes requested a meeting with the supreme commander, Marshal Lobos. In his office, he found Rear Admiral Fork of the operations staff present as well. This he had been expecting; Fork enjoyed a greater share of the supreme commander's confidence than even his chief of staff, Senior Admiral Greenhill. He could usually be found keeping a watchful eye by his boss's side, and lately there were whispers that "the Supreme Commander's nothing but a microphone for the ops staff. When he opens his mouth, it's really Rear Admiral Fork who's speaking."

"This must be about the requisitions from the pacification teams," Marshal Lobos said, rubbing his meaty jowl. "Whatever it is, I'm busy enough even without it, so make this quick."

One didn't get to the rank of marshal by being incompetent. Lobos was a man who knew how to get results on the front lines, methodically process paperwork in the rear, lead large forces, and manage staff. Or at least he *had* known, until some point during his forties. Now, however, his decline was plain to see. He was lethargic in all things, and his lack of energy was especially noticeable when judgment, insight, and decision making were called for. Which was probably why Rear Admiral Fork was being allowed to do as he pleased, making all the decisions.

There were a number of theories as to what had caused this once-gifted commander to end up like this. Some said that the strain he had put on his mind and body as a young man had resulted in the onset of encephalomalacia, or softening of the brain; others said that it was chronic heart disease, or that he had never gotten over losing out to Sitolet in the race for the director's seat at Joint Operational Headquarters—the uniformed men unfolded wings of imagination as they gossiped with one another.

When those wings spread too far, theories emerged such as the one where Lobos—who had never met a pretty girl he didn't like—had caught some horrible disease from a woman with whom he'd shared a night. That particular thesis came with a special extra: the claim that the woman who had given the marshal his ignominious illness had been an imperial spy. Dirty smiles would appear for a moment on the faces of those who heard this rumor, after which their shoulders would draw up as though they'd felt a chill.

"I'll be brief, Excellency. Our forces are facing a crisis. A very serious crisis."

Caselnes chanced opening with his sword brandished high and waited to see how Lobos would react. Marshal Lobos stopped the hand that was massaging his chin and shot a doubtful look back at the rear service chief of staff. Rear Admiral Fork twisted his pale lips slightly, though this was merely force of habit.

"What's this all of a sudden?"

There was no echo of shock or surprise in the marshal's voice, but Caselnes wondered if he were not so much calm and collected as emotionally stunted.

"You're aware of the requisitions coming in from the pacification teams?" Caselnes asked, which might have been a rude thing to say. Fork clearly seemed to think so; though he said nothing out loud, the crook of his mouth grew larger. Perhaps he intended to make something of it later.

"I know about them," said Lobos. "I get the feeling they're asking for too much myself, but given our occupation policy, what choice do we have?"

"Iserlohn doesn't have supplies in the quantities they're demanding."

"Then pass the requisitions on to the homeland. The bean counters might go into hysterics, but they can't refuse to send you what you need."

"Yes, sir, they'll certainly send it. But once those supplies have reached Iserlohn, what do you think happens next?"

The marshal started stroking his chin again. *No matter how hard you rub it, it's not gonna scrape off all that fat,* Caselnes thought.

"What do you mean, Admiral?"

"What I mean is that the enemy's plan is to overload our capacity to resupply the force." He spoke in a harsh tone of voice, though what he'd wanted to do was scream, *Can't you even see that!* at him.

"In other words, the enemy is going to attack the transport fleet and try to cut off our supply line—that's your opinion as rear service chief of staff?" said Rear Admiral Fork.

It was disagreeable to be interrupted, but Caselnes nodded.

"But everything from here to the front lines five hundred light-years away is under occupation by our forces. I don't think there's any need to be so worried. Though, ah, of course we'll attach an escort, just in case."

"I see. Just in case, huh?"

Caselnes said that with all the sarcasm he could muster. What did he care what Fork might think?

Yang, please make it back home alive, Caselnes silently called to his friend. He couldn't help thinking, *This is way too stupid a fight to get killed in.*

II

In the alliance's capital of Heinessen, a fierce debate was unfolding between factions supporting and opposed to the large-scale requisitions from the expeditionary force.

Those in favor said, "The expedition's original goal was to liberate a people groaning under the oppression of imperial rule. Rescuing fifty million people from famine is obviously the moral thing to do as well. Furthermore, when people learn that our forces have saved them, that—coupled with their opposition to imperial rule—will cause public sentiment to tilt inevitably in the direction of our alliance. For reasons both military and political, the expeditionary force's requests should be honored and foodstuffs and other necessities be given to the residents of the occupied zone…"

There was also a counterargument: "This expedition has been poorly planned from the start. The initial plan alone required expenditures totaling two hundred billion dinars—that comes to 5.6 percent of the national budget for this year and more than 10 percent of the military's budget. Even with those expenses alone, it's certain we'll be way over budget when financial accounts are settled. Add in securing the occupied zone and provision of foodstuffs for its residents, and fiscal bankruptcy becomes certain. They should end this campaign, abandon the occupied territories, and return to Iserlohn. Just holding Iserlohn is enough to block incursions from the empire…"

Ideological appeals, cold calculations, and emotions all ran together, and it seemed as if this fierce debate might go on forever.

A report—or rather, a cry—from Iserlohn, however, was what settled the matter: "At least give our soldiers the chance to die in battle. If you spend every day doing nothing, nothing awaits them but inglorious deaths by starvation."

Supplies were assembled in accordance with the military's demands, and they began shipping them out, but not long after, additional requisitions came in for almost the same amounts as the previous ones. The occupied zone expanded, and the number of people residing within it swelled to one hundred million. Naturally, there was no way to avoid an increase in the amount of supplies needed…

Those who had supported the earlier requisitions felt humiliated, as one might expect. The opposing side said, "Didn't we try to tell you? There's no end to it, is there? Fifty million has turned into a hundred million. Before long, a hundred million will turn into two hundred million. The empire intends to destroy the finances of our alliance. The government and the military blindly walked right into this and are not going to be able to avoid responsibility. We have no other options left. Withdraw!"

"The empire is using the innocent civilians themselves as a weapon to resist our force's invasion. It's a despicable tactic, but considering that we're doing this in the name of liberation and rescue, one can't help admitting it's an effective one. We should go ahead and withdraw. Otherwise, our force is going to stagger along under the weight of all the starving civilians it's carrying and ultimately be pummeled by a full-on counterattack when its strength gives out."

So spake João Lebello, chairman of the Finance Committee, in the High Council.

Those who had supported the mobilization said not a word. Instead, they merely sat in their seats looking glum—or rather, shell-shocked.

Madam Cornelia Windsor, chairwoman of the Intelligence Traffic Committee, was staring at the ashen screen of a computer terminal displaying nothing, her comely face gone rigid.

By this point, even Madam Windsor knew all too well that there was nothing else to do but withdraw. Nothing could be done about the expenditures thus far, but the nation's finances could not endure further expenses.

However, if they pulled out now without having achieved any kind of military successes at all, she would lose face for having supported it. Not only those who had opposed this deployment from the start, but also those of the prowar faction presently supporting her, would no doubt seek to hold her politically accountable. The seat of council chair that she had longed for since she first decided to go into politics would recede from her as well.

What were those incompetents at Iserlohn doing? Madam Windsor was seized with a fearsome anger; she ground her teeth and clenched her fists, and her beautifully manicured nails dug into the palms of her hands.

There was no choice but to withdraw, but before that, even if only just once, how about showing everyone a military victory over the Imperial Navy? If they did that, she herself would save face, and this campaign might also avoid being held up as a symbol of folly and waste by future generations.

She glanced over at the elderly council chair. That old man who so thickheadedly, unconcernedly occupied the most powerful seat in the nation...

The head of state, ridiculed as "the one nobody chose." At the end of a graceless game produced by the mechanics of the political sphere, he had come out on top through no effort of his own, like a fisherman coming upon a sandpiper fighting with a clam, easily taking both. *I was fooled into supporting this because he talked about the next election.* She hated the chairman from the bottom of her heart for throwing her into this mess.

On the other hand, Defense Committee Chairman Trünicht was feeling quite pleased with the clarity of his own foresight.

It had been obvious to him that things would turn out this way. At its present level of national and military strength, there had been no way the alliance could have successfully invaded the empire. In the very near future, the expeditionary force would meet with miserable defeat, and the current administration would lose the support of the masses. However, Trünicht himself had opposed that ill-conceived deployment, and thus having shown himself a man of true courage and discernment, would not only emerge unscathed by this, he would likely gain the reputation of a true statesman. That would leave only Lebello and Huang to compete with, but they had no support among the military and defense industry. Which meant that, ultimately, the seat of High Council chair would go to Trünicht.

That was what he wanted. In his heart he was smiling with satisfaction. It was he himself who would be called "the greatest head of state in the history of the alliance...the one who brought down the empire." There was no one save himself who was worthy of the honor.

In the end, the argument for withdrawal was rejected.

"Until some sort of result has been achieved on the front, we shouldn't do anything that would shackle our forces."

This was the prowar faction's argument, delivered in a slightly shame-faced tone of voice. That "result" would for Trünicht be an altogether splendid thing. Although naturally, the sort of result he was counting on was a very far cry from the one the hawks were hoping for.

III

"Until supplies arrive from the homeland, each fleet should procure the supplies it deems necessary locally."

When that directive was relayed to the leadership of each of the alliance fleets, faces turned red with anger.

"Procure supplies locally?! Are they telling us to plunder?"

"What's Iserlohn thinking? Do they think they've become pirate chieftains?"

"When your supply plan fails, it's the first step on the road to strategic defeat. Militarily, that's just common sense. They're trying to force the front lines to take the blame for it."

"Didn't Supreme Command HQ say the supply system was perfect? What happened to all their big talk?"

"They're telling us to somehow procure something that was never even here in the first place!"

Though Yang did not join in with this chorus of rumbling complaints, he fully agreed with them. Supreme Command HQ was behaving extremely irresponsibly, but since irresponsible motives had been behind this deployment from the get-go, it had been too much to hope for that there would be any responsibility in its execution and operation. He hated to think what Caselnes must be going through.

Even so, we're at our limit, he thought. Thanks to its having continued to feed residents of the occupied zone, the Thirteenth Fleet was now just about to reach the bottoms of its stores. The unease and dissatisfaction of Captain Uno, the supply chief, exploded:

"The civilians aren't looking for ideals or justice. All they care about is their stomachs. If the Imperial Navy were to bring in foodstuffs, they'd bow themselves to the ground, shouting, 'Hail to His Highness the Emperor!' They only live to satisfy their base instincts. So why do we have to starve in order to feed them?"

"So we don't become Rudolf."

Giving only that for an answer, Yang called Sublieutenant Frederica Greenhill and had her open an FTL comm channel between himself and Admiral Uranff in the Tenth Fleet.

"Well, if it isn't Yang Wen-li," said the descendant of ancient horse clans from the comm screen. "It's rare to hear from you. What's going on?"

"Glad to see you're looking well, Admiral Uranff."

That was a lie. The strong and sharp-eyed Uranff was showing the shadows of weariness and exhaustion all over. Although he came highly praised as a courageous commander, it seemed that problems of an altogether different dimension from that of courage and military strategy were driving the man to his limits.

When asked how his stockpile of foodstuffs was holding out, Uranff's disgust went up another notch.

"There's only one week's worth left. If there's no resupply before then, we'll have no choice but compulsory requisi—no, there's no point dressing it up—to *plunder* from occupied territory. The liberation force is gonna be shocked when they hear that. Assuming there's anything down there to plunder."

"About that, I've got an opinion I'd like to share..." Yang said. "How about we just chuck these occupied zones and withdraw?"

"Withdraw?" Uranff's brows twitched slightly. "Before we've exchanged fire even once? Isn't that a little passive?"

"We should do it while we still can. The enemy is draining our supplies and waiting for us to starve. And why do you think that is?"

Uranff thought for a moment. "Most likely, they'll hit us with everything they've got. The enemy has the home-field advantage, and their supply lines will be short."

"Hmm..." Uranff was famed for his daring, but it was no surprise that a chill seemed to have run down his spine. "But if we withdraw in a chaotic rush, we'll just end up inviting the enemy offensive, won't we? In which case, we'll make matters a whole lot worse."

"The big prerequisite is being prepared to fight back. If we pull out now, we can do that, but if we wait until our men and women are starving, it'll be too late. The most we can do is retreat in an orderly fashion before that happens."

Yang made his case vehemently. Uranff listened in silence.

"Also, the enemy will have their forecast for the time they think we'll be getting really hungry. If they see us pulling out, interpret it as a full-fledged retreat, and come charging after us, there'll be any number of ways we can fight back. On the other hand, if they think it's a trap because we're leaving too early, well, that's fine, too—we might just be able to withdraw unscathed. The odds of that are not very high, though, and they'll only get lower with each passing day."

Uranff thought about it, and it didn't take long to reach a decision.

"All right. You're probably right. We'll begin preparations for withdrawal. But how should we go about informing the other fleets?"

"I'm about to put a call in to Admiral Bucock. If I can get him to contact Iserlohn, it should carry more weight than if I do it..."

"Very well, let's both make this happen as fast as we can."

As soon as Yang had finished conferring with Uranff, an urgent communiqué arrived.

"A civilian riot has broken out in the Seventh Fleet's occupation zone. The scale is extremely large. It was caused by the military's suspension of food distribution."

Frederica wore an agonized, frustrated expression as she gave the report.

"How did the Seventh Fleet deal with it?"

"They put it down temporarily by using infirmity gas, but it apparently started up again the minute the effects wore off. It's probably just a matter of time before the military escalates its methods of resistance."

Yang couldn't help thinking, *This whole thing has turned into a tragedy.*

An alliance invasion calling itself a liberation force—a force for protecting the people—had turned the masses into its enemies. At this stage of the game, there was probably no longer any way to dissolve the mutual distrust. Meaning that the empire had succeeded splendidly in tearing the alliance forces and the occupied people apart.

"Absolutely splendid, Count von Lohengramm."

I couldn't have done this . . . taking it this far, this thoroughly. Even if I knew I could win if I did it, I just couldn't. That's the difference between Count von Lohengramm and me, and that's the reason he terrifies me.

Because someday, it may well be that difference that leads to disaster . . .

When Vice Admiral Bucock, commander of the Free Planets Alliance Fifth Fleet, made an FTL call to Supreme Command HQ at Iserlohn, it was the pallid face of Operations Staff Officer Fork that appeared on his comm screen. "I asked for an appointment with His Excellency the Supreme Commander. I don't remember saying that I wanted to talk to you. Ops staff shouldn't stick their noses into places where they haven't been invited."

The voice of the old admiral was scathing. In force and gravitas, there was no way Fork could come close to matching it.

The young staff officer was taken aback for just an instant before haughtily retorting, "Appointments with His Excellency the Supreme Commander, as well as reports and the like, all go through me. What is your reason for requesting an appointment?"

"I don't have to talk to you."

Even Bucock forgot his age for a moment, assuming the posture of someone spoiling for a fight.

"Then I can't connect you."

"What . . . ?"

"No matter how high your rank, you have to observe the rules. Shall I end this transmission?"

You made up those rules yourself, didn't you! thought Bucock, though in this case he had no choice but to concede.

"All the fleet commanders on the front lines want to withdraw. I'd like to obtain the supreme commander's consent in this matter."

"Did you say 'withdraw'?" Rear Admiral Fork's lips twisted into the very shape the old admiral had been expecting. "Admiral Yang might say something like that, but I didn't expect to hear someone as renowned for his courage as you, Admiral Bucock, arguing for withdrawal without combat."

"Stop it with the cheap shots," Bucock said. "We wouldn't be in this mess if you people hadn't come up with such a slipshod deployment proposal in the first place. Try feeling just a little bit responsible."

"This is the perfect chance to slaughter the Imperial Navy in one fell swoop. What are you so afraid of? If I was in your shoes, I wouldn't withdraw."

That insolent and thoughtless remark set off flashes like supernovas in the old admiral's eyes.

"Is that so? Fine, then—I'll switch places with you. I'll come back to Iserlohn, and you can come to the front in my place."

Fork's lips were reaching a point at which they could twist no further.

"Please don't suggest the impossible."

"You're the one insisting on impossibilities. And you're doing it without budging from the safe place where you're sitting."

"Are you insulting me, sir?"

"I'm just sick and tired of listening to lofty-sounding words," Bucock said. "If you want to show your talent, you should do it with a record of accomplishments, not eloquent speeches. How about giving command a try and finding out whether or not you've got what it takes to give orders to others?"

The old admiral fancied he could hear the sound of the blood draining from Fork's narrow face. What he saw, however, was not his imagination. The young staff officer's eyes lost focus as confusion and terror spread out over his features. His nostrils flared, and his mouth opened into a bent quadrilateral. He raised both his hands, hiding his face from Bucock's view, and after a pause of about one second, a cry rang out that was somewhere between a moan and a scream.

Bucock looked on speechlessly as the image of Rear Admiral Fork sank down below the bottom of his comm screen. In Fork's place, he saw figures running back and forth, but for the moment there was no one to explain what was going on.

"What's happened to him?" he asked Lieutenant Clemente, the aide who was standing off to one side.

But Clemente didn't know either.

The old admiral was made to wait in front of the screen for about two minutes.

At last, a young medical officer in a white uniform appeared on the screen and saluted.

"Sir, this is Lieutenant Commander Yamamura. I'm a medical officer. At present, His Excellency Rear Admiral Fork is being treated in the infirmary. Please allow me to explain the situation."

Something about Yamamura struck Bucock as a little self-important. "What's wrong with him?"

"Neurogenic blindness brought on by conversion hysteria."

"*Hysteria*?"

"Yes, sir. Feelings of frustration or failure caused him to become abnormally agitated, and this temporarily paralyzed his optic nerves. He'll be able to see again in about fifteen minutes, but at times like this it's possible for episodes to happen any number of times. The cause is psychological, so unless the cause can be removed—"

"What can be done about it?" Bucock demanded.

"You mustn't oppose him. You mustn't engender any feelings of failure or defeat in him. Everyone should do as he says, and everything needs to go his way."

"Are you being serious, Medical Officer?"

"These are symptoms we sometimes see in small children who grow up in environments where they always get their way, and develop abnormally large egos. It's not a problem of good and evil. The only important thing is that his ego and desires be satisfied. Therefore, it won't be until the admirals apologize for their rudeness, give their all in executing his plan, and realize victory so that he becomes an object of praise... that the cause of his illness will be resolved."

"Well, I'm awfully grateful to hear that." Bucock was in no mood for losing his temper. "So thirty million soldiers have to stand in the jaws of death in order to cure this guy's hysteria? That's just wonderful. I'm so moved I think I'm just gonna drown in a sea of tears."

The medical officer made a weak smile. "If we focus on the single point of curing His Excellency Rear Admiral Fork's illness, that is what it will take. If we widen our view to include the entire military, a different way of solving the problem presents itself, naturally."

"Exactly—he should resign," the old admiral barked. "It may be for the best this has happened. The imperial military would be dancing for joy if they learned that the strategist in charge of thirty million troops has the mentality of a kid crying for chocolate."

After a slight hesitation, Yamamura said, "In any case, I'm not authorized to speak on any matter outside of his medical condition. I'll put on His Excellency the Joint Chief of Staff…"

Disgusted, Bucock thought, *So the unofficial wedding of politicians hoping for an election victory and a bright young soldier given to childish fits of hysteria has resulted in thirty million troops being mobilized. You'd have to be a self-intoxicated masochist or one serious warmonger to hear that and genuinely want to fight harder.*

"Admiral…" The man who replaced the medical officer on the comm screen was Senior Admiral Greenhill, the expeditionary force joint chief of staff. There was a deep shadow of anxiety on his handsome, gentlemanly face.

"Well, Admiral Greenhill, I'm sorry to bother you at such a busy time." It was one of the old admiral's virtues that people just couldn't hate him, even when he was being openly sarcastic.

Greenhill smiled the same sort of smile that the naval doctor had. "I'm sorry as well that you had to see such an unsightly moment. We'll need the supreme commander's sanction, but I think we'll be giving Rear Admiral Fork some R & R right away…"

"In that case, how about the proposal from the Thirteenth Fleet to withdraw? I'm 100 percent in favor. The men on the front lines are in no shape for combat, mentally or physically."

"Wait just a minute. This also requires the supreme commander's sanction. Please understand, I can't give you an answer right away."

Vice Admiral Bucock gave him a look that said he had had about enough of bureaucratic answers.

"I'm aware this may sound indiscreet, Admiral, but I wonder if you could arrange for me to speak directly with the supreme commander?"

"The supreme commander is taking a nap right now," Greenhill said.

The old admiral's white eyebrows drew together, and he blinked his eyes rapidly. Then, slowly, he asked: "What did you just say, Admiral?"

Senior Admiral Greenhill's reply was all the more solemn. "The supreme commander is taking a nap. His orders are not to wake him for anything outside of an enemy attack, so I will relay your request to him when he wakes. Please, wait until then."

To that, Bucock made no attempt at answering. His eyebrows quivered so slightly that the movement was almost undetectable. "Very well. I understand very well."

Well over a minute passed before the old admiral continued, in a voice of tightly restrained emotion. "I'm just carrying out the duty I have as a frontline commander toward the lives of my subordinates. Thank you for your trouble. When the supreme commander wakes, please tell him that Bucock called and hopes he had pleasant dreams."

"Admiral..."

Bucock cut the transmission from his end, staring with a heavy expression at the comm screen, which had become a monotonous shade of grayish white.

IV

Reinhard finished reading the reconnaissance team's report, nodded once, and summoned the red-haired vice admiral Siegfried Kircheis. To him, he assigned a mission of great import.

"A fleet of supply ships will be dispatched from Iserlohn to the front lines. That's the enemy's lifeline. Take all the forces I've given you and go smash it. I'll leave the details to your own discretion."

"As you wish."

"Use whatever intelligence, organizations, and supplies that you need."

Kircheis saluted, turned on his heel, and started to leave, but Reinhard suddenly called him to a halt. His friend looked back mistrustfully, to which the young imperial marshal said, "This is to win, Kircheis."

Reinhard knew. He knew that Kircheis was critical of the harsh tactic he'd employed, of letting the people in the occupied territories starve in order to shackle the enemy's hands and feet. It didn't show in Kircheis's face, let alone in his words, but Reinhard understood only too well. He knew the kind of man that Siegfried Kircheis was.

Kircheis saluted once more and left the room. Then Reinhard informed the rest of the admirals.

"While Admiral Kircheis is knocking out the rebel supply fleet, our forces will launch an all-out assault. At that time, I'll put out a false report that the delivery fleet came under fire but is now safe. That's to prevent the rebel force from losing its last hope and resorting to the actions of a cornered animal. At the same time, it's also to keep them from realizing we've gone on the offense—naturally, they'll realize at some point, but the later the better."

He glanced over at the man who was sitting by his side. Before, it had always been a tall, redheaded youth at his side. Now it was a man with half-silvered hair—Paul von Oberstein. Though he had made the decision to put von Oberstein there himself, it still felt a little strange.

"Furthermore, our supply corps will provide food to the people the moment the occupied territories are recovered. Although this was permitted in order to oppose the rebel invasion, driving His Majesty's subjects to starvation was never our military's wish. Furthermore, this is a measure necessary to demonstrate to the residents of the frontier that it's the empire alone which is responsible enough to rule them."

Reinhard's true intent was not to win hearts and minds for the empire, but for himself, although there was no need to go out of his way to tell them that here and now.

The alliance transport fleet, under the command of Admiral Gledwin Scott, consisted of one hundred transport vessels in the hundred thousand-ton class and twenty-six escort craft. Regarding the number of escorts, Rear Admiral Caselnes, the rear service chief of staff, had argued, "That's not enough—at least give them a hundred!" but the request had been denied.

The reasons given had been that the empire seemed unlikely to send a very large force to attack a transport fleet and that dispatching too many ships would leave Iserlohn's security forces shorthanded.

What kind of excuse is that, when you're sitting far removed from the front lines in an "impregnable" fortress? Caselnes was so angry he was about to burst.

Admiral Scott was far more optimistic than Caselnes. When Caselnes had told him just before departure to be on the lookout for enemies, Scott had brushed off the admonition, and even now he wasn't on his bridge but in his cabin enjoying 3-D chess with a subordinate.

When fleet staff officer Commander Nikolsky came to get him, his face was as white as a sheet. Scott, who had been just about to put his opponent in check, asked crossly, "Something happen on the front? I hear a lot of noise out there."

"On the front?" Commander Nikolsky stared back at his commander in disbelief. "*This* is the front. Can you not see that, Excellency?"

Held in his fingertips, a small panel connected to the bridge's main screen was showing a rapidly expanding cloud of white light.

Admiral Scott was speechless for a moment. Not even he could believe those were friendlies. A surprisingly large enemy force was enveloping them.

"This many . . ." Scott finally squeezed out. "I can't believe it! Why this many for one measly transport fleet?"

As he was racing down the corridor to the bridge in a hydrogen-powered car driven by Nikolsky, the admiral kept asking stupid questions. *Don't you understand the point of your own mission?* Nikolsky was about to say, when the cry of an operator burst from the hall speakers:

"Multiple enemy missiles, closing!"

An instant later, that cry became a veritable scream.

"Unable to respond! There are too many!"

Imperial flagship *Brünhild*—

A communications officer stood up from his station chair and turned toward Reinhard, face flushed with excitement. "Message from Admiral Kircheis! Good news, sir. Enemy transport fleet annihilated. In addition, twenty-six escort ships destroyed. Our side's losses limited to one battleship with moderate damage and fourteen walküren..."

Shouts of joy filled the bridge. Though the Imperial Navy's repeated pullbacks had been born of strategic necessity, it had nonetheless been in retreat ever since the fall of Iserlohn, and for its soldiers, this was the thrill of victory that had been missing for far too long.

"Mittermeier, von Reuentahl, Wittenfeld, Kempf, Mecklinger, Wahlen, Lutz: follow the plan, and hit the rebel forces with everything you have."

Reinhard gave the assembled admirals who were standing by their orders.

The admirals responded with a hearty "Yes, sir!" and were about to depart for the front lines when Reinhard called them all to a halt and ordered an attendant to bring wine for each of them. It was an advance celebration of their victory.

"Victory is already assured. But more than that, we have to make this victory a perfect one. The conditions are all in order. Do not allow those rebel upstarts to return home alive. May the favor of our great lord Odin be upon you. *Prosit!*"

"*Prosit!*" the admirals shouted in chorus. Then, after draining their glasses, they hurled them to the floor as was the custom. Innumerable shards of light danced brilliantly across the floor.

After the admirals had left, Reinhard stared fixedly at his screen. There he could make out a cluster of sterile, inorganic lights that were infinitely colder and more distant than the scattered flecks of light upon the floor. He loved those lights, however. It was to take hold of those lights and make them his own that he was where he was right now...

V

October 10 of the Standard Calendar, 1600.

Admiral Uranff, who was positioning his fleet in orbit above Planet Lügen according to gravity-gradient stabilization, could tell that the enemy attack was coming. Of the twenty thousand reconnaissance satellites that had been positioned throughout the region, about one hundred of them in the two o'clock direction had ceased transmitting images after displaying countless points of light.

"Here they come," Uranff murmured. He felt a current of tension running through him all the way to his terminal nerves. "Operator, how long until contact with the enemy?"

"Between six and seven minutes, sir."

"All right, then. All ships: prepare for all-out war. Communications officer: send messages to Supreme Command HQ and the Thirteenth Fleet. 'We have met the enemy.'"

Alarms rang out, and orders and responses flew back and forth across the bridge of the flagship.

"The Thirteenth Fleet will eventually be coming to assist us," Uranff told his subordinates. "That's 'Miracle Yang.' When that happens, we can catch the enemy in a pincer. Don't doubt our victory."

Sometimes commanders had to make their subordinates believe things that they didn't even believe themselves. *Yang will probably be under attack by multiple enemies at the same time we are and not have the luxury of coming to assist the Tenth Fleet,* Urannf thought.

The Imperial Navy's massive attack had begun.

Sublieutenant Frederica Greenhill looked up at her commanding officer, tension evident in her white face.

"Excellency! There's an FTL from Admiral Uranff."

"They're under attack?"

"Yes, sir. He says combat with the enemy began at 1607."

"So it's finally started…"

An alarm rang out at that moment, drowning out the tail end of his words. Five minutes later, the Thirteenth Fleet was exchanging fire with an imperial force led by Admiral Kempf.

"Enemy missiles closing from eleven o'clock!"

At the operator's cry, Captain Marino, captain of the flagship *Hyperion*, made a quick-witted response: "Eject decoys! Heading nine o'clock!"

Yang remained silent and focused on his own job, which was operational command of the fleet. Defense and counterattack at the individual ship level was the job of the captain; if a fleet commander were to involve himself to that extent, first of all, his nerves would never hold.

Missiles tipped with laser-triggered fusion warheads bore down on them like ferocious hunting dogs.

To counter them, decoy rockets were fired. These emitted tremendous amounts of heat and electromagnetic radiation to fool the missiles' detection systems. The missiles in the cluster turned their noses at sharp angles and went after the decoys.

An ominous glow was steadily filling the black void as energy collided with energy and matter clashed against matter.

"Spartanians, stand by for launch!"

The order was relayed, and a pleasant tension ran through the minds and bodies of several thousand spartanian crew members. These were children such as the war god Ares might grant his petitioners, possessed of fierce confidence in their skills and reflexes, to whom the fear of death was but an object of ridicule.

"All right, let's head out and go around!"

The man who gave this enthusiastic shout aboard the flagship *Hyperion* was ace pilot Lieutenant Waren Hughes.

Hyperion was carrying four aces. Besides Hughes, there were lieutenants Salé Aziz Cheikly, Olivier Poplin, and Ivan Konev. To show off their titles, each had had an ace mark of spades, diamonds, hearts, or clubs stenciled in special paint onto the hull of his favored spartanian. Having nerve enough to think of warfare as a sport was likely one factor that had kept them alive this long.

After leaping into his spartanian, Poplin shouted out to the mechanic, "I'm shooting down five, so start chilling the champagne!"

But the answer that came back wasn't what he'd expected:

"There's no way that's happening, but I'll at least get you some water!"

"At least try and play along," Poplin grumbled, as he and the other three pirouetted out into the space together. The wings of the spartanians shone with rainbow hues, reflecting the light of distant explosions. Missiles rushed toward them with hostile intent, and beams came racing in to attack.

"Think you can hit me?!" Poplin shouted.

All four men were making similar boasts. It was the pride of warriors who had crossed the lines of death any number of times and yet lived to tell the tale that was making them do so.

Showing off divine skill, they banked sharply, dodging past missiles. The slender trunks of the missiles that attempted to follow them, unable to endure the sudden shift in g-force, broke apart from their centers. Up ahead, imperial walküren danced into view, tilting their wings back and forth as if in ridicule as they came in spoiling for a dogfight.

Hughes, Cheikly, and Konev met them gladly, and one by one enemy craft exploded into balls of flame.

One of the alliance aces—Poplin—was flushed crimson with anger and suspicion, however. At a rate of 140 rounds per second, he was firing on the enemy with uranium-238 rounds. These had excellent armor-piercing ability and became superheated and exploded upon striking a target—yet all his shots were merely being swallowed up by the void, hitting nothing.

Without his help, the other three had already drawn first blood, destroying a total of seven enemy fighters.

"What's the matter with you?" Vice Admiral Kempf, commanding officer of the imperial force, said with a sharp exhalation of disgust.

Kempf was an ace pilot himself—a hero of many battles who in his silver-winged walküre had flung dozens of enemy craft at the Grim Reaper's feet. Though he was extremely tall, the breadth of his body was such that people didn't really notice. His brown hair was cut short.

"Why are you wasting time on enemies like that? Form half-envelopment formations to their afts and drive them into firing range of the battleships!"

Those instructions were right on target. Three walküren assumed a half-envelopment formation to the aft of Lieutenant Hughes's spartanian and skillfully maneuvered him into a battleship's firing range. Realizing the danger, Hughes banked sharply and sent a hail of U-238 rounds into the cockpit of one enemy fighter, and then tried to thread his way through the gap he had opened. However, he had failed to take into account the enemy battleship's auxiliary cannons. Beams flared, erasing both Hughes and his ship from this world in a single shot.

Cheikly was also felled using the same tactic. The remaining two aces barely managed to shake off their pursuers, and ducked into a blind spot of the battleships' cannons.

Poplin's sense of self-respect had been hopelessly wounded. It was bad enough that Konev had sent four enemies to their graves already, but Poplin, unable to shoot down a single enemy, had done nothing but run, dodging back and forth.

When he discovered the reason why not a single round had hit its target, his sorrow blazed forth into fury. When he returned to the mother ship, he jumped down from the cockpit, ran toward a mechanic, and grabbed him by the collar.

"Bring out that murdering chief mechanic! I'm gonna kill him!"

When Tech Lieutenant Toda, the chief mechanic, came running, Poplin gave his vitriol free rein.

"The sights on my guns are nine to twelve degrees off! Are you even servicing them, you salary-thieving—!"

Tech Lieutenant Toda's eyebrows shot upward.

"I'm doing my job—I take good care of them. After all, a human you can make for free, but a fighter craft costs a lot of money."

"That supposed to be funny, jackass?"

Poplin flung his pilot's helmet to the ground; it caromed off the floor and went high up into the air. Poplin's green eyes burned with anger.

In contrast, Toda's gaze narrowed and sharpened. "You wanna go a round, dragonfly?"

"Bring it on. I've lost count how many imperials I've killed, but every one of 'em was a better man than you. I'll even give you a handicap—one hand's plenty for the likes of you!"

"Listen to you! Trying to shift blame for your own mistakes!"

There were shouts at them to control themselves, but by that time the punches were already flying. Blows were exchanged two or three times, but finally Toda, driven into a purely defensive fight, began to stagger. Just as Poplin's arm was drawing back again, however, someone grabbed hold of it.

"Enough of that, you fool!" said a disgusted Commodore von Schönkopf.

Things settled down right away. There was no one who failed to acknowledge the hero of the capture of Iserlohn. Though naturally, for von Schönkopf himself, it was terribly disappointing to have no other role in the fighting but this.

The commanding officer of the imperial force attacking Urannf's Tenth Fleet was Vice Admiral Wittenfeld. He had orange-colored, longish hair and light-brown eyes, and his narrow face seemed somehow out of balance with his body's firm build. His combative demeanor could be seen in his furrowed brows and the fierce gleam of his eyes.

Furthermore, all vessels under his command were painted black and known collectively as the *Schwarz Lanzenreiter*, or Black Lancers. This force was the very embodiment of swift and violent strength. Uranff had fought a tough, shrewd battle, delivering a steady stream of damage to this force. However, he had taken just as much in return—not percentagewise, but in terms of raw numbers.

Wittenfeld had a larger force than Uranff did, and furthermore, his troops hadn't been going hungry. Both the commanding officer and his subordinates were fresh and full of energy, and although they were taking considerable casualties, they succeeded at last in fully enveloping the alliance fleet.

The Tenth Fleet, unable to advance or retreat, had no way to avoid the concentrated fire of Wittenfeld's fleet.

"Fire at will! If you shoot, you're bound to hit something!"

The imperial force's gunnery officers rained a monsoon of energy beams and missiles down on the densely clustered vessels of the alliance fleet.

Energy-neutralization fields ruptured, and hulls were pounded by unendurable shocks. The concussions finally breached the interiors, filling the ships with explosions, and soldiers and officers were vaporized by hot, murderous gales.

Pulled by the planetary gravity, shattered vessels that had lost propulsion were now falling. Among the planet's inhabitants, children forgot their hunger for a brief while, enthralled by the ominous beauty of the countless shooting stars screaming across the night sky.

VI

The Tenth Fleet's armed potential was just about exhausted. Conditions were terrible: 40 percent of all vessels had been lost, and half of the ships that remained were unable to continue fighting.

Rear Admiral Cheng, the fleet's chief of staff, turned toward the commander with a face gone white as a sheet.

"Excellency, it's no longer possible to continue combat operations. All we can do now is decide whether to surrender or run."

"So it's one dishonor or the other, is it?" Vice Admiral Uranff said, showing a hint of self-deprecation. "Surrender is not in my nature. Let's try to run. Relay the order to all ships."

But even to run, they would need to blaze a bloody trail through enemy lines. Uranff reorganized his remaining force into a spindle formation and slammed all of it at once against one point of the encirclement. Uranff knew how to concentrate his force and use it.

Using this bold and clever maneuver, he succeeded in extricating half his subordinates from the jaws of death. He was killed in action himself, however.

His flagship had stayed in the encirclement to the last, and at the very moment it had attempted to break through, had taken a direct hit from an enemy beam up one of its missile tubes and blown apart.

All across the lines of battle, alliance forces were lapping the bitter soup of defeat.

Vice Admiral Borodin, commander of the Twelfth Fleet, under assault by Vice Admiral Lutz, had fought until a scant eight gunships remained to him, and when both battle and escape became impossible, had shot himself through the head with his own blaster. Fleet command had passed to Rear Admiral Connally, who stood down and surrendered.

The other fleets were also under attack—the Fifth Fleet by von Reuentahl, the Ninth by Mittermeier, the Seventh by Kircheis (who had already destroyed the transport fleet), the Third by Wahlen, and the Eighth by Mecklinger—and pullback had piled upon pullback.

The sole exception was Yang's Thirteenth Fleet. He had employed a clever half-moon formation against Kempf's fleet, dodging the enemy's attacks and bleeding them with alternating strikes on their port and starboard flanks.

Surprised at the unexpected amount of damage he was taking, Kempf had decided that it was better to grit his teeth and choose drastic surgery than to stay the course and die miserably from blood loss. He elected to retreat and regroup his forces.

Seeing the enemy pulling back, Yang made no attempt at using the opening to go on the offense. *What matters in this battle is surviving it, not winning it,* Yang was thinking. *Even if we were to beat Kempf here, the enemy would still have the overall advantage. In the end we'd just end up getting pounded from all sides when the other regiments ganged up on us. The thing to do is run as far from here as we can while the enemy's pulling back.*

In a grave and solemn voice, Yang addressed his forces:

"Attention! All ships: run away!"

The Thirteenth Fleet ran away. But in an orderly fashion.

Kempf couldn't help being surprised when the enemy—which had the advantage—not only did not give chase, but began a rapid pullback. Though he had been bracing himself for considerable losses when they pursued and attacked, he had been duped instead.

"Why don't they use their advantage and attack?"

Kempf was both soliciting opinions from his staff officers and wondering aloud.

His subordinates' responses were split into two camps—the hypothesis that "the alliance force must be rushing to the aid of another force that's in trouble" and the hypothesis that "their aim is to deliver a killing blow by showing us an opening and inviting us to thoughtlessly go on the offense."

Ensign Theodor von Rücke, a young officer fresh out of officers' school, opened his mouth fearfully. "Sir—I mean, Commander—I think it's possible that they don't want to fight and are just trying to get away."

This suggestion went completely ignored, and Ensign von Rücke backed down, alone and red-faced with embarrassment. No one—himself included—understood that he was closer than any of them to the truth.

Kempf, who had a lot of common sense as a strategist, arrived after much thought at the conclusion that the enemy pullback was a trap, and giving up the idea of a second counterattack, set to the regrouping of his fleet.

Meanwhile, Yang Wen-li and his forces continued their escape, arriving in a region of space the imperial forces called War Zone C. There, imperial forces engaged them again, and a new battle began to unfold.

Meanwhile, the Ninth Fleet, commanded by Admiral Al Salem, was under withering assault from Mittermeier's imperial fleet and had been set to flight repeatedly. Admiral Al Salem was struggling desperately to prevent the chain of command from collapsing.

The swiftness of Mittermeier's pursuit and assault was such that the vanguard of the pursuing imperial fleet and the rear guard of the fleeing alliance fleet actually got jumbled together, with ships of both forces flying side by side in parallel. One soldier after another was flabbergasted to see the markings of enemy vessels up close through the portholes.

Also, the high matter-density readings detected in that narrow region of space sent the collision-avoidance systems of every ship into overdrive. Whatever direction they tried to turn, however, they found the way was blocked by both enemy and friendly ships, and some vessels had even started spinning as a result.

They did not exchange fire. It was plain to see that if vast energies were released with the ships packed so closely together, an unstoppable chain reaction would result, and all of them would perish together.

Still, bumps and collisions did occur. This was because collision-avoidance systems, unable to find a safe direction in which to advance, had been driven to a horrid state of autonomy, causing some ships to switch over to manual piloting to keep them from going mad.

The astrogators were sweating hard, and this had nothing to do with the temperature-control function of their combat suits. Clinging to their control panels, they could see the enemy right in front of them, struggling with the shared goal of avoiding collisions.

The chaos finally ended when Mittermeier ordered his subordinates to drop speed and increase the distance between the two fleets. Of course, all this meant for the alliance forces was that the enemy fleet was regrouping and would presently return to its strategy of pursue and attack. As the imperial force put a safe distance between itself and the enemy fleet, the alliance's ships and soldiers were steadily lost amid the deluge of enemy fire.

The hull of the flagship *Palamedes* was damaged in seven places as well, and the fleet commander, Vice Admiral Al Salem, was injured, with broken ribs. His vice commander, Rear Admiral Morton, took over in his stead and just barely kept the remaining force together, treading a long road toward defeat.

The hardships of the path to defeat were of course not theirs alone.

Each of the alliance fleets was enduring that same sorrow now. Even Yang Wen-li's Thirteenth Fleet was no longer an exception.

By that time, Yang's Thirteenth, having retreated to a distance of six light-hours from the site of the initial battle, had been forced into a fight with enemies four times more numerous. Moreover, Kircheis, commander of the Warzone C imperial forces, had already set the Seventh Fleet running for their lives and was committing forces and supplies to his front line constantly in order to wear down Yang's fleet through uninterrupted combat.

This tactic was an orthodox one—not the product of some clever strategy—but it was extremely reliable when put into operation, causing Yang to sigh, "No opening to attack, no opening to run. It seems that Count von Lohengramm has some excellent people working for him. Nothing strange or flamboyant—just good tactics."

He couldn't help being impressed. For although he was using orthodox tactics, it was clear that his numerically inferior alliance force was being driven to defeat.

After thinking about it, Yang decided on the tack he should take: abandon the space they had secured and yield it to the enemy's hands. However, Yang's orderly retreat would draw the enemy into the midst of a U formation, and then, when their ranks and supply lines were stretched to the breaking point, he would counterattack from three sides with all his forces.

"There's no other option. And naturally, it depends on the enemy going for it..."

If he'd had the time to accumulate force strength and perfect independence of command, Yang's strategy might have both secured some measure of success and put a stop to the imperial force's advance.

However, he was ultimately unable to do either. While enduring the fierce onslaught of imperial forces approaching in overwhelming volume, Yang was struggling to regroup his fleet into the U formation when new orders arrived for him from Iserlohn.

The 14th day of the present month,
Concentrate forces at Point A of the Amritsar star system. Cease combat immediately and change course.

When Yang heard those instructions, Frederica saw a shadow of bitter disappointment flash across his face. It was gone in an instant, but in its place he let out a sigh.

"Easy for you to say."

That was all that he said, but Frederica understood how hard it would be to retreat under these circumstances, right in front of the enemy. They were not up against an incompetent, either. Kempf was in the same position: if he could have pulled back, he would have done so from the start. He was fighting on because he couldn't do otherwise.

Yang followed his orders. But during that difficult fighting retreat, the casualties among his fleet were doubled.

On the bridge of *Brünhild*, supreme flagship of the imperial fleet, Reinhard was listening to von Oberstein's report.

"Though the enemy continues to flee, they're retaining such order as they are able and would seem to be making for Amritsar."

"That's near the entrance to the Iserlohn Corridor. But I don't think this is merely an attempt to flee inside. What do you think?"

"That they likely intend to gather their strength and take the offensive again. Though it's a little too late, it looks like they've realized the foolishness of spreading their forces so thinly across our space."

"It is indeed too late."

Scratching with well-formed fingers at the golden hair that spilled down from his forehead to his eyebrows, Reinhard smiled a cold little smile.

"How shall we respond, Excellency?"

"Naturally, we'll gather our forces at Amritsar as well. Why deny the enemy their wish, if it's to make Amritsar their graveyard?"

CHAPTER 9:

I

The voice of the star Amritsar was ever raised in a soundless roar. In its fearsome inferno of nuclear fusion, countless atoms collided, split apart, and reformed, and the tireless repetition of that cycle spilled unimaginable energies out into the void. Varied elements produced multicolored flames that erupted in dynamic bursts of motion measured in the tens of thousands of kilometers, painting the worlds of its respective onlookers in reds, yellows, or purples.

"I don't like this."

Vice Admiral Bucock's whitish eyebrows were drawn together as he peered at the comm panel.

Yang nodded in agreement. "It's an ominous color," he said. "No doubt about it."

"Well, the color is, too, but it's the name of this star I don't like."

"Amritsar, you mean?"

"The initial is *A,* same as Astarte. I can't help thinking it's an unlucky letter for our side."

"I hadn't thought about it enough to notice."

Yang was in no mood to make light of the old admiral's concern. After half a century spent in the empty depths, there were special sensitivities and heuristics that men such as he developed. Yang was more inclined to put stock in the superstitious words of the old admiral than in the decisions of Supreme Command Headquarters, which had designated Amritsar as the site of the decisive battle.

Yang was hardly feeling high-spirited at this point. Although he had fought hard and well, this retreat had cost him one-tenth of the ships under his command, while also putting an end to his attempt at a counterattack. All that he felt now was exhaustion. While his fleet was being resupplied by Iserlohn, while the wounded were being sent back to the rear, and while the formation was being regrouped, Yang had gone to a tank bed to rest, but mentally it hadn't refreshed him in the slightest.

This isn't going to work, he thought. The Tenth Fleet, having lost its commander and more than half of its force strength, had also been placed under Yang's command. It seemed even Supreme Command HQ had in some way acknowledged his ability—in managing the remnants of defeated forces, if nothing else—but he wasn't feeling grateful for the added responsibility. There were limits to both his abilities and his sense of responsibility, and no matter how much might be expected of him—or how strongly his arm might be twisted—the impossible was still impossible. *I'm not Griping Yusuf, but confound it, why do you have to give me such a hard time?*

"At any rate," Bucock had said just before ending the transmission, "I wish that bunch at Supreme Command HQ would come out to the front themselves and have a look around. They might understand just a little bit of what the men are going through."

He had called to discuss adjustments to the positioning of their ships, but the conversation's latter half had turned into an excoriation of Supreme Command Headquarters. Yang hadn't felt like telling him he'd gotten off the subject. He, too, felt the same sense of exasperation.

"Please have something to eat, Excellency."

Yang turned around from the now blank comm panel and saw Sublieutenant Frederica Greenhill standing there holding a tray. On it was a roll of roast gluten stuffed with sausage and vegetables, winged bean soup, a slice of calcium-fortified rye bread, fruit salad smothered in yogurt, and an alkaline drink flavored with royal jelly.

"Thanks," he said, "but I've got no appetite. I sure would like a glass of brandy, though . . ."

The look in his aide's eyes denied the request. Yang looked back at her, broadcasting objection.

"Why not?" he finally said.

"Hasn't Julian told you you drink too much?"

"What, you two have ganged up on me?"

"We're concerned about your health."

"There's no need to be that concerned. Even if I drink more than I used to, it's still just barely what the average person does. I'm a good thousand light-years from hurting myself."

Just as Frederica was about to answer, though, the harsh, grating voice of an alarm rang out: "Enemy ships closing! Enemy ships closing! Enemy ships clos—"

Yang lightly waved one hand toward his aide.

"Sublieutenant, enemy ships would appear to be closing. If I live through this, I'll make it a point to eat healthy for the rest of my life."

The alliance's force strength had already been halved. The death of a daring and brilliant tactician like Admiral Uranff had come as a particularly hard blow. Morale was not good. How long could they hold out against a thoroughly prepared Imperial Navy that was coming against them, on the heels of victory and ready to employ all the proper tactics?

Von Reuentahl, Mittermeier, Kempf, and Wittenfeld—courageous admirals of the empire—lined up the noses of their battleships and charged forward in a tight formation. Although this had the appearance of the sort of brute-force assault that ignores the finer points of strategy, Kircheis was leading a separate force to circle around to the alliance's back side, so it in fact both disguised the empire's intent to catch the enemy in a pincer movement and was the sort of ferocious attack needed to avoid giving the alliance a chance to catch its breath.

"All right," Yang ordered. "All ships: maximum combat velocity."

The Thirteenth Fleet began to move.

The clash of the two forces was on. Countless beams and missiles hurtled past one another, and the light of nuclear explosions seared the darkness. Hulls were rent asunder and sent flying through the empty space, tumbling in mysterious dances, borne along by winds of pure energy. Across their eddies the Thirteenth Fleet haughtily sped, racing toward the enemy that lay ahead of them.

The Thirteenth Fleet's assault was carried out according to a schedule of decelerations and accelerations that Fischer had calculated with utmost precision on Yang's directive. The Thirteenth Fleet rose fearsomely up from the light of Amritsar's immense flames, like a tattered corona sent flying from its sun by centrifugal force.

As the swift assault leapt toward them from that unexpected angle, the Imperial Navy commander who undertook to meet it was Mittermeier. He was a courageous man but had undeniably been taken by surprise; he had let Yang take the initiative.

The Thirteenth Fleet's first attack was quite literally a blistering one for Mittermeier's regiment.

Its firepower was concentrated to an almost excessive density. When a single battleship—and a single spot on the hull of that battleship—was struck by half a dozen laser-triggered hydrogen missiles, how could it possibly defend itself?

The region surrounding Mittermeier's flagship was made an enveloping swarm of fireballs, and Mittermeier, taking damage on his own port side as well, was forced to pull back. Even in retreat, however, his remarkable skill as a tactician was plain to see in the way he was flexibly changing his formation, keeping the damage he took to its barest minimum, and watching for his chance to strike back.

Yang, on the other hand, had to content himself with dealing a limited amount of damage, as he dared not pursue the enemy too far. *Damn,* Yang thought, *just look at all these talented people Count von Lohengramm has! Although if we still had Uranff and Borodin on our side, we could have probably fought the empire on equal footing...*

Just then, Wittenfeld's regiment came rushing in at high speed, interposing itself in the space between the Thirteenth and Eighth fleets—a region called Sector D4 for convenience's sake. It was a move that could only be described as daring or foolhardy.

"Excellency, a new enemy has appeared at two o'clock."

Yang's response—"Uh-oh, that's a problem"—could hardly be called a proper one.

Yang had a strong point in common with Reinhard, though. He recovered his wits quickly and started giving orders.

On Yang's command, the fleet's heavily armored dreadnoughts lined up in vertical columns to form a protective wall against enemy fire. From the gaps between them, gunships and missile ships—weakly armored but with mobility and firepower to spare—laid down a ruthless barrage of return fire.

One after another, holes opened up all over Wittenfeld's regiment. Even so, he didn't drop speed. His return fire was witheringly intense and caused Yang's blood to run cold when one part of his dreadnought wall crumbled.

Even so, there was no serious damage to the Thirteenth Fleet as a whole, although the wounds suffered by the Eighth were deep and wide. Unable to counter Wittenfeld's speed and fury, columns of ships were being shaved off the Eighth Fleet's flank, and it was steadily losing both its physical and energy-based means of resistance.

The battleship *Ulysses* had taken damage from imperial cannon fire. This damage was of the "minor but serious" variety. What had been destroyed was the microbe-based wastewater treatment system, and for that reason, the crew was forced to continue fighting with their feet drenched in regurgitated sewage. This would surely make for a delightful war story if they ever returned home safely, but if they died out here like this, it was hard to imagine a more tragic and ignominious way to go.

Yang could see before his very eyes an allied fleet on the verge of dissolving into the depths. The Eighth Fleet was like a flock of sheep, and the Wittenfeld regiment a pack of wolves. Alliance vessels flew this way and that trying to escape, only to be destroyed by vicious, incisive attacks.

Should we go and help the Eighth Fleet?

Even Yang had his moment of hesitation. Judging by the enemy's spirited action, it was clear that if the Thirteenth Fleet made a move to assist them, things would degenerate into a rough-and-tumble brawl, and their systematic chain of command would not hold. That would be the same as committing suicide. In the end, there was nothing he could do but order more concentrated cannon fire.

"Forward! Forward! Nike, goddess of victory, is flashing her panties right in front of you!"

Wittenfeld's commands could hardly be called refined, but they certainly raised his men's morale, and heedless of fire incoming from the side, the swarm of Schwarz Lanzenreiter utterly dominated Sector D4. It looked as though the forces of the alliance had been split in two.

"It would appear we've won," said Reinhard, allowing just the faintest hint of excitement to creep into his voice as he looked back at von Oberstein.

Looks like we've lost, Yang was thinking at almost the selfsame instant, though he couldn't say so out loud.

Since ancient times, the utterances of commanders had possessed a seemingly magical power to make the abstract concrete; whenever a commander said, "We've lost," defeat would inevitably follow—though examples of the opposite were extremely rare.

Looks like we've won.

It was Wittenfeld who was likewise thinking this. The alliance's Eighth Fleet was crumbling already; there was no fear now of being caught in a pincer movement.

"Good, we've got a step up on them. Now it's time to finish them off."

Wittenfeld was thinking eagerly, *The Thirteenth Fleet has preserved a lot of its strength, but I'll deliver a killing blow in a dogfight.*

"Have all vessels that can function as mother ships deploy walküren. All others, switch from long-range to short-range cannons. We're going to fight them up close."

That aggressive intent, however, had been anticipated by Yang.

When the imperial force's firepower temporarily weakened, Yang instantly intuited the cause: a switchover in their attack methodology. Even though it might have taken them longer, other commanders could also have guessed what Wittenfeld intended. He had moved too early. When Yang saw the error, he determined to put it to maximum use.

"Draw them in," he said. "All cannons, prepare for a sustained barrage."

Minutes later, the roles had reversed, and it was the imperial forces of Sector D4 that were facing imminent defeat.

Seeing this, Reinhard spoke out unconsciously: "Wittenfeld blundered into that. He sent out his walküren too early. Can't he see that they've become easy prey for the enemy fusillade?"

It seemed that a chink had appeared in even von Oberstein's icy demeanor. His naturally pale face looked as if it were illuminated by a comet's tail. "He wanted to secure victory with his own hands, but..."

The voice in which he answered was nearer a groan than anything else.

The alliance forces, having drawn Wittenfeld's regiment into range for a point-blank attack, were dealing out destruction and slaughter at will. Launched from magnetic-rail cannons, artillery shells of superhard steel pierced the armor of enemy ships, and bursts of fusion shrapnel and photon rounds reduced walküren, and their pilots, to microscopic particles.

Colorful and colorless flashes overlapped with one another, as every instant saw the opening of gateways to the netherworld, through which ever more soldiers were passing.

It seemed that the black of the Schwarz Lanzenreiter—Wittenfeld's pride and joy—was coming to suggest the color of burial shrouds.

The communications officer turned toward Reinhard and shouted, "Excellency! Communiqué from Admiral Wittenfeld—he's requesting immediate reinforcements."

"Reinforcements?"

The communications officer recoiled from the young, golden-haired marshal's pointed response.

"Yes, Excellency, reinforcements. The admiral says he's going to lose if battle conditions continue to worsen like this."

The heel of Reinhard's boot sounded harshly against the floor. If there had been an unsecured station chair nearby, he would have probably been kicking it over.

"What is he thinking?" Reinhard shouted. "That I can pull a fleet of starships out of my magic top hat?"

An instant later, though, he had his anger under control. A supreme commander had to remain calm at all times.

"Message to Wittenfeld: 'Supreme Command has no surplus forces. If we send in ships from the other lines of battle, the whole formation will become unbalanced. Use your present forces to defend your position with your life, and execute your duties as a warrior.'"

No sooner had he closed his mouth than he issued a new command.

"Break off all communications with Wittenfeld. If the enemy picked that up, they'll realize the difficult spot we're in."

Von Oberstein's eyes followed Reinhard as he turned his gaze back toward the screen.

Harsh and cold, but the correct thing to do, thought the silver-haired chief of staff. *Still, could he take the same action toward any man, without respect of person? A true conqueror must have no sacred cows he's unwilling to grind into hamburger...*

"They're doing well, aren't they?" Reinhard murmured as he stared at the screen. "Both sides, I mean."

Though their supreme command was far to the rear and their overall command structure lacked smoothness, the alliance forces were putting up a good fight nonetheless. The Thirteenth Fleet's maneuvers were particularly impressive. Yang Wen-li was their commander, Reinhard had heard. It was often said that a great general never had weak troops. Would that man always appear standing in his way on the road he must travel?

Reinhard unconsciously looked back at von Oberstein.

"Has Kircheis arrived yet?"

"Not yet."

The chief of staff answered simply and clearly, but then asked a question which, intentionally or no, had a ring of sarcasm to it. "Are you concerned, Excellency?"

"I'm nothing of the sort. I was just checking."

Swatting aside the question, Reinhard closed his mouth and stared at the screen.

At that moment, Kircheis, leading a huge force amounting to 30 percent of the entire fleet, was taking a wide detour around the Amritsar system's sun and swinging around toward the rear of the alliance forces.

"We're a little later than planned. Hurry!"

In order to escape detection by alliance forces, Kircheis's regiment was flying near the surface of the sun, but its navigational systems had been affected by magnetic and gravitational fields more powerful than anticipated, to the point that the astrogators had been forced to work out their courses using primitive percom calculators. That was why his forces had lost speed, although now they had finally reached the region of space they were bound for.

To the rear of the alliance force lay a deep, wide minefield.

Even if imperial forces were to circle around to their aft, they would find their advance blocked by forty million fusion mines. That was what the alliance leadership believed. Yang was not entirely persuaded, but he figured that even if the enemy did have an effective means of getting through the mines, they couldn't do it quickly, so it would be possible to prepare a formation for fighting back by the time they arrived at the battlespace.

However, the empire's tactics surpassed even Yang's expectations.

Kircheis's order was relayed down the chain of command: "Release directional Seffl particles."

The imperial military, one step ahead of the Alliance Armed Forces, had succeeded in developing Seffl particles that could be aimed in a single direction. Their first deployment? This battle, now.

Pulled along by spy vessels, three tube-shaped emission devices drew near to the minefield.

"Do it quickly," Captain Horst Sinzer, one of the staff officers, said in a loud voice, "or there may not be any enemies left for us."

Kircheis showed a hint of a wry smile.

The densely clustered particles penetrated the minefield like a pillar of cloud in the interstellar medium. The heat and mass detection systems with which the mines were equipped did not react to them.

A report arrived from the ship at the front of the vanguard: "Seffl particles have penetrated to the far side of the minefield."

"Very well. Ignite them!"

At Kircheis's cry, the lead vessel carefully aimed three beam cannons, each in a different direction, and fired.

An instant later, the minefield was speared by three enormous pillars of fire. After the white-hot light had subsided, holes had been bored through the minefield in three places.

Three tunnel-shaped passages—two hundred kilometers in diameter and three hundred thousand kilometers long—had been created in the very midst of the minefield in hardly any time at all.

"All ships, charge! Maximum combat velocity!"

Driven by the commands of the young red-haired admiral, the thirty thousand ships under his command raced through these tunnels like swarms of comets and bore down upon the alliance's undefended rear.

"Large enemy force sighted aft!"

The swarm of luminescent objects was so great that their numbers were impossible to determine, and even as alliance operators were detecting them and crying out in alarm, hole after hole was beginning to open in the alliance's ranks due to cannon fire from the vanguard of Kircheis's regiment.

Astonished, the commanders of the alliance forces lost their wits. Their terror and confusion, amplified many times over, infected their crews—and in that instant, the alliance lines crumbled.

Ships broke ranks, and the imperial forces rained down cannon fire against alliance vessels beginning to scatter in disorder, pounding them mercilessly, smashing them into pieces.

The victor and the vanquished had been decided.

Yang looked on in silence at the sight of his allies in full rout. *It just isn't possible for human beings to anticipate every situation,* he realized belatedly.

"What do we do, Commander?" asked Patrichev, making a loud noise as he swallowed hard.

"Hmmm . . . It's too early to run away," he replied in a voice that somehow sounded like he was talking to himself.

On the other hand, victory was in the air on the ridge of the imperial flagship *Brünhild.*

"I've never seen a hundred thousand ships set to flight before." Reinhard's voice was like that of a youth as it rang out. Von Oberstein responded prosaically:

"Shall we bring the flagship forward, Excellency?"

"No, let's not. If I were to intercede at this stage, I'd be accused of robbing my subordinates of opportunities to distinguish themselves."

That was a joke, of course, and it showed just how fully at ease Reinhard was.

Though the battle itself was building toward its final curtain, the intensity of the slaughter and destruction showed no sign of waning. The fanatical attacks and the hopeless counterattacks were repeated again and again, and in localized pockets there were even imperial units that found themselves at a disadvantage.

At this stage, no one was even thinking of how much meaning there was in tactical victory; those who had victory before them were apparently striving to make it more thorough, while those on the verge of defeat seemed to be praying that they might atone for their ignominy, even if by taking just one more enemy soldier with them.

But what was bleeding the victorious imperial forces even more than this insanely intense combat was the organized resistance of Yang Wen-li, who was staying behind on the battlefield so that his allies might escape to safe territory.

His technique involved concentrating his firepower on local-ized regions so as to divide the empire's force strength and disrupt their chain of command, then dealing blows to the separated forces individually.

The intoxicating feelings that made noble, tragic beauty out of self-destruction and shattered jewels were utterly alien to Yang. While covering the flight of his compatriots, he was also securing an exit route for his own forces and watching for his chance to withdraw.

Von Oberstein, glancing back and forth between the main screen and the tactical computer panel, spoke a warning to Reinhard: "Someone needs to reinforce Admiral Wittenfeld—Admiral Kircheis or anyone will do. That enemy commander is aiming for the weakest part of the envelopment. He's planning to break through with one sudden push. Unlike before, our forces can afford to spare some ships now, and should do so."

Reinhard scratched his golden hair and swiftly shifted his gaze: to the screen, to several different panels, and to his chief of staff's face.

"You're right. Even so, confound that Wittenfeld—his failure was his alone. May he be cursed forever for it!"

Reinhard's orders leapt across the void via FTL. Receiving them, Kircheis stretched out his ranks, attempting to deploy another line of defense to the rear of Wittenfeld's regiment.

Yang, who had still been watching for his chance to pull out, noticed this movement of imperial forces and for an instant felt like his blood had stopped flowing. His way out was being shut off! Had he been too late? Should he have made his escape at some earlier time?

However, luck was on Yang's side in this.

Seeing the sudden movement of Kircheis's regiment, the alliance battleships that happened to be in the path of that advance were seized with panic, and paying no heed to the fact that they were near large masses, warped out.

This was not necessarily an unusual occurrence. Starships that knew it was impossible to flee would sometimes choose the fear of the unknown over certain death and flee into subspace with courses still impossible to compute. When flight was impossible, surrender was also an option, and the signal for indicating such intent was also known to both sides. But sometimes people in a frenzy of terror didn't think of that. What sort of fate awaited those who fled into subspace, no one knew. It was like the world of the dead; there was no consensus opinion.

Nevertheless, they chose their fates with their own hands, and for the others, this spelled grave misfortune. Operators in every regiment of the imperial fleet shouted warnings at the tops of their lungs as they detected ships ahead of the formation vanishing, accompanied by the eruption of violent quakes in space-time. Those cries were overlapped by shouted orders for evasive maneuvers. The forward half of the fleet got caught up in those chaotic undulations, and several ships collided amid the confusion.

For this reason, Kircheis had to spend time reorganizing his fleet, which meant that precious minutes were given to Yang.

Wittenfeld, eager to recover his honor, was leading a numerically inferior number of subordinates in courageous battle. However, each move he made was in response to an enemy that appeared in front of him—not with an eye toward the tide of the battle as a whole.

Had he been paying attention to Kircheis's movements, he might have been able to guess what Yang was planning, even with communications with Reinhard shut off, and thus effectively cut off Yang's path of retreat.

Lacking an organic connection with his allies, however, his force was merely a numerically smaller unit and nothing more.

That was the state of Wittenfeld's regiment when Yang suddenly slammed all his remaining force strength against it.

In his eagerness to make up for his prior blunder, Wittenfeld was filled with fighting spirit, and he was an able commander as well. But at that moment, he also suffered from a critical lack of the force strength necessary to make the most of those qualities.

And he was out of time.

In the space of an instant, ships just a few rows down from Wittenfeld's flagship had been shot through and destroyed. Even so, the commander was still shouting for a counterattack, and if staff officers like Captain Eugen had not held him back, his forces would have likely faced literal annihilation.

Yang led the Alliance Armed Forces Thirteenth Fleet away from the field of battle along the escape route he had secured. Both Reinhard and Wittenfeld were looking on as that still-orderly river of lights flowed away into the distance—Wittenfeld from nearby in stunned silence, Reinhard from afar, trembling with rage and disappointment.

In the space between them were Mittermeier, von Reuentahl, and Kircheis, the last of whom had had to give up on blocking their retreat. Those three young, capable admirals opened comm channels and began to speak with one another.

"The rebel forces have quite a commander."

Mittermeier praised him in a straightforward tone of voice, and von Reuentahl agreed.

"Yes, I look forward to meeting him again."

Von Reuentahl was a very handsome man. His dark-brown hair was nearly black, but what surprised people when they first met him was the fact that his eyes were different colors. His right eye was black and his left eye blue—a physiological condition called heterochromia.

Nobody said, "Let's go after them."

They all knew that the last chance for that had been lost and had sense enough to avoid chasing after them too far. A thirst for battle alone could not keep them alive, nor could it keep alive their subordinates.

"The rebel forces have been driven from the empire's territory, and they will probably flee to Iserlohn. That's enough of a victory for the time being. They're not going to feel like launching another invasion for quite a while and have probably even lost the strength to do so."

This time it was Mittermeier who nodded at von Reuentahl's words.

Kircheis was following the disappearing lights with his eyes. *What will Reinhard think?* he wondered. *Just as in the Battle of Astarte, his perfect victory was flung to the ground in the very last stage. He's not going to be in as magnanimous of a mood as last time, is he?*

"E-gram from Supreme Command!" said the communications officer. "'Make your way back while mopping up the stragglers.'"

II

"Gentlemen, you've all done a superb job."

On the bridge of the flagship *Brünhild*, Reinhard expressed his appreciation to his returning admirals.

One by one, he gripped the hands of von Reuentahl, Mittermeier, Kempf, Mecklinger, Wahlen, and Lutz, and praising their heroic deeds, promised them promotions. In Kircheis's case, he simply clapped him on the left shoulder and said nothing, but between the two of them, that was enough.

It was when von Oberstein informed him of Wittenfeld's return to the flagship that the shadow of displeasure crept into the graceful countenance of the young imperial marshal.

Fritz Josef Wittenfeld's regiment—if it could even still be called such at this point—had just returned with heads hung low. No one in the imperial military had lost more subordinates and ships in this battle than he had. His colleagues von Reuentahl and Mittermeier had both been in the thick of fierce combat, so for his part, it was impossible to lay the blame on others for his heavy losses.

The joy of victory yielded its seat to an awkward silence. Pale faced, Wittenfeld walked up to his senior officer, and, as if bracing himself for the worst, hung his head low.

"This is where I want to say that the battle is won, and you, too, fought heroically, but I can't even do that."

Reinhard's voice rang out like the crack of a whip. Brave admirals who would not budge an eyebrow in the face of a huge enemy fleet unconsciously drew in their necks, cringing.

"Understand this: impatient for glory, you charged ahead at a moment when you shouldn't have advanced. That one misstep could have thrown off the balance of our entire line of battle, and our fleet could have been defeated before the other force arrived. Moreover, you've done needless harm to His Imperial Majesty's military. Have you any objection to what I've just said?"

"None, milord."

His reply was pitched low and devoid of spirit. Reinhard took one breath and then continued.

"A warrior clan is upheld by rewarding the good and punishing the evildoers. Upon our return to Odin, I will hold you accountable. I'm putting your regiment under Admiral Kircheis's command. You yourself are confined to quarters."

Everyone must have been thinking, *That was harsh.* A wordless stir rose up like a cloud, until Reinhard cut it off with the word "Dismissed!" and stalked off toward his quarters, taking long strides.

The colleagues of the unfortunate Wittenfeld gathered around him and began speaking words of encouragement. Kircheis glanced at them and then followed after Reinhard. As he did so, he was being carefully observed by von Oberstein.

He's a capable man, the chief of staff said silently to himself, *but it will be problematic should his relationship with Count von Lohengramm come to be seen as one of excessive privilege. A conqueror should not be bound by personal feelings.*

In an empty hallway that led only to the private quarters of the supreme commander, Kircheis caught up with Reinhard and called out to him.

"Excellency, please reconsider."

Reinhard whirled around with fierce energy. A fire burned in his ice-blue eyes. The anger he had been holding back in front of others he now let explode.

"Why do you want to stop me? Wittenfeld failed to carry out his own responsibilities. There's no point pleading his case. It's only natural he be punished!"

"Excellency, are you angry right now?"

"What of it if I am!"

"What I'm asking you is this: what is it that has you so angry?"

Unable to grasp his meaning, Reinhard looked back at the face of his red-haired friend. Kircheis calmly accepted his stare.

"Excellency..."

"Enough with the 'Excellency,' already—what do you want to say? Tell it to me clearly, Kircheis."

"In that case, Lord Reinhard, is it really Wittenfeld's failure that you're angry about?"

"Isn't it obvious?"

"I don't believe it is, Lord Reinhard. Your anger is really directed at yourself. At you, who have secured Admiral Yang's reputation. Wittenfeld is merely caught in the cross fire."

Reinhard started to say something but then swallowed it. A nervous shuddering ran through his clenched fists. Kircheis let out a light sigh and stared unthinkingly at the golden-haired youth, eyes filled with kindness and consideration.

"Is it really so maddening to have made a hero of Admiral Yang?"

"Of course it is!" Reinhard shouted, clapping both his hands together. "I managed to endure it at Astarte. But twice in a row and I've had enough! Why does he always appear right when I'm on the verge of complete and total victory, to stand in my way?"

"He probably has his complaints as well. Like, 'Why can't I face Count von Lohengramm at the start of the battle?' "

To this, Reinhard said nothing.

"Lord Reinhard, please understand that the road isn't level and smooth. Doesn't it go without saying that there will be difficulties along the way when climbing toward the highest of seats? Admiral Yang is not the only obstacle on your path to conquest. Do you really think that you by yourself can eliminate all of them?"

For that Reinhard had no answer.

"You can't win the hearts of others by ignoring their many achievements for the sake of one mistake. With Admiral Yang in front of you and the highborn nobles at your back, you already have two powerful enemies. On top of that, you're making enemies even within your own ranks now."

For a time, Reinhard made not the slightest of movements, but at last with a deep sigh, the strength drained out of his body.

"All right," he said. "I was wrong. I won't seek redress against Wittenfeld."

Kircheis bowed his head. It was not just for Wittenfeld himself that he was so relieved. He was also happy to know for sure that Reinhard had the broadness of mind to accept frank words of reproof.

"Could you relay that to him for me?"

"No, that won't do."

At Kircheis's prompt refusal, Reinhard acknowledged what he was getting at and nodded.

"That's true. It will be meaningless unless I tell him myself."

If Kircheis were to pass along word of Reinhard's intent to forgive, Wittenfeld—having been reprimanded by Reinhard—would likely continue to hold a grudge against him, while feeling gratitude toward Kircheis. Human psychology was like that. For that reason, Reinhard's indulgence would ultimately have had no meaning, which was why Kircheis had refused.

Reinhard started to turn on his heel but then stopped and spoke once more to his trusted friend and aide.

"Kircheis?"

"Yes, Lord Reinhard?"

"…Do you believe I can seize this universe and make it my own?"

Siegfried Kircheis looked straight back into his dear friend's ice-blue eyes.

"To whom but Lord Reinhard could such a wish be granted?"

The forces of the Free Planets Alliance had formed up into ranks of browbeaten remnants and set out on the path to Iserlohn.

The dead and the missing numbered an estimated twenty million. The numbers their computers output chilled the hearts of the survivors.

In the midst of the life-and-death struggle, the Thirteenth Fleet alone had preserved a majority of its crew alive.

Yang the magician had worked a miracle even here—already a light akin to religious faith shone in his subordinates' eyes as they looked at the young black-haired admiral.

The object of that absolute trust was on the bridge of the flagship *Hyperion*. Both his legs were ill-manneredly propped up on top of his command console, the interlaced fingers of both hands rested on his stomach, and his eyes were closed. Beneath his youthful skin, there stagnated a heavy shadow of exhaustion.

"Excellency…"

He cracked his eyes open and saw his aide, Sublieutenant Frederica Greenhill, standing there a bit hesitantly.

Yang laid one hand on his black uniform beret.

"Pardon me, acting like this in front of a lady."

"It's all right. I thought I might bring you some coffee or something. What would you like?"

"Tea would be lovely."

"Yes, sir."

"With plenty of brandy, if possible."

"Yes, sir."

Frederica was about to start walking away when Yang unexpectedly called her to a halt.

"Sublieutenant… I've studied a little history. That's how I learned this: In human society, there are two main schools of thought. One says there are things that are more valuable than life, and the other says that nothing is more important. When people go to war, they use the former as an excuse, and when they stop fighting, they give the latter as the reason. That's been going on for untold centuries… for untold millennia…"

Frederica, not knowing how to respond, gave no reply.

"You think we've got untold millennia of that ahead of us too?"

"Excellency…"

"No, never mind the human race as a whole. Is there anything *I* could do that would make all the blood I've spilled worthwhile?"

Frederica just stood there, unable to answer. Suddenly Yang looked slightly at a loss, as if he had noticed her discomfort.

"I'm sorry, that was a weird thing to say. Don't give it a second thought."

"No, it's all right. I'll go make tea—with a little bit of brandy, was it?"

"With plenty."

"Yes, sir, with plenty."

Yang wondered if Frederica was letting him have brandy as a reward, though he wasn't watching her as she left. He closed his eyes again and murmured to himself:

"Could Count von Lohengramm be aiming to become a second Rudolf...?"

Of course, no one answered.

When Frederica came back carrying a tray with the tea, Yang Wen-li was fast asleep in that same position, his beret resting on the top of his face.

CHAPTER 10:

A NEW PROLOGUE

I

The series of battles that had come to be called the Battle of Amritsar—based upon the name of the stellar region in which the final encounter took place—had concluded with utter defeat for the military of the Free Planets Alliance. The alliance's expeditionary force completely abandoned the more than two hundred frontier star systems that, thanks to the Galactic Empire's strategic pullback, they had temporarily occupied, and just barely managed to secure their first prize of the conflict: Iserlohn Fortress.

The alliance had mobilized a force over thirty million strong, but the survivors returning home by way of Iserlohn numbered less than ten million, and the percentage of those not returning at all was just shy of a disastrous 70 percent.

This defeat naturally cast an immense shadow over every facet of the alliance's politics, economy, society, and military. The financial authorities turned a ghastly pale as they calculated the expenses so far and the expenses yet to come—including lump-sum payments to bereaved families, as well as pensions. The losses incurred at Astarte had been nothing compared to this.

Blistering criticism and censure rained down on the government and military from bereaved families and the antiwar faction for having launched such a reckless campaign. The rage of citizens who had lost fathers and sons because of a trivial election strategy and a hysterical staff officer's lust for advancement hammered the government and the military down to the ground.

Among the prowar faction, even now there were apologists who defended the invasion, saying, "You speak of the great cost in lives and treasure, but there are things worthy of even greater regard than these. We mustn't fall into war-weary ideologies based on emotion."

However, they could do nothing but fall silent as the responses drove them into their corners:

"Never mind the money! What exactly are you talking about that's worth more than human lives? Protecting those in power? Military ambition? So you're saying that while twenty million soldiers were shedding their blood for nothing—while many times that number were shedding tears for them back home—human life wasn't something that deserved your respect?"

The prowar faction could not answer, because aside from a very small number of people not furnished with consciences, everyone felt somehow ashamed of the simple fact that they were living in safety.

The members of the alliance's High Council submitted their resignations en masse.

The popularity of the prowar faction plummeted, which meant that the antiwar faction entered the limelight to a similar degree. The three councilmen who had cast their votes against the invasion were lauded for their insight, and Defense Committee chairman Trünicht was named interim head of the ruling administration and would occupy that seat until the following year's elections.

In the study at his home, Trünicht raised a glass in celebration of his own foresight. He wouldn't have much longer to wait before the word "interim" vanished from his title.

In the military, Marshal Sitolet, director of Joint Operational Headquarters, and Marshal Lobos, commander in chief of the space armada, resigned together. Scuttlebutt had it that Lobos had, through his own failures, ruined his rival Sitolet.

Vice Admiral Urannf and Vice Admiral Borodin, the two fleet commanders who had died courageously on the battlefield, received special double promotions and were posthumously granted ranks of marshal. In the alliance military, there was no rank of senior admiral, and marshal was next in the hierarchy above full admiral.

Admiral Greenhill was shuffled off to the Defense Committee secretariat-general, where as director of field investigations he was removed from the front lines of the effort to counter the empire's military activities.

Rear Admiral Caselnes was transferred as well and departed the capital of Heinessen to become commander of Supply Base 14, located inside the alliance's territory. Somebody had to take responsibility for the failure of the supply effort in the Battle of Amritsar. Leaving his family behind in the capital, he departed for a frontier land five hundred light-years distant. His wife took their two young daughters and moved back in with her parents.

After recuperating, Rear Admiral Fork was ordered to join the reserve, and there it seemed his ambition had met its end.

All of this caused an alarming shortage of human resources in the leadership of the Alliance Armed Forces. Who was there who could fill those seats?

Assuming the seat of director at Joint Operational Headquarters— and in the process being promoted from vice admiral to full admiral—was Cubresly, who had served until that time as the First Fleet's commander.

As he had not participated in the battles at Astarte or Amritsar, he accordingly bore no responsibility for the defeats there. He had built a sound record of solid results in providing security for the capital and defending public order domestically, as well as in his traditional role of suppressing the space pirate cartels and maintaining the safety of the shipping lanes. He had graduated with excellent marks from Officers' Academy, where it had been viewed as a given that he would one day rise to the highest pinnacle of the military. That prediction had now come true with a speed that the man himself had never dreamed of.

Replacing Cubresly as commander of the First Fleet was Vice Admiral Paetta, who had been recuperating from his wounds in the Battle of Astarte.

Bucock was installed as commander in chief of the space armada and, naturally, promoted to full admiral in the process. This seasoned admiral had at last taken up a post worthy of his experience, and his appointment was highly praised both inside and outside the military. No matter how famous Bucock might have been, he had worked his way up from an ordinary soldier, and without circumstances being what they were, he likely never would have made commander in chief of the space armada. In that sense, something ironically positive had come out of the misfortune of their miserable defeat.

How Yang Wen-li was to be rewarded was not decided upon right away.

He had brought over 70 percent of those in the Thirteenth Fleet back home alive—a survival rate vastly higher than that of any other regiment in the expeditionary force. No one had been able to accuse him of having hidden elsewhere in safety. The Thirteenth Fleet had been right in the midst of intense combat all along and had stayed on the battlefield to the very last, giving its all so that allies could escape.

Cubresly was hoping to make Yang his staff commissioner at Joint Operational Headquarters. Bucock had told Yang directly and with certainty that he would ready the seat of general chief of staff of the space armada for him.

On the other hand, the crew of the ships in the Thirteenth Fleet could no longer imagine having any commander but Yang over them. As von Schönkopf aptly put it, "Soldiers want a commander who comes with both ability and luck. To them, that's the best way to survive."

While things were still up in the air about his next assignment, Yang took a long vacation and went to the planet Mithra. Things were now such that if he stayed at his official residence in Heinessen, he wouldn't be able to set foot outside his door without being thronged by civilians and journalists wanting to meet the undefeated hero, and with his visiphone constantly ringing as well, it was impossible to get any rest.

His text transmitter began spitting out letters that came only seconds apart. One of these was a brief note from the headquarters of the Patriotic Knight Corps—"We extend our praises to a great admiral of our beloved homeland"—at which Yang burst out laughing, while one from the mother of a Thirteenth Fleet soldier who had been killed in action—"You're just a friend and ally of murderers, too"—left him deeply discouraged. It really was just six of one and half a dozen of the other. Honor and glory were things built only atop the piled corpses of unknown soldiers...

Julian had proposed the vacation getaway because he felt like he had to do something. In addition to feeling depressed, Yang had increased his drinking dramatically. Yang wasn't the type to get drunk and do bad things, like disturbing the peace or getting in fights, but he wasn't drinking for enjoyment either, and there was no way his level of consumption could be good for his health.

Yang, perhaps with some degree of self-awareness about this, meekly accepted Julian's suggestion. Yang spent three weeks surrounded by lush, green natural beauty, lost his interest in alcohol, and returned to the capital to find his letter of appointment waiting.

Iserlohn Fortress Commander / Iserlohn Patrol Fleet Commander / Alliance Armed Forces Supreme Staff Council Councilman.

That was the new status that Yang Wen-li had been given. He was also promoted to full admiral. There were a number of past examples of people who had made full admiral in their twenties, but this was the first time anyone had been promoted through three ranks of the admiralty in the space of one year.

Because the Iserlohn Patrol Fleet had been created by combining the old Tenth and Thirteenth fleets, the commonplace term for it, "the Yang Fleet," came to be recognized officially.

It was fair to say that the Alliance Armed Forces had displayed its utmost affection for the young national hero. However, every last bit of it was the opposite of what Yang really wanted. He had been hoping for retirement rather than promotions, and a peaceful life as a civilian rather than honor as a warrior.

And yet Yang departed for Iserlohn, where he took full command of his homeland's front line of defense.

Naturally, this put an end to his life on Heinessen, and the question of what to do with young Julian gave Yang a lot to think about. He even thought about getting Mrs. Caselnes's family to take him in, but Julian had absolutely no intention of leaving Yang's side.

From the very start, Julian had made up his mind to accompany his guardian. Yang saw him getting ready, and despite some hesitation, ultimately decided to take him along. Eventually, an orderly would be assigned to Yang to look after his personal needs, and if that was the case, then leaving that job to Julian felt somehow more comfortable. Although he didn't want to make the boy walk the same path that he did, Yang didn't want to part with Julian either. Julian was made a civilian worker for the military and treated as the equivalent of a lance corporal. He was paid a salary as well.

Naturally, however, it wasn't just Julian who followed Yang to Iserlohn.

His personal aide was Frederica Greenhill. Vice commander of the Iserlohn Patrol Fleet was Fischer. And von Schönkopf was there as well, as commander of fortress defenses. Murai and Patrichev came with him as staff officers, as did Lao, who had assisted Yang at the battle of Astarte. The captain of the First Fortress Spaceborne Division was Poplin. In addition, staff officers from the old Tenth Fleet came with him. The lineup of the Yang Fleet was steadily taking shape.

Now if I can just get Caselnes to take over the clerical duties, Yang thought, deciding to call him on over as soon as he was able.

What bothered him, though, were the movements of the Imperial Navy. Count Reinhard von Lohengramm aside, there were other admirals—scions of great noble houses—who had been inspired by his military exploits; might they not be plotting incursions even now, aiming to strike at a time when the Alliance Armed Forces' ability to fight back was weakened?

Fortunately, however, that unease never manifested in reality, for a pressing situation had arisen within the Galactic Empire which left them with no leeway for launching distant campaigns.

Emperor Friedrich IV had died suddenly.

II

Having won a spectacular victory at Amritsar, Reinhard returned to the imperial capital of Odin to find its surface practically buried under forests of mourning flags.

The passing of the emperor!

The cause of death was said to be acute heart disease. Not only had the emperor's body been weakened by debauchery and neglect for his health, the bloodline of the von Goldenbaum imperial family itself had grown dark and muddy, and he had died all too suddenly, as if to demonstrate what weak and inferior life-forms the family had become.

Friedrich is dead? Reinhard murmured in his heart, with as stunned an expression as might be expected as he stared at the assembled admirals under his command. *Heart disease... a natural death? Wasted on that man. If he could have lived another five—no—two years longer, then I would have showed him a death befitting his many sins.*

He turned his gaze toward Kircheis and met eyes filled with similar emotions—not as intense as Reinhard's, but running possibly even deeper. The man who ten years ago had robbed them of their kind and beautiful Annerose was dead. Viewed through the light of recollection, all those years that had gone by shone dazzlingly bright and seemed to be dancing wildly all around them...

"Excellency," said an exceedingly cold voice that yanked Reinhard up onto reality's shore. There was no need to confirm it was von Oberstein. "*Friedrich is dead* and there is no successor named."

All of the admirals save Reinhard and Kircheis drew in their breaths for an instant, shocked at how brazenly he had just dropped His Highness's titles.

"Why so shocked?" the staff officer said as he looked around at all of them, artificial eyes flashing with inorganic light. "The only man to whom I swear loyalty is His Excellency, Imperial Marshal von Lohengramm. Emperor though he may have been, Friedrich wasn't worthy of flowery titles."

After this declaration, von Oberstein turned to face Reinhard.

"Excellency, Friedrich has died without naming his successor. Clearly, a struggle for succession will erupt among his three grandchildren. Whatever is decided in the short term will only be temporary. It may come early or it may come late, but this is not going to be settled without blood."

"You have the right of it," Reinhard said after a moment.

The young imperial marshal nodded toward him with the look of a fierce and intelligent schemer. "And my fate as well will be determined by which of the three I support. So tell me, then, which of those men who lurk behind the three grandchildren will come forward and extend his hand to me?"

"Marquis Lichtenlade, most likely. The other two have military forces of their own, but the marquis does not. He must be craving Your Excellency's forces most earnestly."

"I see." Reinhard's attractive features seemed to glow as he flashed a different kind of smile from the one reserved for Kircheis. "In that case, let's see just how much we can lease them for."

It was widely expected that the standing of Count Reinhard von Lohengramm would be not a little shaken by the sudden death of the emperor.

However, the outcome turned out to be just the opposite. This was because Erwin Josef, the emperor's five-year-old grandson, had been made the next emperor by the hand of Minister of State Lichtenlade.

The child was a direct descendent of Friedrich IV, so there was nothing unusual about his succession in and of itself. Even so, he was far too young to rule, and above all had no backing from the powerful highborn nobles. For these reasons, he had been thought to be at a disadvantage.

In a case like this, it would not have been unusual for either Elisabeth, the sixteen-year-old daughter of the Duke and Duchess von Braunschweig, or Sabine, the fourteen-year-old daughter of Marquis and Marchioness von Littenheim, to become empress with the backing of her father's family and power. There were a number of precedents. Were that to happen, the father of the all-too-young empress would likely assist her as regent.

Duke von Braunschweig and Marquis von Littenheim had both confidence and ambition, and so predicting such a situation initiated unofficial—but very energetic—maneuvers at court intended to make their predictions come true.

In particular, powerful aristocratic families with young unmarried children were courted by these machinations. "If you'll support my daughter for accession to the throne," they were saying, "I'll consider making your son the husband of the new empress."

If spoken promises were strictly honored, the emperor's two grand-daughters would have both been forced to marry dozens of husbands. Even if the girls had already had boyfriends, their wishes would have doubtless been ignored.

However, it was the Marquis Lichtenlade who administered both the imperial seal and the issuance of imperial decrees, and he had no inten-tion of letting powerful maternal relatives turn the empire into their private property.

Lichtenlade was concerned about where the empire was headed, and more than that, he loved his own position and power. He made up his mind to put forward Erwin Josef, heir of the late emperor Friedrich's heir, but the thought of the great power wielded by those who would be opposed to his plan left him feeling a pressing need to strengthen his own camp. His guard dog would need to be strong and, moreover, easy to manage.

After giving the matter much thought, Marquis Lichtenlade settled on one man, although it was hard to say this individual would be easy to manage. In fact, he was a rather dangerous man. But in terms of raw strength, he had no room for objection.

That was how Count Reinhard von Lohengramm was advanced to the rank of marquis by Lichtenlade, who himself became a duke. It was also how he came to occupy the seat of commander in chief of the Imperial Space Armada. When the accession of Erwin Josef was announced publicly, the highborn nobles—starting with Duke von Braunschweig— were at first aghast, then disappointed, then infuriated.

But the axis of power created by a handshake that had for mutually selfish reasons been exchanged between Duke Lichtenlade and Marquis von Lohengramm turned out to be a surprisingly firm one. This was because the former needed the latter's military forces and popularity with the commoners, the latter desired the former's authority in national governance and influence at court, and both of them needed to utilize the new emperor's authority to its utmost to cement their respective positions and power.

When Erwin Josef II's coronation ceremony was held, the two representatives of his chief vassals respectfully swore their allegiance to the child emperor, who was held sitting in his nurse's lap. Representing the civil authorities was Duke Lichtenlade, who took up the job of regent, while the representative for the military authorities was Reinhard. Though it pained them to do so, the assembled aristocrats, bureaucrats, and military officers had no choice but to acknowledge the two of them as twin pillars of this new order.

The highborn nobles who had been excluded from the new order were quite literally grinding their teeth. Duke von Braunschweig and Marquis von Littenheim were bound together by their shared hatred toward it.

Duke Lichtenlade, they thought, was a worn-out old man who should have ended his role in national affairs and exited the stage with the death of Emperor Friedrich IV. On the other hand, who was this *Marquis* von Lohengramm? A shining service record he may have, but what was he really but an upstart whelp from a poor family of nobility in name only, who had used the emperor's favor toward his sister in order to rise to prominence? *Should we just stand by and let people like that monopolize our national government?* The highborn nobles turned their private outrage into public outrage and longed for the overthrow of this new order.

So long as they shared such powerful, common enemies, the Lichtenlade-Lohengramm axis would likely remain firm as a steel fortress and strong as an iron wall. There was simply no other option.

Reinhard, now Marquis von Lohengramm, immediately promoted Siegfried Kircheis to the rank of senior admiral and named him vice commander in chief of the Imperial Space Armada.

Duke Lichtenlade actively supported this appointment as well, still not having given up on the idea of putting Kircheis in his debt.

The one who held misgivings about this was von Oberstein. He had been promoted to vice admiral and now doubled as Imperial Space Armada chief of staff and Lohengramm admiralität chief secretary, and one day he met with Reinhard to give him some candid advice.

"It's well and good to have a childhood friend, and well and good to have a capable second-in-command. But having both in the same person is dangerous. First of all, there was no need to make him vice commander in chief. Don't you think you should treat Admiral Kircheis the same as you do the others?"

"Know your place, von Oberstein, I've made up my mind already."

The young commander in chief of the Imperial Space Armada put the staff officer with artificial eyes to silence with this single displeased remark. It was von Oberstein's clever scheming that Reinhard was paying for; he did not regard the man with silver-streaked hair as a friend with whom he could share his heart. It did not put him in a pleasant mood to hear vaguely slanderous words spoken against the one who was his other self.

After the emperor's death, Annerose, the Countess von Grünewald, had removed herself from court and moved into a mansion in Schwarzen that Reinhard had readied for them to share. When he welcomed his sister, Reinhard had spoken like an overeager boy.

"You're never going to have hard times again, so please, be happy, always."

Coming from Reinhard, this was a rather unimaginative line, but one suffused with sincere emotion.

However, Reinhard had another face—the face of a heartless, ambitious schemer—that he didn't want Annerose to see.

He was aware of the alliance that had secretly been formed between Duke von Braunschweig and Marquis von Littenheim, and in his heart of hearts he welcomed it.

Let it explode. I'll have them executed as rebels against the new emperor and in one fell swoop purge the highborn of their strength and influence.

If he could destroy both of Friedrich IV's highborn sons-in-law, then all the rest of them would be able to do nothing save yield before Reinhard's ambition. All of their lordships would bow to the ground and swear obedience to him. And when that happened, he would naturally be able to break his alliance with Duke Lichtenlade. *You sly old fox, at least for now, celebrate having risen as high as you can.*

By the same token, Duke Lichtenlade was certainly not thinking of making his axial relationship with Reinhard a permanent one, although like Reinhard, he was counting on Duke von Braunschweig and Marquis von Littenheim's scheming to eventually explode. Using Reinhard's military might, he would crush them. And once that job was done, he would have no further use for a dangerous individual like Reinhard.

On Reinhard's orders, Seigfried Kircheis was moving steadily ahead with military preparations against what was expected to be an armed uprising by a federation of highborn nobles, with Duke von Braunschweig and Marquis von Littenheim at its head.

Kircheis was aware of von Oberstein's cold, dry gaze against his back, but as there seemed to be no cracks in his relationships with either Reinhard or Annerose, he had nothing to be ashamed of and decided to take no greater precautions than necessary.

Kircheis was working hard at performing his duties, while at the same time enjoying opportunities to meet with Annerose that had increased beyond compare with those of years prior. This made the passing of his days fulfilling and blissful.

If only such days could go on forever...

III

Around the time that the two camps in the empire and the alliance had finally formed new power structures and begun to climb, wheezing, the stairway to the future, Landesherr Rubinsky sat in an inner room at his private residence in the Phezzan Dominion and decided to make a call.

The room had no windows, and sealed tight behind walls of thick lead, the space itself was polarized.

He flipped a pink switch on his console, and a communications device activated. It was hard to pick out that device with the naked eye, the reason being that the room itself *was* the communications device, created to bridge several thousand light-years of interstellar space, changing Rubinsky's brain waves into the distinctive wavelengths of FTL transmissions, and sending them to their destination.

"It's me. Please respond."

His thoughts would assume the structure of definite language during these periodic, top secret transmissions.

"Which me is 'me?'"

The reply that came to him from beyond the reaches of space could not have been haughtier.

"Landesherr of Phezzan Rubinsky. How is your Holiness, Grand Bishop? Are you in good spirits?"

Rubinsky spoke with a humility that was hard to believe.

"I've no reason to be in good spirits...not when my beloved Earth has yet to reclaim its rightful position. Until the day that Earth is worshipped by all mankind, as in our distant past, my heart will not be unclouded."

Rubinsky could sense in his thoughts the heaving of a great sigh that used the whole of the bishop's rib cage.

Earth.

The shape of a planet floating in the void three thousand light-years away rose up in the back of Rubinsky's mind to become a sharp, vivid image.

A backwater planet, abandoned after thorough subjection to humanity's plunder and destruction. Decrepit and devastated, exhausted and poor. Ruins dotting its deserts, rocky mountains, and sparse forests. A small number of people just barely eking out a living, clinging to polluted soil that had forever lost its fertility. Dregs of glory, and precipitated grudges. A world so powerless that even Rudolf had left it alone. The third planet from its sun, which had no future and nothing but past...

However, it was this forgotten world that was Phezzan's secret ruler. For it was from the supposedly impoverished Earth that Leopold Raap's capital had come.

"For a long interval of eight hundred years, Earth has been looked down upon unfairly, but the day of her humiliation's ending is at hand. It is Earth that is the cradle of humanity and the center from which all the universe is ruled, and sometime during the next two or three years, the day will finally come for those ingrates who abandoned the mother world to know it."

"Will it be that soon?"

"You doubt me, Landesherr of Phezzan?"

His brain waves played the melody of low and somber laughter. The laughter of Earth's religious and political ruler, known as the Grand Bishop, terrified Rubinsky and made every hair on his body stand on end.

"The flow of history is a thing that accelerates. Particularly in regard to the respective camps of the Galactic Empire and the Free Planets Alliance, the convergences of their political authorities and military powers are moving forward. To that, we will presently add a new mass movement among the people. The spiritual movement to return to Earth that has been lurking unseen in both camps will soon appear on the streets. The work of organizing them and raising capital has been left to you Phezzanese, and there must be no mistakes."

"Of course."

"It was for this purpose that our great master selected the planet Phezzan, sent people loyal to Earth there, and set them the task of amassing wealth. Through force of arms, you cannot stand against either the empire or the alliance. It's only through economic might attained through careful use of its special position that Phezzan dominates the secular sphere, while it's through faith that our Earth rules the spiritual...The galaxy shall be recaptured for Earth without a shot being fired. It's a grand project that has taken centuries to be realized. And now, in our generation, will the wisdom of our master bear fruit...?"

At that point, the polarity of his thoughts reversed, and he called out sharply:

"Rubinsky!"

"Uh...yes?"

"Don't ever betray me."

If even one person who had known the Landesherr of Phezzan had been present, his eyes would have snapped wide open at the realization that even this man could break out in a cold sweat.

"Th-that's something I never dreamed I would hear you say."

"You've both ability and ambition...I was merely warning you so that you do not succumb to temptation. Surely you are sufficiently aware of the reason why the illustrious Manfred II, as well as your own predecessor as landesherr, had to die."

Manfred II had believed in the ideal of peaceful coexistence between the empire and alliance, and had attempted to implement that as policy. Rubinsky's predecessor Walenkov had hated being controlled from Earth and had tried to act independently. Both of them had attempted acts disadvantageous for Earth.

"It's because of Your Grace's support that I was able to become landesherr. I am no ingrate."

"If that's the case, then all is well. That praiseworthiness will protect you."

Some time later, the transmission came to an end, and Rubinsky went out onto the marble terrace, where, standing still, he looked up into the starry night sky. That he could not see Earth was fortunate. The feeling of relief, as if he had returned to reality from some other dimension, was gradually restoring his usual indomitable confidence.

Had Phezzan belonged to Phezzan alone, it might well have been he himself who was the de facto ruler of the galaxy. Unfortunately, however, the reality was different.

To the monomaniacs who were trying to reverse eight hundred years of history and make Earth capital of all the assembled stars once again, Adrian Rubinsky was nothing but a manservant.

However, would that be true in perpetuity? Nowhere in the universe was there an absolute and just reason why that had to be so.

"Well then, who's going to be the last one standing? The empire? The alliance? Earth...?" As Rubinsky was talking to himself, the corners of his mouth turned upward, just like the mouth of the fox that was his other namesake.

"Or will it be me...?"

IV

"We aren't going to be able to avoid a decisive battle with the highborn. It's a battle that will likely divide the empire."

At Reinhard's words, Kircheis nodded. "I'm in consultation with Mittermeier and von Reuentahl," he said, "and operations planning is coming along nicely. There's just one thing, though, that worries me."

"'What will the rebel forces do?'"

"Exactly."

What would happen if, while the empire's internal forces were divided between the Lichtenlade-Lohengramm axis and the Braunschweig-Littenheim camp, the alliance's military were to take advantage of the state of civil war and launch a second incursion? Even Kircheis, who was confident in the planning and execution of his operation, was feeling uneasy about that point.

The golden-haired youth gave his red-haired friend an easy smile.

"Don't worry about it, Kircheis. I have an idea. No matter how much skill Yang Wen-li may boast as a strategist, this measure will ensure that he won't be able to leave Iserlohn."

"And your strategy is...?"

"In short, it's this."

Ice-blue eyes flashing enthusiastically, Reinhard launched into his explanation.

∨

"I can feel the temptation," Yang murmured. Lost in thought, he had not so much as touched the tea that had been brought in for him. When Julian came in to take away his cup, he stared at Yang wide-eyed, but something in the air prevented him from asking what was wrong. He said nothing.

Although the empire's political situation appeared to have gotten a brief reprieve because of the swift establishment of the Lichtenlade-Lohengramm axis, there was no way that the present configuration was going to transition into a period of stability. The Braunschweig-Littenheim camp was going to rise up with armed force or, more precisely, be driven into a corner from which it would have to rise up. A civil war was going to break out and divide the empire.

And when that happened, Yang would come up with an ingenious reading of the situation and intervene—for example, suppose he joined forces with von Braunschweig's people to defeat the Marquis von Lohengramm in a pincer movement and then repaid von Braunschweig's side with a single blow to slaughter them. The Galactic Empire would likely fall.

Or maybe he could give his plans to von Braunschweig, let him do half the fighting against Reinhard, and then hit them both when both sides had reached the limits of exhaustion—that he could probably do himself. For his part, Yang was actually rather disgusted that he prided himself so on his mind as a tactician. When he had murmured, "I can feel the temptation," that was what he had been talking about.

If he were a dictator, that was what he would do. But what was he but one soldier of a democratic nation? There were, of course, restrictions on what he could do. To exceed those restrictions would only make him Rudolf's successor . . .

When Julian had taken away the cup of cold tea, brewed a fresh pot, and set it on Yang's desk, Yang noticed at last.

"Oh, thank you," he said.

"Did you have something on your mind?"

Upon being asked directly, a boyish look of embarrassment appeared on the face of the youngest full admiral in the Alliance Armed Forces.

"It's not the kind of thing I can talk about with other people. I mean, honestly, if all people think about is winning, there's no bottom to how low they can go."

Not quite understanding what Yang was getting at, Julian remained silent and waited for him to continue.

"By the way," said Yang, "I understand von Schönkopf's been teaching you how to shoot. How's that coming along?"

"From what the rear admiral says, I'm apparently 'a natural talent.'"

"Oh, that's good to hear."

"But, Commander, you never practice marksmanship at all. Is that really all right?"

Yang laughed. "I don't seem to have any talent for it. Don't care to make an effort, either, so at present I just might be the worst marksman in the service."

"Well, in that case, how do you protect yourself?"

"A fight where a commanding officer has to take up a gun to defend himself is already lost. All I'm thinking about now is how to not end up in that situation."

"I see. In that case, I'll be the one to defend you."

"I'll be counting on it." Smiling, Yang picked up the cup of tea.

Watching the young commander, a thought occurred to Julian: *He's fifteen years older than me. In the next fifteen years, can I reach his level?*

The boy had the feeling that it was too great a distance.

The galaxy turned, carrying with it thoughts, beliefs, and hopes beyond number.

It was SE 796, IE 487, and neither Marquis Reinhard von Lohengramm nor Yang Wen-li had foreseen any of what still lay ahead for them.

ABOUT THE AUTHOR

Yoshiki Tanaka was born in 1952 in Kumamoto Prefecture and completed a doctorate in literature at Gakushuin University. Tanaka won the Gen'eijo (a mystery magazine) New Writer Award with his debut story "Midori no Sogen ni..." (On the green field...) in 1978, then started his carrier as a science fiction and fantasy writer. Legend of the Galactic Heroes, which translates the European wars of the nineteenth century to an interstellar setting, won the Seiun Award for best science fiction novel in 1987. Tanaka's other works include the fantasy series The Heroic Legend of Arslan and many other science fiction, fantasy, historical, and mystery novels and stories.

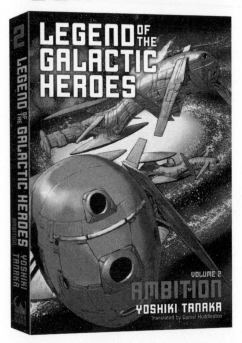

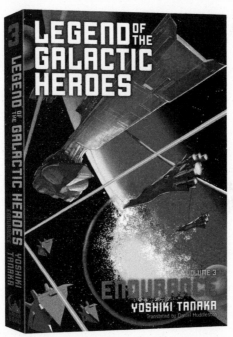

HAIKASORU

THE FUTURE IS JAPANESE

TRAVEL SPACE AND TIME WITH HAIKASORU!

USURPER OF THE SUN—HOUSUKE NOJIRI

Aki Shiraishi is a high school student working in the astronomy club and one of the few witnesses to an amazing event—someone is building a tower on the planet Mercury. Soon, the Builders have constructed a ring around the sun, threatening the ecology of Earth with an immense shadow. Aki is inspired to pursue a career in science, and the truth. She must determine the purpose of the ring and the plans of its creators, as the survival of both species—humanity and the alien Builders—hangs in the balance.

THE OUROBOROS WAVE—JYOUJI HAYASHI

Ninety years from now, a satellite detects a nearby black hole scientists dub Kali for the Hindu goddess of destruction. Humanity embarks on a generations-long project to tap the energy of the black hole and establish colonies on planets across the solar system. Earth and Mars and the moons Europa (Jupiter) and Titania (Uranus) develop radically different societies, with only Kali, that swirling vortex of destruction and creation, and the hated but crucial Artificial Accretion Disk Development association (AADD) in common.

TEN BILLION DAYS AND ONE HUNDRED BILLION NIGHTS—RYU MITSUSE

Ten billion days—that is how long it will take the philosopher Plato to determine the true systems of the world. One hundred billion nights—that is how far into the future Jesus of Nazareth, Siddhartha, and the demigod Asura will travel to witness the end of all worlds. Named the greatest Japanese science fiction novel of all time, *Ten Billion Days and One Hundred Billion Nights* is an epic eons in the making. Originally published in 1967, the novel was revised by the author in later years and republished in 1973.

WWW.HAIKASORU.COM